W9-CAD-830
3 5674 02246846 7

A
SPY
AT THE
GATE

VALERIE
GRAY

St. Martin's Press
New York

"For Colin who helped, and for Antonia, Sophie and Fred, who hindered, with love."

 For information, address St. Martin's Press, 175 Fifth Avenue, New York, N.Y. 10010.

Library of Congress Cataloging in Publication Data

Gray, Valerie.
A spy at the gate.

I. Title.
PS3557.R3337S6 1987 813'.54 86-25972
ISBN 0-312-00191-6

First published in Great Britain by The Book Guild Limited.

First U.S. Edition

10 9 8 7 6 5 4 3 2 1

Contents

Chapter 1
Two Wards

The heavy spring rain beat relentlessly upon the large and cumbersome carriage as it lurched and jolted its way along a narrow lane in a fold of the Sussex downs. The lordly coat of arms was all but invisible on the mud-bespattered door panel and the coachman shivered as he hunched miserably on the box. The horses ploughed bravely on, dragging the carriage through ever-deepening ruts and puddles. Not for the first time the two young ladies inside this ponderous equipage picked themselves up from the floor, shook their skirts and took a firm hold on the hand straps, while Jenny, their maid, who had been suffering agonies from travel sickness, cried, "Lawks, miss, we'm going to have an accident, for sure!"

"Hush, Jenny, don't take on so," exclaimed the smaller of the two ladies, patting the dark curls which framed her vivacious, heart-shaped face. "Lord, Marietta," she continued, turning to her companion, "It can't be much further. I know I saw Shawcross on the signpost at that last turning and according to the guidebook Huntsgrove Priory is but two or three miles beyond the village."

The lady thus addressed sighed wearily as she pulled her brown travelling cloak more closely about her. Her voice trembled a little as she replied, "I hope you may be right, Stephanie. I fear we have gone astray. We seem to have been wandering in this miry, uncomfortable wilderness for hours. If only we could have stayed in London. This countryside is so bleak and inhospitable. I wish Lord Montfort had been able to accompany us, as he originally intended". Stephanie shook her dark head vigorously.

"Well I do not, my dear. Our guardian made it clear that we were much in the way and his manner was most abrupt and unwelcoming — just like the climate of this wretched country. Why, Marietta, we had scarce time to catch our breath after that long journey from the Continent before we were hustled into yet another carriage, with no time to repair our wardrobes, or visit the sights of the City, or attend any social functions. To be fair, our arrival did take his lordship by surprise and we could hardly remain in his bachelor household — but one might have hoped for a warmer reception. I hope that he found time to notify his mother of our imminent arrival at the Priory — I must confess that I am a little daunted at the prospect of meeting Lady Elizabeth. I wonder if she will be anything like her formidable son."

Marietta's china blue eyes rested on the rain streaming down the windows as she reflected wistfully, "I thought Lord Montfort most handsome, did you not? If only his manner had been a little more amiable — but those green eyes of his made me shiver — quite deliciously, of course".

Stephanie giggled, "You make him sound like some hero from a Gothic romance. You read too many novels, Marietta".

That young lady lifted her chin to reveal a fair rounded face, of some nineteen summers, a pleasant face, though somewhat lacking in humour. She was about to make a dignified reply when the carriage gave an unexpectedly severe lurch, swayed perilously towards the ditch beside the road and staggered to a halt. Jenny gave a scream as they landed once more in a tumbled heap on the floor. They could hear the whinneying of frightened horses and muffled curses from the coachman as he jumped down and tried to soothe the poor beasts. Stephanie sat up with decision saying, "Come, Marietta, Jenny, we are not hurt, but we cannot remain here. I think we are stuck in the mud and Coachman Thomas will need help to extricate the carriage. Let us see if we can find help and shelter nearby". She reached out a hand to Marietta, and Jenny scrambled up behind them. With some difficulty Stephanie pushed open the door and gasped at the rush of biting wind and rain. Undismayed, she glanced up and down the lane, happy at the prospect of movement, after so many hours of inaction.

"I can see the chimney of a cottage a little way down on the left behind a high hedge," she reported. "It doesn't look far. Would you like to remain here with Jenny, Marietta, while I go and enquire?"

"Oh no, love, I cannot let you go alone. We will all come," responded Marietta bravely.

With some difficulty the three girls jumped down and felt the ominous squelch of mud and water in their light town boots. Stephanie told Thomas to remain with the horses and promised to send relief as soon as possible. The old man touched his tricorne with his whip and nodded dolefully. Stephanie's cheeks sparkled with the zest for adventure, even a small one, but Marietta huddled within her hood and exhibited no such exhilaration. Jenny sniffed miserably in the rear as they stumbled over the stones to the cottage gate.

Here the bedraggled trio halted a moment to catch their breath. They observed the cottage doubtfully. It was larger than they had imagined and presented a trim appearance, with a neat path, bordered by lawns, leading to the front door. There were several well-spaced fruit trees, pink and white in full bloom and daffodils clustered around their trunks, swaying in the wind, while to the left at the side of the cottage they caught a glimpse of flowerbeds filled with a profusion of spring flowers, a side gate leading to a vegetable garden, and beyond that a barn or stable. The cottage itself was built of local cobbled stone, with a thatched roof and raindrops sparkling on the latticed windows. The door was framed by a trellised porch containing two white bench seats. A gust of wind snatched at their bonnets and Stephanie hesitated no more. The latch clicked beneath her fingers and she stepped firmly up the path, followed by Marietta and Jenny.

The door swung open almost immediately, revealing a smiling maid-servant dressed in black, with a clean white apron and cap. Her eyes widened as she took in the two strange young ladies, but with only an instant's hesitation she opened the door yet further and begged them to step inside. They found themselves in a panelled hallway, narrow, but smelling sweetly of beeswax and lavender. There was a light step on the stairway and a voice called, "Who is it Martha? I was not expecting any visitors today". The speaker came into view and paused as she took in the scene below her. Looking up Stephanie and Marietta had a brief impression of a slender lady in her mid to late twenties, dressed in a somewhat crumpled green day-dress, with abundant brown hair wound in a loose coronet. The lady brushed several stray tresses back impatiently with her left hand as she ran quickly down the stair. Her air of abstraction vanished as she advanced and to the girls' relief she spoke pleasantly, in well-modulated rather deep tones.

"Do forgive my appearance, I have been working. I am Hester Vane. How do you do."

Stephanie stepped forward and curtseyed gracefully, despite her dishevelment.

"Indeed ma'am, it is we who should beg your forgiveness for coming upon you so unexpectedly and in such a state. We had the misfortune to suffer an accident to our carriage in the lane outside your gate and have made so bold as to come and seek aid for ourselves and for our coachman. May I present my cousin, Marietta von Sapsburg?"

Marietta made a curtsey. Stephanie continued.

"And I am Stephanie de Beauclerc. We are the wards of my Lord Montfort and are travelling to stay with his mother, Lady Elizabeth, at

Huntsgrove Priory. I fear that in the rain we must have missed the way for we have no idea where we are. Our carriage is half overturned in a muddy ditch and — and we are quite at a loss how to proceed," she finished lamely.

Miss Vane nodded sympathetically and then said briskly, "What a very unpleasant occurrence, although unfortunately not infrequent. We have true Sussex roads round here and they are notoriously the worst in the kingdom. However, I am sure we can soon set all to rights. Martha," she turned to the hovering figure of her maid, "Please conduct these ladies to my bed-chamber and give them all they require to make themselves comfortable. Then take their maid to Cook". She smiled kindly at Jenny and added, "Mrs. Blossom will take good care of you. I will send George Hamble, my coachman, to aid your man and Miss Stanhope, my companion, and I will be delighted if you will take tea with us when you have recovered a little. I will send a message to the Priory so that Lady Elizabeth is not alarmed. You are not far from your destination, it is but three miles the other side of Shawcross village".

The two ladies appeared quite bewildered and Hester put her hand to her brow with a comical gesture of dismay and said in a different tone, "What a feat of organization! My dear Jane Stanhope will be quite impressed. But do not let me detain you, pray go with Martha and ask her for anything you need". Miss Vane watched Stephanie and Marietta mount the stairs, then turning on her heel, swept off to the nether regions in search of Mrs. Blossom and George Hamble.

Having set all in train for the comfort of her guests and tidied herself by the simple expedient of rewinding her shining coronet and bathing her hands and face in rose water, Hester stepped softly into the sitting room. As she expected, she found Miss Stanhope dozing by the cheerful fire with her cap askew and her embroidery frame on the floor beside her. Hester took up a quill pen from the writing table in the corner and tickled Miss Stanhope behind her ear. The lady sat up indignantly and glanced around. Her eye fell upon Hester standing innocently by the window and she hastily pulled her cap to rights as she exclaimed, "Good Heavens, child, what a fright you gave me! Why aren't you upstairs writing? Surely it's not teatime already? Is something amiss?"

Hester smiled down affectionately at the sharp-faced, thin little lady who had been her governess and was now her dear friend and companion.

"No, Jane dear, nothing is amiss, but we have unexpected visitors, two young ladies who suffered a carriage accident upon our doorstep.

They are wards of Lord Montfort and will be staying at Huntsgrove. I have sent them upstairs to refurbish a little and they will be joining us for tea in about half an hour." Hester paused and Miss Stanhope nodded brightly.

"Poor young things," she remarked, "But a welcome diversion on such a dull day. I was not aware that his lordship had any wards. Life is full of surprises. What can he be thinking of to let them travel alone? The countryside is full of unsavoury characters these days. Sussex has become a warren of smugglers since Bonaparte closed the French coasts."

Hester laughed, "I think our two guests may be from across the water. One of them is a de Beauclerc and must be related to Lady Elizabeth, for I believe that was her maiden name. They speak English very well, but their clothes are of foreign cut".

"Indeed, now you mention it I believe Lady Elizabeth was born in Luxembourg. Has not that unfortunate Duchy been incorporated into the new France? How dreadful to be obliged to live in indefinite exile from one's native land and at the mercy of foreigners. I declare I am grateful to be a freeborn Englishwoman, beholden to no-one." Here Miss Stanhope sniffed, and then added with a slight shiver, "Just imagine, my love, what a chilly reception that haughty Montfort and his retinue of town servants must have given them".

"Oh!" Hester protested, "We must not condemn him unheard. Besides, I daresay young ladies from the Continent are rather more accustomed to a certain stiffness and formality than we are. I noticed during my season in London that the French émigrés were very proud and unapproachable, despite their impoverished circumstances. I do not think that Hugo . . ." she caught herself and amended, "I mean, my Lord Montfort, would be unkind to young ladies of his own family however he may behave towards strangers. He used to be most attached to his mother and I have seen him unbend quite remarkably in the company of his friends. But, of course, that was six years ago and I have no recent knowledge." Hester turned abruptly and rather awkwardly rearranged a bowl of daffodils and pussy willow.

Miss Stanhope eyed her shrewdly for a moment and then said tartly, "Well that's as may be. You were better acquainted with him than I, but I must say that I do not consider a man with his reputation to be a fit guardian for two young ladies. His behaviour towards you was most reprehensible".

Hester's slender form relaxed and she giggled youthfully. Miss Stanhope reflected that if only the silly chit would take more care with her appearance she would be a very attractive woman. Her mouth was a little too wide and her features too irregular for classic beauty, but her complexion was good and the lines of mirth around her long-lashed eyes gave her expression warmth and character. She sighed as Hester chuckled, "Oh, Jane, you are too severe. One would think that Hugo Jermyn had offered me a slip on the shoulder and I assure you he did no such thing".

"I should hope not! To the best of *my* recollection he paid you no more than the barest attention which civility demanded. You know how your Mama and Lady Elizabeth had the match all but settled between them, and yet he was so preoccupied with raking about Town and squandering his inheritance that he barely found time to dance with you at Almacks or escort you to the theatre . . . when I think of how he bolted abroad after your Father died, leaving you and your Mama to struggle under all those debts . . ." Miss Stanhope hesitated, wondering if she had said too much. It was not a subject which Hester cared to discuss, and she closed the topic by stating simply, "Lord Montfort was under no obligation to assist me. There was no understanding between us. I much appreciated your support at that time, Jane dear, and indeed I am very content and happy as I am. To my mind my present existence is most satisfying and fulfilling. I enjoy writing novels. Our small household is easy to run and places no burden on my scatterbrained self. I am grateful for my lovely garden and to be able to live in the part of the country which I love best. I do not regret my old home. Shawcross Manor is a beautiful old house, but it is well-cared for by the Crossleys, and I have the freedom of the Park whenever I wish it. I have enough capital to live comfortably, if modestly, and Mortimer is provided for through my uncle's will. What more could I possibly wish for?"

"A husband," replied Miss Stanhope firmly, "Yours is a generous nature and it will not do for you to dwindle into an old maid, revolving around that scapegrace brother of yours. Mortimer will be down from Oxford very soon and must make his own way in the world. You should go to Town for the Season. Eligible *partis* are thin on the ground in the Sussex countryside."

"Hush Jane, not another word! I can see that you are pining for a visit to Brighton or the Metropolis. I promise that when the sequel to *The Master of Crumbling Keep* is finished we will go to pay a visit to my Aunt, Lady Marchant, and enjoy a change of scene. But I think I hear our guests . . . excuse me." Hester crossed lightly to open the parlour door as Stephanie and Marietta descended the stair. She greeted them, smiling as she ushered the two young ladies before her.

"I trust you are somewhat restored. Do come and meet my companion, Miss Jane Stanhope."

Introductions were duly made. The ladies curtseyed and settled themselves by the fire as Martha entered with a dainty tea tray. Miss Stanhope poured tea, while Hester persuaded Stephanie and Marietta to taste Mrs. Blossom's freshly baked scones topped with strawberry jam and cream. They ate heartily with youthful appetites and were soon chattering easily to their kind hostess and her friend, who listened sympathetically to the tale of their flight from the Continent and subsequent events.

It appeared that the two girls were related to Lord Montfort through his mother's family. Stephanie was the niece of Lady Elizabeth, her father, Count Henry de Beauclerc, being her ladyship's elder brother and lord of the family estate in the Duchy of Luxembourg. Marietta, Stephanie's cousin, was the child of her mother's brother. She had been orphaned at an early age and had grown up in the Beauclerc household and shared Stephanie's English governess, Miss Lamb. That lady had not returned with the girls to her native land, for she had married the Count's steward and had elected to remain in Luxembourg, even when it was taken over by the French after the Peace of Lunéville in 1801. The three years since then had been unhappy ones. Count Henri and his wife Eloise had both died in a carriage accident, and the estate had passed to a distant relative who truckled to the French and had a large family of daughters.

Count Henri had always spoken with affection of his sister, Elizabeth, and with considerable courage the two girls had decided to run away to the unknown English relatives, who were also their nearest kin. They had been assisted by Miss Lamb, now Madame Junot, and her husband, who pitied the girls in their unwanted position at the great house, and feared that they might be obliged to marry Frenchmen, a fate not to be thought of. At some risk to themselves, Monsieur and Madame Junot had arranged for the girls to be transported to the Coast near Ostend and thence smuggled to England and safety. It had been a long, trying journey and Stephanie and Marietta had arrived in London only three days since.

At this point in their narration Miss Stanhope interruped to exclaim, "I can see from Hester's rapt expression that you are giving her a story for her next novel. But tell me, my dears, did you venture on this journey alone?"

"Not quite, ma'am," replied Stephanie. "Our old nurse, Bathilde, accompanied us to the Coast, and her son, André, drove the carriage; they were not missed, for my relatives were away visiting their old home and the estate servants are very loyal and would not betray them. Bathilde waited in Ostend while André escorted us across the Channel in a fishing boat. We engaged Jenny when we landed in Dover, she is the daughter of the landlord at the inn where we stayed overnight before proceeding to Lord Montfort's London house. Of course Cousin Hugo was not expecting us, the mails are so slow that our letters had not reached him and we took him by surprise. I do not think he was very pleased to see us," she finished wistfully. Marietta nodded in agreement, her large blue eyes growing even rounder as she recalled their reception in Grosvenor Place, and his lordship's grim aspect.

"He was most put out to see us," she murmured, "I think he had an important engagement, a dinner party with Mr. Pitt."

Hester's mobile face expressed astonishment.

"With Mr. Pitt? Good heavens, I did not realize that Lord Montfort was interested in foreign policy. It is rumoured that Mr. Pitt may return to office as the head of a Tory Ministry." Hester glanced apologetically at Stephanie and Marietta, "Forgive my interruption, we are so starved of news here in the country. Do pray continue".

Stephanie tossed her curls and sniffed, "There is little more to add. Cousin Hugo said that it was not 'comme il faut' for us to remain with him, as he had no lady in his household to chaperone us. The weather was terrible and we could hardly venture outdoors. After the first shock of our arrival Hugo was quite kind, but he was much engaged and we were tired after our journey, so we had little opportunity to further our acquaintance". She turned to Hester, "You spoke just now as if you knew my cousin, Miss Vane. Perhaps you also know his mother, the Lady Elizabeth?"

"I do not know her well, she is an invalid you see and is not seen much in society. Occasionally, when the weather is good, she attends Morning Service at Shawcross Church. At other times, our vicar, Mr. Stone, visits her at the Priory. Lady Elizabeth and my mother were schoolfriends, but since my mother died and Jane and I moved to this cottage from the manor I have not met her ladyship socially."

An awkward silence ensued, and Miss Stanhope made haste to replenish the tea cups.

Stephanie hesitated, her colour rising, as she persisted in her enquiry, "Excuse my curiosity. It is perhaps not polite, but we have had so many qualms and misgivings since coming to your country. Do you think that Lady Elizabeth will welcome us? Is she a very proud person? We know nothing of what is before us, you understand?"

Hester smiled kindly and replied with composure, "Yes, of course, but I assure you there is no need to be apprehensive. I have always found her very considerate and easy to talk to, her manner is not at all stiff. In her youth she was very beautiful and spent most of her time in London, where she was much courted. Then she married Lord Montfort and they lived very happily in the country. She suffered a riding accident when the present Lord Montfort was about ten years old and since that time she has been unable to walk. Her husband died several years ago and this has naturally affected her greatly. She now devotes her time to her garden and her various charities, in which she is assisted by her companion, Mrs. Penelope Bishop, a distant connection of the Jermyns. I believe she is sincerely attached to her only son, although Lord Montfort spends little time at Huntsgrove. However, I have heard that his lordship has ordered substantial renovations at the Priory, and it is rumoured that he may be contemplating matrimony".

"Thank you ma'am," said Stephanie, "I hope things may be as you say, we have lived such quiet lives that some society would be most welcome. Cousin Hugo said we would not be far from the fashionable seaside resort of Brighton, but I do not see how we can go there if Lady Elizabeth cannot accompany us."

Hester nodded sympathetically at the two eager faces.

"I am sure something can be arranged. Miss Stanhope and I may be visiting the town in a few weeks and perhaps Lady Elizabeth would allow you to accompany us. We will be staying with my aunt, Lady Marchant. In the meantime, I hope that you will visit us whenever you wish. I am usually writing in the mornings, but my book is almost finished and I propose to take a short holiday and enjoy the spring weather. It does not always rain in England."

"Oh, dear Miss Vane, you are so kind, and you too ma'am," cried Marietta looking from Hester to Miss Stanhope with a warm smile. "Already England appears more attractive. Do you write books, indeed, Miss Vane? I adore novels — especially those of the Gothic kind. The selection was sadly limited in Luxembourg and those which were obtaintable were written in French. There was nothing to equal Mrs. Radclyffe. I was so vexed to be unable to visit the London booksellers."

"It was probably just as well, you would have been having nightmares for weeks. Do you think the Priory will stimulate her romantic imagination, Miss Vane?" queried Stephanie mischievously, with a sidelong glance at her blushing companion.

"It certainly has possibilities," agreed Hester, but taking pity on her younger guest she continued lightly, "I must admit that the Priory was frequently in my mind when I wrote *The Master of Crumbling Keep*. I see no reason not to paint my backcloths from nature, although I try to avoid drawing portraits straight from life. Somewhere in my pocket guide to the *Beauties of Sussex* I have a description of Huntsgrove Priory. Excuse me one moment."

Hester rose and went to her desk. The volume which she sought did not appear to be in the tottering pile of books that swayed precariously above her papers. However, with a brief exclamation of annoyance she swooped and retrieved it from its position on the floor where it had done duty as a foot-rest. Miss Stanhope shook her head reprovingly and Hester smiled contritely, "Yes Jane, shockingly careless, but I am sure you agree that books are there to be used and not to collect dust on the shelves".

"No fear of that when you are about," retorted Miss Stanhope, "but what an opinion you will be giving these young ladies of our housekeeping."

"And quite correct where I am concerned," nodded Hester, with her head bent over the book, as she rifled quickly through its well-thumbed pages. "Ah, here we are 'Huntsgrove Priory, Principal seat of Lord Montfort. The Priory was a royal gift to the 10th Baron, Gervase de Montfort at the time of the Dissolution of the Monasteries in 1536. Built in a number of styles, having been improved by successive owners, the Priory today is a delightful home, set in a fold of the Sussex downs, but visible from the road at the end of a long drive lined by elms. There is a large park where sheep graze, and a well-stocked trout pond. In addition to the formal flower and kitchen gardens there is an interesting topiary planted by the 1st Lord Montfort after the Battle of Blenheim. Four thriving farms mark the outer boundaries of the estate'." Hester paused for breath, just as Martha tapped gently and entered to inform her mistress that, "The ladies' carriage do be out o' that nasty old ditch now, ma'am, and their cloaks be all nice 'n dry and waitin' for 'ee by the fire".

"Thank you, Martha," said Hester. Then she turned to Stephanie and Marietta adding, "My dears, it has been such a pleasure to meet you both. I hope that we may meet again soon. I frequently drive out to visit local places of interest in search of new matter for my pen and if you would care to accompany me on some of these expeditions I should be delighted. Perhaps you would like to bring your sketch books? I do my best, but I am not gifted, I fear."

Stephanie beamed and glanced fondly at her cousin, "Marietta is very talented, she can draw anything. I'm sure we shall both be very happy to avail ourselves of your kind invitation, ma'am. But it grows late and we should not trespass any longer on your time. We do apologize for so interrupting your work; even I will be sending for a copy of *The Master of Crumbling Keep* at the first opportunity," she finished with a grin. Marietta nodded vigorously in agreement, as Martha entered with their cloaks and hats and everyone rose to their feet.

"I shall request my publisher to send you a copy," laughed Hester, as she and Miss Stanhope took their leave of the two girls amid renewed thanks.

When Martha opened the cottage door they found that the rain had ceased, the air smelled fresh and sweet and a glorious rainbow arched in the western sky.

"It will be a fine day tomorrow," commented Hester, glancing up at the scudding clouds tinged with red, as she stood at the trim gate, watching Stephanie and Marietta mount the carriage steps in a flurry of trailing cloaks. Jenny dropped a shy curtsey before taking her place, Thomas flourished his whip and the vehicle rolled away down the lane towards Shawcross.

Hester watched it out of sight, heaved a small sigh, straightened her shoulders and followed Miss Stanhope indoors for more tea and a comfortable coze by the parlour fire, in the course of which they agreed that the young ladies would be a welcome addition to their limited country circle.

Chapter 2
The Masked Man

Early that same evening, Hester, feeling restless and unsettled, decided to channel her energies in a useful direction. Accordingly she donned thick boots, warm clothes and gardening gloves and armed with the necessary implements, descended on the vegetable patch and began forthwith to hoe, weed and even dig vigorously. Thus busily occupied she allowed her mind to wander over the sparse information concerning Hugo Jermyn imparted by Stephanie and Marietta. Of an uncomfortably honest disposition, Hester acknowledged to herself that she had been unreasonably disturbed at the prospect of further contact with Lord Montfort through his young cousins. Although she lived but a short distance from the Priory, Hester had had no intercourse with its inhabitants since her father's death. As she had told the girls, Lady Elizabeth was virtually a recluse and frequently confined to the house by ill-health. On the rare occasions when Lord Montfort was in the neighbourhood Hester had studiously avoided the possibility of any chance meeting by remaining at home and she doubted whether his lordship was aware of her presence in Shawcross; he had certainly made no attempt to seek her out and she had considered their former association and friendship at an end. She had accepted with equanimity the local gossip that the extensive work at the Priory must imply his lordship's imminent marriage. Now she wondered how he would fare in that state, recalling his long-upheld aversion to being leg-shackled. However, he was close to thirty and she presumed that he must be sensing his family obligation to provide an heir.

At this turn in her thoughts Hester gave her trowel a particularly vicious twist and the handle broke. With a little cry of vexation she sat back on her heels gazing pensively at a large cabbage butterfly which hovered nearby.

They had both been so young, she reflected, absentmindedly stacking her tools in an untidy heap and seating herself by the well. Hugo had just returned from his Grand Tour and she had been a privincial miss newly arrived in London for her first season. Hugo had been a most eligible bachelor, handsome and heir to a great estate, and much sought after by matchmaking mamas and their dutiful offspring. Perhaps his head had been a little turned by all the adulation he received, but he had been charming to all and had shown no marked preference for any particular lady. He had been attentive to Hester in the casual friendly manner of an old family acquaintance, but he had changed during his two years on the Continent and she could no longer perceive any sign of the easy camaraderie which had existed between them as children and young adults in the country. In the years while Hugo had been abroad, Hester's father's debts had mounted at an alarming rate and she realized that she would not be able to remain in London for another season. Hester knew that their respective parents had planned a match between them while they were still in their cradles. Apart from the schoolgirl friendship of their mothers, it had seemed a sensible arrangement since their family estates marched side by side. However, rumours of Sir Montagu Vane's difficulties reached Hugo's father and a sudden coolness sprang up between the two families.

Hester shivered in the gathering dusk as she recalled the weeks before her father's sudden death. She had despised the machinations of the 'marriage mart' which reinforced her long-felt abhorrence for unions wherein there existed no real affection on either side. She was uncertain of her own emotions and of her ability to manage a large household. Once she was fully aware of her father's circumstances pride had prevented her from encouraging any suitor and to hide her hurt she had adopted a cool, stiff manner calculated to rebuff any but the most ardent young man. Hugo had responded in kind and their meetings had been artificial and forced in the extreme. Yet there had been the rare occasion when the barrier between them had dropped for a moment and they had laughed together in complete accord. She recalled the day when Hugo made a morning call and the cook's cat appeared to deposit her small howling kittens at their feet. Her aunt, Lady Marchant, who also happened to be paying a call, was terrified of cats and had leapt upon a convenient sofa with more haste than dignity — much to her niece's and Hugo Jermyn's amusement. Hester smiled and sighed at the memory. If only worldly goods did not matter so much! But the world of the 'haut Ton' could be fickle, cruel and censorious and she had had no wish to be labelled as a fortune hunter. Hugo might be a kindred spirit, but he was also an exceedingly wealthy man with every prospect of making a great match.

Matters had taken a darker turn shortly after the incident with the kittens. Her father was killed by a fall from his horse, while taking part in a race in which he hoped to recoup his losses by winning against all odds. Hester had been much attached to her feckless parent and she sorely missed his gay company. She was left with his debts and her shattered mama to cope with almost alone. Her young brother Mortimer was away at Eton and was not of an age to provide much support. Her Aunt Annabelle Marchant was kindness itself. She had tried to persuade Hester and Lady Vane to make their home with her, but they resolutely refused. Jane Stanhope had been a pillar of strength and had insisted upon accompanying the two stricken ladies to Sussex. She had helped Hester to deal with all the sad arrangements and she had gone with her on the unpleasant, final visit to Mr. Garth, their solicitor, after the sale of Shawcross Manor. As a result of this visit Hester found herself with a modest competence, sufficient to their needs if they lived quietly in the country. This they were quite content to do: they had left London in haste and although they received many messages of sympathy they did not wish to take advantage of their acquaintances. They found the peace of the country and the unobtrusive friendliness of their old neighbours very soothing. Hester was surprised, however, when the weeks passed and she received no word from Hugo. She wondered if he were ill. Months passed and she heard that, after Hugo had gambled and dissipated away a large part of his inheritance, his father, in desperation, had sent him to America. When his father died three years ago Hugo had returned to England, but she had had little news of him since that time. She knew he had inherited the title, that he now attended to his duties assiduously, was well-thought of in government circles, but that was all the news she could glean from *The Morning Post*.

Hester had also been much preoccupied with her own affairs. Her mother had gradually sunk into a decline and followed her husband to an early grave. This left Hester as sole guardian of her brother, Mortimer, now a young man of eighteen. He had gone up to Oxford soon after their mother's death and was due to complete his studies this month. Fortunately his capital, an inheritance from an uncle, was intact and on attaining his majority he would be quite well beforehand with the world. At present it was his earnest desire to obtain a commission in the Prince of Wales' regiment, the Tenth Hussars, stationed in Brighton, but Hester was uncertain as to the advisability of this course. She frowned, wondering whom she could consult on this vital matter. As to her own life, it was tranquil; she was not unhappy. She had begun to write novels, both for diversion and also to supplement her modest income of £200 per annum. This activity she found an unfailing source of interest and amusement. In pursuit of information she had made many small excursions to local sites of historic repute including churches, wishing wells, Chanctonbury Ring and once to Huntsgrove Priory when seeking a suitable setting for her latest tale. That visit had been made reluctantly, when the present owner, who seldom spent much time there, was away and Lady Elizabeth was indisposed.

Hester roused herself. She could hear the chimes of Shawcross Church clock striking the hour of eight. She rose to go within doors in the gathering dusk, but halted as she heard the clatter of horses' hooves. She glanced towards the gate and was startled to see a figure swaying perilously in the saddle. With a stifled exclamation Hester ran forward and opened the gate, just as the man slipped from the horse with a groan — instinctively she reached out her arms to cushion his fall. The momentum of his fall caused both Hester and the dark-cloaked figure to land in a tumbled heap on the grassy bank beneath the privet hedge. Gasping for breath — his weight had winded her — Hester scrambled to her feet, but the shrouded man did not stir. She bent over him and removed his hat, which was pulled low over his face. In the gloom she could see little beyond the fact that he wore a mask which covered the whole upper portion of his face. She became aware of a light blinking at the cottage door and a voice calling her name. Her fingers trembled slightly, but she did not hesitate as she quickly pulled off the mask and slipped it in her pocket. She glanced up and down the lane, but at that hour it was deserted.

With a quick decisive nod, Hester ran over to the gate to summon help. The light was dim and shadowy, but she had not failed to recognize the lean, pale face in the moonlight. The masked man was Hugo, Lord Montfort.

She opened the gate gently with a minimum of creaking, and sped across to Jane's flickering light by the well.

"Whatever is amiss, child, you look as if you have seen a ghost!", exclaimed Miss Stanhope as she caught sight of Hester's white face and the twigs sticking in her hair.

"Hush Jane dear," murmured Hester, laying a finger to her lips and speaking softly, "There is a wounded man in the lane, please send George to me, then put on water to boil and bring blankets and bandages to, the sitting room. There's no time to explain now, we must see how badly he is hurt and perhaps call Dr. Minton to assist us. George can go for him while we make the gentleman comfortable."

Miss Stanhope's eyes sparkled. She scented a mystery but wasted no time in speculation. She laid a reassuring hand on Hester's arm before picking up her skirts and trotting away rapidly in the direction of George's domain above the stables. Hester could hear her rapping on the door as she knelt once more beside Hugo. He seemed to have recovered from his swoon, for he was lying with his eyes open, gazing blankly at the blood on his fingers, having just removed his hand from his shoulder. He must have heard the soft rustle of her dress, for he transferred his gaze and shook his head. It was now very dark in the shadow of the hedge and Hester realized that he could not see her face. She laid her hand lightly on his brow, which felt very hot to the touch, and whispered,

"Pray do not try to move. I do not know how badly you are hurt, but assistance will be with us directly."

Nodding feebly, he closed his eyes. She could hear his breathing and the sound of a horse's harness jingling as it cropped the lush grass a little further up the lane. She must get George to attend to the horse as soon as possible. A thought struck her. Surely George could not have gone down to the inn this evening? She was just beginning to panic, for Hugo was a large man to move, and she sighed with relief as she heard hurried footsteps. The next instant George Hamble's burly figure was looming above her, his round eyes and grizzled features illuminated by the lantern. He wasted no time in idle comment, but fell to work with sailorly efficiency.

"You bring the lantern, please Miss," he said a moment later, breathing a little heavily, but otherwise seemingly untroubled by the heavy burden across his shoulders. As Hugo made no sound she guessed he had swooned again. They crossed the garden and entered the cottage in a trice. Hester closed and bolted the door before following George and his burden into the warm sitting room. Jane had pulled the shutters to and closed the windows to keep out noxious night draughts. Normally Hester did not approve of this habit, but tonight she made no protest.

"We will attend to him, thank you, George," said Hester, "Do you go and stable his horse and then fetch Dr. Minton. If the doctor is not at home, please leave a message asking him to call as soon as possible." She hesitated, glancing from George's sturdy dependable face to Miss Stanhope's small, sharp countenance. She had known these two since her childhood and they were loyal, tried friends. She decided to take them into her confidence a little, while resolving that the matter of the mask should remain her secret for the moment.

Therefore she continued, "I am sure that you both will have

recognized this gentleman. I think that until we know more about the circumstances of his — his accident, we should be most discreet about the whole affair. We do not want the village folk to be gossiping and I think his identity should be kept from Martha and Cook. I believe we must send a message to Lady Elizabeth at the Priory to say that his lordship is safe with us, but the message should be delivered into her own hands. You may do this after you have spoken with Dr. Minton, George. Go now quickly and see to the horse, before it is observed wandering in the lane."

George nodded solemnly and stumped out, leaving Hester to aid Miss Stanhope in making their patient as comfortable as possible. The room felt uncomfortably warm, Hugo looked very flushed as he lay propped among the cushions on Lady Vane's old chaise longue. Jane had swathed herself in a voluminous white pinafore, which was already stained ominously with streaks of red. In silence the two ladies worked to cut away the sleeves of his jacket and shirt.

"It's a shame to spoil that fine waistcoat," observed Miss Stanhope, glancing down at Hugo's elegant striped creation.

"It will be spoiled anyway," replied Hester practically, "I think we must cut it, or we cannot easily apply the bandage to his upper arm and shoulder. It will certainly hinder Dr. Minton in his examination. Do you think that he will be at home this evening, Jane?"

Miss Stanhope's slightly wrinkled cheeks took on a deeper hue. She and the good doctor had been engaged in a gentle courtship for some years now. Hester could not refrain from smiling as Miss Stanhope answered with asperity.

"Heavens, Hester, however should I know? — yet stay, now that I think of it 'tis his night for reading to old Betsy Jenkins," she sniffed, "Though why he wastes his precious time on that old witch I cannot think."

"Well, I daresay she is lonely, and kind Dr. Andrew is happy when his company is appreciated," remarked Hester provokingly.

Jane looked at her fiercely, but Hester preserved an innocent mien and rolled her eyes at the ceiling.

"Enough minx," snapped Miss Stanhope, "Make yourself useful to this poor young man of yours here and sponge this wound, while I fetch fresh water."

On this parthian note she sailed out of the room, while Hester took up the sponge rather gingerly and applied it gently to an ugly gaping wound in the left shoulder. It was not long before Miss Stanhope returned with Dr. Andrew Minton by her side.

The doctor wasted no time. He merely nodded to Hester as he stripped off his coat and opened his bag of evil-looking instruments. Hester wished that she was made of stronger stuff as she watched Dr. Minton advance on his unfortunate patient. It seemed to her that he was positively brandishing the gleaming knife in his hand.

"Must find out if the ball is still in there," he muttered to Jane, while Hester turned hastily to the fire. She continued to look in that direction for a long time, clasping her damp hands nervously and listening to the subdued sounds behind her. Mercifully Hugo seemed to be unconscious throughout the proceedings, although he groaned several times. At last Dr. Minton straightened with a sigh of relief and said,

"He'll do now. A nasty graze, he lost a great deal of blood and made matters worse by falling from his horse, but he should be as right as a trivet in a few days. The bullet must have passed through the fleshy part of his arm, but it did not become lodged. He may be a little feverish tonight and should rest for a couple of days. I'll look in tomorrow and see how he does. I'll administer a sleeping draught before I leave, but perhaps we had best move him to a bedchamber first."

Dr. Minton addressed his remarks equally to the two ladies and Miss Stanhope replied briskly, with a glance at Hester,

"Certainly, I'll see that a bedchamber is prepared at once. Then you can take a little refreshment with us until George Hamble returns to help us move the poor gentleman. Do you wish to remain in here, or would you prefer to sit in the breakfast room?"

Before Hester could answer, Andrew Minton sank into a deep wing chair by the fire saying,

"This'll do fine, m'dear. You run along and Missie here can tell me what all this is about."

Thus summarily dismissed, Miss Stanhope drew herself up to every one of her five feet two inches and departed with her head in the air. Dr. Minton grinned at Hester conspiratorially, fumbling in his pocket for his pipe and tobacco pouch.

"Always did like a woman with spirit, but it's a rare thing to meet one as ready to fly up into the boughs as our Jane," he remarked as a satisfying cloud of smoke wreathed about his head.

"She usually responds to provocation," admitted Hester with a smile. She had seated herself on a low footstool after extinguishing the candles near the patient. Her face sobered and she cast a troubled glance at the sleeping figure of Hugo.

"Do you think he is in any danger?" she whispered.

"Not from my treatment, young lady. But there's something devilish havey cavey about the whole business, if you ask me," he responded bluntly. Dr. Minton looked at her keenly beneath his bushy brows. He wore an old brown, wide-skirted coat and brown riding breeches, with his own grey hair tied back with a black bow. He was a lean, capable, hard-working man, with enough of the Scotsman about him to despise those who lived idly and softly at the expense of other men's labour. In his youth he had run through a considerable fortune with ease, and had then learned the hard way to make his own living. In his despair after losing the family estates in Scotland, which he had never even visited, the young Minton had attempted to commit suicide by throwing himself beneath a carriage. He failed in his object, for although severely injured, he was taken up in the carriage which happened to contain an eminent and fashionable surgeon, Dr. Roderick Marvel. Dr. Marvel took a fancy to the young Andrew in the course of his treatment, which took place in the doctor's own house. As he grew stronger Andrew watched his rescuer at work, learning a deep respect and affection for him. Dr. Marvel shared his time and energy between all his patients, regardless of their ability to pay, and he spent an hour each day at Newgate Prison, the great debtor's prison, treating the unfortunate inmates who had succumbed to various prison ailments. Finally Andrew decided that he would like to make a career in medicine, aided and encouraged by Dr. Marvel. After practising successfully for some years in London, Dr. Minton contracted smallpox and when he recovered he decided to remove to the countryside in Sussex for he found that many of his wealthy patients were repulsed by the scars. He had been living in Shawcross for some fifteen years and was a widely respected member of the community, which fully appreciated its good fortune in having such an able practitioner in a rural district.

Stirring uneasily beneath his gaze, Hester reached out to throw another log on the fire. She spread her hands to the blaze, regarding them thoughtfully as she replied,

"I do not know. I was working in the garden when suddenly I heard horse's hooves and saw a figure swaying in the saddle. I caught him as he fell, but he was in great pain and soon became unconscious."

"Mmmm. I see. And he was alone? Did he say anything or give any indication of what may have occurred? Even in these troubled times people do not usually shoot gentlemen on horseback in this quiet part of the country. Especially lords!" he added, with a humorous quirk of his eyebrow.

Hester smiled perfunctorily, but it was obvious to Andrew Minton that her thoughts were elsewhere.

"I have a feeling that you are not telling me everything, but I shall not press you," he said, as Hester raised her hand in a gesture of protest. "Ah, here comes the promised refreshment. A glass of canary, thank you," in answer to a questioning look from Miss Stanhope, "And one of Mrs. Blossom's excellent little cakes."

"You need someone to give you more substantial fare than little cakes," sniffed Miss Stanhope as she proffered the canary wine, "You're as lean as a rake and out at all hours, in all weathers."

"But of course, that is my profession," responded the doctor mildly. Then he added, "I should be happy to have someone provide more substantial fare — you have but to say the word, m'dear".

Miss Stanhope's small frame grew rigid with disapproval,

"Let us debate the subject no further, sir. How does your patient?"

"Well enough, but I must be off soon. Do you think Hamble will be long?"

"I thought I heard hooves in the stable yard a few moments ago. Excuse me, I will go and see." Hester rose and quitted the room with relief, pressing her fingers to her aching temples. She seemed to have been in the warm, close atmosphere for hours. In the kitchen she found George Hamble seated at the well-scrubbed table, a tankard of ale at his elbow. He rose at the sight of her, and Hester smiled.

"Did you see Lady Elizabeth, George?"

"Ar, right enough, Miss Hester, ma'am. In a proper taking she were not even knowin' his lordship was hereabouts, but I explained that 'twere nothing serious loike and she calmed down, poor lady, and axed me to thankee fur yer trouble, Miss and if you would be so good as to send 'er word how 'is lordship be doing tomorrow morning."

"Yes, of course. Had the two young ladies arrived, did you notice?"

"Yes, indeed, Miss, but I think they must have bedded down early. Her Ladyship were alone when I saw her, but she's 'eard as how I'd 'elped her coachman with the wheel and arl. She thanked me very kindly and gave me a crown."

"Well, that is a relief. What a day of excitement. Could you do one more service for me, George? Dr. Minton wishes the gentleman to be moved upstairs. Where are Martha and Mrs. Blossom?" she concluded, glancing around in surprise.

"I think Miss Stanhope sent them to bed, Miss. I 'eard 'er telling 'em to be off as I was taking me boots off on the step."

"Very well. Come with me then, George, and softly."

Hester returned to the parlour with George at her heels. A stretcher was contrived from a blanket and with some difficulty his lordship was removed above stairs. Dr. Minton administered a sleeping draught and took his leave, promising to return the next day. The ladies cleared away all traces of the evening's activities in companionable silence.

"Do you go to bed now, Jane," said Hester when they had finished. "It must be very late. I will sit up with his lordship in case his condition should deteriorate during the night."

Miss Stanhope opened her mouth to protest, but gave a hearty yawn instead.

Perceiving her advantage, Hester pressed,

"You see how weary you are. You would fall asleep at the bedside. Besides you have already done your share of help this evening. You and Dr. Minton worked like a perfect team!"

"Naughty puss!" exclaimed Miss Stanhope, "Very well, have it your own way, but leave the door ajar and call me if you need me."

The two ladies took up their candles from the hall table and mounted the stair together. They parted at the door of Miss Stanhope's bedchamber and Hester went on down the passage to her own room, where she collected a shawl and a volume of Pope's poetry to keep her company through the long night hours. She then returned to the passage and went up two steps to the little box room under the eaves. Opening the door softly, she tiptoed to the bed. All was still; retreating, she curled up in a comfortable little chair by the window. The shutters were open and she could see the crescent moon peeping fitfully from behind the chasing clouds. For a while she mused on the strange coincidences of the day, the arrival of Marietta and Stephanie, her own memories of Hugo Jermyn and then the advent of that same man, wounded, followed by Dr. Minton's visit. She withdrew the mask from her pocket and examined it. She could find nothing very remarkable about it. It was made of plain black velvet, with two slits to see through. It was the kind of mask which she had worn herself to a masquerade, covering the top half of the face only and she could not imagine why Lord Montfort would find it necessary to wear such a thing in the depths of the country. She slipped the tell-tale object back in her pocket. Her tired mind revolved around the puzzle, but she could think of no satisfactory explanation. More questions occurred to her — what was he doing in the country when he had told his wards that he was detained by business and could not leave town? Who had shot him and why? In her own experience the local country people were law-abiding folk, apart from some occasional contraband dealings late at night — and this incident must have occurred quite early in the evening.

An owl hooted in the distance and the man in the bed stirred restlessly. Wringing out a damp cloth, Hester gently bathed his forehead. His eyes flew open but he gazed at her without recognition. Suddenly he said in an astonishingly normal voice,

"Oh lord, I've missed the boat. What will become of the mission? Better tell Ned, he will know how to contrive."

A few moments later he started up from his pillow, exclaiming,

"The message must be in France by the 25th!"

Hester bent over him saying soothingly,

"Certainly, my lord, but you must rest now or you will reopen your wound."

Hugo looked up and regarded her questioningly for a long moment. He murmured,

"Sure we've met, but — can't tell — where I have had the — pleasure. . .," his voice trailed away drowsily, after a few incoherent mutterings he subsided into a deep sleep.

Hester retired to her chair and remained wide awake and thoughtful, though poor Mr. Pope was quite disregarded, until Miss Stanhope appeared with a cup of hot chocolate at half past six in the morning. They exchanged a few quiet words concerning the patient's welfare before Hester allowed herself to be persuaded that she must take some rest. She fell asleep as soon as her head touched the pillow and knew no more for several hours.

Chapter 3
Tea For Two

When Hester awoke it was mid-afternoon. She rose hastily and tidied herself, taking more pains than usual with her appearance. She chose a dainty, nearly new, sprig muslin dress, which showed off her slender figure to advantage, and disdaining her usual braided coronet she tied her hair high in a loose bunch of curls. She decided not to ruin the whole effect by swathing herself in her favourite Indian shawl. Instead she clasped her mother's heart-shaped locket about her throat and ran downstairs briskly to counteract the slight shivering brought on by her short puffed sleeves and thin muslin.

Hester found Miss Stanhope in the sitting room. It appeared that Dr. Minton had but just now taken his leave. He had found Lord Montfort much improved when he examined him and changed the bandages. His lordship was possessed of a strong constitution; the doctor considered that after another day or two of rest he should be well enough to travel the short distance to the Priory.

"Is his lordship conscious? Has the fever left him? Has he said anything?" enquired Hester.

Miss Stanhope's eyes widened slightly as she observed Hester's lavender muslin, her second best, taken out from its mothballs so early in the year, but she made no comment beyond saying,

"Yes, to all three questions, my love. His lordship will know that spring is definitely upon us when he sees you!"

Hester coloured, laughed and then said defiantly,

"Well it is spring, even if it does not feel like it, and I did not wish to be caught unawares in my old working clothes again today, should anybody call to ask after his lordship."

"A wise precaution to be sure," nodded Miss Stanhope imperturbably, "But his lordship has been asking to speak with you."

"Does he know who I am?" queried Hester, a trifle dismayed.

"Of course. He asked me when I took up a bowl of thin gruel for his luncheon if I were the lady who had sat up with him last night. I took pity on his confusion, introduced myself, and explained that he was in the house of Miss Hester Vane. He frowned when I mentioned your name but merely said, 'So I did not imagine it. Pray present my compliments to Miss Vane and request her to favour me with a few moments of her time, when convenient.' I told him that you were still sleeping after keeping watch at his bedside all night, but promised I would give you the message. Then he smiled at me so sweetly that my heart quite turned over — so unexpected with those beetling brows — and he fell asleep like a baby. Would you like to take your tea upstairs with him?"

"Well, I was thinking of finishing my chapter and then walking to the village to beg Mrs. Lightfoot to let me have a bottle of her elderberry wine for Mortimer to come home to. He is so fond of it."

"Nonsense child. Mortimer will not be home for some days yet and you can finish your chapter this evening. Lord Montfort will be awake by now and feeling neglected I'll be bound; invalids need pampering, you know. He will find an old woman like me quite an inadequate substitute for a charming young lady like yourself at his tea table."

Hester threw up her hands in a comical gesture of despair,

"Very well, ma'am. If you are to be his champion I see that all is lost. I will gather a few flowers to brighten his sickroom and we will take tea in a quarter of an hour."

"Good girl!" chuckled Miss Stanhope as Hester quitted the room, "I hope she does not muddy her skirts traipsing about in the garden after so much rain."

Meanwhile Hester gathered a nosegay of violets and pansies. These she arranged in a small brown earthenware jug. Then she tapped softly on the door of the sick room. There was a firm "Come in" and she entered, her heart beating a little fast.

Holding the flowers before her, rather as if she expected to ward off a blow, Hester approached the bed. Her chin well up, she told herself to be quite cool and detached. Unfortunately for her good resolutions she tripped over the hook rug and deposited her floral offering in a damp heap in the middle of the coverlet.

"Oh, good heavens, how clumsy I am!" she cried in dismay. Not daring to glance at the silent figure propped among the pillows, Hester seized the damp cloth which she had used during the night and began to mop furiously. Miss Stanhope choosing to appear at this juncture with the tea tray, her experienced eye took in the situation in a moment. Over Hester's bent head her eyes met those of Hugo Jermyn. His stern face was transfigured by a sudden irradiating grin, and Miss Stanhope was forced to compress her lips tightly to suppress a giggle.

"Miss Jane, do set down that most welcome tea tray and come to our aid!" said Hugo calmly.

"Yes, of course, my lord, Hester dear, damp sprig muslins may be 'all the crack' as they say, but I fear you will catch your death of cold if you sit about drinking tea in that state. Do go and change and I will set all to rights here."

"Yes, er . . . thank you," gasped poor Hester, "I won't be a moment." Pressing her fingers to her hot cheeks she rushed to her room and gazed at herself in the mirror. Whatever is the matter with me, I'm behaving like a schoolroom miss, she admonished herself. Hastily removing the clinging lavender gown, she pulled out her green watered silk. Some frenzied rummaging unearthed a rose sash and matching hair ribbon. Thus attired, she carefully bathed her face with rosewater and triumphantly returned to take tea with Lord Montfort all in the space of five minutes.

The scene was peaceful. Miss Stanhope had disappeared leaving the flowers in a small glass on the window seat. Hugo was waiting for his tea. With some constraint, Hester approached the bedside once more, made a slight curtsey and said,

"Good afternoon, my lord Montfort. You may recall that I am Hester Vane. I trust that you are feeling better?"

Hugo gazed up at the face above him, noting the warm brown hair, the laughter lines around the eyes and the firm, yet gentle mouth. His green eyes met and held Hester's grey ones for a long moment. Somewhere below, a clock chimed the hour of four. It was a sweet musical sound and imperceptibly the atmosphere in the room lightened. A bumble bee buzzed past the open casement, the spell was broken and Hester seated herself at the table. She began to pour the refreshing brew into the delicate bone china cups.

Abruptly Hugo said,

"I am feeling much restored today and I understand that it is largely to you that I must offer my thanks. Miss Stanhope tells me that you were the lady who found me and sat up with me through the night."

"So much one does in common humanity, my lord, no special thanks are due to me." Then, feeling that she had been perhaps a little ungracious, she added, "'Twas Dr. Minton who treated your wound, with the aid of my good Jane."

"But the flowers were all your own idea?", he insisted pettishly.

"Both idea and execution," granted Hester, laughing despite herself.

"I have some questions which I must put to you," stated his lordship, a grim note in his voice.

"Presently, my lord. It is unwise to vex yourself with problems in your weak condition." She pretended to be preoccupied with her task, adding conversationally, "I am aware that few gentlemen share my view, but I assure you that this is a peculiarly fortifying beverage when taken hot and well-sweetened." Her attempted diversion succeeded; Hugo watched aghast as three spoonfuls of sugar were measured into his cup. Satisfied, Hester rose gracefully to set the nauseating liquid within easy reach of his hand. She offered him a plate of dry biscuits. His lordship accepted one with a resigned grimace.

"You're taking advantage of my feebleness," he protested, "Nothing but thin gruel for luncheon and now this. How is a man to get body and soul together again on such insubstantial fare?"

"I was not aware that the two had yet separated, my lord," observed Hester with composure, "However, be that as it may, Dr. Minton was quite adamant that strong flavoured food, especially meats, would inflame the fever. I believe he remarked that a day of starvation would do no harm to a man of your iron constitution."

Hugo grunted, "Did he indeed, damn his impertinence!"

Hester sought for some subject of innocuous conversation.

"I had the pleasure of making the acquaintance of your two wards, Miss von Sapsburg and Miss de Beauclerc, yesterday. They took refuge with us when their carriage broke down in the lane near my cottage. You will be relieved to hear that they arrived at the Priory without further incident. My coachman, George Hamble, called on Lady Elizabeth to reassure her concerning your own safety late last night and naturally enquired about the young ladies."

"My family seem to have put you to a great deal of inconvenience yesterday. Quite a day of accidents," he remarked dryly.

"It was no inconvenience at all," Hester assured him politely, "Your cousins were charming and I hope that I may see them again. Life in the country can be a trifle dull at times. I expect that is why I write novels."

Hugo gave her a startled glance, followed by a wry grin.

"That accounts for it then," he remarked with satisfaction, nibbling a biscuit. When further elucidation was not forthcoming, Hester prodded suspiciously,

"Accounts for what, pray?"

"Your air of abstraction and, ah . . . ineptitude with household tasks. Miss Jane tells me that you are sadly scatterbrained. But forgive me, I do not mean to be uncivil," he added hastily as Hester's expressive countenance clouded, "The circumstances are somewhat unusual."

A darker mood enveloped them. Hugo moved restlessly on the

pillows and muttered, half to himself,

"I cannot stay here, I have urgent business to attend to."

Impatiently, he tried to sit up unaided, but fell back with a gasp. Hester was dismayed at the pallor of his face. She went quickly to the small chest beneath the window seat, poured a glass of cordial and took it to him. Hugo sipped a little, the colour gradually returning to his cheeks. Hester reproached herself for staying so long, but when she made a move to withdraw he caught her hand in a surprisingly strong clasp.

"Cease fencing with me, Miss Vane, if you please and kindly explain exactly what occurred last night. By according me sanctuary you may have placed yourself in considerable danger."

Hester was puzzled and alarmed by his earnest manner. Gently she removed her hand, saying firmly,

"My lord, you will suffer a relapse if you excite yourself so. I promise that I will do my best to satisfy your curiosity when you are recovered, but I am sure you should rest for a while. If you wish I will return after dinner. Can I get you anything to make you more comfortable?" He shook his head peevishly, but as she reached the door he called after her,

"One moment, Miss Vane. I beg you to forgive my boorish behaviour. It is a poor return for your kindness. I should like to peruse a copy of your most recent work, if you have one readily to hand."

"I will fetch you one with pleasure," replied Hester. "Dr. Minton tells me he finds novels remarkably efficacious in sending him to sleep. Perhaps mine may perform the same service for you. Excuse me, I shall not be away long."

When she returned with *The Master of Crumbling Keep* Hester found Lord Montfort fast asleep. She placed the volume on the table and looked down at the well-remembered features. In repose his face seemed more youthful and vulnerable, much as it had been before he left for the Continent and their ways had parted. With a small sigh of regret, she tiptoed downstairs.

Feeling indisposed for conversation, Hester was tempted out of doors by the late afternoon sun. She wandered idly down the lane in the opposite direction to the village until she reached a small stone bridge across a stream. Here she sat down upon the broad parapet and leaned back on her hands, closing her eyes, and revelling in the surprising warmth of the sun on her bare arms and face.

She still loved Hugo, she admitted to herself. It was strange that the attraction remained after so long a separation. She thought that she had forgotten, achieved tranquillity. She did not need this disruption in her well-ordered existence, she mused resentfully, recalling nonetheless the way her spine had tingled at the touch of his hand. This was foolish, Hester scolded herself, at her age one should have more control over one's emotions. Hugo Jermyn was not for her and she must avoid his company as much as possible. It had been made quite clear years ago that the penniless daughter of an old neighbour was quite unworthy of his attention. Yet he did not behave like a mercenary man, he had never been on the catch for an heiress and had always treated his bits of muslin with generosity and consideration, if all one heard was true. Scandalized at the turn which her thoughts had taken, Hester opened her eyes. Not sorry to have her reverie interrupted, she rose to welcome a little girl coming down the lane with a tall man.

"Good afternoon, Mr. Stone," Hester greeted the Vicar of Shawcross, "And how are you today, Sally?" she asked the little girl, whose long, fair hair hung down below her thin shoulders. Sally Lightfoot was small for her ten years and delicately made. Her mother was the housekeeper to Mr. Jedediah Stone. Sally was a general favourite in the neighbourhood, being blessed with a warm and helpful disposition. At her mother's insistence, she wore a thick brown cloak over her blue woollen dress, and her small feet were encased in ankle boots. A lively black terrier named Toby frisked at her heels. The two were inseparable companions.

Sally made a curtsey, while Mr. Stone stood a little to one side, watching the lady and the child wistfully.

"I'm very well, thank you ma'am. Toby and I are keeping Mr. Stone company because he gets lonely sometimes, all by himself in that big, ugly old house." Sally gave a little shiver, thinking of the ancient vicarage, damp and musty with age and shrouded by yew and laurel like the church-yard which it adjoined. Sally lived with her mother in a cosy cottage beyond the church, overlooking the village green.

"Sally is very good company, Miss Vane," said the vicar, smiling down at them both from his considerable height. "We have been trying to tickle a trout for my dinner in the old mill pond, but without much success I am afraid."

"Well, I'm sorry for you and happy for the trout," remarked Hester, as she turned to accompany them down the lane towards the village. "Fishing has always seemed to me a very barbarous activity, second only to hunting some unfortunate hare or deer — and I'm not even sure I should make that distinction."

"I understand your attitude, although I do not share it. Hunting and being hunted, it is all a part of the order of nature — and fishing is a most soothing occupation, lending itself, as it does, to long periods of meditation. And I very rarely catch anything," he concluded with a rueful smile. Hester shook her head.

"My dear sir, how rude of me. I did not intend to be so uncivil. It is merely that hunting is a subject on which I happen to feel strongly."

Mr. Stone put his hand lightly beneath her elbow to assist Hester to surmount a muddy pitfall in the middle of the track.

"I like a young lady who will speak her mind, Miss Vane, so refreshing. Yours is a delightfully independent spirit."

"Not a trait of which most clergymen approve in the weaker sex," rallied Hester, for she thought Jedediah looked tired and worried. He was a well-built man in his early thirties, with hair and eyes of a soft, indeterminate brown. This apparent softness was belied by a square jaw and large, hooked nose. He was attired in clerical black and presented a rather sombre appearance. Hester had known him since he came to the parish soon after her father's death. She had found him a firm friend, and an unusually diligent cleric. He did not confine his activities to a weekly sermon, nor did he seek to ingratiate himself with the local gentry. He was willing to help any member of his flock, at times in quite unorthodox ways, but in one respect he steadfastly refused to follow in the tradition of his predecessors: he refused adamantly to become involved with the local smuggling fraternity or to accept any gifts as the price of silence though his income was meagre. However, he had been known to pray earnestly beside some wounded smuggler, and to render what practical assistance he could until the doctor arrived. He was well-liked and respected by the poorer folk and the rank and file among the smugglers, but it was rumoured that the leaders were dissatisfied with this situation and were again pressing for rights of way through the churchyard. These whispers had reached Hester by devious routes and it would not do to speak of them, but she did sympathize with his predicament.

They parted at her cottage gate, Sally having run ahead with Toby. Hester waved after their retreating forms and hurried indoors to tidy herself before dinner.

"His lordship wishes to leave us tomorrow. Do you think he will be well enough?" enquired Hester of Miss Stanhope as she toyed with a dish of roast lamb and pickled cucumber.

"I daresay. If he insists. There is nothing wrong with his appetite at least, I'll be bound."

"Good heaven, you did not allow him to have lamb this evening?"

exclaimed Hester in dismay.

"No, no, I am not so foolish. He ate merely two or three poached eggs, some of Mrs. Blossom's freshly baked bread with our own honey, an apple tartlet and some sherry wine."

"To be sure, a very light repast," agreed Hester.

Miss Stanhope chose to ignore the irony in her tone and changed the subject by asking,

"Did I hear Mr. Stone's voice outside before dinner?"

Hester nodded, lifting her napkin to her mouth to hide a smile. Miss Stanhope thought Mr. Stone a very worthy young man, and in default of anything better she had for some time considered him in the light of a suitor for Hester's hand. Hester liked him well, but she had no desire to exchange her snug cottage for the gloomy vicarage and she knew that she would make a very bad vicar's wife. She had also noticed how Mr. Stone was attracted by the bright eyes of Susan Garth from Hatch End and she had no wish to throw a rub in their way. However, she humoured Miss Stanhope and confirmed that she had indeed met Mr. Stone with little Sally, when she had stepped out for a moment for some fresh air.

Miss Stanhope nodded absentmindedly, then startled Hester by announcing,

"I'm sorry, my dear Hester, but he will not do for you. A Vane of Shawcross Manor may look higher than a country vicar, be he never so worthy."

"Jane, I am shocked." declared Hester roundly. "You forget that I am no longer a Vane 'of Shawcross Manor' as you put it. If I loved Mr. Stone and he loved me I should not allow social distinctions to weigh with me for a second!"

"Hoity toity, miss. Such romantic notions are all very well between the covers of a novel from the circulating library. They cannot be indulged in your situation."

Hester was obliged to laugh,

"Do not ring such a peal over me. I have no intention of marrying anyone at present. And Jane, pray do not be transferring your matchmaking designs to his hapless lordship, for I assure you that fish will not fry."

"Hester, where do you learn these vulgar expressions? From young Mortimer, I presume. When I think of all those years I spent trying to instil in you some measure of ladylike decorum, I could weep."

"I should advise strongly against it my love, for it will make your eyes all red, recollect Dr. Minton is coming to play backgammon with you."

"Why so he is. I had quite forgotten. Could you ring for Martha to clear and bring the coffee." Miss Stanhope consulted her big old-fashioned timepiece, a legacy from her father, "It is nearly eight o'clock already. We are very late tonight."

"What a good thing you decided to put on that very fetching lavender cap. I will ring for Martha while you pinch your cheeks, you know how Dr. Minton admires an apple-cheeked complexion," said Hester wickedly.

When all was tidy and the ladies were sipping their coffee, Hester remarked casually,

"As you have company this evening I think I will retire early. I could look in on Lord Montfort for a few minutes to see if he requires anything for the night and then you will not need to disturb him later on."

Miss Stanhope's brows drew together and she gave Hester a penetrating glance, but made no comment beyond a nod of assent. They heard footsteps on the path and a few moments later Martha ushered Dr. Minton into the parlour. Hester exchanged greetings and a few words concerning the progress of their patient with the doctor, finished her coffee and waited until the two old friends had their heads together over the backgammon board. Then she slipped upstairs, smoothing her skirt and tumbled curls as she went. She found his lordship awake, reading the novel which she had left for him. He appeared to be straining his eyes to get the last ounce of daylight.

Hester seated herself quietly, content to wait until he had finished the paragraph. After a short interval, Hugo closed the book, first marking the place carefully. Then he looked up with a grin and exclaimed,

"Thank you for not interrupting. An unusual characteristic in a female. My dear Miss Vane, this has entirely captivated me. I cannot think why I have not encountered your works long since. I had not realized that there was so much fire hidden beneath that calm exterior!"

"I should not have suspected your lordship of indulging in such light entertainment," retorted Hester, amused, "My characters are quite independent creations you know. They may throw less light on me than you suppose."

Hugo nodded wisely, "Of course. But may I borrow a copy to take for my mother's perusal. This is exactly the kind of book which she admires, full of sound common sense despite its superficially romantic air."

Hester smiled,

"Of course you may borrow it for Lady Elizabeth if you think that it would give her pleasure. I have already promised to request my publisher to send a copy to your two wards, as that is the only copy I have by me at present. I did not realize *The Master of Crumbling Keep* would be in such demand in Shawcross. Most of my friends disapprove of my 'scribbling' as Jane calls it."

Hugo raised his brows in polite disbelief, but commented, "I cannot deprive you of your personal copy. Tell me, am I correct in thinking that I detect a vague resemblance between Crumbling Keep and Huntsgrove Priory, or is that merely a figment of my parochial imagination?"

Hester flushed a little as she admitted,

"No, it is not your imagination. I hope you do not object? I am careful never to employ real people as models for my characters, but I have fewer scruples in regard to location. I did take some liberties and I changed a number of architectural details, but *au fond* Crumbling Keep is the Priory as I imagined it might be, had it been neglected for a long period."

Hugo eyed Hester quizzically for a moment.

"No, I do not object, Miss Vane. Indeed, I assure you I am flattered that my home should find its place in literature! But you say you have promised a copy of your work to Stephanie and Marietta. That I do find disturbing. Do you have the impression that the young ladies are much addicted to the 'genre'?"

Disconcerted, Hester answered cautiously,

"I trust I am not betraying a confidence, for I should not wish to prejudice you against either young lady; Miss Marietta appeared to be the 'addict'. Miss Stephanie declared roundly that in general she has no time for such nonsense, but she promised to read my work for curiosity's sake!"

Hugo put his hand to his brow in an exaggerated gesture,

"You relieve my mind, on one score at least. But I was not aware that you had visited the Priory recently. Your memory is remarkably accurate if you have not been there since we were children."

It was the first reference made by Lord Montfort to their earlier acquaintance and Hester stiffened. She replied coolly,

"Your housekeeper, Mrs. Poole, is an old friend of mine. She was good enough to show me over the gardens and the formal rooms, to refresh my memory when I was writing the book last year. I was interested to hear that you are renovating the old wing." Hester finished on a questioning note and Hugo nodded easily.

"Oh yes, it is time I took the place in hand. Otherwise it will be in very truth a crumbling keep!"

Hester laughed and their eyes met and held. Once again Hester was conscious of a prickling sensation. Abruptly, she rose to leave, murmuring that the hour was late.

"One moment, I beg," Hugo spoke softly, but firmly.

"Yes?" Hester halted in the middle of the room, one foot tapping impatiently.

"Miss Vane, I must ask that you describe to me the events of last night. Also, there are some other questions concerning our former relationship which puzzle me but I will not press you on that head, if you do not wish it."

Thus addressed, Hester decided that offence was the best method of defence and she said steadily,

"I am at a loss to understand your latter remark, my lord! that episode in our lives is over and best forgotten. With regard to your injury there is little I can tell. I was sitting in my garden, I heard your horse, and saw you swaying dangerously in the saddle. I ran out in alarm. Fortunately, I was in time to act as a buffer, when you slipped to the ground. My man, George Hamble, assisted me to bring you within doors and we called Dr. Minton. The rest you know."

"I see. Then you were alone when you found me? Did anyone else observe my arrival?"

"Not to my knowledge. It was almost dark, but I did not hear any sounds in the lane. Now, my lord, I am very fatigued. I do not wish to probe into your affairs and I intend to remain equally reticent concerning my own. I have always been taught that 'least said, soonest mended'."

Hester swept a deep curtsey before crossing to the door. With her hand upon the knob she added significantly,

"Pray remind me to return your mask when you leave. I hope that you will have no further use for it. It seems to be a dangerous article of apparel. Good night, my lord."

Hugo was left staring at the closed door. With a wry grin he muttered,

"Wretched perverse female!"

It was some time before Lord Montfort and Miss Vane, in their respective chambers, fell asleep that night.

Chapter 4
A Chance Meeting

Hester awoke the next morning to an agitated scratching at her door. She rolled over indignantly and blinked as Miss Stanhope loomed above her, waving a piece of paper.

"Why Jane, is the house afire? Are we besieged? Your cap is all askew. Pray compose yourself and tell me what is wrong."

"He's gone, Hester. His lordship left the house this morning before the servants were astir. He was not sufficiently recovered to leave his bed and I cannot imagine how he contrived to saddle that great black brute without assistance. He left this missive for you on the hall table. Oh what a foolish young man he is! Do you think that we should send word to the Priory to see if he is returned safely?"

Hester frowned, and shook her head.

"No, I am sure that he would dislike it above all things. We are not even sure that he is gone to the Priory. But perhaps his note will enlighten us."

She took the single folded sheet of paper and scanned it quickly. In a bold scrawling hand she read,

"My dear Miss Vane,

I beg that you will excuse the incivility of my abrupt departure. I have unfinished business which must be attended to immediately. I would like to express my gratitude to Miss Jane and to yourself for your great care and kindness. I will do myself the honour of waiting upon you both at an early date to convey my thanks in person. At that time I will reclaim any personal effects which I may have overlooked in my haste.

My compliments to Miss Jane.

Your sincere friend and servant,

Montfort."

"Good Heavens!", exclaimed Hester in dismay, "Surely he did not leave this open upon the hall table, where anyone might read it. I trust that he managed to depart unobserved. Do you think that anyone would recognize his mare — Cassy did he not call her?"

"Yes, yes," cried Miss Stanhope impatiently, "But what does he say? I cannot understand what he is about. Why should he wish to depart unobserved?"

Reluctantly, Hester collected her racing thoughts and set herself to soothe her companion,

"Now Jane, surely you must remember that he wished his identity to be kept from the servants. He did not desire the whole village to be gossiping about his mishap. His note is most civil, he presents his compliments to you and will call upon us soon."

"Well it is all most mysterious; I have a feeling that you are keeping something from me. But I will not tease you. What do you propose to do today?"

Hester considered, "I believe I will take the trap and drive into Pendleton. Do you wish to accompany me, or shall I take George for escort? He was telling me that we need a new scythe."

Miss Stanhope nodded briskly, "A good idea, my love. Take George, by all means. I feel a trifle done up this morning and would be glad of a little quiet. I have neglected my sewing box sadly and I think I will make over my green pelisse if we are to visit Lady Marchant in the near future. Perhaps you would be kind enough to purchase some gold braid for the trimming. Do you have many commissions to execute?"

"No, not really," replied Hester, "I intend to call at the post office. It is time that we received a letter from Mortimer. Then I need some new gloves, for my old ones are much worn and I am quite ashamed of them. I saw Mrs. Crossley looking at them pointedly only last Sunday. She mentioned that primrose or lavender kid are all the mode in Town this year."

"Hum!" sniffed Miss Jane, "That Mrs. Crossley takes too much upon herself. And as for those daughters, always giving themselves airs, as if their family had lived at the manor for generations. Vulgar upstarts in my opinion. No true lady would boast of her grand acquaintance as Mrs. Crossley does. But then, of course, her father made his fortune in trade, clay pots or some such thing."

"How harsh you are today," protested Hester, "Quite out of sorts. I agree that we do not have much in common with the Crossleys, but they are most good natured and eager to be of service. Mr. Crossley has already offered to put his carriage at our disposal whenever we wish to travel to Brighton or London. Now Jane, do go down and have some breakfast and I am sure you will feel better. I will join you directly."

She reached for her wrapper as Miss Stanhope departed with a flounce. Hester glanced through the window as Martha entered with hot water and fresh towels. It was a bright, sunny day and she chided herself for feeling a trifle flat.

"This will never do," she said aloud, making haste to complete her toilette. Some half an hour later she was seated beside George in the trap jogging sedately along the country lane. She was fetchingly attired in a modish brown pelisse, with a matching bonnet, ornamented with an orange ostrich feather.

"'Ee do be right purty as a picture Miss Hester," declared George with his slow smile. Hester smiled back,

"Thank you, George, that is very good for my morale. You remarked, I presume, that his lordship left us this morning?", Hester raised her brows and regarded her companion inquiringly.

"To be sure, mistress. I helped him saddle Cassy, for 'is left shoulder were so weak he dropped the bit and then fell over a bucket and swore something 'orrible. So I woke up and come down to see what were goin' on. 'is lordship were that apologetic and begged me ter give 'im an 'and. Well, I were all fer fetchin' you, Miss, but he wheedled and commanded and afore I knew it, he were mounted and ridin' off, leavin' me with a crown, a'scratchin' my haid and wonderin' if I'd done right. I wanted to accompany 'im, but he said he'd go quicker and safer alone and that I should stay and watch over you. He did say he thought you might be in some danger from the local 'gentry' for 'arborin' him." George lowered his voice and glanced around cautiously as he spoke. Despite herself, Hester felt a prickle of unease at these words and she too scanned the rolling downlands as she replied,

"What foolish talk is this? I am well known in this county and have done nothing to offend any of our neighbours. In common humanity I could scarce refuse to help a man in distress."

"His lordship grew up in this county too, Miss Hester," retorted George calmly, "Yet he was shot only a short distance from your door. Something's afoot in the village and everyone's afeared to talk of it. Yon Mr. Stone, 'ee be shunned by many folk. 'Tisn't wise to be seen talkin' with 'im too free," he finished warningly and flicked his whip as they emerged from the small lane on to the main road to Pendleton. 'Merrylegs,' the bay mare, quickened her pace and they were soon bowling along at a very creditable pace.

Hester tossed her head, compressing her lips firmly. The light vehicle jolted in a rut and she was obliged to hang to the side to steady herself.

"This is nonsense," George, she burst out scornfully, when the rocking had subsided and they were once more jogging along smoothly between neat hedgerows. "I will not be intimidated. Why, Mr. Stone is well liked and respected throughout his parish. I certainly have no intention of avoiding his company — I had no notion of this state of affairs. I despise rumour and gossip of all things. Why did you not tell me of it before?"

"'Cos I knew how it would be," said George Hamble resignedly, "I remember how you were, as a little mite, up at the Manor, all fire and spirit, defending them little rascals from the cottages at Downend whenever there was any trouble. Don't 'ee recall the time that old bull of Squire's got in among the turnips an' you said 'twas your idea — I do know fur a fact 'twas young Thomas Bates as did it. And then you tried to persuade the Master the lad should go to school and he ran away to sea and was drownded, so 'twere all fur naut." Hester laughed ruefully,

"Yes, I remember it well. It was the only time Father ever whipped me. But I meant it for the best. It always seemed so unfair that I should have so much, when those children had so little. But I see what you would be at and I will not be distracted. What is amiss in the village and why are folk afraid to speak of it?"

George shook his head and loosened his glowing red neckcloth for the day was growing warm.

"I don't know much, Miss, but from what I can gather, there be a new leader among the 'gentry', no-one knows who he be. He's after makin' 'is fortune fast, and he dabbles with dangerous matters, papers and such, not just reg'lar trading like it used to be, you see Miss? There's many a lad comes home bloodied and bruised, but everyone's afeared to say anything. Mr. Stone, bein' a true gentleman, he won't have no truck wid such doings and there you are."

Hester knitted her brows thoughtfully,

"Thank you for telling me, George. This puts a different complexion on the situation. It will not do to meddle, I quite agree. Do you think his lordship could be involved in any way?"

"I don't know, Miss. All I know is somebody shot 'im tother night and he said to watch over you after you cared for him."

Silence fell between them. George Hamble chewed ruminatively on a straw, while Hester digested the information which she had just received. In due course they entered the little town of Pendleton and rattled over the cobbled streets until they reached the market place. It was not market day, but the morning had lured many people out of doors obliging them to thread their way slowly to the door of 'The Lamb' hotel. Here George assisted Hester to alight. It was settled between them that they would make their separate purchases and meet in an hour's time. George led 'Merrylegs' through the archway to the stables and Hester, cheeks aglow at the pleasurable prospect of making frivolous purchases, retraced her path across the square. She glanced around and felt a thrill of delight at the busy scene. For the moment her worries were forgotten and she revelled in the familiar sights and sounds: prosperous sheep farmers, with their dogs at their heels; a little old lady, all in black, sitting at the foot of the market cross with a basket of lavender at her feet; some urchins playing fivestones in the gutter beside the horse trough, waiting for an opportunity to earn a penny by watering some gentleman's horses; a trim maidservant in earnest conversation with a young ostler; the chant of youthful voices reciting in unison wafting through the open windows of the old Elizabethan Grammar School behind the Church, and the distant quacking of the ducks in the old mill pond beyond 'The Lamb'.

Hester halted a moment to allow an elegant carriage to sweep past her, then proceeded at a faster pace until she arrived at a small, bowfronted shop bearing a faded sign in a genteel script: 'Miss Milsom's, Fine Millinery and Haberdashery'. She entered to a soft tinkling of bells and found two ladies before her at the counter. She observed them with interest. They were obviously mother and daughter. Both ladies were fashionably attired in high-waisted round gowns, but the original simplicity of their design was lost in a welter of Indian shawls, scarves, necklaces and bracelets. Indeed, so abundant was the profusion of articles that Hester could not imagine how they could possibly require any more. She seated herself a little to one side and waited patiently as they examinded tray after tray of feathers and ribbons. Clearly they found the selection provokingly provincial, for when poor Miss Milsom had displayed every item at her command the younger lady exclaimed pettishly,

"Come Mama, we are wasting our time. Miss Eliza insists that cocquelicot ribbons are all the rage in Town this season. *The Lady's Magazine* was quite adamant on that point and nothing else will suffice to trim my white muslin."

"As you wish, my dear. For myself I can see nothing among these plumes to equal, let alone surpass, those on Mrs. Simmon's turban last Sunday. Let us try Mr. Brown's establishment on Church Street. I told you we should have gone there in the first place. Good day, Miss Milsom."

Amid a flurry of skirts and a flutter of shawls, mother and daughter departed. Hester rose and smiled at Miss Milsom sympathetically. The little milliner returned her smile shyly, while her small mittened hands hovered helplessly over the trays, sorting and rewinding rather aimlessly. She was dressed in a plain black gown, her only ornament a simple gold chain. Her soft grey hair curled in tight ringlets about her face, and her expression was sweet and youthful, despite the fact that she was well past middle age.

Miss Milsom's violet blue eyes met Hester's grey ones and she shook her head resignedly.

"Pray excuse this confusion, Miss Vane. How may I be of service?"

"I am seeking some new kid gloves. I have a fancy for some in a primrose shade and I also require some braid for trimming a pelisse."

These articles presented no problem and Hester made her selection with ease. She added a yard of lace to finish some cambric handkerchiefs which she was making for Miss Stanhope's birthday.

"This lace is very fine," she observed, fingering a length idly, "Surely it is not from Nottingham. Is it imported?"

Miss Milsom nodded complacently.

"Yes, ma'am. It is pure Valenciennes. I keep it for my special customers."

Hester stiffened, alerted by the other lady's tone.

"I see. It must be difficult to obtain."

"Why no, ma'am. I receive my shipment regularly once a month by Mr. Garth's carrier." Miss Milsom's hand flew to her cheek in dismay, "Oh, heaven's I should not mention names. I am not usually such a chatterbox, but I am a little upset this morning. You must have heard, Ma'am, of the robbery at Staleybridge, and the poor gentleman attacked in his carriage only a mile or two outside Pendleton. Those two ladies were speaking of it just before you came in. One hears such strange tales recently." The little lady shivered, adding belatedly, "But it does not do to speak too freely, there are spies everywhere."

Hester was about to reply when the door bell jingled and a stout lady entered, accompanied by her maid. Miss Milsom busied herself in wrapping Hester's packages, and the moment for confidences was past. Hester took her leave and continued thoughtfully up Church Street, oblivious now to the press of humanity around her. She was puzzled by the milliner's obvious fear, and by her reference to 'Mr. Garth'. Hester knew only one Mr. Garth of any consequence in the neighbourhood. He was her solicitor and his sister, Susan, was her good friend.

The church clock struck twelve as she entered the post office across the street. The clerk handed her a letter and glancing hastily at the superscription she recognized her brother's careless hand. She slipped the letter in her reticule to read at leisure and decided that she had just time to call at the Circulating Library before returning to the hotel. Consequently she turned left on leaving the post office and slipped through a narrow alley to emerge on Hill Street where lived the wealthy and fashionable townsfolk of Pendleton. Tall, imposing houses flanked the steep street, with wrought iron railings beside the steps and intricate fanlights above the doors. One house was clearly unoccupied. There were no curtains at the windows, no primroses in the window boxes. The paintwork looked new and the brass door knocker gleamed brightly. A carriage stood before the door, and as Hester drew level, a lady and gentleman stepped down from the vehicle and prepared to mount the steps. The couple were deeply engaged in conversation and did not appear to notice Hester, but she let fall an involuntary exclamation of surprise for they were the Garths, the brother and sister about whom she had been thinking only a few moments ago.

The carriage horse pawed the ground nervously, causing Miss Garth to look back. Perceiving her friend, she dropped her brother's arm and ran eagerly across the flagstones to clasp Hester in a warm embrace. She was a small, beautiful creature of some twenty summers, with a profusion of golden curls peeping out from beneath her modish bonnet. Great honey brown eyes dominated her delicate oval face. She was very short-sighted and had to stand on tiptoe to peer into her friend's smiling grey eyes.

Hester gently disengaged herself and turned to greet Stephen Garth, standing impassively to one side, with an air of detached boredom on his rather harsh countenance. He was not a tall man, but his shoulders were broad and he gave an indefinable impression of hidden strength. He was ten years older than his sister and bore little resemblance to her, either in feature or manner. His thick, light brown hair remained unruffled by the wind, as he bowed over Hester's hand.

"Good day, Miss Vane. This is an unexpected pleasure." He straightened and stepped back, evidently feeling that he had made all the concessions to civility that were required. He was ever a man of few words. Susan threw up her hands in mock despair.

"Stephen, is that all you can say to my dear Hester, when we have not seen her this age? — apart from Sundays and I do not regard such meetings for one can never say anything of any consequence in that draughty old churchyard." She smiled at Hester and continued, "But let us ignore him, he is like a bear today. What are you doing in Pendleton? Why do you never visit us at Hatch End any more? Have you news from your brother? How is dear Miss Stanhope? Do tell me everything."

Before Hester could comply with this sweeping request, Mr. Garth grinned suddenly and his whole expression was transformed.

"Miss Vane, a thousand apologies. Sukey is quite right, I am indeed in an ill-humour today. Certain business ventures are proving troublesome. Also, time presses and we are come to view this house, for Susan finds that she is too isolated at Hatch End when I am obliged to be away on business."

"I think that a splendid idea," replied Hester, "Pray do not let me detain you. I was on my way to the Circulating Library and took a short cut through Colliers Row."

Susan broke in to say, "You go ahead Stephen, I will join you directly. I am sure that you do not truly need my advice and I like the situation already".

Stephen Garth nodded his head in agreement and bowed slightly in Hester's direction,

"Very well. Bye the bye, Miss Vane, there are one or two matters which I should like to discuss with you, at your convenience. I shall be passing through Shawcross tomorrow afternoon. May I do myself the honour of calling upon you at — shall we say four o'clock?"

Hester frowned thoughtfully, her head tilted a little to one side. She was quite unaware of the enchanting picture she made, with the bright sun shining on her fresh complexion and a strand of hair blowing across her eyes. She raised her long, dark-fringed lashes and met Stephen's intent gaze. It made her feel vaguely uncomfortable, as she had before in his company. She knew that she was both attracted and repelled by the magnetism of his forceful personality. Some small doubt lurked in the back of her mind. She tried to recollect what Miss Milsom had said about Mr. Garth and his carrier. Could it be that Stephen Garth was connected with the smuggling fraternity? Surely not — and yet, he was, she knew, a man of considerable power and influence, despite the fact that he came from an impoverished county family and had been obliged to earn his own living. If the Garths were considering moving from Hatch End to Hill Street they must be coming up in the world.

The silence lengthened between them and Hester made haste to reply, pushing aside the wayward lock.

"I am delighted to see you at any time, sir, but I am puzzled to know what affairs we can have to discuss. I am not in any difficulty at the moment, and if the matter is not urgent I can easily call at your office when I am next in town."

Stephen Garth's countenance assumed a firm, almost grim, expression.

"I must emphasize, Miss Vane, that it is a matter of some importance and I wish to discuss it with you in private as soon as possible."

"So be it then, Mr. Garth. Until tomorrow, at four o'clock." Hester held out her hand, he bent and kissed it before she could withdraw. He turned abruptly and ran up the steps, throwing an admonition to his sister not to keep Miss Vane gossiping too long.

Susan had been observing her brother with interest. No sooner had he disappeared inside the elegant portal than she said mischievously to her friend,

"I do believe Stephen is developing a 'tendre' for you. I have never known him behave so strangely before!"

Hester blushed, frowned and finally laughed,

"What nonsense you do talk, my dear. I observed nothing unusual in his manner."

Susan remained unconvinced.

"Mayhap you did not, but I have noticed that he mentions you frequently of late and always with a decided partiality in his tone. How delightful it would be . . ," she began impetuously and then paused, arrested by Hester's obvious embarrassment.

"I will not tease you, Hester dear. Let us talk of something else. Tell me, have you seen Mr. Stone recently? I was confined to bed with a migraine last Sunday and was unable to attend Morning Service."

It was Hester's turn to smile mischievously. She had long been aware that the Vicar of Shawcross was deeply in love with Susan Garth and she suspected that the affection was mutual. However, Stephen Garth was his sister's guardian until she came of age and Hester suspected that he opposed the association. Jedediah Stone had many attributes, but since wealth was not among them it was understandable that Stephen should caution prudence. His sister was impressionable and her circle limited. It occurred to Hester that this might be a major factor in the proposed removal to Pendleton.

She said simply,

"I remarked your absence, as I am sure did others, with regret. We will miss you sadly at our tea parties and sewing circles if you come to live on Hill Street."

Susan's expressive face darkened. Hester was troubled by the hopelessness lurking in the beautiful brown eyes.

"I have no choice. Stephen is quite determined to leave Hatch End, although we shall not sell the property, merely rent it to reliable tenants. I do not think I could bear to part with the old house completely. I have lived there all my life. But Stephen needs a hostess to entertain his business friends and he feels that I would be safer here. He was most alarmed by the dreadful attack on that unfortunate London gentleman the other day. He does not like to leave me alone, though to be sure there are the servants and the dogs. Did you hear of the incident at Staleybridge? Everyone is talking of it."

Without giving Hester time to reply, Susan plunged into her tale. It seemed that a gentleman travelling alone from London to Brighton had been waylaid at the Staleybridge fork and had lost a number of valuable articles to a highwayman, known as the 'Beau Chevalier'. The authorities had proclaimed that this wicked robber was wanted 'dead or alive' and a handsome reward had been offered for information, much more than was usual in such cases. It was thought that perhaps the London gentleman had put up the capital. Little was known of the 'Beau Chevalier', although it was suspected that he was an émigré Frenchman, for he was said to speak with a strong, but educated, French accent.

A vague sense of unease grew upon Hester.

"When did this incident take place?", she enquired casually, after expressing her horror at the perils now awaiting unwary travellers.

"Let me see," Susan pondered a moment, her dimpled chin resting on one delicate finger, "Today is Thursday. I believe it must have been last Monday, early in the evening. Yes, I am sure that is right, because Stephen was away. He spent the night here in Pendleton and so heard the news. He told me of it when he returned home on Tuesday morning."

Susan chattered on, not observing the arrested expression which had dawned in her friend's eyes.

Hester learned that the highwayman was believed to have been wounded by the gentleman in the coach, a Mr. Hyde Abercromby. Here Susan darted off at a tangent to relate the interesting fact that Mr. Abercromby was a relative of the famous General Abercromby who had been killed at the Battle of Alexandria, in which the French were defeated. Of course it had all been in vain because now that monster Napoleon had determined to be Emperor of the French and his ambition knew no bounds; had Hester heard the new rumour that he planned to invade England next month? 'Twas said he had a great army at Boulogne and poor Admiral Nelson dare not set foot on land, so busy was he protecting England's shores.

"And who knows?" she concluded despondently, "The harvests have been so bad, and many poor people lack even their daily bread. One could not blame them if they felt the temptation to follow the example of those terrible *sans culottes.*"

Rather bewildered by this sudden change in tone, Hester made an effort to reply bracingly,

"Lud my dear, how solemn you are. 'Tis not like you to be such a Jeremiah. Tell me, if Mr. Abercromby managed to fire at the 'Chevalier', did he then get a glimpse of him? Could he identify him again?"

Susan shook her head doubtfully,

"I think not. The road is thickly wooded near the fork. After the rogue escaped, Mr. Abercromby drove on into Pendleton and put up at the 'Lamb'. Somewhere along the way he met my brother, and Stephen gathered from the gentleman that he could see only a tall, dark outline on horseback in the shadows. The only distinctive features which he remarked were the man's laugh, which was rich and deep, and of course, his accent."

Hester's heart began to beat rapidly and she put a hand to the railings to steady herself. Susan's voice seemed to come from some distance away.

"My dear Hester, are you faint? I should not have kept you talking so long on the steps. Won't you come in and sit down on the window seat, while I procure some water?"

Hester rallied and the colour rushed back to her cheeks. She put out a restraining hand as Susan prepared to mount the steps and summon her brother to their aid.

"No, I am quite recovered. I beg you will not disturb Mr. Garth. Indeed I have detained you far too long and I am sure there are many matters concerning the domestic arrangements on which you will wish to confer with your brother. I will rest a few moments at the Library before returning to the hotel."

Reluctantly Susan took affectionate leave of her friend and disappeared inside the house. Left to herself, Hester soon succeeded in regaining her composure. It was most unlike her to be so easily overset, and she was puzzled at her own reaction. Certainly she had received much food for thought, but she did not have time to dwell on it. A glance at her watch, which she carried on a thin gold chain around her neck, informed her that it wanted but a few minutes to the hour. Hastily she adjusted her bonnet, smoothed her gloves and retrieved the packages from Miss Milsom's, which had slipped unnoticed to her feet. She wondered fleetingly if she had been well-advised to buy gloves, perhaps a muff might have been more serviceable? She dismissed the notion resolutely, reminding herself that the muffs this season were even larger than those carried last year and she preferred to retain her freedom of movement. Muffs were so awkward, though vastly fetching with the right ensemble. While inwardly debating the rival merits of gloves and muffs, Hester bent her footsteps towards the large, beautiful horse-chestnut tree, which marked the lower end of Hill Street. She hesitated for a moment outside the Library, then entered quickly and chose at random a book on Natural History for Miss Stanhope and a volume of Addison's Essays for herself. She did not usually favour Essays, but Dr. Minton had recommended those in 'The Spectator' only last week. He had thought that the gentle admonitions and strictures addressed to ladies (and gentlemen) of an earlier age, couched in elegant, outmoded phrases, would appeal to Hester's wit and intellect. Hester would have liked to linger and browse through the latest copies of *The Lady's Magazine* and *La Belle Assemblée*, but George would be waiting patiently and she had promised herself that she would work diligently on the intricate unravelling of her plot that afternoon.

Hester crossed the market place feeling well content with her morning's work. She had made some useful purchases, gleaned some interesting information and shaken off the unaccustomed mood of depression which had afflicted her when she left home. She found George seated by the horse trough; both horse and man appeared well-baited and refreshed. They mounted and soon the light vehicle was rattling along the country lanes once more, with 'Merrylegs' snorting happily as she kicked the town dust from her hooves.

"Rackon they must've put somethin' in 'er oats," remarked George Hamble with a grin. "Did 'ee get all 'ee was wantin' in town?"

George had served the Vane family since before Hester was born and had taught both Hester and her brother to ride. They had been apt pupils and the three had shared many happy hours together. Therefore Hester exclaimed aloud with pleasure as she remembered the letter from Mortimer reposing in her reticule. She drew it forth; it was rather crumpled and contained only a single sheet, which she scanned quickly.

"Will we be seein' Mr. Mortimer shortly, Miss Hester?", enquired George hopefully, as she looked up smiling.

"Yes, is it not delightful? Much sooner than I had expected. Tomorrow in fact. This letter must have been slow in coming for he sent it from my aunt's house in London nearly ten days ago."

Hester scrutinized the letter more closely.

"Ah, I see. He came down from Oxford early, owing to an outbreak of sickness in college. Cousin Tom persuaded him to stay in London in order to witness a bout of fisticuffs between the — Good Heavens, can this be right, George? — the 'Battersea Bruiser' and 'Fearless Finnegan, the Fighting Irishman' — they sound quite gruesome. And so does this!" she continued, laughing merrily, "He has purchased a new white satin waistcoat with thin cherry stripes and has had his hair cropped *à la Titus*. I did not know he cared for such things. But George, we must hurry home. There is nothing prepared and he will be on the Brighton Stage tomorrow afternoon. All being well he will hire a horse at the 'Horse and Groom' and cover the remaining miles to Shawcross in time for dinner."

"Ar, 'twill be good to have the young master at home again," said George, flourishing his whip with the practised twirl, which young Mortimer had tried and failed to emulate on more than one occasion.

They made good time and it was not until they turned off the main road and were almost within sight of Shawcross, that Hester thought to ask if George had heard anything of the Staleybridge robbery.

"Why yes, miss, 'twere a rum do by all accounts. The ostlers were saying that theer 'Bow Chevaleer' is grown mighty bold and owdacious o' late. 'Twere lucky for the Lunnon gennelman that Mr. Garth 'appened by so fortunate and scared the rascal away with a flea in 'is ear, beggin' your pardon, miss."

"I suppose so, though the version I heard was a little different. I believe Mr. Abercromby had frightened off the rogue before Mr. Garth arrived," Hester remarked thoughtfully, "But what became of Mr. Abercromby: Do you know if he is staying hereabouts?"

"I don't think so, miss, not long leastways. He do be a fashionable gennelman and took hisself off to Brighton next day to join the Prince o' Wales and his lady friend, Mrs. Fitzherbert." George pursed his lips and an expression of deep disapproval marred his craggy features.

Hester smiled mischievously within the brim of her large bonnet but she ventured no further questions. She knew from experience that old George regarded her as a delicate flower and would refuse to sully her ears with scandalous tittle-tattle.

It was not long before they reached home. George took 'Merrylegs' around to the stables while Hester ran indoors with her packages, eager to set all in a bustle to prepare for Mortimer's reception on the morrow. Other preoccupations were forgotten for the moment in happy anticipation of her brother's homecoming.

Chapter 5
Two Visits

It was eleven o'clock on Friday morning; Hester had been awake early and had been busily engaged in setting her small household by the ears, in her anxiety to have everything spick and span for Mortimer's arrival. When Miss Stanhope descended at her usual hour of nine, she had found Martha in tears and Mrs. Blossom waiting to give in her notice. Having soothed these two indispensable souls, she had gone in search of Hester and found her seated on the sitting room floor surrounded by a sea of papers. Capable Miss Stanhope soon brought order out of chaos and succeeded in convincing Hester that the most useful task which she could accomplish would be to finish her remaining chapters as rapidly as might be, thus leaving herself more time to devote to her brother and his entertainment.

Accordingly a somewhat chastened Miss Vane had retired to her room to spend the morning in diligent composition. She had just reached the point where her young heroine was awakened at dead of night by the sound of ghostly laughter, when she was disturbed by the rattle of carriage wheels in the lane outside her window. A few moments later Miss Stanhope put her head round the door and announced briskly,

"My lord Montfort is come to call with the two young ladies. Do make haste and join us for heaven's sake, child, don't forget to take that duster from your head and remove your apron. Why you will persist in wearing that drab old grey dress I cannot think. It should have been relegated to the attic years ago. I'll go down and order some refreshment. They will be all at sixes and sevens in the kitchen no doubt, but I have some china tea put by from the last consignment and a little sherry wine for his lordship."

She trotted away. As soon as she'd gone Hester jumped to her feet and ran to the looking glass. She had not expected Hugo to come so soon; no, it would never do, she decided eyeing her appearance with disfavour. In a remarkably short space of time she had changed into a becoming morning gown of white sarsenet, threaded with blue ribbons.

She dragged a comb through her unruly curls, slipped a fringed shawl about her shoulders, and without pausing to consider the whole effect too closely, descended to the sitting room, quite forgetting that she was still wearing her old slippers.

She was greeted gaily by Stephanie and Marietta; with more reserve by their guardian. Lord Montfort remained standing until the ladies were seated. Stephanie sat beside Hester on the blue velvet love seat and Marietta chose a comfortable arm chair opposite them. The girls were in good looks this morning and Hester thought what a charming contrast they made, Stephanie, small and dark in a gown of lemon and a ribbon of the same shade running through her silky tresses, while the fair Marietta was dressed in soft pink muslin sprigged with small white daisies. Hester glanced round and discovered his lordship seated on the uncomfortable old chair by the bureau in the corner; he appeared to have detached himself from his surroundings. Hester frowned, wondering why he had troubled to call if he was not prepared to pay the ladies a modicum of courtesy. She recalled that he had frequently been charged with being intolerably 'high in the instep', but she had always found him quite approachable and was at a loss to explain his demeanour.

She became aware that Stephanie was chattering on happily and she decided to ignore her silent guest. Perhaps his wound was still bothering him, she concluded charitably.

". . and we knew that you worked in the mornings and did not wish to interrupt you," finished Stephanie, smiling at her seraphically.

Hester replied politely that she was delighted to be interrupted.

"I am finding it difficult to work this morning, for you see my young brother, Mortimer, has written to say he will be arriving tonight in Shawcross. I have not seen him since Christmas and so am quite excited at the prospect. He has been staying with my Aunt Marchant in London; he appears to have divided his time equally between his tailor and accompanying Cousin Thomas to those terrible prize fights."

"How does my Lady Marchant?" enquired Hugo suddenly. The ladies turned to him in surprise.

"Very well, I believe my lord. She is not a good correspondent, but Mortimer mentioned nothing amiss. Jane and I are hoping to visit her soon." Hester was about to say more when Miss Stanhope tripped in, with Martha in her wake, bearing a dainty tray of biscuits, tea and a wine decanter and glass for Lord Montfort.

Miss Stanhope seated herself at the tea table and began to pour, talking volubly the while on such random topics as Mortimer's imminent arrival, the weather, and the absence of their usual orderly morning routine. Lord Montfort rose to assist Miss Jane in passing the cups. His lithe, athletic figure seemed to fill the room. He was formally attired in a cut-away square-ended coat of dark blue superfine. He wore white close-fitting pantaloons and sported an immaculate red and white striped waistcoat; his silk cravat was tied in an intricate knot, which Hester recognized from her last London visit as the one called 'orientale'. She frowned; it seemed to her that it was an unnecessary affectation in the country, where such subtleties were normally eschewed in favour of comfortable stocks, except among the young sons of the local gentry who aspired to varying degrees of dandyism, much to Dr. Minton's amusement: 'dem young macaronis' he called them with old-fashioned bluntness. A fleeting tremor crossed Hester's expressive countenance at the thought; Hugo chose this moment, when the other ladies were occupied in examining Miss Stanhope's newly completed tapestry fire screen, to murmur in her ear,

"It is good to see you smile. You were regarding me so severely just now that I feared I was quite in your black books. I hope you received my note and have forgiven me for departing so unceremoniously."

He glanced around, but the other ladies still sat with their heads bent, deep in conversation. He continued in an undertone,

"My wards are not aware that I suffered an accident and was obliged to impose on you and Miss Stanhope. I have explained the whole to my mother, but in general it is, as you once remarked, a case of 'least said, soonest mended'. I trust Miss Jane will not betray me by some chance word."

"So do I," replied Hester. "I did impress upon her the need for discretion and I imagine she will wait for you to raise the matter, if you so wish." She raised her voice a little and enquired if the young ladies had heard of the Staleybridge robbery, casting a mischievous glance in Hugo's direction as she did so. Hester was not a little curious to see how he would react to a discussion of an issue which, she suspected, touched him very nearly. She was disappointed, however, for he gave no sign of any emotion beyond a mild interest; his handsome features remained impassive as he remarked blandly,

"Why yes, we heard of it firsthand last night over dinner. The unfortunate gentleman in the coach is my very good friend, Hyde Abercromby, and he was on his way to visit me when the incident occurred. After the attack he changed his plans and went first to Pendleton and then on to Brighton in order to set the forces of law in motion. I gather that he did so most effectively, he has every expectation that the fellow will be laid by the heels in the near future. Abercromby decided not to delay in Brighton, but came to the Priory last night. He lost several items of considerable value and is this moment in Pendleton taking futher action. He will remain as my guest for a few days in order to be on hand should any clue come to light, before returning to Town. In fact, Abercromby's presence at the Priory is the second reason why we have called upon you this morning — the first reason, as you must know is to extend our heartfelt thanks for your kindness to Stephanie and Marietta the other day." Hugo bowed towards Miss Stanhope and Hester in turn, then continued rather hastily as he saw Miss Stanhope about to speak.

"I am commissioned by my mother to invite you both to Huntsgrove for dinner tomorrow evening. We keep country hours and my carriage would call for you at five o'clock. I hope you will overlook the absence of formality, but it would give me pleasure if you would allow me to introduce Abercromby to you while he is in the County."

His lordship paused and awaited their reply with an anxiety which was new to him. It pained him to acknowledge to himself that Hester Vane might well refuse his invitation; he could understand that she might not wish to renew a friendship which had been allowed to lapse in uncomfortable circumstances. After all, it was now six years since there had been any social intercourse between the Vanes and the Montforts, six years in which many things had changed on both sides. Hugo was naturally a considerate man; he was also wealthy, arrogant, and accustomed to having his slightest wish obeyed to the letter. His green eyes sought Hester's with a penetrating stare, while he awaited her answer to his invitation. She met the green gaze unwaveringly and guessing something of his thoughts, determined to tease him a little.

"My lord, it is most kind of you to bring us this invitation from your mother. Nothing could afford us greater pleasure than to meet the hero of such stirring adventures upon the highway. I understand Mr. Abercromby actually winged the villain?" This was a question which was vexing Hester's mind considerably, for if, as she had guessed, Hugo and the 'Beau Cheavalier' were one and the same person, why would he attack his friend's coach and risk recognition? Indeed, when one thought of it, why would a man in Hugo's position do such a thing at all? — He was not a young buck to be kicking up such a dangerous lark from sheer boredom. Perhaps she was wrong, but his mother had taught him French as a child and he could easily assume an émigré accent of the sort attributed to the masked man, and there was no gainsaying the fact that he had arrived, wounded and masked on her doorstep, on the evening of the Staleybridge affair. She could not fathom the mystery, but resolved to make a push to provoke an explanation, should the occasion arise.

"Two shots were fired," his lordship was saying calmly, "Apparently, after the robbery, Hyde seized his pistol and fired through the carriage window and Mr. Garth of Hatch End providentially arrived on the scene. He also fired at the retreating form of the robber. The details are hazy, but it seems certain that one of the shots did achieve its mark."

"Was it not dreadful?" broke in Marietta, her blue eyes growing dark at the thought, "And to think that we crossed that bridge only a few hours earlier!"

"Yes, indeed," agreed Miss Stanhope, her sharp eyes flickering from Hester to Hugo. She sensed undercurrents, but wisely held her tongue for the time being as she concentrated on the matter in hand, "I never travel with anything of value upon me and I would have something to say to any young man who tried to remove my gold locket, the only item which I treasure, for reasons of sentiment." A martial light sparkled in her eye as she fingered that trinket, and Lord Montfort raised his quizzing glass to observe it more closely. An appreciative grin suddenly transformed his features.

"My dear Miss Jane, 'twould be an intrepid soul indeed that dared assail you. Do say you will bear us company tomorrow," he continued coaxingly, "Miss Vane hesitates, and if you will not bring reinforcements to my aid I fear all is lost."

Miss Stanhope chuckled.

"Do not seek to cozen me, my lord. 'Twas but a trifling service we rendered after all." She glanced meaningfully at his arm and he had the grace to flush slightly under his tanned skin. Miss Stanhope liked him the better for it; she turned doubtfully to Hester,

"What do you say, my love? We are not quite at liberty tomorrow evening, for 'twill be Mortimer's first day at home."

Before Hester could speak, Stephanie intervened to say gaily,

"But it would be delightful if Sir Mortimer could join us, also. Is that not correct, Cousin Hugo?", she looked to Lord Montfort for corroboration.

"Quite. I was about to say the same thing myself. Can we now consider the matter settled?" Hugo turned enquiringly from Miss Vane to Miss Stanhope and back again. Hester smiled reluctantly; mentally apostrophizing his lordship as a very tiresomely persistent man.

"I have no other objection. It is very good of you to include Mortimer in your invitation, my lord. Please convey my compliments to Lady Elizabeth and tell her that we accept most gladly."

"Hum," grunted Hugo, looking at Hester suspiciously. She met his gaze with an expression of limpid innocence.

"A little more sherry wine, my lord?" asked Miss Jane.

"No, I thank you ma'am. We must take our leave. I regret that we have disturbed you, when you must be fully occupied in preparation this morning." His purpose achieved, his lordshop wasted no further time in small talk. He rose abruptly; obligingly Hester pulled the bell and requested a flustered Martha to bring the ladies' spencers and muffs. However, incensed at having been outmanoeuvred, Hester commented more sharply than she intended,

"You put us country bumpkins to shame; I wonder you did not drive yourself this morning, Lord Montfort?" she allowed her gaze to rest meditatively on the third button of his lordship's elegant waistcoat. Surprised and puzzled at the unexpected attack, he responded coolly,

"Why no, Miss Vane. It is not my practice to ride *ventre à terre* about the countryside when I pay a morning call with two young ladies. My light town curricle would soon land in a Sussex ditch after the recent rains. I find driving in the country incredibly tedious." Hugo bowed over her hand and drew on his gloves. Hester flushed with mortification; somehow Hugo had seen through her implied criticism of his modish attire and had neatly turned the table, with a light rebuke. She hurried from the room while Lord Montfort and his wards took courteous leave of Miss Jane. Breathing deeply, Hester led the way. In the porch she stopped short in astonishment, treading on his lordship's toe. His good arm gallantly went out to steady her, while Stephen Garth, who had tethered his horse just beyond the Montfort conveyance, stepped ominously towards the cottage, his face as black as a thundercloud.

Momentarily forgotten, Hester intercepted the look of intense dislike which passed between the two men, while the other three ladies were yet lingering for a final word.

"Good day to you, Garth," Hugo nodded distantly. He turned to summon his charges. Obediently Stephanie and Marietta joined their cousin, who curtly performed the necessary introduction. The indefinable air of hostility vanished as Stephen Garth bowed low to the young ladies and Miss Stanhope.

"How do you do, Mr. Garth," said Stephanie, dimpling bewitchingly and fluttering her long lashes, beneath the shade of her becoming straw bonnet. Hester heard Hugo mutter 'minx' as he strode off down the path, glowering in a sulky manner, which made him appear oddly youthful. She was tempted to laugh, but stiffened when Stephanie continued,

"Dear sir, can it be . . . are you the Mr. Garth of Hatch End who rescued poor Mr. Abercromby (la, how difficult is this name for my poor tongue!)?"

Stephen Garth started and frowned; then looked at Stephanie more closely. There was a distinct air of menace as he asked abruptly,

"Who told you of this?" Stephen glanced accusingly at Hester, "Was it Miss Vane?"

Before Hester's lips could frame an indignant denial, Stephanie's elegant little profile tilted proudly,

"I do not gossip," she replied firmly, stung by his tone, "Me, I had this information from the lips of Mr. Abercromby himself. He is my cousin's guest at Huntsgrove."

Marietta tugged at Stephanie's hand. She was quite pale and it was clear that the short altercation had alarmed her.

"Stephanie, we must go. Cousin Hugo awaits us."

Stephen raised his hand in a protesting gesture, but Stephanie ignored him as she made a quiet farewell to Hester and Miss Stanhope. She swept down the path, a 'grande dame' in every inch of her short figure. In a trice the three visitors had mounted, the steps were put up and Lord Montfort's small tiger had sprung to his post on the box. The carriage disappeared and Hester relaxed. Miss Stanhope slipped quietly indoors; Stephen smiled at Hester ruefully. It was a charming smile and moved by curiosity, she allowed herself to be guided to a small wooden bench, which stood in a secluded corner of the garden. They seated themselves and a short silence ensured, which Hester made no attempt to break.

"Miss Vane, what can I say? My behaviour to your guests was unpardonable," declared Stephen at last. "I have no excuse to offer beyond the fact that I was disappointed not to find you alone, when I had something of particular importance to say to you. Sukey is quite right when she tells me that my hasty tongue will be the cause of my downfall sooner or later."

Hester remained silent, turning his speech over in her mind. She was not at all satisfied with his explanation. It seemed to her that if she could but sweep aside the mists of obscurity which shrouded the events that had transpired at Staleybridge the other evening, then she would be well on the way to solving the problem.

"I was not aware that you were so well acquainted with his lordship," she remarked neutrally.

"To the devil with his lordship," burst out Stephen impetuously. He jumped up and paced to and fro across the lawn several times in an agitated manner, reminding Hester forcibly of a caged lion which she had once seen on display when a travelling circus had visited Brighton. All at once he seemed to reach a decision; he halted before Hester and dropped to one knee. This was so unexpected that she could scarcely credit the evidence of her own eyes. He took her hand, causing an involuntary shudder to run through her. His eyes searched her face, as he held her hand firmly between his own large ones, not giving her an oppotunity to withdraw.

"Miss Vane, Hester, I think you cannot be unaware of the very high esteem and regard in which I have held you for several years. I am now in a position to marry. My present condition and prospects are excellent and I have high hopes of supplementing my income considerably in the very near future. I was a trifle annoyed at meeting you in Pendleton yesterday, for I wished my town house to be a surprise, everything arranged to the best advantage before you saw it. Hester, I am buying the house for you. Will you do me the honour of becoming my wife?"

Hester's eyes flew to his face and she was shaken by the depth of passion which she found there.

"But, Susan," she faltered, "I thought you were buying the house for her?"

"My dear girl," he exclaimed in amused exasperation, "You know as well as I do that Sukey would much prefer to remain at Hatch End. She needs to get away from that demmed parson. But you two deal well together. I will not curb your activities, m'dear, you can still write your romances, if you wish. I'll even make no objection if you and Sukey go off to Brighton for the season. We could take a house on the Steyne," he finished on a pleading note.

For a moment Hester was tempted. It would be so pleasant to relinquish all cares; to shift the burden of Mortimer management to more capable shoulders and to be a lady of consequence onec again. Her steady grey eyes rested wistfully on the strong hands clasped in her lap. The breeze gently ruffled her hair and she thought of another hand which had seized her own so recently: the hand of Hugo Jermyn as he lay in bed in the small box room just above her head.

Gently she detached herself and said resolutely,

"Dear sir, I am deeply flattered by your kind offer, but I cannot accept. I regard you as a good friend, but I do not love you as I should wish to love my husband. If I married you it would be for the wrong reasons, because I wished for protection, for advice, for security. Marriage for such motives could not bring happiness. But I trust we can remain friends. I rely on you for advice in your official capacity."

Hester was alarmed at the wave of strong emotion which passed over Stephen Garth's stern features as she spoke. She rose and sped across the lawn until she reached the sanctuary of the shady porch. Stephen followed her and before she could prevent him, he had caught her in a crushing embrace; his eager lips met hers hungrily demanding, and for a brief moment she surrendered; then, with a grasp, she freed herself and shrank back, desperately seeking the elusive door handle.

"Hester," Stephen cried thickly, "I cannot live without you. You will be mine whether you will or no."

He advanced purposefully towards her, but mercifully the door opened to reveal Miss Stanhope, her bright eyes darting from one flushed face to the other.

"Mr. Garth is — is just leaving, Jane," stammered Hester, overcome with relief and confusion, "Pray excuse me, sir, there is so much to be done today with my brother arriving tonight. My fondest love to Susan. Farewell, sir." She slipped inside and Jane Stanhope closed the door with unladylike force.

Hester remained motionless until she heard footsteps retreating down the path and the creak of the garden gate.

"I heard all, my love," declared Miss Jane, dramatically, "I vow, 'twas as good as a play. What a very rough man he is to be sure!"

Hester could not forbear from laughing, albeit rather brokenly, as Miss Stanhope followed her into the cosy parlour. The mid-day sun fell on a large bowl of pansies, their soft velvet faces open to face the warmth. Hester crossed to the round table by the window and touched them gently; she remarked in a detached way that her hands were trembling.

"Drink this, 'twill steady you," ordered Miss Stanhope, firmly propelling her into a seat by the table and setting a glass of sherry beside her. Obediently Hester sipped the amber liquid. Its restorative properties soon caused her to stop shaking. After a little her sense of the ridiculous completed her recovery. She shook her head at her companion.

"Jane, how could you eavesdrop so unashamedly. I would never have suspected you of such a thing. But I feel much better now, and I was so glad to see you at the door that I must forgive you." Her face clouded, "What a strange morning! I am sure Mr. Garth did not intend to come until this afternoon. I invited him for tea at four o'clock. That dreadful meeting should never have happened. I declare I was ready to sink when Miss Stephanie gave him that setdown."

"Nonsense, not a thing you could have done. It was most unlike him not to come at the appointed hour, but I suppose his impatience was — er, understandable?"

Miss Stanhope looked at Hester uncertainly.

"I suppose so," conceded that young lady wryly.

"Well, I think I will just finish this rosebud before lunch," remarked Miss Stanhope, seating herself placidly and taking up her needle, "Miss Marietta much admired my tapestry, but I have the impression that Miss Stephanie does not care for such sedentary occupation. She told me that she is more at home in the stables than in the drawing room. Hoever, she is a taking little thing; I expect she will soon have all the young men in the neighbourhood at her feet. 'Tis a pity she and Lord Montfort are so closely related or they might make a match of it," Miss Stanhope bent her head to hide a sly smile.

Hester was not deceived.

"You wretch!", she exclaimed; then could not resist adding loftily, "Of course it is all one to me, but I did not observe any signs to indicate that his lordship was in any way smitten. I should imagine that the disparity in their ages and temperaments would preclude such an eventuality."

"It's been done before," Miss Stanhope retorted with an emphatic nod, "But let us speak of other matters. Do you believe that you and Stephen Garth can continue to be friends? 'Twould be most awkward if we were obliged to change our lawyer, for I do not know of another reputable man nearer than Lewes or Brighton. Mr. Garth does not strike me as one who will accept his dismissal easily; he has always cherished an excessively high opinion of himself and he is very ambitious, but to be fair, I am sure that he would treat his wife well and generously. Are you absolutely convinced that you would not suit?"

Hester had been gazing through the open window while she listened, her fingers mechanically twisting and untwisting a skein of embroidery thread. Now she dropped the thread and ran to sit on the little footstool at Miss Stanhope's feet. Unexpectedly she began to weep, her tousled head in her friend's lap. Miss Stanhope's worn, nimble fingers touched Hester's bright curls in an unwontedly maternal gesture, for she was not naturally a demonstrative person.

The storm of weeping passed, Hester sat still, her face buried in her sleeve. In a muffled voice she gave Miss Jane to understand that she was quite happy in her present single state; that she would never marry

Stephen Garth for she felt that they shared few, if any, interests and that she utterly refused to become the slave to any man's passion. At this juncture she raised her head to ask accusingly,

"Do you realize, my dear Jane, how many of my school-fellows now have a nursery full of children and a husband whom they rarely see? Oh lord, what a witch I sound, but it is quite true that the majority of husbands go out through the window when their children come in through the door — or do I mean the other way about? However it may be, it is not the life which I would lead. If truth be told, I am a little afraid of Mr. Garth; his personality is so forceful that I feel myself quite submerged in his presence."

Miss Stanhope shook her head reproachfully.

"There is no need to be so vehement, my love. I am entirely of your opinion with regard to the marriage of convenience; but in a situation where true affection exists, I am persuaded that the married state is a most enviable condition. Forgive me, but I feel I must speak *in loco parentis* since you have no close relatives to turn to for advice. You are no longer just out of the schoolroom, but you are still one of the most eligible ladies in the neighbourhood. As a child you were prone to seek perfection and to suffer endless frustration because you could not be satisfied with a little less. My dear, spinsters are a thorn in everyone's flesh. After middle age they became either amiable eccentrics or embittered eccentrics, but in both cases they become unwanted hangers-on of society, useful in times of crisis, but otherwise largely ignored."

Miss Jane paused for breath and Hester interrupted, in genuine amusement,

"My own dear sour puss, what a terrifying picture you paint with such a broad brush. You will have me at my last prayers if you rattle on much longer in this lugubrious manner. But there are so few eligible gentlemen in the vicinity. Shall I set my cap at Dr. Minton? No, don't scratch my eyes out, I know well it is a lost cause. He cannot look at me when you are by. I have it — Mr. Hyde Abercromby. I wish I had thought to question his lordship concerning his friend's age, appearance, interests and vices."

"Hester, enough! What a shocking romp you are. But there is something in what you say. We must take special pains with your appearance tomorrow night at dinner." Miss Stanhope's eyes narrowed, as she mentally reviewed Hester's wardrobe. "I have it, thank heaven the warm weather seems to be settled for a few days. You can wear your blue chemise dress with the beautiful shawl Lady Marchant sent for you at Christmas. What a fortunate circumstance that you purchased some new evening slippers in Brighton last October. They are hardly worn at all."

Miss Stanhope's taste was infallible and Hester nodded in agreement, tacitly accepting the diversion from more serious subjects. The good lady paused to consider her own ensemble.

"My lilac tunic dress will do very well. I was reading only the other day in Mrs. Crossley's latest issue of *The Lady's Magazine*, that the braiding at the hem is more ornate than ever this season, so I shall add the gold braid which you had from Miss Milsom yesterday. Oh dear, do you recall, my love, when we dined at the Manor on Twelfth Night, how that clumsy footman of theirs spilt a drop of soup on my black silk shawl. The mark did not come out, though I tried every remedy that Mrs. Lightfoot could suggest. It will have to be my grey wool, so much less elegant, but rather warmer. Those large rooms at the Priory can be draughty at night, I doubt not . . . What say you to my black lace cap?"

"Very becoming," replied Hester, "At least Dr. Minton remarks on it every time he sees it. But perhaps your purple turban with a little gold trimming might be better for a formal occasion. I note that you plan to sit snugly in your cosy grey shawl, while I shiver in my blue dress. If I contract an inflammation of the lungs I shall know at whose door to lay the blame!"

She glanced at the handsome timepiece on the mantelshelf, a gift from her father to her mother on their wedding day.

"It is one o'clock already and I have done nothing this morning. Mortimer will have accomplished more than half his journey by now. Is all in readiness?"

"Yes, of course. Mrs. Blossom is making some of those custard tartlets that he always asks for and there is a fine saddle of mutton. As it is Friday the sole is particularly fresh, but I will concoct some of my parsley sauce to make it a little more festive. Do you think he would relish carrots or parsnips as an accompaniment?"

"Oh, I don't know, both . . ." said Hester absently. "You know, Jane, I have just thought that his lordship did not once mention his wound. Of course, it is true that he did not wish Miss Stephanie and Miss Marietta to be alarmed for they know nothing of his mishap. Did he look quite well to you?"

Miss Stanhope clucked her tongue in dismay.

"How remiss of me. It did not occur to me to enquire. Now that I think of it he was a trifle pale, but he seemed to move his arms without difficulty and he was wise enough to refrain from driving."

It was Hester's turn to look dismayed. She exclaimed disjointedly,

"You are right . . . so rude of me to taunt him with his fine town dress; oh dear, what will he think? . . . What can I do to make amends?"

Miss Stanhope considered for a moment, while Hester rose abruptly and took an agitated turn about the long, low room. It seemed to the older lady that Hester's reaction was out of all proportion to the offence. She decided to tread warily. She sat back, her elbows resting lightly on the arms of her favourite upright chair. It was an uncharacteristic gesture for she rarely allowed her back to relax against a support, even in solitude. At length she spoke calmly, her fingertips pressed together in a judicial manner:

"You are making a mountain out of a molehill, Hester. It may be that your conduct was a little wanting in propriety towards his lordship, but in this instance I believe it was excusable. After all Lord Montfort left us quite unceremoniously yesterday morning; consider, my love, the circumstances of your previous meeting were unusual. I am persuaded that he is too much the gentleman to bear a grudge for some trivial remark. Do not forget that he stands in your debt. Besides," she finished lightly, "A little teasing will do him no harm; I believe his lordship is quite human beneath that crusty shell which he shows to the world. You have a talent for penetrating such armour. Only consider Mr. Garth's performance."

Miss Jane gave a youthful giggle, oddly at variance with her grey hairs. Hester laughed too and bestowed a light kiss on the birdlike little lady's brow.

"You are a sane, prosaic creature, Miss Jane, and quite the best antidote to my distempered freaks. However, my various emotions have been sorely tried of late. It is a relief to know that Mortimer will accompany us to Huntsgrove tomorrow; he will provide a welcome diversion. Indeed I am fortunate to have such a brother, one can always rely on his cheerful disposition. It will be so pleasant to have his company for a while. If only he did not wish to go into the Army . . ." Hester's soft, deep voice trailed away.

Miss Stanhope nodded sympathetically.

"Perhaps his lordship will advise you. He must have military connections, you know."

"Very true, I may consult him if an oppotunity arises. But now I must get on. Will you excuse me if I have my luncheon on a tray? I have left my poor heroine in such a plight that it is almost beyond my feeble wits to extricate her."

The two ladies separated to go about their separate tasks and the customary atmosphere of tranquility enveloped the sunny cottage.

Chapter 6

"The Horse and Groom"

It was late on Friday afternoon when the London coach arrived at 'The Horse and Groom'. The ponderous conveyance had been delayed earlier by a cracked shaft and the driver dared not linger if he were to reach Brighton by nightfall. The single passenger, a young man with an air of the Quality about him, was deposited with more haste than ceremony; the coach rattled on its way through the windswept hedgerows and was soon out of sight. The weather changed rapidly so near the coast and an unexpected storm had blown in from the sea; fast moving grey clouds had dimmed the sunny splendour of the morning and the first heavy raindrops had begun to fall an hour ago.

The young man wore a high crowned hat, with a many-caped greatcoat flung carelessly about his broad shoulders. He lifted his head to scan the sky, taking deep breaths of fresh air; a relief after the hours of confinement in the stuffy vehicle. The rain fell unheeded as his eyes took in the scene; his keen gaze roved over the tops of the downs, noting the sheep huddled in the hedgerows, the old gnarled trees bent in the wind, and the fresh green fields on the lower slopes; in the distance he could dimly discern a cluster of chimney pots, but the cottages were hidden from view by the ancient hedges which tunnelled their way through every fold of the downs; of people there was no sign. He turned to survey the inn and a smile curved his wide, generous mouth as he took in the familiar half-timbered frame, the snug latticed windows set deep in the thick walls and the stout oak door. It was a large, rambling building set well back from the road. There were flowers in pots on the window-sills and the whole effect was charming despite the dismal weather.

The faded inn-sign creaked above his head, rousing him from his reverie. With a sigh of satisfaction the gentleman stooped to pick up his bags, leaving a small box beside the mounting block to be fetched later. He walked purposefully across the cobbled yard and plied the brass knocker vigorously. There came a sound of footsteps on the flagstones, a comely maidservant opened the door and peeped out.

She let out a little shriek of surprise.

"Lud, Sir Mortimer, what a start you gave me a-hammerin' on the door. There bean't many folk about this afternoon, along of this larmentable rain. But come in, sir."

She stood back and her eyes widened as she took in his baggage.

"Did you come on the Lunnun coach, sir? The master will be that put out to 'a missed it. He wanted to send a package to Brighton. Mr. Potter's down in the cellar — I'll fetch him directly. Step into the parlour, sir, and let me take your wet things."

Mortimer Vane followed the trim figure down the dark panelled passage. They turned to the right, Sir Mortimer ducked low to avoid the lintel, and emerged in the common tap-room. The maid passed through and entered a smaller room at the far end known as the 'Snug'. A welcome fire of seacoals spluttered brightly in the wide hearth and Mortimer cast a longing glance at the comfortable, high-backed settle in the ingle-nook. Bessie fussed around him, taking his gloves, hat and scarf and assisting him to remove his dripping coat. Presently he stood revealed in a splendid waistcoat of pale blue and silver stripes, adorned with small silver buttons. His coat was of a darker blue and his buff-coloured inexpressibles seemed to be moulded to his form.

Bessie absorbed this vision, a twinkle in her eye.

"You do be as fine as fivepence, sir," she remarked, "Can 'ee sit down by the fire while I go and seek Mr. Potter. What will 'ee take to drink Sir Mortimer?"

"*Can* I sit down?" repeated Mortimer, a boyish grin creasing his handsome, regular features and lighting his deep-set hazel eyes, "What do you mean, Bessie lass? Enough of your impudence. I'll have you know I had this outfit from the Prince of Wales's own tailor — all the crack these waistcoats ye' know." He squinted down at that item admiringly, then seated himself nonchalantly on the settle. "I'll take a tankard of old Ned's home brewed ale, spiced and hot, if you please."

"Very good, sir. I won't be but a moment." Bessie bobbed a curtsey and departed, carrying Mortimer's wet garments over her arm.

Left alone, Mortimer leaned back, lazily watching the fire and listening to the steady tick of the large, old-fashioned grandfather clock which stood in the corner beside the dresser. It was very quiet, for this room was on the side of the inn sheltered from the fury of the storm. The solitude and the feeling of displacement which a journey often brings induced a mood of unwonted introspection. In general he preferred a life of action to the more sedentary pursuits of the gentleman scholar. His sojourn at Oxford was now ended and he wondered, a little anxiously, how he should spend the rest of his days. He had just indulged a short bout of dandyism in the Metropolis, in company with his more sophisticated cousin, Tom Marchant. Tom was endowed with a comfortable fortune and no gambling instinct or proclivities, much to his parents' relief. Tom appeared contented with his limited round of the fashionable clubs, drawing rooms, assemblies, theatres, and other diversions of the 'beau Monde'. After a few weeks, Mortimer had found it stifling; he yearned to lead a more adventurous existence and his childhood ambition to obtain a commission in the Prince of Wales's Own regiment, stationed at Brighton, returned to him with redoubled force.

He sighed. He was no longer certain that the Brighton Camp was the place for him. For years now the Prince's Own had entertained the townsfolk and fashionable visitors with a constant round of parades, field days, grand reviews and sham fights — such things were all very well; they had thrilled him as a boy, but now it occurred to Mortimer that the regiment had been involved in very little real action. There was a rumour circulating in the London clubs that the Prince had again tried and failed to obtain the King's assent to his engaging in active service. He acknowledged to himself that he would enjoy the gay life and civilian admiration which would be his lot in the Tenth Light Dragoons, but now that England was at war once more with France surely it was one's duty to tangle with those Frenchies and beat them once and for all. Besides it would be expensive, living in Brighton. The Prince's Regiment was the most popular in the Army among fashionable young men and most of the officers were the Prince's own friends. Mortimer shook his head regretfully. His modest fortune was held in trust until he came of age in two years' time and there was his sister, Hester, to consider. In due course he intended to purchase a small estate in his beloved downland country, but he was not yet ready to settle down and in a few years Hester might be married. With brotherly candour he recognized that Hester was not beautiful, but she possessed more character and sweetness of disposition than was common in a female. Well, he would do his best to persuade her to accept their Aunt Marchant's invitation to spend the little season in Brighton — perhaps the sea air would clarify his prospects, he concluded with youthful optimism.

Mortimer ran a hand through his thick, curly brown hair, brushed modishly forward. That ale was an unconscionably long time in coming. He rose to ring the bell, but halted with his hand raised, as he heard footsteps in the outer room. A moment later he was shaking hands with his old friend, Ned Potter, landlord of 'The Horse and Groom'.

The short burly man beamed at Mortimer hospitably.

"It be that good to see you, Sir Mortimer, though unexpected loike. Here be your ale, sir. One moment whiles I take a poker to it."

The landlord squatted on his heels before the glowing fire and carefully inserted a short poker into the heart of the blaze.

Mortimer's brows knitted in perplexity.

"Unexpected, Ned? How can that be? I sent word to my sister two weeks' ago. Though now I think of it I believe I wrote that I would hire a horse from you to save George Hamble the trouble of coming over with 'Merrylegs'. I shall need a horse to ride while I am in the district. Do you still have 'Vixen' eating her head off in your stables?"

It was Ned Potter's turn to look troubled. He hesitated before replying,

"Yes, well — er, no. That is to say she is already hired by a gentleman tonight, Sir Mortimer, but she should be back first thing in the marning. In fact, sir, I don't have a horse in my stables at the moment."

"Damnation, why ever not man? I've never known you to be in such a plight before. Why, last time I was here there were at least six horses in Peter Lightfoot's care." Mortimer eyed the landlord's back suspiciously as Ned plunged the red hot poker into the pewter tankard, causing it to foam and spill over on to the highly-polished surface of the massive refectory table, which dominated the centre of the room. Ned wiped the base of the tankard carefully on his leather apron and stooped to place it at Mortimer's elbow. The light was dim, but it seemed to Mortimer that Ned Potter's face assumed a remarkably sheepish expression. Not for nothing had young Sir Mortimer been born and raised in the Sussex Downs.

"So that's the way of it," he said good-humouredly, taking a sip of ale and setting it down with care in case he should mark his cherished waistcoat. "Well, I hope those gentry take good care of my 'Vixen'. She's a fine mare, not cut out for stumbling about in rabbit holes in the dark. Ought to know better than to send her out on such an errand," Mortimer finished severely.

"Indeed, Sir Mortimer, I doan't loike it any better 'an 'ee do," declared Ned unhappily. "'Tis the first time they've taken 'er and it'll be the last; but my other mare, 'Lassie', she cast a shoe and I had to leave her at the blacksmith's until tomorrow over Pendleton."

"I must make the best of it," said Mortimer resignedly, "'Pon my soul, 'tis demmed inconvenient. There's my sister expecting me for dinner and no way of informing her; but never mind, since there's no help for it I'll not deny 'tis pleasant to stay by your cozy fire on such a wild night. Can you have a bedchamber prepared and dinner in, say, an hour?"

"Of course, sir. You finish your ale and I'll send Bessie up to air Number One, 'tis the best we have, sir."

"Splendid. What can you offer me for dinner, Ned? I'm ravenous, I must confess. I've had nought to speak of since early this morning. I lose my appetite in Town, too many late nights and afternoon teas, dancing attendance on the ladies. When I think of Mrs. Blossom's custard tartlets . . but I will not repine if you can produce me a stew like the one I had when I left last January. A vision of that stew has lingered in my palate's eye through many a jaded meal in Oxford."

"I'm happy to hear you say so, sir. If you'll excuse me I'll bustle to set all in motion for your honour's comfort."

Some half an hour later the landlord reappeared.

"Your bedchamber be all prepared, if you'll just follow me, Sir Mortimer. Would you care to come down, or will you take dinner in your room, sir?"

Mortimer shivered as they left the warm fire, crossed the empty taproom and began to mount the narrow, winding stair.

"Oh, I think I'll come down. Devilish dull up here on my own, you know. How are Mistress Potter and Alice? I haven't seen them about. In fact, now I come to think of it, I haven't seen anyone about. It's as close and quiet as a plaguey oyster. Is aught amiss, man?"

Mortimer reached the head of the stair and scrutinized the landlord closely in sudden concern. The candle flickered and a splash of wax fell to the floor as Ned shook his head, nurmuring that all was well; that the wife and daughter Alice had gone over to Pendleton to visit old Mrs. Potter and would be back after market tomorrow. An inward conviction seized Mortimer that the landlord was hiding something from him; was even afraid of something. He noticed Ned casting several furtive glances over his shoulder into the eerie shadows beyond the candle's warm glow. Decidedly there was something wrong.

The inn was old and rambling; they went up and down several odd steps, rounded two corners and tripped over a linen basket before they reached the best bedchamber. Although Mortimer had often dined at the inn in his journeyings to and from school and college, he had never stayed overnight before.

"I shall need a guide to find my way downstairs again," he observed.

Ned Potter lit two candles above the fireplace and gave the newly-lit fire a prod with the toe of his boot. The landlord was his usual cheerful self as he responded,

"No need for that sir, jest follow your nose. There's a lovely mutton stew a-bubbling on the range. Bessie will lay it up for you in the 'Snug' in about half an hour. Is there aught else I can get for you, Sir Mortimer?"

A quick glance revealed his bags standing neatly side by side under the window; steam rose from the ewer on the marble-topped wash-stand with clean towels close by; a round bulge indicated a warming pan between the sheets.

"Is it safe to leave that thing there?" enquired Mortimer in some alarm. In general he scorned such mollycoddling, but the night was unseasonably chill.

"I'm not sure, Bessie must ha' forgotten," Ned Potter was doubtful.

"Best take it out then. I don't want the whole inn to burn down on my account."

When the landlord had departed, clutching the bright copper pan by its wooden handle, Mortimer made haste to tidy himself. He rummaged in his travel bag for his tortoiseshell comb and brushes, whistling softly between his teeth; he was bending before the low looking glass, struggling with the rumpled folds of his cravat when a sudden draught extinguished the candles. The shutters rattled and Mortimer crossed to the window to fasten them more securely. He paused, his hand on the casement, and peered out into the night. The moon appeared fitfully between dark, scudding clouds; he could hear the swaying trees creak and the pitter-pat of raindrops on the stable yard below. He was about to draw in his head when there came the sound of a heavy door slamming directly beneath his window. Instinctively Mortimer drew back into the shadows; there was a soft clatter on the cobbles and a muffled curse as a tall figure swathed in a dark cloak tripped over some unseen object, probably a pail judging by the noise it made. Mortimer could discern vaguely a pinpoint of moving light, which he took to be a shuttered lantern. It disappeared through the stable door. Seconds later the man reappeared leading a horse. Briefly the dark figure lifted the lantern and raised his hand in a gesture of farewell; Mortimer was puzzled for the face beneath the shadowy low-crowned hat did not shine pale in the faint light. With a swift intake of breath, he realized that the man wore a mask; could it really be so, or did his eyes deceive him? Yes, it must be, for a muffler would have presented a much bulkier appearance. The lantern light vanished; the man swung into the saddle and bending low to avoid the trees, turned sharply to the right and trotted briskly along the bridlepath which eventually led to Shawcross.

Mortimer's curiosity was aroused. He was also annoyed: that masked man had been riding 'Vixen' and at such a pace would be lucky if he did not lame the plucky little mare in the dark and the rain. The door shut softly below. Mortimer reflected that it was a fortunate chance that his candles had been extinguished by the draught; gently he closed the shutters and slipped the rough wooden peg in place. He finished his toilette, took up a candle and locked his door behind him. As Ned had surmised, the appetizing smell of mutton stew was sufficient guide to bring Mortimer once more to the 'Snug'. Here he found Bessie waiting to remove the covers, while his host replenished the fire and lit more candles.

Mortimer seated himself at the table, shaking out his napkin, while Ned Potter poured a glass of wine.

"Do you think the storm will blow itself out before morning?" he enquired casually, "This weather seems to be very bad for custom." Mortimer regarded the silent tap-room thoughtfully.

"Rackon it will, sir," replied Potter easily, "Trade is never very brisk on a night loike this, but some o' the reg'lars will be in presently. There's some meeting over at the Church tonight."

Mortimer nodded and turned his attention to his dinner. He made a hearty meal, then strolled over to the inglenook settle.

"I'll have a bottle of your best port and a half a cheese, Ned."

The landlord departed to the nether regions, leaving Bessie to clear the covers. Mortimer watched her, idly at first, then more searchingly. Her round, pretty face was flushed and her full lips parted with excitement. The girl must have sensed his regard for she raised her dark brown eyes to meet his; they were sparkling. Mortimer was not vain and he did not flatter himself that he had engendered this flutter in her maidenly bosom.

He asked bluntly,

"What's to do, Bessie? You look like the kitten that ate the cream."

She started, pressing one work-roughened hand to her slender throat.

"I don't know what you mean, sir," she said as she plucked nervously at the lace of her kerchief.

Bessie half-turned from the table; her elbow caught the edge of the dresser and she gave a sharp little cry of pain. Mortimer leapt to her side, tilted her chin firmly beneath his long fingers and planted a kiss squarely on her full lips. The next instant he was recoiling from a stinging box on the ear.

They stood facing one another, Bessie panting a little and Mortimer ruefully rubbing his ear.

"Really sir, I would not ha' thought it of 'ee, but I hopes I didn't hurt 'ee," said Bessie reproachfully at last.

"Lord, Bessie, of course it hurt. But that's not the point; now I know for certain 'twas not I brought that sparkle to your eye tonight. It puzzles me and I do not like mysteries. Could it perhaps be connected with the dark stranger who rode off on 'Vixen' a short while since?"

The girl hesitated, then whispered,

"In a way, sir, but 'tis not what you think. He be Quality like yourself, an' I know my place. But 'ee's such a kind gentleman. He brought me a message from my Peter; we're to be wed come Michaelmas, sir."

"Hum!" Mortimer rubbed his chin meditatively, "You mean Peter Lightfoot, the ostler?"

"Yes, sir," Bessie smiled happily and began stacking plates on a tray.

"Peter and I were good friends. We played together as boys in Shawcross."

"I know, Peter told me. He often speaks of you, sir," said Bessie quietly.

Mortimer retreated to the settle and stretched out his long legs, one gleaming boot crossed over the other.

"I wish you both very happy. But tell me, is Peter involved with the gentry hereabouts? You can speak freely; as I said Peter is my good friend, but he was always one to be falling into scrapes." Mortimer grinned reminiscently.

A troubled frown wrinkled the maid's smooth brow.

"I don't know, sir, and that's the truth. Something is bothering him, but he won't tell me. I believe it's to do with Miss Alice an' her fine lawyer friend, but I'm only guessin' after all. Peter says it's too dangerous for me to get caught up in . . ." Bessie halted abruptly. The door to the tap-room opened and Ned Potter appeared bearing the port and cheese. He was followed by several of the village folk, come to refresh themselves after the meeting. Bessie bustled away, leaving Mortimer alone in the 'Snug'. He consumed the port and a large portion of cheese in a leisurely fashion, brooding the while on the subject of his interrupted conversation with the little maid. Bessie's good-tempered face had looked quite vicious for a moment when she spoke of Alice Potter, the landlord's daughter. Could she be jealous? He dismissed the thought as unworthy — obviously Bessie had eyes for no-one but Peter. He racked his brains but could think of only one lawyer in the neighbourhood: Stephen Garth, his own solicitor in Pendleton. Garth came of a good family and Mortimer could recall numerous instances of his ruthlessness and ambition. He did not think such a man would be satisfied with an innkeeper's daughter. He concentrated his thoughts on Alice Potter. She was about his own age and had been an accomplished flirt almost before she quitted her cradle. He had never liked her above half, but he acknowledged that on the rare occasions when he had spoken with her (since they grew up) she had been pleasant and obliging. The local menfolk clustered round her like bees round a honey pot and her absence tonight probably explained the almost uninhabited tap-room. Alice was the Potters' only child and she had been much indulged. She was sent away to a Ladies' Seminary in Horsham and had returned a year ago with a set of airs and aspirations far above her present station and expectations. Alice was no beauty, but her manner was lively and her taste exquisite. She had a sharp tongue, but usually reserved it for members of her own sex, preferring to keep her claws sheathed when gentlemen were present.

Mortimer stirred restlessly. He had an uncanny knack of seeing to the heart of a situation, which frequently gave him a wisdom beyond his years. He sensed that in some obscure way Alice's relationship with Garth was the clue to a puzzle, but too many pieces were missing. He yawned; comfortably drowsy, he dismissed all problems from his mind and was soon fast asleep. He was roused by a muffled thumping sound. Sitting up stiffly, he noted that it was very quiet. The villagers must have departed long since. The candles were guttering low in their sockets; a glance at the clock revealed that it wanted but a few minutes to eleven.

"Best be off to bed," muttered Mortimer to himself, stretching and preparing to rise.

There came a further thudding on the stout inn door. Thoroughly awakened, Mortimer's curiosity was aroused. It was too late for casual visitors; country folk went early to bed. He subsided in the darkest corner of the old settle and closed his eyes, feigning sleep. His straining ears caught the sound of stealthy, hurried footsteps, the soft rattle of bolts being withdrawn and the faint click of a key in a well-oiled lock. Mortimer remained still, every sense alert: a hushed colloquy seemed to be taking place in the passageway; the door to the tap-room burst open, the candles flickered in the draught and a tall man, shrouded in a black cloak, staggered in supported by Ned Potter, with Bessie close behind.

Chapter 7
The Midnight Visitor

Mortimer lounged motionless in his corner, giving vent to an occasional gentle snore; with an effort he kept his eyes shut and the landlord, after one quick glance in his direction, decided to ignore him. The man groaned and Ned Potter wrung his hands in dismay, momentarily at a loss.

He whispered to the hovering Bessie,

"He cannot remain here, he said the Runners are close on his heels."

"But his wound has opened again," protested Bessie, "Look 'ere, Mr. Potter, 'tis blood on his 'and and shoulder. You get him settled in the panel and I'll run for water and bandages. I wonder where 'Vixen' can be; I'll take a quick look in the stable. Oh, if only my Peter were 'ere."

Mortimer heard the girl's retreating footsteps; a good girl that, steady head in a crisis. He turned his attention to the two men and ventured to open his eyes. The stranger was sprawled on the bench by the table, his head pillowed on his right arm. His right hand clasped his left shoulder and through his fingers there oozed a slow trickle of blood. Odd, there seemed something vaguely familiar about the unconscious form. Mortimer noted a large signet ring on the man's right hand, but it was too dark for him to make out the details of the design.

Meanwhile, Ned Potter had taken up a candle and was hurriedly running his hand over the panelling on the opposite side of the hearth to Mortimer's inglenook. An intricate frieze, with a Tudor Rose motif, bordered the low ceiling; after a short delay Potter found the knob he sought, two roses to the right of the larger central one. He pressed firmly, noiselessly a panel slid open beside him. Mortimer closed his eyes hastily as the landlord turned back into the room; Ned had no time to linger and Mortimer watched surreptitiously, beneath lowered lids, as the strong little man half-dragged, half-carried the limp figure to the gaping hole. He swung round to back into the secret panel and for a second Mortimer was afforded an excellent view of the front of the man's body, his head slumped forward on his chest; there was no doubt that it was the same man who had clattered away beneath his window earlier in the evening — and he still wore a mask. What was it Bessie had said of him? ah, that was it!, "Quality like yourself" and he had brought her a message from Mortimer's old friend, Peter Lightfoot.

A level-headed young man, Mortimer was not one to rush willy nilly into action, but his interest was aroused, and he was wondering how best to proffer his aid when Bessie reappeared. She had just set the water down on the table when there came a thunderous knocking on the door. Her hands shook, spilling some of the brandy over her snowy white apron. All in a moment Ned Potter slipped back into the room, seized the bottle, water and bandages and hid them behind the panel. He pressed the knob to close the panel.

"Go lass, and open the door, but not too quickly," he commanded the pale maid. His gaze swept round the room to see that all was tidy and his mouth fell open in a comical expression of dismay as he encountered young Sir Mortimer's keen hazel eyes, wide-awake and twinkling.

There was no time for comment. Two scarlet-coated Bow Street Runners pounded into the 'Snug', with Bessie bringing up the rear. They halted just inside the narrow doorway, sniffing the air like hounds scenting their quarry. Mortimer felt compassion stir for the hunted man; he raised a languid eyebrow in the direction of the two men, before ignoring them to address the landlord peremptorily,

"By all means bring me some more of that excellent brandy. But bring it yourself this time man, I'll not have that clumsy wench slopping it about. I thought that I had requested a private parlour, what are these men doing here? Surely you are not still serving customers at such an advanced hour?" Mortimer raised his ornate quizzing glass and surveyed the Runners haughtily.

"We're no ordinary customers, sir," said the elder of the two men, stepping up to the table and producing a folded paper, which he waved under the indignant Ned Potter's nose. He spoke with a marked London accent. "My name's Watson, Bill Watson o' Bow Street and this 'ere," he continued, tapping the paper impressively, "This 'ere is a warrant to search this inn. Accordin' to information received this inn is an 'aunt of the no-tor-ioos 'ighwayman 'oo terrorizes these parts, a Frenchy some call the 'Bew Cheevaleer', the same bein' in league wiv smugglers and other unlawful in-diwiduals."

"We nearly 'ad 'im an hour agone, but 'ee gave us the slip," broke in the other Runner, a sturdy young man, with sandy hair, freckles and bristling side whiskers. Clearly, he was impatient with his senior's ponderous approach. "He galloped off in this direction and turned aside just as we reached the little stream about 'alf a mile down the road. We delayed to search the 'edges 'n ditches in the wicinity, 'til I remembered the tip we 'ad about this 'ere inn . . ."

"That's enough, Tom," interrupted Watson authoritatively, "You go and search them stables, I'll stay 'ere and conduct a few enquiries."

The man addressed as Tom subsided, somewhat abashed. When he had gone Watson sat sdown heavily in the chair lately vacated by the wounded stranger. His shrewd little black eyes rested thoughtfully on the three other occupants of the room. He drew forth a well-thumbed black-covered notebook and licked a stubby pencil.

Ned Potter decided it was time to assert himself.

"Go get the gentleman his brandy, Bessie,— if that's all right with you, sir?" Ned turned a bland, enquiring face towards Mr. Watson.

"Make it two, girl," nodded the Runner absentmindedly.

"What's this, drinking in the course of duty, officer?", Mortimer asked sarcastically, "What was your name again, Watson, was it? Such a lapse should be reported to his superiors, don't you agree landlord?"

Ned Potter nodded, grinning from ear to ear.

The Runner shook his head reproachfully,

"Now sir, I 'aven't touched a drop all day, as young Peabody can vouch. And what's more I don't intend to, 'til this 'ere hinterview is over, but I'm not getting eny younger and 'tis a filfy night. 'Twouldn't be 'uman not to take a drop'o cheer ter keep the chill out." Watson eyed Mortimer suspiciously. He muttered musingly, "Tall, dark, broad shouldered, gent. o' the Quality." Watson rose and approached the ingle seat, where Mortimer lounged, his face half hidden in the shadows. Excitement quivered in his voice as he exclaimed,

"Bring those candles 'ere landlord. Now you can explain to me, my fine young sir, what you're doin' in these remote parts on such a night."

Mortimer slowly lifted his heavy lids and met Watson's stare. He assumed a tone of ineffable boredom with the whole affair. Addressing Ned Potter, who stood a little to one side, holding aloft a branched candelabra, he drawled,

"Potter, my good fellow, I believe this er . . . limb o' the law wishes to know my credentials. Be so kind as to set his mind at ease before he carries me off to the nearest gaol."

His round, wrinkled face devoid of expression, the landlord turned to the Runner.

"Rackon you must a' bin drinkin', officer. This gentleman's Sir Mortimer Vane o' Shawcross. He's well known in the neighbourhood and anyone can vouch for him."

Watson was not easily shaken.

"If, I say if, that be so, what is a gentleman o' quality doing lurkin' in a wayside tavern, 'stead o'lyin' snug abed in 'is own 'ome?", he persisted.

"Enough o' this foolery, man," Mortimer was irritated. "My affairs are my own business, but this much I will tell you: I arrived on the London Coach this afternoon. The coach was delayed and I arrived late. I therefore decided to spend the night here, the weather being so inclement. I intend to join my sister, Miss Hester Vane, in Shawcross, tomorrow morning. I trust that you are satisfied?"

"In my line o' work one's rarely satisfied, sir," responded Watson calmly, as he scribbled a note in his little black occurrence book, "Since you've told me so much, perhaps you wouldn't mind tellin' me just 'ow you hintend to reach Shawcross, Sir Mortimer?"

Before Mortimer could reply that he meant to hire a horse from the landlord, Ned Potter intervened hastily,

"Miss Vane sent Sir Mortimer's 'orse over from Shawcross yesterday, officer. She's a black mare. Your friend will find her in the stables."

Fortunately Bessie returned with the brandy at that moment; Ned Potter shot a pleading glance at Mortimer, while the Runner's attention was distracted. The maid was closely followed by the second Runner, Tom Peabody.

"One black mare, quite fresh and not ridden for some time," reported Peabody.

Bill Watson glanced wistfully at the glasses of brandy which Bessie was pouring at the table. He straightened and grasped his knotty baton with a firm grip.

"Dooty calls," he announced, "We will proceed to search the inn. You lead the way landlord."

The two Runners were about to quit the room with Ned, when Sam, the Potters' ginger cat, sidled in. Without hesitation the cat crossed the room to the secret panel and commenced sniffing at the wainscoting.

No one moved or spoke. All eyes were fixed on the heedless Sam, scratching in a most determined fashion.

The Runners' eyes gleamed; Peabody raised his truncheon to rap on the hollow panel; the movement was arrested as Mortimer stood up, saying coolly to Ned.

"Drat it, man, your cat is a poor mouser; I saw a sleek, fat mouse enter the hole by my foot some while since." He yawned, "Well, I'm for my bed. Perhaps, officer, you would be good enough to search my chamber first, I'm tired after my journey and minded for bed."

Peabody still hesitated, uncertainly; Sam, the cat, tired of his investigation, stretched out on the hook mat before the fire. Watson prodded his colleague with the tip of the crown, which surmounted his baton of office.

"Sir Mortimer's in the right of it, Tom me lad; 'Tis late indeed," he said testily, "You remain on guard at the foot o' the stair, whiles I go with Sir Mortimer to his chamber. Lead the way, Mr. Potter."

The little procession crossed the darkened tap-room, the uncarpeted boards creaking beneath their feet. Bessie remained behind to dampen the fire, lest a chance spark should tinder a blaze. Mortimer paused in the passageway to take up his night candle, which Ned solemnly lit with a taper. The wind whistled eerily along the hall; Mortimer did not envy Tom Peabody his solitary vigil. The best bedchamber presented a pleasant contrast to the cold, dark passage; Bessie had found time to turn back the sheets and lay out his nightshirt, a small fire blazed merrily setting their shadows leaping on the wall, Mortimer seated himself on the side of the bed and began to pull off his boots. Ned Potter stationed himself by the door, his face a mask of disapproval, while the Runner poked his nose in every nook and cranny. There was nothing perfunctory about his search; Mortimer waited patiently, suppressing an inner qualm. Never before had he sought to obstruct the forces of law and order. He wondered what had moved him to do so on this occasion. However, it was too late to withdraw now; he had acquiesced in Ned's account of his horse in the stables, something very queer about that, he could have sworn there had not been time to unsaddle and rub down the stranger's mount; nothing for it but to hope the Runners would not pursue their enquiries to Shawcross where everyone knew that his sister did not possess a black horse.

Watson was lifting the lid of the old oak linen chest at the foot of the four poster. Over the man's head Mortimer and Ned exchanged glances. The landlord shook his head, putting his finger to his lips warningly. Mortimer smiled reassuringly; after all Ned Potter was an old friend of his, an erstwhile sailor and, Mortimer was prepared to swear, honest and loyal, though not above a little illicit trading on occasion. He could not betray him to this officious little man from London.

At last Watson was finished. Mortimer closed the door behind the two men and leaned against it, emitting a long sigh of relief. He crossed to the bed, undressed rapidly and slipped an elegant, brocade dressing gown over his nightshirt. Seating himself in the comfortable arm chair by the fire, he determined to remain awake. From time to time he heard muffled bangings and thumps and once the sharp squeal of a cat. He must have dozed for when he came to himself, his shoulder aching from his awkward posture, the first pale streaks of dawn light were piercing the cracks in the shutters. Mortimer was chilled; he jumped to his feet and ran to the door, the events of the previous evening flooding back to him. He shivered. All was quiet, he could not even hear the wind. Cautiously he descended the stair and made his way to the 'Snug'. The dying embers of the fire rustled gently. He hesitated, there was no sign of any struggle. In all probability the Runners, eluded by their quarry, had long since departed through the inhospitable night. There was a footstep behind him, Mortimer whirled around and found himself face to face with Ned Potter. In his passing through the outer room he had neglected to notice his host outstretched upon a low bench by the window.

"Your pardon, I did not mean to disturb you," said Mortimer, feeling absurdly at a disadvantage, like a child caught in the pantry. He hurried on,

"I tried to stay awake to see if I could be of any further assistance, but I'm afraid tiredness overcame me."

"And a good thing too, y'r Honour," declared Ned bluntly. Carefully he replaced the ancient blunderbuss, which he had snatched from the wall when awakened by the intruder, "The less you knows o' the business the better. I'm that sorry I had to involve you at all, but there was no help for it wi' them red-coated rascals poking their long noses in every corner." He smiled reminiscently. "Led them a merry dance, I did. The older one, he banged 'is 'ead in my cellar an' they were both as black as chimney sweeps afore I'd done. I rackon they won't come 'ere again in an 'urry."

Mortimer grinned.

"How of the, er . . . gentleman? he asked, "Was he much hurt?"

"Not really, sir. 'Twas an old wound reopened you see. It looked worse than it was. Bessie and I soon set 'im to rights. I have to thank you, Sir Mortimer, for not betrayin' the old panel and fer keepin' quiet about the horse."

"Ah yes, I wanted to ask you about that, Ned. How do you explain a fresh horse in your stable, when you'd told me earlier there were none to be had? What happened to 'Vixen'?"

"Well, you see, sir, the gentleman left his own horse here, and borrowed my 'Vixen' — we found her tethered down in the copse near the stream. I couldn't lend you a horse which did not belong to me, now could I, sir?", Ned Potter finished pleadingly.

Mortimer ran a hand through his curly hair, then he clapped the landlord on the arm,

"No, I suppose not. But 'tis the devil of a coil, Ned. What happens if those Runners question my sister?"

"Oh, Lord, Sir Mortimer, I didn't think o' that. But I doubt they will, since they found nought in the way o' evidence. What I'd like to know is who suggested to those men that this might be a good place to look for High Tobymen and other sich villains," Ned concluded, knitting his craggy brows, "Folks are pretty loyal hereabouts."

Mortimer burst out laughing.

"What a hypocrite you are, man. So demmed virtuous no one could possibly suspect Ned Potter of harbouring mysterious strangers."

"I don't, sir, as a rule. This were a bit of an emergency, loike. But you'll take cold down here, can I get you some coffee or a nice 'ot toddy?"

"I wouldn't say no to some coffee. I don't feel much like sleep now. Think I'll make an early start. I assume 'Vixen' will be available in an hour or so?"

"Yes indeed, sir. I'll see to it right away. Bessie will still be abed, so I'll jest set the coffee on to boil. Excuse me, sir." Ned knuckled an eyebrow, sailorly fashion and departed, leaving Mortimer in the tap room. He was debating within himself whether to return to his chamber or await his coffee in the 'Snug', when there came a rustle and soft thud from the inner parlour. Mortimer swung round in time to see the panel slide open. He stood quite still, watching the tall stranger emerge blinking in the early morning sunlight.

The wounded man was pale, but he no longer wore a mask.

Their eyes met. Mortimer gave a gasp of surprise. No wonder the fellow seemed familiar.

"Good morning, my lord Montfort," he said quietly.

For an instant the older man frowned in an effort to gather his scattered wits. He looked penetratingly at Mortimer, then recognition dawned and he advanced smiling.

"Sir Mortimer Vane, is it not? We met at Lady Marchant's drum last month. You are very like your sister, sir. Forgive me if I do not shake your hand, I had the misfortune to suffer an accident recently and my shoulder is a trifle stiff this morning."

"I thought it was your left shoulder which was injured," Mortimer exclaimed impetuously.

"Hum, I believe you are right, though I feel as if I had broken every bone in my body . . .," Hugo ceased abruptly; he raised a hand to his brow and Mortimer noticed the signet ring on the third finger; it bore an ancient heraldic device, a sable dragon rampant.

Mortimer nodded sympathetically,

"Daresay you're not feeling quite the thing. Potter didn't have too much time to attend to your wound, with those Runners on your heels."

Hugo's eyes flew to Mortimer's face.

"You were here last night? It must sound very foolish, but I can't recall . . ., where's Ned Potter? Surely he was not apprehended?"

"No, no," replied Mortimer soothingly, "He's in the kitchen brewing coffee. He should be back directly. Why don't you sit down in that chair by the fire, you don't look altogether in prime twig, you know. I'll endeavour to get a blaze."

Hugo acquiesced without protest; he sank gratefully down on the settle, while Mortimer, careless of his handsome dressing robe, dropped to his knees on the mat and applied himself vigorously to the embers. With a little coaxing he achieved quite a tolerable fire. He sat back on his heels and held his hands to the blaze.

The two men maintained a neutral silence for several minutes; both were curious as to the other's rôle in last night's drama, but were uncertain how to proceed. They hailed Ned Potter's appearance, bearing a laden tray, with undisguised relief.

"Ah, Potter, just what we need," pronounced Hugo, "Toast too, splendid, I haven't felt so ravenous in months."

The worthy landlord looked from one to the other, then shrugged his shoulders and turned his attention to the coffee pot.

"No need to look so glum, Ned, Lord Montfort and I are already acquainted," said Mortimer, his eyes glinting mischievously.

"'Tis a case of least said, soonest mended," responded Potter dourly, "You should ha' waited for me to open yon panel, my lord."

"'Least said, soonest mended'", repeated Hugo meditatively. "'Tis the second time in a week that that saying has been addressed to me. You are quite right, old fellow, my apologies. I woke up in that dark hole; it felt stifling and I pressed the knob unthinkingly. I must have been unconscious for some hours. What exactly occurred last night? I remember little beyond arriving at your door with the pursuit close behind. I trust I did not bring trouble upon you?" His lordship regarded the trusty innkeeper with concern.

"Why as to that, my lord, 'twas a close shave, and 'twas Sir Mortimer here what headed the Scarlet coats off," Ned smiled reluctantly as he glanced at Mortimer, placidly munching toast and honey at the table.

"I am in your debt, Sir Mortimer, pray how was this achieved?"

"Quite easily. The Runners mistook me for you — tall, dark, gent o' the Quality was, I believe, their description. Distracted them, you know. I enjoyed it — enlivened a plaguely dull evening. But I tell you what, m'lord," added Mortimer severely, "Won't do, running around in demmed loo masks, bound to get caught sooner or later."

"Very true, my lord," corroborated Ned, shaking his grey head, "The risks are too great. Someone must've betrayed you — why else would those scarlet weskits be on yer trail, all the way from London."

Hugo frowned and sipped his coffee.

"I haven't the ghost of a notion," he confessed at last. "Can't think straight this morning. Almost as if I had a hangover."

"You probably have. I gave you enough brandy to put courage into a fleet." Ned glanced at the tall grandfather clock, "Sirs, it's almost five o'clock. Thank heaven Mistress Potter 'n Alice are away over in Pendleton. But Bessie will be astir any moment.'Twould be best if she didn't find us here."

"Right, I'll retire to my chamber," agreed Mortimer, rising to his feet. He sketched a bow to Montfort, no mean feat in a dressing gown and nightshirt. "I wish you a speedy recovery, my lord. Don't doubt you have your reasons for your night-time activities, not my business o'course, but if I were you, I should stay home at nights for a while." Having delivered himself of this speech, Mortimer flushed boyishly; Hugo's rather stern, taciturn features relaxed and a smile of singular charm softened his clear green eyes.

"I thank you for your advice; I will try to mend my ways. But to speak of pleasanter things, I believe that I am to have the pleasure of entertaining you for dinner at Huntsgrove tonight — today is Saturday, is it not?"

"Yes, I believe it is, but I was not aware of a dinner engagement. Of course, I have not seen my sister, I was er — delayed last night. I did not know you and she were on visiting terms . . .," Mortimer stopped confused; now that he thought of it he dimly recalled some affair long ago between Hester and Montfort. He could have bitten his unwary tongue.

Hugo took pity on his embarrassment.

"I regret to say that my mother and I have seen little of your family of late. My mother is an invalid and does not get about, while I have spent most of my time in London or abroad. However, my two young wards have recently fled from the Continent to make their home with us. Your sister assisted them when they suffered a carriage accident on her doorstep and I was delighted at the opportunity to renew our acquaintance."

Mortimer nodded happily,

"Oh if that's the way of it . . . I'll be most happy to accompany Hester this evening. Good morning, my lord." He executed a dignified departure, leaving Hugo to smile ruefully at Ned Potter.

"Foolhardy, that you be, my lord," sighed Ned, "Let me tend that shoulder. Do you think you can ride?"

"Peace, man, never fret, if you can saddle my 'Cassy' I'll be off. Can those Runners be lingering in the vicinity? I have no fancy to tangle with them again."

"How did they come upon you last night, my lord?" asked Ned, deftly bathing the afflicted shoulder and replacing the bandages.

"Ah! Have a care, Ned! not too tight. Yes, that is better. How did they come on me — it's hard to recall, I was fatigued, probably a trifle careless, for I was feeling that pleasant glow of a mission successfully accomplished (I gave the message into Cartwright's own hand, bye the bye he sails tonight). Then, of a sudden, as I was quitting Pendleton by the water meadow, a gruff voice bade me halt and those two Runners leapt out from the shade of a tree. They rode well, for men of their stamp, especially the one with whiskers, and I was hampered by my shoulder. I did not succeed in giving them the slip until I reached the crossroads a mile North of here. By that time I was so faint with the exertion that I had no choice but to come to you. 'Twas not well done in me, but believe that I am grateful."

"You did quite right, my lord, and no harm done, thanks to young Sir Mortimer. A very proper young gentleman that, my lord, stood up to them bullies as cool as a cucumber. But I'd give a deal to know 'oo set the Runners on your tail." Ned Potter's round face assumed an unwontedly grim expression.

"'Tis a matter which must be investigated — and soon," agreed his lordship, shrugging into his russet brown riding coat with a grimace of pain, "Go saddle 'Cassy', there's a good fellow and let me know when the coast is clear. I'll rest here."

"Best wait in the panel, my lord, 'tis safer," declared Ned firmly.

Reluctantly Hugo allowed himself to be shepherded to the dark hole. He disappeared within; the panel slid into place and Ned Potter made haste to remove the stained bandages. A few moments later the landlord was in the stables, saddling the mettlesome black mare quickly and surely. Ned whistled softly between his teeth as he worked; there was no sign of Peter Lightfoot, the ostler, though he should have been back by now. He turned over Lord Montfort's account of last night's attack in his methodical, country mind. Odd that it should have happened in Pendleton while the wife and Alice were there. His face softened as he thought of his daughter, but he sighed too; she was a rare handful and no mistake since she came back from that fine seminary. Ned hoped she was not losing her heart to the lawyer-fellow Garth, that she spoke of so often these days. With simple wisdom Ned could see that it would do her no good to set her cap at Stephen Garth; his hands clenched as he thought of the fellow taking advantage of a young girl like Alice. A seemingly irrelevant thought struck him with the force of a blow. He pulled the girth too tight and the mare whinneyed in protest. He loosened it and stood up, frowning: It had occurred to him that Stephen Garth had been present on the night of the Staleybridge attack.

Unwillingly, he considered the matter, but shied away from the implication. It was always possible that a chance word from Alice to Garth had set the forces of law in motion. Ned did not believe that his daughter would wittingly betray him; but Garth seemed a cunning rogue, good at asking questions, too, in his line of business. There had been some rumours circulating concerning Garth recently; he was known to be generous and he lived in a style beyond the means of most of his profession. Ned was not one to gossip and he had not lent more than half an ear to the tap-room whispers; still, a few enquiries might be useful. Ned finished his task rapidly and crossed the yard, glancing about him keenly. He resolved to say nothing of his suspicions to Lord Montfort.

Ned returned to the 'Snug'. All was quiet, but he could hear Bessie singing in her chamber overhead. The village would be astir; there was no time to be lost. It was the work of a moment to release his lordship. Ned assisted him to wrap his long, old-fashioned travelling cloak about his tall, athletic form. Hugo clapped his hat upon his head, drew on his gloves and took up his whip. The two men parted at the kitchen door with a quick handclasp and a whispered word of farewell. Seconds later, Cassy's hooves clattered on the cobbles and Lord Montfort rode out of sight, leaning low in the saddle and urging his willing mare to a pace which Miss Vane might well have described as '*ventre à terre*'.

Chapter 8
The Homecoming

The hands of the grandfather clock had advanced to the respectable hour of eight, when Mortimer ran lightly down the stair and entered the tap-room. He had discarded his modish town gear in favour of a dark green riding coat and buff-coloured breeches. While making a hearty second breakfast he raised an enquiring eyebrow and asked the hovering Ned Potter if all was well.

"Aye sir, all's bowman," nodded the landlord, with a wink.

"Meant to be down earlier, ye know," confided Sir Mortimer, "But, stap me, I fell asleep again. Can you have Vixen ready in half an hour? I just have to throw my traps in my bag. Oh, and Ned, would you arrange for the carrier to convey my box to Shawcross when next he calls."

"No difficulty, sir. I'll send it over Monday."

"Is Peter Lightfoot returned?" pursued Mortimer, finishing his coffee, and dropping his napkin on the table.

"Indeed he is, Sir Mortimer. He came in ten minutes ago, with a couple of nags that I'd hired to Mr. Garth over at Hatch End."

"Splendid, I'd like a word with him."

The meal completed, Mortimer was in haste to be off. He collected his bag, paid his shot and stepped out into the sunny morning. It was a pleasant, fresh spring day, with that indefinable tang of sea salt in the air. The young man's spirits rose as he passed the horse trough and entered the stables.

He found Peter Lightfoot in Vixen's stall, engaged in slipping the bridle over the mare's head. Peter was a blonde giant, with more than a touch of the Viking about him. He wore a leather waistcoat and breeches, with a white, full sleeved shirt, open at the neck to reveal a bronzed skin. He had a lean, good-humoured face, piercing, blue eyes and even white teeth, which flashed in a warm smile of welcome as he observed Mortimer standing at the end of the stall. The two had been friends since boyhood, when George Hamble had taught them both to ride in the Manor park. Peter's mother had gone into service at the

Manor as a young maid; she had risen to the position of housekeeper and retained her position after she married, for her sailor husband was often away at sea. She had not quitted her post until the Crossleys replaced the Vanes at Shawcross Manor. By that time her husband was dead; Mrs. Lightfoot had used her comfortable legacy to move into Vine Cottage, and found occupation for her busy hands by mothering Mr. Stone at the Vicarage. Peter did not follow in his father's footsteps, preferring a life spent on land, and he had been happily employed as ostler at 'The Horse and Groom' for some years.

"Good to have you home, Sir Mortimer," said Peter, taking his friend's outstretched hand, and shaking it heartily.

"Thanks, old fellow, 'tis good to be back in Sussex," drawled Sir Mortimer, flushing with pleasure, "What's this I hear from Mistress Bessie, that you two are to be wed on Michaelmas Day?"

"'Tis true enough, I rackon," admitted Peter, reddening in his turn.

"No need to look so sheepish, man," laughed Mortimer, "Where will you live? How does Mistress Lightfoot take the news?"

"Oh, she and my Bessie, they be as thick as thieves, no trouble there, thank the good Lord. As for where we shall live, there's a cottage in Pen village over yonder, 'tis the one that belonged to old Widow Blake, afore she died. There's some work to be done on it, but 'twill all be ready come Michaelmas and I'll not be sorry to have me own home. Things have been a mite uncomfortable around 'ere o' late," he finished darkly.

Mortimer nodded understandingly.

"Yes, I gathered from Bessie that she and Alice Potter do not always see eye to eye; and then there seems to be so much night-time activity — I can't remember the last time I spent such a deuced wakeful night at an inn, not even in the centre of London."

Mortimer stroked the mare's velvety nose pensively. Peter shot him a sharp glance, but ventured no reply. They emerged into the sunlight, Vixen between them. Mortimer paused with one foot in the stirrup,

"Have you seen your Mother and Sally recently? Is there any message which I can convey for you?"

He vaulted lightly into the saddle; Peter stood back, his broad, capable hands resting on his hips, his head thrown back, eyes narrowed to shield them from the sun's glare.

"Thankee kindly, Sir Mortimer. If so be you should see them give them my love, and tell them I'll be over next Monday with the carrier; and tell Sally I have a gift for her from the tinker." Peter glanced around the yard, but it was empty save for themselves and an old collie dog, lying by the kitchen door. He put a hand to Mortimer's bridle, pretending to adjust the strap; in a suddenly hushed voice he muttered,

"Mum's the word on last night, sir, for all our sakes."

He stepped back,

"That should be all right now, Sir Mortimer, a safe journey and my respects to Miss Hester."

Mortimer raised his whip in acknowledgment.

"I'll be careful. Farewell, Peter."

He trotted out of the yard, his brow furrowed as he pondered the young ostler's parting words; unable to reach any satisfactory conclusion, he characteristically declined to brood, but turned his attention instead to the beauty of the morning. In a little while he emerged from the leafy lane and followed the bridle path across the fields. He proceeded at a steady pace, going gently uphill, until he reached a small eminence which afforded a fine view of the rolling hills. Here, Mortimer drew rein, breathing deeply and delighting in the profound peace and harmony of his native downland. Away below him he could see smoke curling from the chimneys of the inn and the cottages in Pen village. In the distance, on his right, he recognized the squat Norman tower of Shawcross Church; he turned in the saddle and perceived, yet further to his right the wooded elms, which marked the main approach to Huntsgrove Priory. The Priory itself was hidden from his view by a fold in the downs. A fine red admiral fluttered by; the butterfly caused the mare's ears to twitch.

Slowly the horse and man descended the hill. They crossed the highway which ran to Lewes in the East and Arundel in the West, and followed the rough cart track which led to Shawcross.

The clock on the church tower was striking ten as Mortimer entered the village. He rounded the Green and took the lane which ran at right angles behind the church — a familiar short cut to home.

Mortimer found his sister in the garden, tying up the flowers which had been beaten down by last night's storm. Hester jumped up at his approach and ran to meet him, laughing at her dishevelled state. Mortimer leaped down at the gate, kissed his sister heartily and kept an arm around her slender waist as he leant back to look at her.

"Best of sisters, how blooming you are!" he declared, adding wickedly, "Even the very mud of the garden attaches itself to your charming nose."

Hester rubbed hastily at the offending feature, exclaiming happily,

"Horrid boy, you know I am a sight. Let me go and tidy myself, while you take your horse around to the stable. Then we can have a comfortable prose. Have you breakfasted? How late you are, we expected you yesterday?"

Mortimer laughed.

"Don't bombard me with questions, my sweet. Just let me rid myself of my dust and all will be explained. I breakfasted some hours since, but a tankard of ale would not come amiss."

Some half an hour later Hester and Mortimer sat down together on the sunny window seat of the parlour, each brimming with news, not having seen one another since Christmas.

"You begin," said Hester generously. "Jane is in the village, taking comforts to old Mrs. Jenkins, who is still bedridden. She will be home for luncheon."

"Well, first my dear, I have a letter for you from our Aunt Annabelle. I am commissioned by her to say that she depends upon your company in Brighton for the season. She has hired a villa on the cliff because she wishes to be removed from the bustle of the Steyne. She preserves her naturally indolent disposition and is relying on you to keep her supplied with the latest *on dits* —' twould not be a particularly onerous task if you take Jane along, and I dare swear the change of air and scene would do you good," he concluded with the air of one making a great discovery.

Hester regarded him with affection, somewhat taken aback by this display of brotherly solicitude.

"And how of you, Tim, do you plan to accompany us? No doubt you will find country life sadly slow, after all your gay doings in town," Hester's innocent tone caused Mortimer to look at her sharply; he had not failed to remark the use of his nursery nickname, which Hester reserved for occasions when she wished to take him down a peg or two.

He grinned, raising his hand in a mock gesture of defense.

"Touché. I'll not deny 'twas in my mind to escort you. Cousin Tom will be there and we plan to visit the Camp and scout around. Tom has several acquaintances among the officers there."

"I see. How did you leave my Aunt? I trust she was in good health."

"Oh, aye she was in prime twig — er, I mean in excellent health, apart from a bout of influenza last month. She declares she is quite worn down with entertaining Uncle Marchant's political friends, but really she thrives on it. She is going to Brighton so that she can keep an eye on the Carlton House set, for 'tis understood the Prince is to be in residence at the Pavilion for most of the season, and with the King in such poor health it behoves her to sway with the wind. My uncle remains in Town; Mr. Pitt needs all his supporters on hand it seems."

Hester nodded thoughtfully.

"Is not Lord Montfort a close friend of Mr. Pitt?"

"Now that you mention it, I believe he is. Odd thing that — I ran into the fellow at 'The Horse and Groom' where I was obliged to rack up last night." remarked Mortimer casually.

Hester's interest quickened,

"What a strange coincidence; we are to dine at Huntsgrove tonight, if you do not object? How did you find his lordship?"

"Very charming, not at all high in the instep. He mentioned the dinner engagement himself; told him I'd be delighted to accompany you. Bit of a rum go, ain't it?; can't remember when we were last singled out for such an attention? How did it come about, do you have him in your toils, m'dear?" Mortimer asked quizzingly. To his surprise Hester blushed and fiddled with the letter from Lady Marchant, which was lying in her lap.

"Nonsense, 'tis no such thing. I happened to be of service to his two wards, Miss Stephanie and Miss Marietta, when their carriage broke down the other day." Hester observed the look of dismay which crossed Mortimer's good-natured features. She hurried on, "You will like them, I'm sure. They have not been in England for long, but their English is excellent. They were obliged to flee from Luxembourg and had most romantic escape. I know that in general you do not care to dance attendance on young ladies, but I think you will find them interesting and not quite in the ordinary style. Miss Stephanie in particular has a great deal of character and vivacity. Jane was much taken with them and she is not at all easy to please."

Mortimer smiled humorously.

"No indeed, she is quite a dragon. But, tell me, has Lord Montfort suffered an accident recently, his shoulder seemed to be paining him?"

Hester hesitated, uncertain how much to reveal of a secret which was not hers alone.

She replied cautiously,

"Yes, as a matter of fact there was some mishap the other evening. The details are vague, but I gather he was hit by a chance shot, possibly fired by the men pursuing the robber who attacked a coach at Staleybridge the same night; but his lordship does not like to discuss the incident and I beg you will not mention it to anyone."

Mortimer scented a mystery, but forebore to question his sister further.

"You have seen his lordship recently then?"

"Why yes," responded Hester calmly, "He called here yesterday morning with the young ladies, to thank Jane and myself for our services and to invite us to dinner."

Mortimer sipped his ale, and recrossed his shapely legs.

"Speaking of invitations, do you mean to accept Aunt Annabelle's offer of hospitality?" he enquired.

Hester nodded,

"Oh yes, I believe so. My book is almost finished and I have already promised Jane that we will take a little holiday. The weather has been so terrible this spring; we are quite moped with so much confinement. I shall be ready to go in a fortnight or so. When does our aunt intend to quit London?"

"I'm not certain, but no doubt she has informed you in her letter. There was some rout party that she wished to attend next week, so she will probably remove early the following week. But what of the local news? Does Dr. Minton still court our Jane?"

"Assiduously. They play at backgammon or whist at least once a week, and Jane often accompanies him on sick visits. He makes little progress I fear. I suspect 'tis because Jane has some foolish notion that she cannot desert me until I am wed, though she will not admit it. Incidentally, on the subject of courtship, I met with Susan Garth and her brother in Pendleton recently; it seems Mr. Garth wishes to purchase a town house there, he finds Hatch End too remote from his place of business. Susan hinted that her brother would like to limit her friendship with Mr. Stone, by setting a barrier of distance between them."

Hester refrained from mentioning Stephen Garth's proposal of marriage to herself, for she knew that Mortimer had always instinctively disliked their solicitor and had dubbed him a 'pettifogging lawyer' on more than one occasion.

They continued their discussion on topics of mutual interest until Miss Stanhope returned and luncheon was announced. It was a leisurely meal; Mortimer responded patiently to all Miss Stanhope's eager questions concerning the latest modes and gossip of the Metropolis. At length the good lady retired to her chamber to rest in preparation for the dinner party that evening and Mortimer suggested to his sister a stroll to the village. He proposed that they should call at Vine Cottage to give Mrs. Lightfoot the message from her son. Hester agreed readily to this plan and they soon set out, taking with them a jar of Mrs. Blosson's cranberry jelly and some sweetmeats for Sally.

As they walked Mortimer told Hester of the Runners' visitation at 'the Horse and Groom'. He narrated the whole incident, omitting only the presence of Lord Montfort in the panel. Hester listened closely and when he had finished his account she asked,

"But did you not say that you met with my lord Montfort at the inn? Was he present when these Runners arrived?"

Mortimer hesitated, temporarily at a loss. He had forgotten that he had mentioned Hugo Jermyn's arrival earlier.

"Well, yes," he replied uneasily, "But he arrived before the Scarlet Coats, you know, and er, kept out of their way. I gather he had his own reasons for not confronting them; his business was of a rather private nature with Ned Potter. Shouldn't have mentioned the matter at all, trust you won't repeat this information, Hester."

"My lips are sealed, since you wish it, my dear. Let us speak of other matters. Was Peter in good spirits? Will he be coming over to Shawcross soon?"

Mortimer turned with relief to safer ground.

"He said he'd come over on Monday with the carrier; he can fetch Vixen and it will save George the journey. Did you know that Peter and Bessie Appleby are to be wed?"

"Of course," smiled Hester, "Mrs. Lightfoot can talk of nothing else. Since Bessie is an orphan the ceremony is to be performed here in Shawcross; it will be quite a large party if Peter's mother has her way. But here we are," she added as they skirted a corner of the green and arrived at the pretty vine-covered cottage, nestling beside the old church, but not close enough to be overshadowed by it. Sally Lightfoot was swinging on the gate; she jumped off, bobbing a cheerful curtsey when she saw the visitors.

"Mama," she called, skipping lightly up the path ahead of them, "Here be Miss Vane and Sir Mortimer come to call." Sally's little terrier, Toby, barked in welcome, his short tail wagging furiously.

Mrs. Lightfoot must have heard the commotion for she soon appeared at the door, with a welcoming smile on her comely face; she had always been devoted to the Vane family and young Sir Mortimer was her particular favourite.

"Come in, my dears," she cried, standing aside hospitably to allow them to enter. She received the jar of cranberry with voluble thanks and busily dusted two chairs before waving her visitors to be seated. Hester settled herself in the chair nearest the window, but Mortimer seized the matronly figure and swung her around, as if — she exclaimed — she had been a sack of feathers. Mortimer set her down and planted a resounding kiss on her plump cheek, before releasing her. He then flopped down astride the other chair, placed near the table and regarded Mrs. Lightfoot with a wicked grin, as she fumbled to set her cap straight on her grey-brown curls and smoothed her apron.

"You grow more handsome every time I see you, Mrs. Martha," declared the incorrigible young man. He sniffed, "Hum, do I smell cakes — delicious. I found nought to equal your angel cakes in the whole of Oxford."

"Aye, sir, I've always been a dab hand wi' light pastry," Mrs. Lightfoot smiled complacently, "My poor Edward proposed to me after eatin' one o' my apple and cinnamon pies. 'Tis surely true that the way to a man's heart is through his stummick. Seems like only yesterday . . . and now I'm thinking of making the wedding cake for Peter and Bessies. How time does fly. But don't they feed you proper up in Oxford, Sir Mortimer? You look a little pale and in need o' fattening' up. I'll send over some o' my calves' foot jelly; yon Polly Blossom was a clumsy wench in the kitchen." Shaking her head she turned away to set the kettle on to boil, while behind her back Mortimer and Hester exchanged amused glances. The feud between the two good ladies had been raging with unabated vigour ever since they had been young maids in service at Shawcross Manor.

"Lord, what's this talk of calves' foot jelly?" protested Mortimer, "I'm not yet at my last prayers, I hope. However, I'm very willing to do justice to these dainty morsels." So saying, he sampled several of the little cakes which Mrs. Lightfoot placed at his elbow. The ladies sipped their tea, while Mortimer, his appetite assuaged, delivered Peter's message. An hour passed in easy conversation and at length Hester rose to leave, explaining that they must be back in good time to change for dinner at the Priory.

"If Mortimer eats any more of your lovely cakes he will not be able to squeeze into his fine new waistcoat," she added teasingly.

Mrs. Lightfoot hesitated, glancing through the open window, to where Sally could be seen, playing ball with Toby in the garden.

"Thankee again, my dears, for the jelly and sweetmeats, they be a rare treat for Sally." She lowered her voice, "Take heed, sir and ma'am to avoid passing through the village after ten o'clock at night. Be sure and leave the Priory in good time tonight."

Intrigued, Hester and Mortimer enquired the reason for such caution. Mrs. Lightfoot shook her head and muttered darkly about strange doings over by the churchyard. Abruptly she fell silent, placing a finger over her lips to ensure their discretion, for at that moment a voice was heard hailing Sally cheerfully, a shadow passed the window and a tap came upon the cottage door. Perforce Hester and Mortimer delayed their departure to exchange civilities with the new arrival,

Mr. Stone, The Vicar.

They all sat down once more; Jedediah Stone's wistful gaze swept briefly around the whitewashed cottage, bright and shining as a new pin, with its rows of gleaming pewter on the dresser, well-scrubbed table and gay hooked mats. His eyes rested appreciatively on a large brown jug, filled with wild flowers, collected by Sally on her rambles in the fields. No amount of hard work could achieve the same welcoming effect in his dark vicarage.

Mr. Stone sighed; it was not that he minded so much for himself, although he had an instinctive love for all beautiful things. He could contrive without material comforts, but he feared a lady like Susan Garth might well be unhappy in his present environment. He shook off his abstraction and turned to his housekeeper.

"I trust you will forgive my intrusion, Mrs. Lightfoot," he said in his pleasant, cultured tones. "I happened to spy Sir Mortimer and Miss Vane's arrival from my study window, while I was wrestling with yet another new work attacking the Established Church, lent me by Dr. Minton. It is very difficult to keep one's head these days when so many of our scholars and even eminent theologians are infected by the radical, anti-christian ideas circulating on the Continent. But I must not bore you with my problems. Tell me Sir Mortimer, what were men talking of in town? Is it true that Mr. Pitt is back in London? I began to despair that he would ever stir from Walmer Castle; no doubt his work with the Kentish Volunteers was very valuable last year when the invasion from across the Channel seemed imminent, but in my humble opinion a man of William Pitt's abilities should be at the helm when the nation is in peril."

Mr. Stone halted, rather flushed by his peroration, and smiled apologetically at the ladies.

Mortimer nodded sympathetically,

"Many men feel as you do, but I understand the King is still firm in his support of Addington. From what I could make out there is muddle and confusion everywhere. It is difficult to keep the enthusiasm of the Volunteers at fever pitch, when the threatened invasion has been so long delayed. Personally I believe that the moment has passed and Boney will turn his attention elsewhere. The fleet is our bulwark, but it is ill-equipped and overstretched, thanks to St. Vincent's parsimony during the Peace. What we need is more regular soldiers to tackle the French on land; we can never rest secure while that Monster's tentacles stretch from one end of Europe to the other."

"Very true," agreed the Vicar, "I was saying to Minton only the other day that the Ministry made a mistake last year in calling out so many Volunteers, without the equipment to back them up. A handful of trained soldiers are worth a hundred yeoman with pikes."

"Lord Montfort and Squire Crossley ordered some handsome uniforms for our Militia," interjected Mrs. Lightfoot proudly, "A real picture they were a' drillin' on the Green last summer. I took the silver buttons from my husband's best Sunday coat, and sewed them on Peter's scarlet; quite dazzlin' they were, when the sun caught 'em."

"I believe it was easier to find tailors than it was to purchase ammunition," murmured Hester. "For my part, I am thankful that the invasion continues to delay. I used to shudder every time I glimpsed the beacon on Ashbury Down. But surely, their invasion flotilla has not been dispersed?

"No, 'fraid not, Hester," replied Mortimer, "We cannot afford to relax our vigilance or we may be caught unawares."

"I pity the poor sailors at sea for months on end. I have always thought that to maintain a blockade must be the most tedious thing imaginable."

Mrs. Lightfoot nodded in agreement,

"Aye sir, 'tis very true and hard on a man's family when he is obliged to be away so much. I can't say how grateful I were when my Peter decided against the sea, especially after Edward went down at the Battle o' the Nile'." Mrs. Lightfoot dabbed her eyes with the corner of her apron.

"I met Miss Garth in Pendleton the other day," remarked Hester, making haste to change the subject. "She was distressed that she had not been able to come to church last Sunday; she was confined with a migraine, I believe."

"Indeed. I met Miss Garth quite by chance when out walking yesterday, and she told me herself that she had been indisposed. I found her quite agitated by that affair at Staleybridge the other day. You have already heard of it perhaps, Sir Mortimer?" Mr. Stone turned enquiringly to the young man.

"Hester mentioned something of it, but I've not yet got a plain tale. What actually occurred?"

Mr. Stone continued with some deliberation. "There is no plain tale. I myself have received several versions, all based on second or third hand rumour. It appears that a gentleman from London, a Mr. Abercromby, was waylaid in his coach at the Staleybridge crossroads last Monday night. His assailant was the notorious highwayman, known as the 'Beau Chevalier'. Mr. Abercromby was apparently parleying with the man when Mr. Stephen Garth providentially arrived on the scene. Accounts of what followed are confused, but the upshot was that several shots were fired. The highwayman escaped, though thought to be wounded, and Mr. Garth accompanied Mr. Abercromby to Pendleton to report the attack to the authorities. That is all I can tell you with any certainty."

"Very interesting," said Hester and Mortimer together. They stopped and laughed, then Mortimer persisted,

"How was the highwayman described? Has he been in the neighbourhood for long? I do not recall any mention of such a rogue when I was last at home."

"To answer your first question, descriptions are vague. Obviously he does not prey upon travellers in broad daylight. I suspect that his activities have been exaggerated. He is said to be tall and dark, with a marked French accent. Beyond that he is usually well-enveloped in a cloak and muffler. He changes his horses, but most frequently rides a black one. He first made a stir in the neighbourhood about a year ago, just at the height of the invasion scare, when he crossed two of the Prince of Wales's friends on their way to Brighton. He seems to be an unpredictable fellow, weeks will pass without a sign and then there will be a spate of hold-ups. I have noticed that one hears of his presence in a moment of crisis, but that is probably purely coincidental — rather meagre information, I'm afraid. Country tongues are curiously silent. I need hardly add that it would be most unwise and dangerous to become entangled with such a villain. If you will accept a word of advice I would recommend most strongly that you stay close and lock your doors carefully at night; I have reason to suspect that this man is still in the vicinity."

Hester's eyes widened a little as she wondered if she had been observed in her garden on Monday evening. Mortimer ran his finger around a neckcloth which suddenly felt uncomfortably tight.

"We will certainly take every precaution, Mr. Stone; and now, I fear, we must take our leave. By an odd chance we are to meet that very Mr. Abercromby of whom we have been speaking at Huntsgrove this evening. He is an old friend of Lord Montfort." Hester spoke with a composure which she did not feel and stood up, drawing on her gloves.

The Vicar's eyebrows rose, but he refrained from comment.

The Vanes' farewells were soon made. They thanked a rather subdued Mrs. Lightfoot for her refreshments and stepped out into the late afternoon sunshine. Mortimer and Hester walked home in a companionable silence which neither was eager to break, both reflecting on what they had learnt.

Chapter 9
The Dinner Party

Alone in her chamber, Hester succeeded in banishing all disquieting thoughts of the afternoon's interchange from her mind. She found that she was looking forward to the evening's entertainment with an unusual degree of pleasurable anticipation. She had dismissed Martha, her maid, after the girl had dressed her hair and slipped her gown over her head. Her hands felt nervously clammy, as she lifted her small diamond and sapphire necklace from its case and fumbled with the fastening. Hester pulled on her long white gloves; clasped the matching bracelet about her slender wrist and stood back to survey the effect in the looking glass. The high-waisted blue chemise dress, with its short puffed sleeves and low décolletage was admirably suited to her slim figure. Her brown curls were piled high on her head, with several coaxed forward to soften and enhance her high cheekbones and firm, round chin. She wore white satin slippers and a white silk embroidered shawl; in all, she presented a striking appearance.

Hester indulged in a brief pirouette and curtseyed low to her reflection, her grey eyes sparkling with laughter. She straightened, gave her curls a final tweak and slid her delicate ivory fan over her arm before tripping gaily down the stair to join Mortimer and Miss Stanhope, who were awaiting her in the sitting room.

"Admirable, my love, but do endeavour not to bounce in that unladylike way or your hair will tumble down," advised Miss Stanhope, who was seated by the fire in a lilac gown with old gold trimmings; her feet were neatly side by side, her hands demurely folded in her lap and there was a decided twinkle in her eyes. She regarded Hester's trim figure critically, giving that young lady the uncomfortable feeling that she was once more in the nursery, being prepared to be shown off at one of her mother's tea parties.

"'Pon my soul, 'tis vastly becoming," affirmed Sir Mortimer, raising his quizzing glass the better to absorb the vision of loveliness before him.

Hester grinned and swept a grand curtsey.

"I thank you kindly, sir and ma'am, such praise nigh overwhelms me."

She danced over to her brother, her eyes resting mischievously on the intricate folds of his cravat. Mortimer was elegant in a formal evening coat of dark blue velvet, with white silk breeches, white waistcoat and black buckled shoes. He endured her searching examination, giving a slight tug to his jewelled cravat pin.

"My dear, you make a very dashing escort," she pronounced at length.

Mortimer laughed a little sheepishly.

"Oh, as to that, Cousin Tom gave me a few pointers when I was in town. He's up to every rig and tow," he said airily.

Hester raised her brows delicately; when she had last had the pleasure of meeting Cousin Thomas he had been a grubby, troublesome school-boy.

"That must be quite a transformation," remarked Miss Jane tartly, before Hester could speak.

There came a loud rapping at the door. Martha appeared to announce that my lord's carriage awaited them. Mortimer assisted Hester and Miss Stanhope to don their dark evening cloaks and gallantly escorted them down the path, a lady on each arm. They arranged themselves comfortably upon luxurious cushions, the carriage door was shut and they rattled away at a sedate pace through Shawcross Village and on to Huntsgrove Priory, a distance of some three miles. The journey was enlivened by Miss Stanhope's speculations concerning the probable nature of the various courses which would grace the dinner table. Mortimer gamely seconded her in this small talk, while Hester made little pretence at conversation. Her heart was beating fast when they arrived at the imposing front steps of the Priory some half an hour after their departure from Shawcross. The massive dark oak door swung open at once, revealing a well-lit panelled hall of ample proportions. From her previous visits Hester knew this to be the most modern part of the house; the main reception rooms had been largely rebuilt by the de Montfort who returned home from the Blenheim campaign, early in the eighteenth century, with a considerable fortune at his disposal and a rich wife to boot. The family had prospered and the estate had been well maintained, although considerable refurbishment was now essential in the older wings which had fallen into disuse. It was these latter sections of the property which the present Lord Montfort was seeking to modernize.

Simkins the butler bowed before the three visitors, a powdered footman relieved them of their outer garments and they stood a moment blinking in the candle-light.

"Hif you will jest follow me ladies, Sir Mortimer," Simpkins murmered. He led them down the hall towards the sweeping double-sided staircase and threw open a door on the right, announcing sonorously,

"Miss Jane Stanhope, Miss Hester Vane, Sir Mortimer Vane, my lady."

Lord Montfort came forward to greet them, darkly handsome in a green swallow-tail coat and white small clothes. The shade of his coat enhanced the greenish tinge of his eyes; Hester found the whole effect positively saturnine. She hastily gathered her wandering wits as Hugo bowed before her.

"You are even more bewitching than usual tonight, Miss Vane," he complimented her. Hester inclined her head in acknowledgement; she noted with alarm that his left arm was in a sling, but there was no time to comment. Hugo conducted his guests to the fireplace where they found Lady Elizabeth ensconced in a deep armchair, girded about by shawls and scarves. It was not easy to discern any resemblance between the frail lady, with her delicate Dresden fairness and her tall, broad-shouldered son. However, when she raised her long lashes to smile warmly at the two ladies, Hester was taken aback by the vivid sea-green hue of her large eyes. Lady Elizabeth graciously made them welcome; she thanked Miss Stanhope and Hester for their kindness to her nieces and looked around for those damsels, who were discovered standing by the pianoforte, making idle conversation with an unknown gentleman, while they awaited their aunt's pleasure. She summoned them with an imperious wave of her small, heavily ringladen hand. Stephanie and Marietta came forward obediently to make their curtseys and general introductions were performed for the benefit of Mortimer and the other gentleman who was, as they had guessed, Mr. Hyde Abercromby.

"Go away and gossip, all you young things," commanded her ladyship at length, "Miss Stanhope will sit here beside me and we can enjoy a comfortable prose. I am so relieved that you were able to come and support me," she added in a lower tone, as Miss Jane took up a position as far removed from the warmth of the blazing fire as she civilly could, "My companion, Penelope Bishop, has contracted a severe cold and I thought it wiser that she should remain in her chamber this evening. She was most disappointed to miss our litttle party, but I told her that now my nieces are with us there is certain to be another opportunity. It is so dull for the poor young things in the country. I remember when I was their age . . ." Lady Elizabeth launched into a happy flood of reminiscence, in which Miss Stanhope indulged her, privately reflecting that her own experiences had been rather different.

The other members of the party, thus summarily dismissed by her ladyship, were temporarily at a loss, but the lively Stephanie soon had everyone laughing at her account of the girls' hair-breadth escape from a fishing port near Ostend, pursued by French dragoons, and all constraint vanished. The normally reserved Marietta plied Mortimer with eager questions about London, and Mortimer, flattered by their interest, decided to overlook the facts that his lordship's two wards were both foreign and female. Ably supported by Mr. Abercromby (with whom the young ladies were already on good terms), Mortimer gave a sprightly account of an equestrian exhibition which he had recently witnessed at Astley's Amphitheatre. The talk turned to the subject of horses and Mortimer's incipient admiration for Miss Stephanie grew rapidly when he found that she shared his enthusiasm and was remarkably knowledgeable for a female.

Hester, herself a notable horsewoman, sat a little to one side, listening with amused interest to the conversation. She was content to be an observer while she found her bearings. She found that she liked Hyde Abercromby. He was perhaps a little older than Hugo, a man of middle height, with broad upright carriage, suntanned features and a sallow skin, as though he had spent some time in the Orient. He had a humorous, rather square face, with thick dark brows above eyes of a deep blue. Hester noticed that his clothes were well-cut; modish in their elegant simplicity. He looked a solid, reliable person; Hester felt instinctively that she could trust him.

She allowed her gaze to wander around the room, observing everywhere an exquisite taste, combined with comfort, which delighted her. The room justified its name of the Blue Saloon; a plain blue Wilton carpet covered the floor; the walls were white, but surmounted by a delicate blue frieze of Wedgwood design and velvet blue hangings, with heavy gold tassels, hid the long windows at the far end of the spacious chamber. The chair furnishings were of gold brocade and the fine piano held a prominent position near the windows. Spring flowers filled the room, being perched precariously on every available side table. Hester's roving eye reached the marble Adam fireplace and she met the quizzical look of Lord Montfort, who was leaning nonchalantly against the mantle.

Furious with herself at having been caught out in such a barefaced examination of his home, Hester felt her cheeks redden; to hide her confusion she stammered some comment on the beauty of the flowers. Thus addressed, his lordship seated himself beside Hester on the sofa and began to converse easily on horticultural topics. He proved surprisingly well-informed, warming to the theme of his improvements to the Priory estate. Hester learned that both Hugo and his mother were keen gardeners; but whereas Lady Elizabeth favoured the classical, formal style, Lord Montfort subscribed to the more natural, 'Gothic' school, first introduced by 'Capability' Brown and continued by his followers, notably Mr. Humphry Repton. This was an unexpected side to his lordship's character; Hester would not have suspected him of being a 'romantic' in any sense. When she taxed him with this, he replied that in general she was quite right in her assessment, but that in relation to a medieval building, such as the priory, he felt that a certain freedom from restraint in its environs was essential.

"I have retained the rose garden and the topiary in deference to my mother's wishes; if you are interested I would be delighted to show you the gardens and park one day. Or perhaps you have already seen them, when you were here before?" Hugo's mobile eyebrow raised enquiringly. For a moment Hester hoped that the ground would open at her feet; fervently she wished that she did not always feel at such a disadvantage in her dealings with Hugo.

"I did come to explore the grounds, my lord," she replied quellingly, "I would not presume to intrude on the privacy of the family. Simkins was good enough to direct me through the original, gothic ruins and a few old buildings that still survive." She glanced up at Hugo suspiciously, but his countenance remained grave.

"In that event, I hope that you will permit me to show you the gardens," he insisted politely. "I should like very much to hear your comments."

Hester was obliged to return a civil answer, but she brought an abrupt end to their tête-à-tête by pointedly rising and joining the group round the fire, which now comprised all the other members of the party. Stephanie and Marietta seized upon her at once, seeking to obtain her approval to a scheme suggested by Jane Stanhope. Their slight French lisp was more than usually pronounced in their excitement; Mortimer observed Hester's bewildered expression and intervened to explain the situation.

"Fact is, Miss Stephanie and Miss Marietta wish to go to Brighton. His lordship has promised that they shall go as soon as he can find a suitable chaperone and Jane has offered her services, subject to your approval. They will stay in the house which his lordship has hired for the season, while we stay with our Aunt Marchant. Lady Elizabeth thinks it an excellent notion, so it's up to you to say if you have any objection, m'dear."

Hester shook her head.

"Why no, if Jane and her ladyship are satisfied with the arrangements, I can think of no difficulty. It will be very pleasant to be all together in Brighton."

"Capital!" declared Mortimer, while the two girls exchanged happy smiles. As usual they were attired to complement one another, Stephanie in apple green, with pink ribbons and the fair Marietta in pink, with white accessories.

Hyde Abercromby announced that he also intended to visit Brighton, after a short trip to town. Everyone agreed that he would make a welcome addition to their circle. Mr. Abercromby bowed in acknowledgement, before turning to Hugo, who was still seated a little apart, with a rueful smile on his lips.

"How of you, old fellow?" enquired Mr. Abercromby, "Will you join us? Surely you don't intend to rusticate all summer?"

Hugo hesitated, for once at a loss; warm-hearted Stephanie added her persuasions to those of Mr. Abercromby, saying reasonably that there was no point in hiring a house for the season if he did not intend to benefit from it. Even Marietta, who was still a little in awe of her cousin, felt obliged to add her entreaties. The practical Mortimer clinched the matter, as he remarked with a grin,

"Do come, my lord. Your presence will be essential to the ladies' comfort; they'll need a conveyance to get about, picnics and so forth. I daresay you wouldn't care to have anyone else drive your bays, saw you tooling 'em in town, prime bits o' blood."

Hugo capitulated,

"I confess I had not thought of the matter in that light, but there's some truth in what you say." He glanced at his friend, "I'll return to London with you, Hyde, and we can drive down to Brighton together in my curricule; unless you wish to ride?"

Mr. Abercromby shook his head,

"No, that will be a good plan. I can relieve you if your shoulder troubles you. My man can follow with my horse, Argus."

"Then that is settled. Are you sure you do not wish to accompany us, mama?" his lordship turned to Lady Elizabeth and gave his rare, charming smile.

"No, Hugo, I shall do very well here at Huntsgrove. Crowds are so fatiguing and I have never cared for the raffish set surrounding the

Prince." Lady Elizabeth smiled deprecatingly at Mr. Abercromby, "Your pardon, sir, I was forgetting that you are a friend of the Prince of Wales; there are exceptions, I know, but in general I find the atmosphere in Brighton too free. The town is filled with encroaching coxcombs and vulgar upstarts, not to mention the military disporting themselves in grand parades and reviews, when they would be better employed attending to their duties."

Not unnaturally these strictures from the gentle lady had the effect of silencing the company. At length Miss Stanhope remarked judiciously,

"I agree with much of what you say, Lady Elizabeth. It would certainly be better for the country if his royal highness settled down with his lawful wife and eschewed the Catholic society of Mrs. Fitzherbert. But one must consider that the Prince and his regiment are in a difficult position when His Majesty refuses to let his heir take part in active service. For my part I find the sea air most beneficial and I believe that during the season one need not despair of congenial society."

The ladies were unable to pursue the subject; Simkins appeared to announce that dinner was served and everyone filed into the dining room, Mr. Abercromby gallantly escorting the two elder ladies, followed by Mortimer, Marietta and Stephanie, with Hugo and Hester bringing up the rear. As they crossed the hall Hugo remarked to Hester in an undertone,

"You did not add exhortations to the rest just now, Miss Vane. I hope that my presence in Brighton will not discommode you in any way?"

Hester chose to disregard the underlying serious tone in his deep voice. She responded lightly,

"Good Heavens, my lord, what have I to say in the matter? I should suppose that Brighton is large enough to accommodate us both without any undue friction. It is a matter of complete indifference to me."

Lord Montfort frowned and muttered,

"That is what I feared."

They had reached the dining room and there was a little bustle while everyone seated themselves at the table. The problem of seating five ladies and three gentlemen had been neatly resolved to almost everyone's satisfaction. Hugo was at the end of the long rectangular table; Lady Elizabeth faced him at the far end, Mr. Abercromby on her left and Sir Mortimer on her right. Mortimer was happy to find the lively Stephanie beside him, with Jane Stanhope beyond her next to Lord Montfort. Marietta was across from her cousin, though an épergne of massive proportions hid Stephanie from view. Hester found herself on Hugo's right; she could only be thankful that the voluble Miss Stanhope would support her in the burden of conversation.

They began with some skate in oyster sauce, followed by pea soup. The talk turned to books and Hugo asked Hester how her novel was progressing. Hester returned a noncommittal answer. Miss Jane sniffed,

"I do wish that you would give up writing, my love, and follow more ladylike pursuits."

Hester smiled at Hugo, unconsciously looking very appealing in the warm glow of candlelight. Her eyes sparkled like the sapphires at her breast; Miss Jane knew well that the subject of women writers always had the power to rouse her; the older lady sat back and relaxed.

"Jane does not approve of my writing novels, but I notice that she is always eager to read them! Writing has never been an exclusively masculine preserve and there are some subjects upon which women are better able to express themselves than men. Don't you agree, my lord?" she finished wickedly.

"I do, Miss Vane; I have never subscribed to the notion that the term 'weaker sex' should be applied to the intellect. One has only to consider the work of Madame D'Arblay to realize what a contribution women can make to literature. But it is interesting that many ladies are reluctant to publish their name on the title page; can you explain such undue modesty?

Hester finished her soup and put down her spoon thoughtfully.

"I presume such ladies fear the notoriety which they may incur. Many novels contain autobiographical material. In the case of Madame D'Arblay (or Fanny Burney as she was when 'Evelina' was published), I understand that she was a rather shy person, who shrank from the criticism and speculation which her works aroused. But of course she did not long preserve her anonymity and I should imagine she enjoyed the praise which she received. I toyed with the idea of adopting a pseudonym myself, but rejected it. I prefer to take responsibility for my books and to accept whatever credit or blame my readers and critics may offer. I think that I made the right decision, though perhaps a certain mystery would be more appropriate for a writer of Gothic tales." Hester peeped at Hugo slyly and added, "Of course people in many walks of life feel the need for the protection of some disguise."

Lord Montfort had been listening attentively to her comments. Now he raised his napkin to his lips to hide a smile.

"Just so," he admitted, blandly. He sat in silence while the servants removed their plates and set down the meats. Hester's eyes met Miss Stanhope's across the table: the main dishes were as she had guessed: they comprised ham and chicken, a boiled leg of mutton and capers, a roast turkey and fried rabbit. The ladies partook sparingly; when they were served, Hugo introduced a new topic of conversation by enquiring how soon Miss Vane intended to remove to Brighton.

Meanwhile, at the other end of the table, Lady Elizabeth was exerting herself to charm Mortimer and Hyde Abercromby. She was past mistress at the art of being a good listener and she had soon drawn the gentlemen into a discussion of Oxford as a social and scholastic centre. She knew a good deal about the matter for Hugo had spent some formative years at Christ Church College, known to its intimates as 'The House'. When that subject was pretty well exhausted, Mortimer confided his ambition to obtain a commission in the Tenth Light Dragoons.

Mr. Abercromby had been talking easily with Marietta, but on overhearing Mortimer's plan he glanced keenly across the table, and, with a murmured word of excuse to his partner, said firmly,

"H.R.H.'s regiment is certainly an excellent social set if you have the entrée, but if you want action I do not think you will find the Brighton Camp very rewarding. Of course, I may be wrong; you will have heard the rumour that with the resumption of war the Prince's Regiment may go overseas, without their Colonel-in-Chief. However, I strongly suspect that the Brighton Camp will be with us for some time to come. There is always the argument that the Tenth Light Dragoons hold a vital position should the French attempt an invasion."

Marietta and Stephanie exclaimed in horror at the possibility; Hugo intervened to say dampingly that he did not believe that the attempt, if it took place, would be successful.

"Why not?, enquired Hester.

"Because, ma'am, the little Corsican has no understanding of naval matters. He cannot hope to invade our shores with those flat-bottomed Army transport alone. He needs ships of the line. So long as we hold the bulk of our fleet in the mouth of the Channel, Bonaparte's designs will be frustrated."

"It is very comforting to have the protection of the fleet," murmured Miss Stanhope.

"But we cannot sit back and let Boney overrun all the other countries of Europe. We must fight him on land," cried Mortimer, who like Napoleon himself, was too impatient with the vagaries of winds and tides to be a naval man.

"I agree with you," responded Hugo calmly, "But the time is not yet ripe. We need a Prime Minister who is prepared to take the offensive. Also I believe the First Consul will find Russia something of a stumbling block to his designs in the East."

"Let us hope those muddling politicians will soon come to their senses," Lady Elizabeth spoke tartly, "I understand one of Mr. Addington's favourite maxims is 'to doubt is to decide'; that is no principle on which to govern a country in time of war."

Hyde Abercromby turned to her ladyship.

"An increasing number of people are of your opinion, Lady Elizabeth. When I left London the talk at White's was all of a truce between the supporters of Fox and Grenville; it seems Mr. Pitt is at last convinced of the necessity to return to the House, though it goes against his honour to renounce the promises of support which he gave to Addington at the time of the Peace."

Hugo nodded in confirmation of his friend's remarks. Then he addressed himself to Sir Mortimer.

"If you are minded to join the Army, Abercromby and I can give you introductions to several officers at the Brighton Camp who have the Prince's ear. However, I would suggest that before you make a decision you visit Sir John Moore's Light Dragoons at Shorncliffe. Moore is probably the ablest of our younger officers, with the exception of Arthur Wellesley (and I do not imagine you wish to go to India if it can be avoided — Hyde can tell you about conditions in the subcontinent, he was born out there)."

"Army brat," smiled Mr. Abercromby, "But Montfort is in the right of it, Moore is a soldier of exceptional ability. I wager his idea on tactics and especially firepower are equal if not superior to those of the Grande Armée. His men are hand-picked, it's not easy to obtain a commission and he gives his Regulars a hard time."

Mortimer's eyes were shining with enthusiasm, but Hugo noticed that Hester was quite pale and that her hands were nervously clenching and unclenching, while her raspberry puff lay untouched on her plate. Everyone else had by now finished their dessert.

"We must apologize to the ladies for monopolizing the conversation with such tedious topics," he said decidedly.

Lady Elizabeth took her cue. She rose and led the ladies to the Blue Drawing Room, where they found coffee and tea awaiting them. The gentlemen lingered at the table over their port and nuts.

Miss Stanhope had also remarked Hester's subdued spirits and she silently heaped curses on Mortimer's head for distressing his sister when she should have been enjoying the rare treat of civilised dinner party with congenial companions (an infrequent occurrence in their limited circle), unhampered by nagging worries for her brother's future. Miss Jane seated herself between Stephanie and Marietta and began a detailed discussion of the newest modes. Meanwhile Hester accepted a cup of coffee from her ladyship with trembling hands.

"Sit here, beside me, my dear," said Lady Elizabeth kindly. "You are very like your dear mama. We were such good friends when we were girls. You must miss her sorely."

"Yes indeed, ma'am," replied Hester quietly, "But I think she was happy to be reunited with my father. He was a delightful husband and parent. I often wish that he were still with us; Mortimer did not take easily to petticoat government and I fear he is rather headstrong."

"Then a few years in the Army will do him no harm. Young men must have their fling, my dear. I know that your affection for your brother will make it hard for you to part with him, but consider, is it not better for Sir Mortimer to spend some years in the service of his country, rather than in dissipating his health and fortune in a life of idle frivolity? I think it is to his credit that he wishes to join the Army."

Hester raised her large, grey eyes to meet Lady Elizabeth's wise, green gaze. She fumbled in her reticule for a handkerchief and blew her nose defiantly.

"What you say is very true, ma'am," she sniffed, "I confess I had not looked at the matter in that light. It is very good of your son and Mr. Abercromby to offer to help him in making the right contacts. Did Mr. Abercromby spend many years in India?"

"Oh yes, I believe so. He spent his childhood there, but returned to England for his education. When he came down from Oxford he decided to go back to India. He was a younger son and there were few prospects of advancement for him here. He became a good friend of the Wellesleys and worked as a liaison between the British and the native princes. He was connected in some way with the East India Company, made a fortune in trade and decided to settle in England after the Peace of Amiens. Unfortunately his wife and small daughter died of yellow fever on the voyage home."

Hester looked up in amazement,

"How dreadful!" she exclaimed.

Lady Elizabeth agreed, adding,

"His wife was a distant connection of mine and when Hyde returned to this country, rich as a nabob, but quite overburdened with grief, he came to visit me. Hugo had but just returned from overseas himself.

The two found that they shared a similar outlook on life and they became close friends. I am very attached to him myself."

The two gentlemen under discussion now appeared with Mortimer, to join the ladies. Lady Elizabeth filled their cups and conversation became general. After a time, Mr. Abercromby requested Stephanie to favour the company with some music. It seemed that they had been looking through Lady Elizabeth's music selection earlier in the evening, and Stephanie had promised to play Mr. Abercromby one of his favourite airs, Mr. Dibden's 'Tom Bowling'.

Under cover of the music Lord Montfort seated himself near Hester and enquired softly if she would care to visit the Priory gardens one day in the following week, before everyone left for London and Brighton.

"You are very kind, my lord. I should be delighted to come."

"Good, would Wednesday be convenient?"

"Perfectly, I thank you."

"Then that is settled, I'll send the carriage for you and Miss Stanhope at three," declared his lordship, smiling. He looked penetratingly at his companion and added abruptly, "I regret that our military talk at the dinner table should have distressed you."

Hester was touched by his evident concern. She glanced around the room. Mr. Abercromby, Marietta and Mortimer were grouped by the piano. Stephanie had finished her song and Mortimer was urging Marietta to perform. Lady Elizabeth and Miss Stanhope had their heads close together; they were deep in a discussion of village affairs. Hester looked levelly at Hugo and answered frankly,

"You are under a misapprehension. I have not the least objection to a discussion of serious topics, such as politics. I read the *Morning Post* avidly, even when the news depresses me! I was merely being selfish; but your mother has shown me that I must not allow my partiality for Mortimer to interfere with his ambitions. I did not mean to indulge in a fit of the sullens. Do forgive me, my lord."

In her eagerness to explain her position, Hester twisted violently the cord which attached her fan to her wrist. The knot broke and the fan slipped to the floor. Hugo and Hester bent together to retrieve it; their hands touched and they both sat up hastily. Hugo replaced the fan on her lap, his eyes glinting appreciatively as he observed Hester's flushed countenance.

"There is nothing to forgive, Miss Vane. It is not every sister that is so concerned for her brother's welfare. Sir Mortimer is a gentleman of spirit. I am happy to have had the opportunity of making his closer acquaintance. Did he tell you of our meeting last night?"

At this reminder, all the strange events of the past week crowded into Hester's mind. She replied cautiously,

"He did mention something of it, my lord. But I gather you were not there when a very odd incident occurred at the inn. Two Bow Street Runners arrived late in the evening. They were searching for the same highwayman who held up Mr. Abercromby's coach — the 'Beau Chevalier', I believe he is called."

Hester searched Hugo's face anxiously. A grim smile twisted his features.

"Two Runners, you say. That is certainly very interesting. Hyde must have stirred up a hornet's nest when he arrived in Pendleton after the attack. I did not think the Runners would have arrived in the neighbourhood so soon. I gather these men did not succeed in laying the rascal by the heels?"

"Oh no, I don't think so. At least he was not found at the inn. Mortimer said that for a moment they mistook him for the highwayman, but soon realized their mistake. My brother could not assume a French accent to save his life," she finished lightly.

Unconsciously Hugo put his right hand to his shoulder.

"Does your shoulder still pain you?" Hester's voice was troubled.

"A little. It's of no consequence." Hugo rose to his feet suddenly. With a murmured word of excuse he crossed the room to compliment Marietta on her performance. Hester remained where she was, gazing after him in dismay. She jumped when Miss Stanhope tapped her lightly on the arm and suggested that it was time they took their leave. A servant was dispatched to order the carriage and thanks were spoken for a delightful evening. It was a little after ten when the Vanes and Miss Stanhope, in their elegant conveyance, rumbled through the sleeping village of Shawcross.

Chapter 10
The Outrage

All was quiet as they passed the church, though Hester could not repress a shiver when she remembered the warnings of Mrs. Lightfoot and Mr. Stone earlier in the day. In the dimness her hand sought Mortimer's and he gave it a comforting squeeze. She was grateful for his presence and for the useful-looking pistol hanging in its holster above Mortimer's head. She scolded herself for her nervousness, though in truth it was an uncomfortably dark night, and she had lived long enough in the country to know that it behoved one to take 'the gentry' seriously. Hester tried to recall the Montfort's coachman; he had appeared a burly, middle-aged man, not unlike their own George Hamble. With an effort she wrenched her mind from its preoccupations to concentrate on Miss Stanhope's cheerful chatter.

". . . and everything in the first style of elegance," she was saying complacently. "I must ask Lady Elizabeth's cook for that oyster sauce recipe. Did I overhear you remark that we shall be visiting the Priory again soon, my love?"

"Yes, Jane, you did. His lordship has invited us to view the gardens and to take tea with Lady Elizabeth and Mrs. Bishop on Wednesday. I was just wondering if Lord Montfort brought his own chef from town — maybe 'twas he that created the sauce you mention. Are you quite happy with the Brighton arrangement? I hope that you did not allow yourself to be overpersuaded?"

"No, indeed, I shall enjoy it. For you know, Hester, if I come with you I shall be obliged to bear your Aunt company much of the time, and she does not like to stir herself unduly. To be quite frank, I find it tedious to be so much in the house. I prefer to rise at an early hour and I like to be busy. Lady Marchant's household is so well-organized that I am sometimes at a loss to occupy myself; whereas, if I have the run of Lord Montfort's house as well as the charge of Stephanie and Marietta it will be an excellent outlet for my energies. Also, it will be a beneficial change for us both to be not always living in one another's pockets, don't you agree?" Miss Stanhope concluded robustly.

Hester laughed,

"Very succinctly put, Jane dear. I take your point, for I know I am a sore trial to you. But I warn you, you will see me frequently, and also Mortimer, if I mistake not. He will wish to maintain his acquaintance with the young ladies, and to plague his lordship to introduce him to his friends at the military camp, I am sure."

Mortimer snorted in disgust.

"Hey, madcap, what do you take me for? I grant you Hugo and Hyde have been good enough to say they will make certain I get the right introductions, but as for plaguing them, 'tis no such thing, said they'd be glad to do it," he finished naively.

"I see you have advanced to first-name terms already," said Hester calmly, "Your time in Brighton is going to be much occupied. I only hope that I shall be able to prevail upon you to escort me to the occasional assembly."

Mortimer heard the quiver in her voice and eyed her suspiciously,

"There's no need to take a pet. Ye know I'll be happy to do the pretty from time to time. Don't suppose it'll be necessary though, with his lordship's party, and my aunt and Tom around."

"I vow, I'm overcome by your chivalry, brother Tim," snapped Hester.

"Hush, children, cease this sparring," commanded Miss Jane, "We are home. It all looks very dark. Why does not Martha open the door?"

The Montfort coachman, Sam Green, reined in his horses, while the liveried footman sprang down to open the door and hand the ladies out of the carriage. Mortimer followed them. For a moment everyone stood in the lane, uneasily surveying the silent cottage.

"Perhaps I'd better come in with 'ee, zur," growled Green. Hester noticed that he was grasping a serviceable blunderbuss in his right hand. Green continued, "There was a few pack 'osses in the shadders by the church. Could be it ain't too 'ealthy in these parts tonight. His lordship told me to watch out," he added in an undertone. The coachman gave soft orders to the footman, who went obediently to the horses' heads. Then he turned and opened the gate. Hester and Miss Stanhope followed close on Mortimer's heels, despite his wish that they would remain in the carriage. Approaching the door cautiously, they found, to their dismay, that it was not locked. Miss Jane muttered darkly about careless servants and their probable fate. Hester busied herself with lighting the candles.

"This is intolerable," exclaimed Mortimer, "Where is everybody?" He threw open the parlour door. All was quiet, with the fire burned low.

"My desk!" cried Hester suddenly, her eye lighting on the dark corner by the window. She ran to her bureau. Papers were scattered all over the floor in complete disarray.

"Robbers!" shrieked Miss Stanhope, looking wildly around for some lurking intruder.

"You both remain here," commanded Mortimer, in a tone of unwonted authority. He set off down the passage to the servants' quarters, a grim expression on his face. Green followed closely. Hester settled Miss Stanhope in her favourite chair and hunted through her reticule for some smelling salts. The good lady was so overset that for once she acquiesced meekly; she took a vigorous sniff, sneezed and shook her head. Hester was relieved to see the colour coming back to her pale cheeks. It was not long before they heard footsteps in the hall. Mortimer entered, his handsome face flushed with excitement.

"Pray do not be alarmed. All is well now, but I fear I have some disquieting news. The servants were locked up in the cellar by two masked men. I have released them and they are in the kitchen making a cordial; they are quite unharmed. Apparently, they were at supper some two or three hours ago, when the door flew open and the two men burst in thrusting George before them. Martha and Mrs. Blossom were so surprised and shocked that they could make no move. The men tied all three up, gagged them and left them in the cellar while they ransacked the house. So far as I can tell nothing of value is missing, but perhaps it is best if you look for yourselves. Green is leaving in a few minutes, when we have made sure that all is secure for the night." He paused for breath and Hester broke in,

"But, Mortimer, do you think we should allow Green to take the carriage back tonight? If there is trouble abroad I am convinced they would be safer here. It is unlikely that we shall be invaded twice in one night. I cannot think what they hoped to gain by such an outrage! I must talk to Martha. Do you remain here, Jane, and I will bring you a hot posset shortly."

Mortimer accompanied Hester from the room. They parted in the hall, Mortimer saying that he would try to persuade Sam Green to remain overnight. He hastened outside and Hester stood a moment in thought, her hand on the newel post. She realized that she was shaking and that she had not removed her evening cloak. She slipped it off, hung it over the bannister, composed her features and trod firmly down the passage to the stone-flagged kitchen. As she entered Martha jumped and Mrs. Blossom threw her apron over her head and let forth a piercing wail, rocking to and fro in her capacious rocking chair. Pippet, the cat, jumped guiltily from the table, where he had been lapping a jug of cream, and disappeared from view behind the dresser.

"Enough," said Hester sharply, "The danger is past now. I am sorry that you had such a fright, but we must be calm, and set things to rights. Do you have any idea what those men came for or what they looked like?"

She addressed Martha, for Mrs. Blossom was for once beyond the power of speech and kept up a low moaning sound.

"No Miss Hester, they didn't ax us no questions. They jest took us by surprise like, and hustled us down into that nasty spidery ol' cellar as quick as they could. They were big men, wrapped in long greatcoats, with masks and hats, but they blew out the candles and 'twere almost dark, save for the fireglow. They tied us up so tight our 'ands are real sore, see, miss?"

The maidservant held up her wrists for inspection. Red weals still marked her skin. Hester nodded sympathetically.

"You had best find some salve to bring out the bruises, while I heat some milk for a posset for Miss Stanhope. Where is George?"

"He went out with Mr. Green. They said they were going to check the garden and stables, miss."

Mrs. Blossom came to herself abruptly at the sight of Hester with a saucepan in her hand.

"Whatever are you about, Miss Hester?" she exclaimed, scandalized, "You leave Miss Stanhope to me, miss. I know just the thing to make her sleep like a baby." The stout cook heaved herself to her feet, invigorated by the thought of work to be done. Gratefully Hester surrendered the saucepan.

"You'd better make enough for yourself and Martha too, Mrs. Blossom. Mr. Green may be staying the night, Sir Mortimer has gone to speak with him. If he does we will have to make up a couple of beds in the box room. I'm going to run upstairs to check on our rooms and rid myself of this finery. You come with me, Martha and I will find the salve for your wrists."

Hester and the maid went first to the medicine chest in Miss Stanhope's chamber. While she gently applied the ointment, Hester enquired,

"How did the men get in, Martha? Surely you know that the door must be locked after sunset?"

"Why yes, miss, o' course. But ye see, George were comin' in for a bite o' supper, and so when I went to the pump for some water I called to George that we were ready and left the door ajar when I came back in. He were in the stable and said he'd be right along. Those nasty ruffians must ha' caught him as he crossed the yard, for they all came in together. 'Twere all so quick, we didn't hear a thing."

"I see. Well it couldn't be helped. Don't look so downcast. I'm sure that if they wanted to get in they would have found a way, even with the door locked. There, is that easier?" Hester completed her ministrations and glanced enquiringly at Martha.

The maid nodded.

"Good, then we'll take some down for Mrs. Blossom. But first come with me to my chamber and help me remove this gown," Hester rinsed her fingers at Miss Stanhope's washstand and glanced around the room. "Everything seems in order here, I wonder what they were seeking. Just look in Miss Stanhope's jewel case, Martha. What a fortunate thing I was wearing my sapphires tonight." Hester did not believe that the intruders were ordinary robbers, but she did not wish to alarm the maid unnecessarily and it was as well to be certain that their valuables were safe.

"It hasn't been touched, miss," reported Martha, closing the lid of the fine old leather box and replacing it in the chest at the foot of Miss Stanhope's bed.

They proceeded to Hester's chamber and here a very different scene met their eyes. The bed was strewn with clothes from the press; chairs were overturned and the drawers pulled out, with their contents spilled over the floor. It seemed that no corner of the room had escaped unscathed.

"Oh, miss," breathed Martha, stooping to retrieve the broken pieces of an old Sèvres vase, "How wicked!"

After the first shock, Hester rallied her stunned senses. With Martha's aid she slipped out of her blue gown and removed her jewellery. She noted with relief that her jewels were all in place, although the lock was broken. Comfortably swathed in a lemon, chintz wrapper Hester set to work methodically to restore order, ably seconded by Martha. When all was done, she sank into her fireside chair, frowning in puzzlement.

"You're a good soul, Martha," she smiled at her maid. "I cannot find anything missing, which is strange, but fortunate. I am quite at a loss, but I trust the mystery will be solved in due course. You must be very tired. Do you go down to Mrs. Blossom and take your posset. Let me know if Green is staying tonight. I shall be with Miss Stanhope in the sitting room for a few minutes."

Hester found Miss Stanhope much revived by Mrs. Blossom's

posset. She, herself, felt very weary and was happy to find a warm drink awaiting her on the hearth, inside the fender. She settled herself comfortably on the rug before the fire and sipped meditatively.

"Where is Mortimer? Have you seen him?" she asked Miss Jane at length.

"No, my dear, but I heard him talking to the coachman in the hall some time ago. I believe the man elected to return to the Priory, in order to notify his lordship of the outrage. Somebody ought to send to Squire Crossley too — don't you think that as Justice of the Peace he should be informed?"

"Yes, — no, I don't know. Let us wait for Mortimer. At least, you may go to bed if you wish, Jane, your room is quite untouched and I'm sure all is safe now." Hester sighed and leaned her head against the arm of the chair behind her. It was a shabby old chair, covered in gold brocade; once it had been father's favourite resting place and since childhood she had found it soothing to assume her present position when vexed or troubled in any way.

For once Miss Stanhope forebore to chide her by saying, as she usually did, that Hester would become round-shouldered if she remained slumped in that unladylike posture. Instead she remarked with some asperity that she doubted that she could sleep a wink, for fear they should all be murdered in their beds. She determined that she would remain with Hester, in full possession of her faculties, until Mortimer came to reassure them. Miss Stanhope rather spoiled the effect of this declaration by yawning hugely. A few moments later she was sound asleep.

Hester sat quietly, gazing at the fire and listening to the rustle of night time noises in the old cottage. She realized that the invasion of the sanctuary of her home had made her unwontedly nervous; she was uneasy at Mortimer's prolonged absence and was a prey to considerable anxiety before she heard a door slam, followed by her brother's voice bidding the servants 'goodnight'. Immediately she relaxed and Mortimer was a little surprised by the dazzling smile which his sister bestowed on him, when he entered the parlour, still wearing his evening dress, though he had discarded his cloak. Hester laid a finger to her lips, with a meaningful glance at Miss Stanhope. Mortimer nodded understandingly. He seated himself in the old brocade chair, so that he could whisper in Hester's ear, without fear of disturbing the older lady.

"All's well, love," he began. "Green has taken the coach back to the Priory by the longer route, avoiding the village. He has the footman up beside him, with the blunderbuss, and it's not likely that anyone would think it worthwhile to attack an empty carriage. I think I'd best have a word with Squire Crossley after church in the morning. I doubt if the villains will be apprehended, but it would be as well for everyone to be on their guard. I blame myself, I did not take Stone's remarks seriously this afternoon. However, that has been remedied. George Hamble is keeping watch at the moment and I shall relieve him at four o'clock. Did you discover anything missing?"

"No, Tim, Jane's room was untouched. Mine had been ransacked, but my jewels and other valuables were all there. I have been racking my brains to discover some motive for the intrusion; did your investigations yield any clue?"

"Well, this is pure conjecture, mind, but it's my belief those men were the two Runners I met with the other night at the 'Horse and Groom'. George observed that one of the men spoke with a strong London accent. He says they were snooping around the stables, after they tied him up, and 'tis my guess they were checking on the horse. Fortunately the mare I borrowed from the inn is still in the stable till Peter fetches her tomorrow. I only hope those men don't know one black mare from another. The horse they saw at the inn was Cassy, not Vixen." Mortimer paused, a worried frown on his brow. Hester stared at Mortimer in perplexity.

"I think there is something about that night you did not tell me, Mortimer," she observed severely, "Runners can usually obtain search warrants. They do not need to behave in such an unorthodox fashion. I think you had better tell me the whole. I take it Lord Montfort was involved in some way?"

Hester twisted round to peer into her brother's face. He nodded reluctantly. A gentle snore caused them both to glance warily in Miss Stanhope's direction, but that lady slumbered peacefully on. Mortimer bent his head close to Hester's and gave her a detailed sketch of the events at the inn on Friday night. Hester listened carefully, but without surprise to the tale of Hugo's arrival, with the Runners hard on his heels. She raised her eyebrows when she heard of the secret panel, but forebore to interrupt his narration until she learned of Bessie the maid's remarks concerning the friendship between Alice Potter and Stephen Garth.

"How strange!" she cried, "Stephen Garth again. You know that he was at Staleybridge by some odd coincidence when Mr. Abercromby's carriage was stopped. Do you think Alice can have told him of her father's association with the mysterious Beau Chevalier?"

"It did cross my mind, but I had not really thought it through, until this moment," admitted Mortimer. "It seems that Garth has a finger in several pies. But that still does not explain why this house should have been ransacked, unless the Runners were convinced that I was the highwayman after all; they had been told that he was tall and gentlemanly. There is no evidence against me, apart from the fact that I now have Vixen in the stable, when I told the Runners (or rather Ned Potter told them) that you were sending over a horse for me. We had to explain Cassy's presence in the stable at the inn. It seems that Montfort often leaves his mare there, and borrows Vixen."

"Good heaven, how complicated it all is!" exclaimed Hester in dismay. "I have something to tell you also, something which may help to explain why the house was searched tonight. But tell me, was your room ransacked like mine?"

Mortimer nodded.

"Well," continued Hester, "Obviously those men knew where to go. They must have been given detailed instructions by someone who knows the house quite thoroughly. But let me elaborate a little on your story. You must wonder why I was not surprised to hear that Hugo appeared wounded and in disguise at 'The Horse and Groom'. When I told you of my meeting with his lordship and his wards last week, I did not feel at liberty to add that he also spent time in this cottage on an earlier occasion. He arrived here on the night of the Staleybridge robbery, wounded and masked as you have described him. I was in the garden and 'twas I who removed his mask before summoning assistance. No one else knows of this. Jane and George aided me, and we called Dr. Minton to dress the wound. Hugo was in a fever and was obliged to remain here, but we did not reveal his identity to Martha and Cook. He left secretly very early last Wednesday, before the household was astir."

Mortimer listened to Hester's account in amazement. After a pause, he said broodingly,

"I quite fail to understand Hugo's motives. Why would he hold up his friend's coach?"

"Why would he assume such a character at all?" retorted Hester.

Her brother frowned,

"He had no right to place you in such danger. Won't do to abet such unlawful behaviour, ye know Hester. I confess I like the fellow. It's most peculiar. Dem it, he doesn't strike me as the sort to kick up such larks. Did you tax him with question? Did he offer any explanation?"

Hester shook her head regretfully.

"No. Clearly he did not wish to discuss the matter and I did not care to press him. Indeed I have had little opportunity to do so, and after all 'twas no concern of mine."

"But it is now," broke in her brother impatiently, "When our house is invaded, and 'tis not safe to go in the village at night, we have a right to some answers from him."

"Let me think for a moment," begged Hester, laying a restraining hand on her brother's arm, for his voice had risen in his agitation. "I believe that Stephen Garth is involved in some way. There is clear hostility between the two men. They met here the other day, when Hugo called with his wards."

It was Mortimer's turn to look severe.

"It seems to me there's a deal I've not been told, since I came home, sister mine. What was Garth doing here, anyway?"

Hester blushed and hung her head guiltily.

"He came to ask for my hand in marriage," she said softly, at length.

"What!" Mortimer exploded, "Demmed upstart. You'll have none of him, I hope?" He looked down at Hester inquiringly, but she kept her head bent, and he could only see the heavy brown tresses falling forward over her face. Seeing that she said nothing, he pursued firmly, "Just think, child, Garth is nought but a lawyer, even if he does come of good family. In all probability Alice Potter is his mistress. I've never liked him, since I was in shortcoats, nor trusted him. He's a ruthless, cold individual and 'tis my belief he cheated mama and yourself over the settlements, when father died."

Hester looked up in surprise.

"You never said so before, though I must admit I had a little the same suspicion. I had no one to whom I could turn for evidence or help . . . but 'tis no matter now. I confess I wonder how a man circumstanced as he is can afford the fine new town house, which he proposes to buy in Pendleton."

Mortimer emitted a low whistle. A thought struck him.

"Why did you not turn to Hugo for aid at that time? I was used to think there was an understanding between you."

Hester sighed, but replied evasively,

"'Tis all old history now, Tim. There were reasons. But it occurs to me that it may have been Stephen who set the Runners on the 'Beau's' trail so quickly, with his legal connections. He also knows this house very well," she added musingly.

"It all sounds like Good Queen Bess, when she was but a Princess in prison, 'Much suspected of me, nothing proved can be'," pronounced Miss Jane, suddenly, sitting up and setting herself to rights. The brother and sister stared at her in consternation. She nodded brightly from one to the other, her sharp eyes twinkling. "'Tis the most entertaining tale I have heard this age, I vow, and I must say I prefer to have Mr. Garth for the villain rather than his lordship." She shook her curls reprovingly at Hester. "You should have told me the whole, my love. I can be mum as an oyster on occasion, you know."

Hester rallied and smiled at her friend.

"I did not consider that it was my secret to reveal, Jane. I would have continued to keep silence, if this evening's outrage had not carried the problem to our very door."

"Quite right and very loyal, when one remembers that this notorious highwayman is wanted by the law," agreed Miss Stanhope sarcastically.

"I cannot believe that his lordship would harm anyone who did not deserve it. I am sure there is a rational explanation," said Hester defensively.

"Well, I tend to agree with you, but others may not," replied Miss Jane, "Tell me, did it occur to you that those men were seeking specific evidence this evening? What became of the mask which you removed for example?"

"Jane," gasped Hester, "How could you sit there and listen so shamelessly? I would never have suspected you of stooping to eavesdrop like this."

"In general I do not approve of such a practice," responded her mentor calmly, "But on this occasion I believe that three heads may be better than two; even, if I may venture to say so, four heads." She looked from one to another, but her hearers were temporarily bereft of speech. Miss Jane continued placidly, "I did not like to interfere, particularly as I too have a fondness for his lordship. However Andrew and I were not quite without the power of putting two and two together on the night of the accident. You have merely confirmed our suspicions. I trust I need hardly add that we would neither of us speak of this matter to another soul. I do think, however, that it might be prudent for us to bring forward our departure to Brighton, if it can be arranged. We can leave Lord Montfort and Mr. Garth to solve their differences in their own way. I suspect that your presence in the neighbourhood, Hester my love, will only add fuel to the flames of their hostility!"

"Can't help thinking that's a good notion. Very sound," assented Mortimer, "You're a capital conspirator, Jane."

Miss Stanhope chuckled; even Hester could not resist a smile, but she sobered quickly.

"You are indeed, Jane. It is a relief to have you in our confidence. I have the oddest sensation that I am at the centre of a mystery tale equal to any that I could invent; I shall have more sympathy for my heroines in their tribulations in future. But you mentioned the mask and this is bothering me. I slipped it in the pocket of my old gardening gown, meaning to return it to his lordship, but there has been no opportunity. I wonder if it is still there."

She stood up, in quick distress.

"I must go and see. Excuse me."

Her two companions waited impatiently, listening to Hester's light feet running up the stair. In a few moments she returned, her breath labouring with her speed and agitation.

"What shall we do?" she cried, "It is gone!"

Miss Stanhope gave a little gasp of dismay. Mortimer exclaimed,

"Are you quite certain? Did you look elsewhere? Could you have mislaid it with your gardening implements or some such thing? Think carefully, for you know you can be very absentminded upon occasion."

"No, no," declared Hester decisively, "I am sure. You remember that when I found his lordship we came straight within doors to tend his hurt. Afterwards I thought it safer to leave the mask in my old gown, for fear that Martha would discover it if I attemped to hide it in a drawer. It was most remiss of me, I should have taken more care, but I never dreamed that my room would be turned topsy-turvy and to be frank I forgot all about it."

They sat in silence, each preoccupied with their own thoughts for a few moments. The clock on the mantlepiece chimed the hour of one in the morning.

"There is nothing we can do tonight," stated Miss Stanhope at last, "I think we should retire and sleep on the matter. Should you object if I took counsel with Dr. Minton in the morning? His advice is frequently sound and I know that he has numerous sources of information which are unavailable to us. Perhaps he could make some discreet enquiries; there may have been some folk abroad tonight who could shed some light on the subject. After all, a mask is not evidence, though it may serve to confirm suspicion. Many people wear such objects for nothing more incriminating than a masquerade or domestic theatricals. I do not think we should refine too much upon it."

"That is a very sensible thought, Jane, though I would be at a loss to account for its presence in my old dress. However, if the two men were the Runners they cannot use evidence obtained in such an underhand manner; 'tis not as if they knocked on the door with a search warrant and made a legal entry."

Mortimer intervened to remark thoughtfully,

"I am puzzled also. The fact that nothing else was removed implies that the men were searching specifically for that object. This worries me. Do you think that you were seen in the lane with Hugo on Monday night and perhaps observed slipping the mask into your pocket? At that time the Runners were not in the vicinity, so someone must have carried tales — but to whom?"

"Stephen Garth!" said Miss Stanhope and Hester together.

"But why?" persisted Mortimer, "I know the fellow is a lawyer and is fond of Hester, but these are insufficient reasons."

"There is a reward for the capture of the 'Beau Chevalier'" Hester reminded her brother, "And Mr. Garth is the only lawyer of standing and influence nearby."

"'Tis true enough," nodded Miss Stanhope, yawning prodigiously, "But I'm for my bed. We will think more clearly what is best to be done in the morning."

"I agree, Jane dear," murmured Hester, rising also, "And if Mortimer concurs, I suggest you speak with Dr. Minton at the first opportunity."

"Yes do, the more the merrier," grinned Mortimer irrepressibly. On this cheerful note, they took up their candles and wearily made their way to bed. Much against her expectations, Hester fell sound asleep as soon as her head touched the pillow.

Chapter 11
Sunday Morning At Church

Hester awoke to the sound of church bells pealing in the distance. She sat up, feeling alert and refreshed after her sleep; the events of the previous evening crowded in upon her, but she found she could contemplate them with a degree of detachment. She rang for Martha and made her toilette; with some difficulty the maid succeeded in finding a gown of pale pink, trimmed with coquelicot ribbons, which had not been crumpled by careless male fingers. Hester was irritated to find that her new lace-trimmed cambric handkerchiefs had been torn and trampled. She gave orders that Martha should check her wardrobe and make any necessary repairs. This done she crossed to the window to take stock of the weather.

"It appears unseasonably cool today, Martha," she remarked, gazing out on a sky of fitful sunshine and cloud.

"Yes, Miss Hester, there's a keen wind a'blowin', you'd best wear your warm brown pelisse over that flimsy dress, or you'll catch cold for sure."

"Yes, indeed I shall. Thank you, Martha, that is all for now. How are your wrists this morning?"

"Much easier, thank you, miss, that coltsfoot salve worked wonders. Miss Stanhope and Sir Mortimer are already in the parlour, miss."

"Very well, I shall join them at once. I should tell you that we may be leaving for Brighton very soon and I would like you to accompany me. We will have much work to make ourselves presentable within a week or ten days."

Martha's apple-cheek complexion took on an even rosier hue at the pleasurable prospect before her. She bobbed a curtsey, exclaiming,

"Oh yes, miss, I'll do my very best." The little maid then bounded away to begin her duties and Hester went down to breakfast. She found Mortimer partaking heartily of ham and eggs, while Miss Stanhope toyed with her tea and dry toast. Greetings were exchanged. Then Miss Stanhope burst forth with the subject which was uppermost in her mind.

"Hester, something must be done to make the cottage more secure. I declare I could not sleep easy in my bed all night, but started up at every rattle," she pronounced roundly.

Hester replied soothingly that orders should be given to have all the door locks strengthened with bolts and the shutters and window fastenings checked.

"Well, I maintain 'tis all a most splendid adventure," averred Mortimer, "I did not expect life in Shawcross to be so interesting." He requested the toast and marmalade, and fell to happily. His sister regarded him with a mixture of awe and displeasure.

She said tartly,

"For my part, I can dispense quite easily with the excitement of having my home ransacked while I am at a dinner party. Do you suppose they watched us depart? I wonder if they would have made the attempt had we been at home."

"No telling, m'dear," responded her brother, helping himself to a third cup of coffee.

"I see it is useless to expect any sense from you at this hour. I can only be grateful that they were not interested in my nearly-complete manuscript." Hester gestured towards a neat pile of papers, which had fortunately escaped the onslaught on her bureau.

Mortimer sat back with a sigh of satisfaction and tossed his napkin on the table. Hester's expression softened as she observed with affection her brother's neatly brushed hair and cheerful open countenance. In deference to the Sabbath he was modestly attired in a buff-coloured morning coat and breeches, with a plain dark green waistcoat ornamented with silver buttons. His white shirt sported a minimum of frilled ruffles.

"I see that the depredations on your wardrobe were not too severe," she remarked. "I had much ado to find suitable garments that were not hopelessly crumpled, if not actually torn."

"Hum, very aggravating for you, Hester. I was fortunate in that most of the clothes in my room are now outmoded and discarded. My box will not be here until tomorrow when Peter brings it with the carrier. I think I must find a valet when we go to Brighton, I can't think how I have contrived without one for so long."

Hester knew a brief moment of regret for the vanished, towsled schoolboy whom she recalled so well. However, she admitted to herself that the elegant young man, now lounging at his ease across the breakfast table, was a very acceptable substitute.

Miss Stanhope broke in upon her reflections with a cry of horror at the thought of great rough men carelessly inflicting all manner of damage on Hester's apparel. She felt they should depart for Brighton forthwith.

"I sympathize with the impulse, Jane dear, but pray consider: my aunt will not yet be established, our wardrobes are in need of some refurbishment and the Priory party may not be ready to leave at such short notice. I believe that the damage is now already done and it is most unlikely that we will have a further visitation. I must own that it goes against my inclination to quit my own house with such unseemly haste. I suggest that we depart in the middle of next week. Ten days should be ample to make all necessary arrangements. What is your opinion, Mortimer?"

Mortimer thus appealed to, expressed himself in complete agreement with Hester's arguments. Miss Stanhope admitted that she had been a little hasty in her agitiation, and the matter was allowed to drop as they rose from the breakfast table to make ready for attendance at the morning service.

It was a few minutes before eleven when the Vanes and Miss Stanhope set out, clutching their prayer books and their hats in the sharp wind. They followed the footpath through the cornfield in single file, making no attempt at conversation. In the shelter of the lych gate they paused to catch their breath. They were a little late and there was no-one in the churchyard except Stephen Garth and his sister, Susan, who were engaged in close conversation with Mr. Jedediah Stone. The Garths stood within the old stone porch, blocking the entrance to the church. Hester could see that the Vicar was frowning, while Mr. Garth seemed angry and Susan was biting her lower lip, as if near to tears.

The strong wind muffled the sound of their footsteps, as the ladies, followed by Mortimer crunched down the pebbled pathway, flanked by tipsy headstones and a fine row of ancient yews. They were almost upon the little party by the door before they were observed. Susan saw them first and dropped a curtsey, putting up a furtive hand to brush away a tear. Mr. Garth swung round and favoured the Vanes with a brief, curt bow; he then seized his sister's arm and hustled her through the open doorway, while Mr. Stone with a muttered word of greeting and excuse, slipped past them round the corner to the little vestry door. Miss Stanhope, who had not observed all that had passed, owing to her preoccupation with the wind, was inclined to be annoyed at the absence of ceremony, but Hester, in an undertone, begged her to excuse the incivility and they proceeded down the aisle to their pew, with Mortimer at their heels.

It was almost uncomfortably warm in the little church, with its thick stone walls, although the wind made draughty tunnels, which chilled one's feet. Hester settled herself, carefully placing her feet, in their thin slippers, upon a hassock. She glanced around and nodded to several acquaintances within her line of vision, including the family from Shawcross Manor, in their pew across the aisle. Hester exchanged amused glances with Miss Stanhope. The Crossley ladies had defied the keen wind and wore their usual Sunday array of feathers, frills and furbelows. The church was quite full that morning. Hester could hear numerous rustlings and whispers from the villagers behind her. She sighed thankfully. It was always comforting to be seated among the familiar congregation, in the old church which had been a place of worship since Saxon times. The heavy stone font near the door was all that now remained visible of the original edifice, the present structure being largely Norman.

Hester was engaged in seeking the first hymn when there came a slight rustle at the rear. A moment later the party from Huntsgrove Priory took their places immediately below the pulpit and directly in front of the Vanes. Lady Elizabeth remained seated in the aisle in her Bath chair, with Mrs. Bishop at her side. Stephanie and Marietta were seated between his lordship and Mr. Abercromby, and Hester was much amused to note the way in which Hugo stilled the whisperings of his wards with a stern frown. When everyone stood up to sing the first hymn, Hester saw with surprise that Hugo's arm was no longer in a sling. The service proceeded without incident until the time came for parish announcements and the calling of the banns for holy matrimony. Mr. Stone mounted to his pulpit and read this interesting information aloud in a firm voice. All went smoothly for some minutes; Hester was drifting into her own thoughts, when she was abruptly recalled by the words,

"I publish the Banns of Marriage between Susan Emily Garth (spinster) and Jedediah Matthew Stone (bachelor), both of this Parish. If any of you know cause, or just impediment, why these two persons should not be joined together in holy Matrimony, ye are to declare it. This is the first time of asking."

Almost before the announcement was concluded Stephen Garth arose from his seat. All heads turned at the sudden interruption. For a moment there was silence, while Stephen Garth and Mr. Stone glared at one another, oblivious of their surroundings; then Mr. Garth shook his fist malevolently at the unfortunate vicar and stomped down the aisle, slamming the heavy door shut behind him. Poor Miss Garth fell to her knees, her shoulders shaking with a passion of sobbing. Mr. Stone hesitated, his natural instinct to rush to his fiancée's side vying with his duty to his congregation. Hester made a move to go to Susan, but was forestalled by kind Dr. Minton who placed a fatherly arm about the weeping girl's shoulders, and persuaded her to accompany him outside. The little flurry of whispering was hastily suppressed; Mr. Stone made a great effort to achieve his usual calm serenity, but he tossed aside his prepared notes and launched out from Corinthians, Chapter 13, verse 2.

"And though I have the gift of prophecy, and understand all mysteries, and all knowledge; and though I have all faith, so that I could remove mountains, and have not charity, I am nothing."

There followed the most passionate defence of love, and the sacred character of love, that any of that congregation was ever likely to hear: and when he concluded, returning to his text,

"And now abideth faith, hope, charity, these three; but the greatest of these is charity."

There was many an eye filled with unshed tears.

Mr. Stone had always been regarded with affectionate esteem by the villagers, but he had been held a little aloof, as befitted one not born and bred in the district. From this morning forward the inhabitants of Shawcross regarded their vicar in a new light; he had won their hearts, while Stephen Garth, who had previously been regarded with a mixture of respect and fear, was now shunned by his neighbours and aquaintance.

The change was immediately apparent as the buzzing congregation stepped out into the sunshine. The air was warmer and lively gossiping groups filled the churchyard, though, as Mortimer remarked to Hester, not even the January snows could have prevented such an outbreak of chatter on this occasion. The Vicar was surrounded by well-wishers, his clerical vestments fluttering about him. When the throng had subsided a little, Hester and Mortimer stepped forward to offer their congratulations. At the same moment, Dr. Minton appeared with Susan on his arm. She seemed quite recovered as she took her place at her fiancé's side and smiled radiantly up at him. For a space they were quite oblivious of their surroundings. Dr. Minton shook his head in mock despair; Hester knew a brief twinge of envy at such happiness.

As the doctor made a move to depart in search of Miss Stanhope, Susan put out a hand to detain him.

"Dear sir, I can never thank you enough for coming to my aid in that moment of acute distress."

Andrew Minton twirled his empty pipe between his fingers.

Gratitude always embarrassed him.

"Don't mention it m'dear," he said gruffly, "Happy to be of service. Don't let that brother of yours cast you down. You're almost of age and have a right to a life of your own. You can't live forever at his beck and call. I wish ye both very happy I'm sure. Excuse me, but I see a lady I must speak with." He executed a courtly bow, which included Hester and Sir Mortimer, before setting off hastily in pursuit of Miss Stanhope. That lady decided to be perverse for she ceased her idle contemplation of the tombstones and, feigning not to notice the lean Scotsman's approach, she sped down the path to join the Priory party by the gate. Hester could not repress a giggle; the others followed the direction of her gaze and they too broke into merry laughter.

"Such devotion must surely be rewarded," said Susan softly. She turned to Hester, "My dear friend, could I come home with you for a little while? My spirits are so confused that I do not feel equal to confronting my odious brother until his anger has had time to cool. Also, I have something of importance to say to you, if it is not inconvenient."

"It will be a pleasure to have your company," replied Hester quickly. She glanced enquiringly at the vicar, "Perhaps, Mr. Stone, you would like to join us for luncheon?"

"It is very good of you, Miss Vane. I infinitely regret that I am already engaged to dine at the Manor."

"Oh, I am sorry," said Hester sincerely, "We must make another arrangement soon."

Mortimer tapped her arm.

"I believe Lady Elizabeth wishes to speak with you," he remarked, nodding towards the little group waiting patiently by the lych gate. Hester followed the direction of his gaze; Lady Elizabeth waved her hand in a welcoming gesture.

"Forgive me," she exclaimed, "I must not keep her ladyship waiting. Pray accept our heartfelt felicitations to you both. Do you go with me, Susan?"

"Yes, of course." Miss Garth took leave of her betrothed, while Hester, accompanied by Mortimer, moved slowly down the path. They were soon joined by Susan.

Lady Elizabeth greeted them graciously. She then performed the necessary introductions. Hester was made known to Mrs. Bishop; while Susan curtseyed shyly to Stephanie, Marietta and Hyde Abercromby. Everyone congratulated Susan upon her choice. Lady Elizabeth remarked that she was most fortunate in having secured the affection of such an estimable young man.

"His sermon today was truly outstanding," her ladyship announced decidedly. "Now that the weather is more clement, I shall make every effort to attend morning service regularly."

Susan curtseyed again happily, in acknowledgement of Lady Elizabeth's kind words.

"I am truly sorry that I was unable to hear the sermon, your ladyship; but from the comments that I have overheard I am persuaded that I agree with every sentiment which Mr. Stone expressed."

"Well, that is a good beginning," observed Lady Elizabeth, smiling to take any sting from her tone. "When is the wedding to take place? I am surprised that your brother is so opposed to the match. What are his reasons?"

Susan's lip quivered at the reminder, but she replied with commendable composure,

"My brother is very ambitious, ma'am. He wishes me to make a wealthy match with a business acquaintance of his own. He has little patience with tenderer emotions. To him a marriage is a business and social arrangement, no more. However, I shall be of age in July. It is my dearest wish that the wedding shall take place sometime in August."

Lady Elizabeth nodded understandingly.

"I see. You have my sympathies in this predicament. I have known marriages of convenience which have turned out very well, but never I think, when either party's affections are previously engaged. Your brother is your guardian until you come of age, I take it?"

"Yes, ma'am," responded Susan in a subdued tone. She glanced uncertainly at Lady Elizabeth, but was encouraged by her listener's attention to proceed, "I fear that his displeasure may take some violent form. Pray do not misunderstand. We are much attached, but he is so much my senior that he has long been in the habit of exacting instant obedience from me. He cannot bear to be crossed. I am much afraid that he may seek to remove me from the neighbourhood."

Again Lady Elizabeth nodded.

"Forgive me, but would it not have been wiser to wait until after your birthday before making your betrothal public? Your brother can forbid the match, you know; you cannot be married without his consent."

Susan shook her head despondently.

"There were reasons why it was not possible to wait, your ladyship. My brother had discovered our attachment. He has purchased a house in Pendleton for the express purpose of separating me from Mr. Stone's vicinity. We wished to make our betrothal public, but as I said we shall not be wed until August, when my brother has no legal claim on my obedience."

Their conversation was here interrupted by Mrs. Bishop, who enquired if her ladyship wished for another shawl. This hint effectively broke up the party. The Priory carriage was at the gate and Mortimer and Mr. Abercromby hastened forward to assist the ladies. There was some delay while Lady Elizabeth arose from her Bath chair, her companion fussing anxiously with wraps and cushions. Having made her farewells, Hester stood back. She found Lord Montfort at her side.

He said quietly,

"Green told me of your alarms last night when you arrived home. I was much distressed. I trust that the damage was not irreparable?"

"No, I thank you, my lord. At least not in material terms. But it will be long before I can rest easy in my own home at night. My peace is quite cut up. Jane is anxious that we should remove to Brighton as soon as possible." Hester hesitated, but the ladies were not yet settled. She whispered quickly, "Only one item was stolen, my lord. I fear it is something which belongs to you."

Hugo's mobile eyebrows drew together in a quick frown. He murmured,

"It was inexcusable of me to have embroiled you in this situation. I am angry with myself for not accompanying you home last night, but I did not wish to court attention, and I feared that my arm would hamper me in case of need."

Hester replied softly,

"There is nothing to reproach yourself for, I assure you. I took you into my home on my own initiative when you were unconscious. The responsibility on that occasion was mine. But I am happy to see that you are so much recovered from your indisposition," she added more loudly, indicating his left arm, with a slight gesture.

He bowed in acknowledgement. Their brief *tête-à-tête* was interrupted by Lady Elizabeth calling imperiously from the carriage window.

"One moment, mama," responded his lordship. "I must take my leave, Miss Vane," he continued, bending the full force of his penetrating green eyes on Hester's serene, upraised countenance. "I shall see you on Wednesday. I look forward to pursuing our discussion then." He bowed ceremoniously, his hat almost sweeping the path; in so doing he dropped his gloves, which rather spoiled the grand gesture. Hester glanced up from her curtsey, her cheeks dimpling and her eyes sparkling mischievously.

Hugo grinned unwillingly.

"Minx!" he muttered in her ear, as he stooped to retrieve the errant articles. They parted on that note. The carriage party rattled away, with Lord Montfort and Mr. Abercromby riding escort behind.

"What a very fine figure he makes on horseback," declared Miss Stanhope teasingly. Hester swung round, her head tilted enquiringly to one side,

"Mr. Abercromby, you mean? she asked innocently, "Yes, indeed, Jane. I suppose it to be the result of so much polo-playing in India."

Susan Garth had also observed the by-play with interest. Her near-sighted eyes widened a little, but she made no remark. They were the last to leave the churchyard. Mortimer courteously held the lych gate open for the ladies and offered Susan his arm. Hester and Miss Stanhope followed.

"Dr. Minton will be calling upon us this evening," said Miss Stanhope casually, when Susan and Mortimer had walked a little ahead. "I told him that we wished for his opinion on a matter of some importance."

"That is excellent," responded Hester warmly, "He is such a comfortably strong person and his advice is always unbiased and shrewd. I thought that he handled the difficult situation during the service with just the right degree of tact and firmness. Susan was quite distraught. Her brother's behaviour was abominable. I am sure I shall pity his wife, if ever he succeeds in securing one. You did not hear Susan's comment, I think? She remarked that her brother regards matrimony as a business arrangement." She pursed her lips in an expression of disgust. Miss Jane laughed heartily.

"Sisters do not always find it easy to see their brothers in the rôle of lovers, my dear Hester. This also works in the reverse direction, of course," she concluded thoughtfully. No more was said upon the subject, for the ladies had been walking at their customary brisk pace, and were now within earshot of Miss Garth. The Vanes' cottage was soon reached and the party separated to tidy themselves before sitting down to luncheon. Susan Garth accompanied Hester to her chamber, where Martha poured warm water into a bowl and laid out fresh towels. The ladies set aside their outdoor garments, and prayer books, bathed their faces and combed their windswept curls. Thus refreshed, Hester seated herself on the window-seat, and patted the cushion beside her invitingly.

"Come, Susan, let us talk. Luncheon will not be ready for half an hour and here we may be quite private. I am curious to know what is this matter of importance which you wish to discuss with me."

Susan tripped daintily across the room and perched herself on the edge of the wide window seat beside her friend. She plucked nervously at her skirts, seemingly at a loss how to begin. Hester waited patiently; at length Susan gave a small fluttering sigh and murmured,

"You are quite sure we cannot be overheard? I should not have come, my presence here may put you in danger."

Hester was quite taken aback by this unexpected pronouncement; she raised her brows and gestured towards the garden; a wide lawn stretched away beneath them.

"See, my dear, the lawn is quite deserted. Pray do not be so melodramatic. Tell me, why should I be quaking in my shoes?"

Susan threw back her head, struggling for composure. Hester leaned forward and laid her warm hand on her friend's quivering fingers. After a moment Susan gave a little laugh, she sat back and relaxed, fixing her soft, brown eyes on Hester's face with an appealing expression, reminding her of a spaniel which she had once owned.

"You must think me very foolish, but I find it very hard to be disloyal to Stephen. However, I am in such a state of trepidation that I can no longer remain silent." She paused and Hester nodded encouragingly. "You must have realized this morning that my brother is much opposed to my determination to wed Mr. Stone. Unfortunately matters are more complicated than they appear. You see, Stephen is involved with the local smuggling fraternity, in fact, he — oh, Hester, I should not be telling you this — he is the leader of these men. I am so frightened, for since he discovered my affection for Jedediah he has begun to use threats to break up our friendship, unless Mr. Stone consents to allow the church to be used for hiding contraband. Jedediah steadfastly refuses to do so, but he is under great pressure; many local people are involved and there are spies everywhere. I know Jedediah is popular, but the village folk are afraid to support him. I feel there is no one I can trust, except you, and the Lightfoots — although I fear Peter Lightfoot is also a smuggler, or at least somehow involved through working at the 'Horse and Groom'." Susan's voice faltered and she gazed beseechingly at Hester.

"Susan, this is dreadful. I had no idea that Mr. Garth could be so unscrupulous: how wicked to seek to place his own sister and a man of the church in a position of blackmail! I am most sincerely sorry to hear this tale, but I must confess I am also puzzled — in what way can I be of service? Why do you feel you can trust me rather than, for example, Squire Crossley?"

Susan shivered.

"I believe the squire is acquiescent to the 'gentry's' deeds; I fear he is well paid for turning a blind eye when the occasion demands it. It would not do to go to him; Stephen would be alerted at once. He does not know how much I have learned of his underhand dealings. If I went to Squire Crossley they would merely say that I was an hysterical female because my brother opposes my marriage to a poor country parson. Stephen is quite ruthless and cannot bear to be thwarted. I have to warn you, dear Hester, that you, and to a lesser degree Sir Mortimer, are now the object of my brother's displeasure. It is quite true, you must believe me," exclaimed poor Susan, as Hester shook her head doubtfully. "Listen and bear with me a little longer. It is known that you aided a wounded man on the night of the Staleybridge attack. The identity of the man is also known to my brother and his close associates. He is Lord Montfort, alias 'The Beau Chevalier', is he not?"

Hester started, her mind racing. Her first impulse was to deny all knowledge of the affair, but she realized this was futile. She said cautiously,

"It is certainly true that Lord Montfort suffered an accident on the night of the Staleybridge incident. In common humanity I took him in and did all I could to ease his wound. However, that is not to say that he received his injury in any mysterious way. Do but consider, Susan; his lordship is a good friend of Mr. Hyde Abercromby, you must have seen them together in church this morning. Is it reasonable to suppose that Lord Montfort would hold up his friend: indeed, when one examines the question, is it reasonable to suppose that his lordship is in fact a highwayman? The whole idea is absurd, he cannot be in need of funds, and I simply cannot imagine him doing such a thing for a lark, it is not in his character."

Hester sat back with an air of having settled the matter to her own satisfaction. She regarded Susan keenly, pondering her interest in the issue; could it be that she was on a mission for her brother? She knew that Susan feared her brother and she recalled that it was Susan who had raised the Staleybridge affair when they had met in Pendleton soon after the incident. Susan seemed to sense her suspicion; she smiled faintly.

"It is but natural that you should defend his lordship. Let us be frank. I believe that you are in love with him, and I wish that you may be as happy in your choice as I am. I had hoped that you might marry my brother, but that was before I realized his true character. He is quite merciless and is involved in many dubious transactions, not only in smuggling. He is surrounded by an inner ring of cruel blackguards, I can use no other term, and they terrorise the locality, rich and poor alike. I suspect that Lord Montfort is seeking to destroy the cabal; in any event he has crossed my brother in some way and Stephen is very bitter against him. This vindictiveness is increased by your presence, my dear Hester; Stephen is convinced that he and his lordship are rivals for your hand."

Hester opened her mouth to protest, but closed it again as Susan continued,

"The whole situation is now very complicated. My brother has employed two Bow Street Runners to rid him of the scourge of the 'Beau' without letting his own hand appear in the affair. The Runners were foiled the other night at 'The Horse and Groom', partly by the prompt intervention of Sir Mortimer. Stephen is becoming desperate. In addition Mr. Stone continues to oppose him and matters have been brought to a head by the announcement of our impending marriage. My brother is now making dark threats against Mr. Stone and I am terrified for his safety. I am also frightened for you and your brother. The invasion of your home last night was a deliberate attempt to frighten you; of course it was also an effort to obtain evidence of the 'Beau's' presence in your house, so that it could be laid before the Runners."

Hester listened incredulously.

"If that was so, why did these men not come sooner? Evidence obtained in such a manner is of little value."

Susan shrugged,

"I do not know. I presume because last night was the first evening when you were absent from home. Perhaps Stephen wished to be sure of your involvement with Lord Montfort, rather than to obtain evidence."

Hester twisted a lock of hair round her fingers, her mind grappling with a number of unanswered questions. She was convinced of Susan's sincerity, but puzzled on several points in her narrative.

She exclaimed ruefully, "Susan, I am grateful to you for this intelligence. But how did you discover your brother's activities?"

"It has been a matter of slow realization rather than sudden revelation," responded Susan. "As you know, Hatch End is in a very isolated position, but there has been much coming and going at night, and this has occurred with increased frequency of late. I have known for some time that Stephen was a smuggler: indeed he told me so when I returned from Miss Moore's Seminary in Brighton two years ago. He said that he was doing it for me, so that I should have a good dowry and make the splendid match to which my birth entitled me. He swept aside my protestations and I kept silent because I did not know what else to do. In the last year his power and ambitions have known no bounds. There have been violent incidents and the thought of violence sickens me; to all this now are added dreadful apprehensions for my beloved Jedediah and for other innocent people. I can no longer remain silent. I am telling you these painful details because I fear you are in great danger; you must remove from the vicinity immediately and exert your influence to persuade Lord Montfort to do likewise."

Chapter 12
'Tea And Brandy'

Not unnaturally, Hester was stunned by Susan's confidences and by the depth of her knowledge. Susan perceived Hester's hesitation and pressed her advantage.

"Believe me, my dear friend, this is no time to trifle. I would like to run away myself, but Jedediah will not hear of such a thing. He says that it is his duty to remain here and protect his parish as best he may, so I must remain too. But there is no reason why you should not move, and I urge you to do so."

Hester was finally stirred to protest.

"Do not let us exaggerate this out of proportion, Susan. We are living in a civilised country with the rule of law at our disposal. I have lived in this neighbourhood most of my life and I have no intention of being driven from it. I cannot speak for Lord Montfort, but I am sure he is not without influence himself. As for Mr. Stone, I admire his courage, but it is also prudence. If you ran away what would be your means of support? Mr. Stone would never get another living and your lot would be hard indeed."

Susan sighed,

"You still do not understand. Stephen *is* the law here, and he is quite without pity."

A vision of herself in Mr. Garth's passionate, but merciless, embrace, flashed through Hester's mind. She knew herself no match for him in terms of physical strength, but in terms of wit and cunning perhaps there was a chance. She tilted her head in a characteristically determined gesture; forewarned is forearmed she told herself.

"I do not doubt your sincerity, Susan, but I find some aspects of the matter quite incomprehensible. For example, your brother tells me that he is in love with me and wishes to marry me. If this is so, how could he countenance the affair of last night, and, incidentally, how did you hear of it so soon?

Susan's countenance lightened and she grinned, almost mischievously,

"My brother does not perceive the contradiction. He has fastened upon you as the object of his attentions because he admires your independence and spirit; he feels that you would be a challenge to him, but one which he could master. I cannot speak for the depth of his affection, for we have never discussed it. In a more material vein I am sure that he desires to wed you because you come from an old Sussex family, you are well liked and respected in the neighbourhood, and you would provide a gracious and respectable front for his establishment."

For once Hester's sense of humour failed her. She broke in, her voice throbbing with indignation.

"Marriage to Mr. Garth is a challenge which I can well dispense with. Let me assure you that I am not about to contract an alliance with anyone; I do, in truth, prize my independence and even were I contemplating matrimony it would not be to one little better than a housebreaker. Merciful heaven, what a coil is this!"

Susan laughed gaily,

"Methinks thou dost protest too much! But I will not take issue with you on Stephen's behalf. He has many good qualities, but he is infatuated with power, and I share your abhorrence of a man who can seek to blackmail his prospective wife as well as his sister! Seriously, Hester, I should be more grateful than I can say, if you could enlist Lord Montfort's aid in ridding the community of this scourge of terror. I was standing in the shadows outside my brother's library door on Saturday night when he was closeted with his two ruffians. I heard him give orders for the search of your house and he was most particular in describing to them a certain mask which he believed to be hidden in your room. He also required his bullies to seek evidence of your brother's involvement with the 'Beau Chevalier'; he would like to have Sir Mortimer arrested as an accomplice. You see, my dear, if he cannot win you by fair means he will not hesitate to try foul ones, though it pains me inexpressibly to say so."

The two ladies regarded one another solemnly for a long moment. In the silence they heard Martha's footsteps on the stairs. There came a light tapping on the door and the little maid appeared to announce that luncheon awaited them below. Their tense faces relaxed as the friends rose, shaking out their skirts with sighs of relief.

At the head of the stairs Hester hesitated. She turned to Susan saying in an undertone,

"Thank you for telling me so much. I will do what I can to help. May I confide in Mortimer?"

Susan nodded, but cautioned, "Do not let him do anything rash. I cannot emphasise enough how dangerous this affair could become."

They left the matter there. Conversation during the meal was confined to trivialities; Mortimer exerted himself to amuse the ladies and Susan's spirits brightened visibly. When they removed to drink their tea in the parlour Miss Garth was her usual cheerful self. The talk turned, as it often did in that small household, to the difficulties which beset females of intellect who wished to make their own place in the world in some rôle other than the traditional and honourable estate of wife and mother. Susan Garth listened in some bewilderment, but with growing approval and interest, to a discussion which would have horrified her conservative, strong-arm brother. She determined to try some of these subversive ideas on her fiancé at the first opportunity.

". . . I declare, most women's lives are so limited and their acceptance of their lot is so passive, that I despair of any real change, I think I should have been born a man!" Hester was saying in resigned tones. Susan gasped and glanced at Miss Stanhope. She was reassured to see her little eyes twinkling merrily. Sir Mortimer shook his head at his sister in mock reproof; he was lounging at his ease in his father's comfortable, old chair, one leg swinging idly. He tapped his highly-polished boot with his quizzing glass to get their attention. In an accent of feigned humility he remarked,

"Since I am in the minority in the presence of three such charming and articulate ladies I hardly dare to venture an opinion . . ."

"But you will so venture nonetheless, wretch," interrupted Hester, giving his carefully arranged locks a tug as she passed by with swishing skirt to accept a cup of tea from Miss Stanhope's hand. Susan watched this small by-play wide-eyed and thought wistfully of her relations with her own brother, so different from the affectionate teasing of the Vanes; there was nothing relaxed or easy about Stephen, though he could be tender on rare occasions.

"As I was saying," continued Sir Mortimer firmly, rattling his teaspoon on the delicate china cup to give weight to his argument, "In my humble opinion you are much happier as a woman, Hester, dear sister. Your abhorrence of things military is so pronounced that I am persuaded you would find a masculine rôle hard to sustain in these warlike times."

"Nonsense, my love," Hester broke in impatiently, "My attitude would be quite different, I daresay, had I been raised to respect the manly code of duty to one's country, honour, and all these other high notions which frequently strike women (in the privacy of their own minds) as ridiculous and excessive. For myself, waiting patiently and helplessly at home, while you run off to join Sir John Moore at Shorncliffe or the Prince's Regiment, which may leave for the Continent at any moment, I find it hard to talk of glory, when all I see is the waste of our youth; hard to talk of our empire, when all I see is greed."

"Pray do not get heated, Hester, it will impair your judgement," recommended Miss Stanhope, sipping her tea meditatively. "Do you not perceive that Sir Mortimer has thrown you a military red herring, which you have been so obliging as to swallow?"

Hester opened her mouth to protest and then laughed, shaking her fist at the imperturbable Mortimer, "I should know better than to be taken in by such bait. You are quite right, Jane, he was seeking to divert me, but logic in argument is not usually one of my failings! In a sense Mortimer was correct to raise the military issue, physical strength in one form or another has always been the reason why men have retained their dominance. The generality of men are afraid to loosen their grip by acknowledging that in a civilised society women can be equal, if not superior in intellect."

Mortimer winked at Susan, making her giggle delightfully,

"Help me, Miss Garth," he pleaded, "Surely you do not subscribe to my sister's heretical notions? Are you not quite content in your present rôle of housekeeper to your brother and wife-to-be?"

Susan considered the question thoughtfully before replying doubtfully,

"I know you are not serious, but I must admit that there are times when I feel quite downtrodden. I do not think that sufficient allowance is made for the woman's point of view in many instances."

"You see," said Hester, taking up the cudgel to help her friend, "Men hold all the positions of authority and counsel. They are our doctors, lawyers, priests and rulers of the country. Any influence which women exert is almost invariably channelled through a man. Depending upon their station in life, women can exert an indirect influence through a salon like the blue stocking ladies, or by the path of easy virtue for the lower classes of society. Of course, women are largely to blame. For centuries they have allowed men to dictate to them, they have been content to confine their education to domestic concerns and to dissemble in the company of man, so that any intelligence which they might possess is well hidden beneath a cloud of feminine fripperies. I am quite out of patience with my own sex; why, I read somewhere the other day that even the courageous and unconventional Lady Mary Wortley Montagu once acknowledged that women were a lower order of creation, owing obedience and submission to the 'Superior Sex'."

"Quite true," murmured Mortimer wickedly. His sister threw a cushion at him. Miss Stanhope intervened, with an apologetic glance at Susan,

"Peace, children, this is the sitting room, not the schoolroom. For my part, I agree in the main with Hester's diagnosis. It is always an uncomfortable situation to find oneself at odds with the old-established mores of society, as I believe the unfortunate Lady Mary discovered. However, that was some years ago and I can think of a number of admittedly exceptional women who are now respected for their abilities in their own right. As you know, I have spent many years of my life as a governess and I would say without hesitation that education is the key to equality between the sexes. In terms of native endowment there is no reason why they should acknowledge themselves inferior."

"With you and m'sister always before me," broke in Mortimer with a disarming smile, I have never been one to underestimate the Fair Sex, ma'am. Like it or no, any thinking man must realize that petticoat government is with us from the cradle to the grave. Their sphere of influence is all pervasive!"

Hester raised her brows and leaned forward, saying earnestly,

"That may be true, but we are still so hedged about with restraints that I am convinced my original argument holds. I do not dispute the fact that many men enjoy the company of an intelligent female, though I would suggest that an equal number are intimidated by the challenge. But in practical terms, there are few means at a woman's disposal if she wishes to support herself independently. Far too many women resort to matrimony and the shackles of a large nursery; a single woman is little more than an object of pity."

Miss Stanhope smiled kindly at the silent Susan.

"Hester is prone to adopt extravagant positions in debate, my dear Miss Garth. You must not believe all that she says."

Susan smiled back shyly. She had always been a little in awe of Miss Stanhope's sharp tongue.

"Truly, ma'am, from my own observation, I do not think that Hester has overstated her case. In town, gentlemen may pay homage to a lady of wit, but in the country more traditional attitudes prevail. Did not Lady Elizabeth have a noted salon at one time? She must find life at Huntsgrove sadly flat by contrast."

Hester nodded thoughtfully,

"I believe you are right, but it was before my time. Do you remember anything of it, Jane?"

"Yes indeed. Of course I moved in humbler circles, but her soirées were always reported in the Society columns. Her literary coterie rivalled that of Mrs. Montagu and it was once rumoured that she had almost caused Dr. Johnson to abandon Mrs. Thrale and the Streatham set in favour of Grosvenor Place. I will say for the good Doctor that he was ever one to appreciate an intelligent woman. Lady Elizabeth was on excellent terms with most of the Society hostesses."

"What was the secret of her popularity?" queried Hester, rubbing the side of her nose meditatively.

"Well, her continental ancestry may have been, in part, responsible. Most of the blue stocking ladies were singularly provincial in their outlook. In the 60s and 70s of the last century it was customary, indeed almost obligatory, to decry everything French as artificial, while we congratulated ourselves on the 'naturalness' of English taste. Lady Elizabeth achieved a remarkable blend of the two cultures, being equally at home in English and French Society. She departed from the French tradition by inviting both men and women conversationalists to her entertainments, and those on this side of the Channel who admired, for example, the works of Monsieur Voltaire, found a welcome forum and a sympathetic audience in her ladyship's drawing room."

"Why, that is fascinating," cried Susan. Hester, smiling at her brothers attempts to stifle a yawn, added, "I shall ask Lady Elizabeth about it. What a pity that such salons no longer flourish, society being given over wholly to frivolity, gambling and other excesses which I am sure Mrs. Montagu would have denounced."

"I believe you are too harsh, sister," observed Mortimer judicially, sitting up and assuming a wise expression. "If you were to set up a salon in Brighton this Season, I wager you would be all the rage. People would flock to the house of the female pen, and you would be reassured that all feeling for the world of the arts and literature has not yet been extinguished among the 'bon ton'."

"What a challenge. I declare I am almost tempted to take up your gauntlet."

"You will do no such thing, miss," interrupted Miss Stanhope. "Have you forgot that you will be staying with your Aunt Marchant? Her ladyship would not relish her drawing room being filled with a number of idle persons, with nothing better to do than write sonnets to your eyebrow!"

"Oh Jane, condemned out of your own mouth!" cried Hester. "You see, Mortimer, Jane agrees with me that the 'Ton' can think of little but gossip and frivolous things. They would no longer attend a salon to discuss the works of Monsieur Voltaire."

Mortimer preserved an obstinate silence; Hester glanced at him and sighed regretfully,

"Of course the Prince of Wales is a noted patron of the arts. It would be fun to try, but I fear my social circle is too limited. Also my own scribblings are of too insubstantial a character. I could not rival Mrs. Montagu's 'Essay on Shakespeare' or Mrs. Carter's philosophical translations. I wonder what my aunt would say if I suggested a salon entertainment to her."

"She is too indolent and too fond of you to object. She would say 'Very well, my dear, but do be sure to ask an equal number of Whigs and Tories, and do give Alphonse sufficient warning, or he will throw a tantrum and we shall have nothing to eat to aid the muse!'" chuckled Mortimer irreverently, as he mimicked his Aunt's cheerful complacent tone.

Miss Stanhope was obliged to laugh, but she said firmly,

"That will do. If you go on in this vein I shall feel obliged to chaperone you, Hester, and then poor Miss Stephanie and Miss Marietta would have to remain at Huntsgrove. You would not be so unkind, I am sure."

Hester reached out to pat her companion gently on the arm.

"No, no, I was merely teasing. I wish to enjoy my holiday in Brighton; I am not seeking another form of work."

Susan Garth roused herself at these words. She had drifted into a private reverie, but now she glanced towards the window; the cosy room was in shadow and outside the sea mist swirled in the gathering dusk. She jumped up in dismay.

"Good heaven, I have been so pleasantly distracted by your discourse that I forgot the time. Stephen will be furious if I am not home by five o'clock, he hates to dine alone."

Her three listeners glanced at one another, and quickly away, unwilling to voice their common thought that Stephen Garth was already angry with his sister and that his temper would not have been sweetened by her long absence.

"I will go with you, if you will permit me," said Mortimer, stretching his long legs and rising nimbly to his feet.

"I should be most grateful for your company, sir," replied Susan. They made haste to get ready; Susan cast one longing look around the cheerful room, her eyes wide and solemn in the light of the candles which Hester had touched with a taper. She curtseyed to Miss Stanhope; the older lady pecked her cheek and wagged an admonishing finger,

"Do not give way to that brother of yours. Remember your happiness is at stake and that of one you love. If I had followed my own advice my situation today would be quite different." Miss Stanhope nodded brightly and turned aside, blinking away a tear.

Hester was surprised by this unusual insight into her former governess's early life, but she refrained from comment as she stooped to embrace Susan, who was trembling a little.

"Buck up, my dear. I will think well on what you have told me, and I'll find means to communicate when I have consulted his lordship. Do not despair, but if the situation becomes intolerable, come to us. Promise me," she said earnestly, giving her friend a shake.

"I will. Thank you all for your kindness." Susan followed Mortimer and preceded him through the door, which he held wide. Hester and Miss Stanhope stood upon the step, wrapped in shawls, as Mortimer and Susan mounted. With a final wave, they disappeared in the gloom. The ladies shivered and retreated rapidly indoors.

"I would like some more tea," remarked Miss Stanhope, eyeing Hester shrewdly. "You look as if it would not come amiss for you too. Are you uneasy about Mortimer? I think that he can take care of himself."

She rang for Martha and ordered more tea and fresh coals for the fire. Hester took up a volume of Pope's poetry, glanced at it and tossed it impatiently aside.

"You should take up embroidery. It is very soothing to the spirits," observed Miss Stanhope, placidly selecting a silk and commencing to set neat stitches in a tapestry which was destined to replace the present, rather worn, fire screen. She continued to sew quietly for some minutes, until the maid had returned with the tea and made up the fire.

"Do not disturb yourself, I will pour," said Hester quickly, when they were alone again. She filled two cups to overflowing and exclaimed in annoyance at her carelessness.

"Leave it to me," said Miss Stanhope calmly; she set aside her frame and descended upon the tea table. Hester moved sheepishly to her former chair and sat down with a sigh of relief.

"I am sorry to be so clumsy, Jane. In truth I am very restless this evening. When do you expect Dr. Minton to call?"

"At his usual time, a little after six, but he may be delayed. He told me this morning that he expects Annie Trotter to be confined at any moment."

Hester frowned. "That wretched girl. Surely she does not need any more children. She cannot care for the ones she has now. A shrewish remark, but true nonetheless. I do hope she postpones her delivery until tomorrow. I particularly wished for Dr. Minton's advice on a matter of some importance."

Miss Stanhope looked across the hearth to where Hester sat, twirling a pencil, her brows wrinkled in thought. The elder lady was very curious, but forebore to press the matter. Instead she contented herself by pursing her lips and remarking disapprovingly that such a frown would leave a permanent furrow on Hester's brow. A giggle dispelled the obnoxious wrinkles at once; Miss Stanhope's sharp eyes softened.

"Why do you not read me your latest chapter," she suggested, "It will help pass the time, and I am all agog to know how you extricated our hero and his lady from the terrors of the marsh."

Nothing loath, Hester went to her bureau and after a slight search returned with a rustling sheaf of papers. She had a gift for reading aloud and the two ladies were soon pleasurably immersed in the penultimate chapter of her gothic romance. An hour slipped by unnoticed. Miss Stanhope pricked her finger several times in excitement, the fire crackled and the candles burned low. At last Hester looked up.

"Do you think it will pass muster, or is it too outrageously improbable?" she enquired wistfully of her sternest critic. Miss Stanhope sucked a drop of blood from the tip of her finger, composed her animated features in judicial lines and pronounced,

"Of course it is quite improbable. No mere man could run such a gamut of perils and emerge virtually unscathed to find the fair Eleanor still awaiting him after so long a silence. However, my standards are set by the menfolk of today, who appear to be sadly lacking in the spirit of adventure; it is, I suppose, just possible that mediaeval gentlemen rivalled the Greek gods in beauty and valour. Once that leap of faith is made, all else may be assumed plausible, if unlikely. In sum I would say that you have all the necessary gothic ingredients. I trust that you have a plan which will unravel all the tangled threads and arrive at a happy conclusion in the final chapter? I cannot abide unhappy endings. Afflicting deathbed avowals of love or renunciation put me out of all patience."

"I share your prejudice," admitted Hester, adding gleefully, "Though I must say that the redoubtable Eleanor would make a splendid Mother Abbess. What do you think, shall I let the Master sink in a quagmire at her feet? I am sure she could deal quite efficiently alone with the mob at the Keep. Then she could retire to the convent and devote her life to good works."

"Don't you dare!" cried Miss Jane indignantly.

"Very well, I won't. I could not resist a small revenge for your remark that gentlemen today lack a spirit of adventure. Sometimes I wish they did. But it is late, I must see to tidying myself before supper. Thank you for not asking me questions. I have much to tell you, but I wished to wait until Mortimer and Dr. Minton are here. Surely Mortimer should be back soon?"

As if in answer, footsteps were heard in the passage and Mortimer himself appeared in the doorway, still clad in his greatcoat.

"Oh, I am glad you are back safely," cried Hester impetuously, "I was quite worried about you. Is all well? I did not hear your horse's hooves in the lane."

"No need for alarm," replied her brother reassuringly, "I took Vixen instead of your mare, so we were able to jump the ditch and come into the stables the back way through the spinney. Miss Garth slipped in unobserved. There were lights only in the servants' quarters so I presume that Stephen was from home. It's a vile night, misty and drizzling."

He corroborated this statement by shaking himself like a wet dog. Drops of water flew everywhere making the fire hiss and splutter. Miss Stanhope protested vehemently, in a voice redolent of nursery discipline; Mortimer's lean features broke into an impish grin as he raised a hand to protect himself from imagined blows and retreated upstairs, calling for hot water and dry towels as he went. The ladies followed at a prudent distance, to attend to their own toilets.

As the clock struck six they reassembled in the parlour. Miss Stanhope had changed into a dress of warm brown velvet, while Hester wore her favourite deep blue Empire style round gown, with puffed sleeves and a narrow ruff at her throat. The ladies eyed one another complacently and chatted idly of the purchases they intended to make in Brighton, while they awaited Dr. Minton's arrival. Mortimer sat by the fire, his thick hair curling in damp fronds on his forehead and about his ears. His wet clothes had been replaced with a comfortable, if outmoded, brown coat, buff coloured breeches and an unwontedly subdued waistcoat of a mid-brown shade. He was leafing through a week-old copy of the *Morning Post* and giving vent to various snorts and rumbles at frequent intervals, when Dr. Minton was announced.

"You look a little flushed, young man," observed the Doctor, when greetings had been exchanged and everyone was comfortably seated.

"Oh dear, perhaps he has taken a feverish chill from being out so long in the damp," murmured Miss Stanhope, anxiously, "I will ring for Martha to bring you some catmint tea. If you drink it very hot it is particularly beneficial."

"I can't abide the stuff!" declared Mortimer, his expression an equal mixture of horror and disgust at the prospect.

Hester bent hastily to poke the fire, and Dr. Minton intervened saying cheerfully,

"Now then, Jane, don't fuss woman. I'm the doctor around here, and I prescribe a little nip of brandy to keep the cold out or reduce the fever! I wouldn't say no to some myself either."

Mortimer threw a glance of heartfelt gratitude at the doctor, exclaiming thankfully,

"Yes, of course, just the thing. If I am flushed 'tis with annoyance at those fools in the government, so cheeseparing that they are actually cutting back on military expenditure while the French go from strength to strength. And speaking of brandy, how will we afford it, if we have to pay the regular price? Dem it, I'd sooner go without than put any more into Garth's well-lined pockets. There's no help for it, Hester, we'll have to find a new lawyer in Brighton," he finished decisively.

Andrew Minton surveyed the trio in the quiet snug room, his thick brows more beetling than usual. He took a generous pinch of snuff, sneezed and rumbled severely,

"What's this, am I hearing aright? You mean to pay full price for your spirits from now on. There's more to this than meets the eye. Ye'd better let me have a plain tale, for I'm bound to advise you that 'twill do you no good to cross Stephen Garth in this vicinity. Jane's been droppin' dark hints for a week or more. Wait a moment, let me put this snuff away, can't think why I carry it, for it gives me no pleasure, pure addiction. Ah, here's my pipe. Do you object if I smoke, ladies?"

Dr. Minton always asked this question, with unfailing courtesy, on his frequent visits. Both ladies did object, but they were too fond of the doctor to say so, and merely took care to seat themselves strategically upwind of the writhing smoke. Mortimer had not been so farsighted and the first few puffs sent him off into a paroxysm of coughing. However, he made a rapid recovery at the dreaded words 'catmint tea' and staggered over to the side table to pour himself and the doctor generous measures of 'eau de vie'. Hester and Miss Stanhope accepted small glasses of sherry wine. When everyone was settled, Mortimer glanced at his sister.

"You'd better tell the tale, Hester. Did you learn anything from Miss Garth this afternoon?"

Hester nodded and folded her hands in her lap, her eyes on the bright fire. In her soft pleasant voice she recounted from the beginning the story of Lord Montfort's accident, her meeting with the Garths in Pendleton, Stephen Garth's proposal and Lord Montfort's dinner party. Mortimer interjected with his own account of Montfort's night at the 'Horse and Groom', and the search of their cottage on the previous evening. Much of the tale was familiar, but Miss Stanhope amd Dr. Minton listened in silence until Hester concluded with her account of her conversation with Susan and the serious warning which Miss Garth had given concerning her brother, his methods and mysterious night-time visitors.

"You suggest that Susan Garth believes her brother to be the leader of this gang of smugglers and worse, and that Garth knows Lord Montfort to be the 'Beau Chevalier'?" summed up Dr. Minton at length. He chewed his pipe, scowling grimly.

Miss Stanhope was sitting on the edge of her chair, her small slender fingers gripping the arms so that the knuckles showed white.

"It is an intolerable situation. Can nothing be done? And poor Mr. Stone, it must be dreadful for him. One is so isolated in the country, I never thought to have a band of lawless men terrorising the neighbourhood of Shawcross; and to think that even Squire Crossley is in their pay. Well Andrew, what is the solution? To whom can we turn?" Dr. Minton seemed to experience no difficulty in following Miss Jane's agitated train of thought. He rapped out his pipe on the hearth, then stood with his shoulder resting on the mantlepiece. He appeared to her prejudiced eyes a tower of strength as he said decisively,

"Garth is playing a deep game and so, in a different way, is Montfort. You have unwittingly become involved in something far more dangerous than smuggling laces and brandy and the sooner you remove to Brighton the happier I shall be. The local people have an affection for you, but they are frightened and would not protect you from Garth's hired London bullies. The prospect look ugly, there is no disguising the fact. I have a certain degree of influence, everyone needs a doctor upon occasion and there is no other reputable physician for miles around. If anything happens to you or to Jedediah Stone I shall be among the first to hear of it, and will take action immediately, but that is all that I can promise and it is little enough. Your tale fits in neatly with various scraps of information and rumour I have heard. It is widely rumoured that Alice Potter is Garth's mistress, with her mother's connivance, but no-one has yet dared tell Ned Potter, and this shall be remedied. As for the two villains who searched your house, they were not the Runners

Mortimer saw at the inn. They are two London gaol-birds hired by Garth a month ago to keep the village folk quiet while he stalked his various prey, including you, Hester m'dear, and the 'Beau'. The villagers are sympathetic to the highwayman, who often leaves offerings of some magnitude at the Church. They do not know his identity. They are now thoroughly aroused on behalf of Stone and Garth may well need his bullies to protect him these dark nights. Of course, Garth has other enemies too. 'Tis suspected that he keeps double books and that his legal dealings would not bear investigation, but these things take time to prove; lawyers are reluctant to condemn their fellows for fear of precedent." Dr. Minton snorted in disgust, then wagged an admonishing finger at his tongue-tied audience. He proceeded weightily, "Now hark to me. You asked for my advice and this is no time for shilly-shallying or mock heroics. You must go to Montfort and speak to him bluntly, no oblique roundaboutation or maidenly modesty, Hester. If you love him, as I believe you do, you must get through his stubborness for all our sakes. This village is a place of fear while the scourge of Garth rules the community. 'Tis no time for a private feud between the two men. Montfort is the only man with sufficient influence to rid us of Garth. Crossley is a mere cipher in Garth's pay. There will be men hung before this business is over and we can get back to honest smuggling. See Montfort, then let it out that you will be leaving for Brighton in ten days. Depart on Thursday when the moon is full and Garth will be otherwise occupied. No protests, Sir Mortimer, you can do no good here and you'll be needed to guard the ladies in Brighton. 'Tis not so far from Shawcross after all, and Garth's arm is long. That is my counsel, and one final word, young man, have your own and your sister's affairs removed to a lawyer in Brighton as soon as may be. See to it tomorrow. Garth always rides to Hove on a Monday and his partner will give you no trouble. Mention my name, he owes me a favour or two, for 'twas I saved his wife and infant son when they had the smallpox and the Pendleton physician gave them up for lost and refused to go near the house, after one quick examination."

Dr. Minton sat down and relaxed. He sipped his brandy and allowed his stern features to ease into a warm smile. Hester returned the smile, saying softly,

"Dear sir, what should we do without you to guide us? You must not place yourself in jeopardy for our sakes. There seem to be spies everywhere. We shall do as you advise and depart on Thursday." She glanced at Miss Stanhope and Mortimer, who both nodded in quick confirmation of her decision.

"Will you visit us in Brighton, Andrew?" enquired Miss Jane, wistfully. The doctor met her eyes yearningly, as if they were alone in the room, but replied briskly,

"No, Jane. Someone must stay here to hold the fort and keep the wolves at bay. You will want news and someone to keep an eye on the cottage in your absence. I shall contrive to have a word with Montfort when you go; we must have this place safe for your return after the season. Now, let us forget our troubles and play a hand of whist. 'Tis why I came, after all!"

The good doctor's obvious enjoyment of the game lightened the rather tense atmosphere engendered by their earlier conversation. At a little after nine, Hester and Mortimer tactfully retired, leaving the elderly lovers to a brief tête-à-tête. As she closed the door, Hester heard the doctor say, huskily,

"I shall miss our little games of cards. 'Twill be a lonely summer. May I hope for more permanent company in the autumn?"

"Yes, Andrew, we have waited long enough, I think," replied Miss Stanhope, in a low, shy voice which Hester hardly recognized for that of her companion. Andrew Minton enveloped his beloved in a crushing embrace, his fob watch sticking painfully into her ribs. She squeaked protestingly and Hester tiptoed up the stair, leaving them to their happiness.

Chapter 13
The Priory Garden

The next few days passed away in a whirlwind of activity. Miss Stanhope took firm charge of the practical arrangements for their departure on Thursday. A note was despatched to the Priory to inform Lord Montfort and his wards of the change in their plans. Mortimer happily undertook to be the messenger, glad of an excuse to further his acquaintance with the enchanting Miss Stephanie again so soon. He departed early on Monday morning, for it was his intention, after calling at the Priory, to ride into Pendleton to see Stephen Garth's partner. He carried a second letter in his pocket, which he was instructed to forward to his aunt Marchant, by express. It was to be hoped that her ladyship would receive this missive in time to inform her Brighton household of the impending arrival of her nephew and niece, for she was not due to take up residence in Brighton until the following weekend.

Miss Stanhope adjured Mortimer to reveal their early departure only to the Montfort family, for it was above all things undesirable that word of their intentions should reach the wrong ears. Martha was also sworn to secrecy, but the maid readily accepted her mistress's explanation that after the events of Saturday night, Miss Stanhope was in a fever to be gone. Martha could not but sympathize with that point of view and she set to, with a will, sewing and packing under Miss Stanhope's supervision.

Hester took refuge downstairs at her writing table in the cozy, book-lined corner of the sitting room. Resolutely she dismissed all other thoughts from her mind in order to compose the final chapter of her manuscript before leaving Shawcross. With much industry and many blots, she achieved her objective by midday on Tuesday. Contentedly, she packed away the manuscript titled *The Secret of Warburton Abbey*. She would carry it with her to Brighton and there make a fair copy before sending it to her publisher, Mr. Murray, in London.

Mortimer and Hester were just preparing to quit the cottage for a short walk after luncheon, when a messenger in Lord Montfort's russet and orange livery presented himself on their doorstep. Having ascertained her identity, the man made a respectful bow and placed a sealed package in Hester's hands, remarking as he did so that his lordship had been adamant that the package should be left with no-one but Miss Vane herself. No reply was expected and the man bowed again and departed as abruptly as he had come.

The box was large but light. Mortimer raised his eyebrows, as he followed his sister through the open door into the dining room. Ignoring the dining table, which still bore the remains of their meal, Hester tripped gaily over to the window seat. She set the box down carefully and tore open the seals with eager fingers. Mortimer peered over her shoulder as she lifted the lid to reveal a large envelope addressed to Miss Hester Vane in a bold, familiar hand. Beneath the envelope was a thick wad of tissue paper. With fingers which trembled slightly, Hester laid the note on one side and raised the tissue, which made a soft rustling sound.

"Ohh!" she breathed on a longdrawn sigh, for before her lay an exquisite bouquet of yellow and white spring flowers, bound up with an enormous bow of yellow and white striped ribbon.

"Pity we're leaving so soon, ye won't be able to enjoy 'em to the full," observed the practical Mortimer. For a moment Hester stood in silent contemplation of the beautiful offering.

"It does not signify," she said quietly.

Mortimer felt a twinge of misgiving at her failure to respond to his sally.

"Ain't you going to see what he says?" he enquired presently, for Hester seemed lost in a fit of abstraction.

"What?, oh — yes, of course." She reached for the envelope and scanned the single sheet, her brows knit in an effort of concentration. It was not easy to decipher, for his lordship's hand was not noted for its legibility.

At length she looked up smiling.

"How good of him," she said placidly, "See, Tim, his lordship entirely approves our early departure. He insists that we travel in his carriage, with Stephanie and Marietta. He offers to provide a mount for you, and Mr. Abercromby will also accompany us. My dear, you must send word to Pendleton that we shall not require the chaise, but it must be done discreetly. Hugo has thought of everything; he suggests that we drive to visit the Priory gardens and stay for luncheon tomorrow, taking our boxes with us. The second carriage can then be packed and the servants can travel ahead on Wednesday afternoon, leaving us to follow early on Thursday morning. He concludes with the wish that I will find the small gift of flowers acceptable, and he looks forward to our visit on Wednesday. Oh, and there is a postscript for you assuring you that Vixen was safely restored to 'The Horse and Groom' last night. I wonder how he knows that, I trust he was not doing anything foolish."

Mortimer shook his head doubtfully, "Hum, very civil of him, I vow, though I'm surprised ye don't find his orders a trifle high-handed. I made sure you would object to his taking all the arrangements into his own hands, but I see the floral tribute has got beneath your guard. Dashed cunning notion that, must remember it. Females are very susceptible creatures, even the best of 'em."

"You wretch," exclaimed Hester without heat. "You are quite right, but a man in Hugo's position is always high in the instep you know, and you must own that it will be much more comfortable to travel under his protection." She glanced at the note again. "He does not mention that he will be coming with us."

"Not likely he would. We don't wish to make too much of a bustle about our departure. Probably he will go to London in a few days and drive his curricle down to Brighton. That was always his intention, I believe. The roads should be reasonable now, so long as we don't get any more heavy rains. Why don't you put those flowers in water, while I send George to Pendleton with instructions to cancel the conveyance. Then we can take our stroll."

Hester nodded in agreement and Mortimer departed for the stable. She lingered a moment, sniffing her flowers and revelling in their fresh spring scent, elusive yet fragrant. Her eyes strayed to the last lines of her letter and she reread the words which she had omitted in the resume which she had given her brother. Lord Montfort had written,

> "I hope, my dear Hester, that these flowers of spring find favour in your eyes. I cannot tell you with what inexpressible longing (the word was scratched out and 'pleasure' substituted) I look forward to escorting you among their brothers and sisters on Wednesday. There is much which I wish to say to you, but the pen is a dashed (scratched out) feeble instrument and I must trust to my (often unruly) tongue on the morrow.
>
> Ever your devoted,
>
> Hugo."

Hester laughed with a mixture of tenderness and mischief as she gazed at his curiously worded blend of impatience and formality, but she grew serious as she absorbed the use of her given name, and she pondered long on the phrase "there is much I wish to say to you." A vision of the usually immaculate Lord Montfort, with inkstained fingers and untidy, ruffled hair as he toiled in the effort of composition flashed through her mind, but she forced herself to dwell on his strange behaviour six years ago and the long silence thereafter, which he had not attempted to break. Such things one could not forgive too easily; if only there were a rational explanation. She felt all her hard-won tranquillity and composure crumbling, but, try as she would, she could not regret it.

Hester was still engaged in this mental struggle when Mortimer returned from his mission. He regarded her suspiciously.

"What ails you, my girl? I thought we were going out."

"Tim, I beg your pardon, I was wool-gathering," she exclaimed contritely, "I'll be with you in a moment."

So saying, Hester swept up her flowers and rushed out of the room, leaving Mortimer to shake his head in bewilderment and mutter darkly over the incomprehensible ways of females in general and sisters in particular.

The next day dawned clear and fine and at the appointed hour of eleven Hester, Miss Stanhope and Mortimer took their place in the Montfort carriage. Their valuables were packed inside, but they were not too severely discommoded, as a smaller, less impressive vehicle had called for their boxes at an early hour, and had departed discreetly by the back lanes in the direction of Pendleton. Hester wriggled her toes in their neat kid half-boots in pleasurable anticipation. She had taken some pains with her appearance and wore a simple lilac gown, trimmed at wrist and hem with a deeper purple braid: a lemon silk shawl protected her shoulders and her toilette was completed by her new primrose gloves and a charming chip straw bonnet, no longer in its first bloom, but refreshed with a spray of violets.

With a flourish the carriage swept through the open Priory gates, traversed the park at a very fair speed, and crunched to a halt on the gravel before the front steps. Miss Stanhope, who had enjoyed the drive tremendously, felt obliged to protest at the breakneck speed as soon as her little feet were firmly upon the ground. However, she had not time to indulge her displeasure; the great door swung open while she fumbled in her reticule for her smelling salts. His lordship ran lightly down the steps to greet them. Miss Stanhope closed her reticule with a snap and brandished the smelling bottle at him in a menacing way. His eyes twinkled, but his face appeared perfectly grave as he possessed himself of the threatening hand and pressed it to his lips, smelling salts and all. He stood back abruptly and sneezed mightily, for the top had come loose and the contents were potent.

"Good lord, ma'am," he spluttered, while Hester and Mortimer exchanged delighted grins, "Pray tell me at once what I have done to be in your black books. I will make amends at once, for your methods of vengeance are like to prove lethal!"

"'Twas not intended for you, my lord," responded Miss Jane airily. She patted him gently on the back with one black-mittened hand, as he succumbed to a further bout of sneezing. "But 'twill do you no harm, for it vents the spleen in a moment."

Hugo was speechless, but Hester took pity on him.

"Nonsense, Jane, you should leave the physicking to Dr. Minton and not dabble. The fit will pass in a moment, my lord," she continued bracingly, turning to their stricken host, "Do but close your eyes, hold your nose and count to ten." He did as he was bid, and was soon sufficiently recovered to conduct them within doors, only his watery eyes and a certain redness about the ears testifying to his inner sufferings.

"I must remember to beware of that trick in future," he muttered in Hester's ear as the butler relieved them of their shawls and Mortimer's hat and cane. "I declare I would rather face a dozen armed men than Miss Jane and her salts. Does she ever use them herself?"

"Of course not," laughed Hester. She added more seriously, "I have to thank you for my beautiful flowers, my lord, they gave me great pleasure. Also for the arrangements which you have made on our behalf for the journey. It is a relief to have such tiresome matters dealt with so smoothly and competently."

"I wish that I had the right to relieve you of all your burdens," he began impetuously, but checked himself as he observed Mortimer and Miss Stanhope approaching from across the hall, where Miss Stanhope had been making a great bustle of setting herself to rights before the looking glass. Hester threw him a startled glance and her chin tilted a little. This was moving too fast for her. Hugo looked at her keenly.

"Forgive me if I have erred," he whispered, and added aloud, "You must blame the heady effects of Miss Stanhope's salts on one quite unaccustomed to their powers. Shall we join my mother? She awaits you in the drawing room." He ushered his guests before him into a pretty pink saloon overlooking a broad terrace. Here they found the rest of the Priory party, including Hyde Abercromby. When everyone was seated, refreshments were served and the talk turned to the impending departure for Brighton.

"You will not go with us, my lord? enquired Miss Stanhope wistfully.

Hugo, elegant as always in a coat of dark blue superfine and light coloured small clothes, shook his head regretfully. He set down his cup and glanced round at the circle of expectant faces. Hester thought fleetingly that never before had she seen him appear to such advantage, though his capable athletic frame and strong dark face seemed out of place in the small dainty room. Perhaps he felt so too, for he rose abruptly and strode over to the garden door, which opened on to the terrace.

"I fear I cannot, Miss Jane," he said gently, "I must remain here for a few days and will then come to the coast via London. However, we shall all meet again as soon as I have performed certain duties and I shall hope to have the pleasure of driving you in my curricle before the end of next week, by which time you should be quite settled and ready for a little entertainment."

"I have never driven in a curricle in my life, but there is a first time for everything," said Miss Stanhope stoutly. Hester, who knew that the brave little lady was terrified of horses, nodded approvingly. She found Hugo's eye upon her.

"I trust, Miss Vane, that you will ensure that Miss Stanhope leaves her smelling salts behind on that occasion," he remarked wickedly. She smiled mischievously in return, her grey eyes sparkling enchantingly. For a moment their glances locked and held, oblivious to all else. Then Hester heard herself saying lightly,

"I will do my best, but you must engage to drive very gently, for my dear Jane likes to admire the scenery and will have no ambition to see you drive to an inch."

He grinned appreciatively, "That pleasure I shall reserve for you. Miss Jane shall see that my bays can be as gentle as cooing doves."

Lady Elizabeth, who had been listening closely to the light chatter, suddenly patted Hester's hand, as she sat beside her.

"You look quite ravishing today, my dear. You should be out enjoying the fresh spring air. Hugo, why do you not show our guests the gardens before luncheon?"

"Certainly mama," he bowed. "Would you care to come out and sit in the rose garden? It is very warm in the sun and I do not think you could catch a chill."

The delicate lady, ethereal as ever in a rose gown of watered silk, shook her head, as she smiled affectionately at her tall son.

"No, my dear Hugo. I shall do very well here, but do take Miss

Stanhope with you for Penelope can read to me until you return."

Miss Jane demurred, but allowed herself to be persuaded when it became clear that her ladyship usually rested before luncheon. She stepped on to the terrace with Mr. Abercromby beside her. Stephanie and Marietta, aflutter in sprigged muslin with blue and green satin sashes, followed closely with Mortimer, while Hugo stood aside to let Hester pass, her face hidden beneath her chipstraw bonnet with its enormous lemon bow. His lordship pulled the door shut behind him and offered his arm to Hester. They crossed the terrace in the wake of the others and paused at the head of the steps which descended to the rose garden in order to survey the prospect. It was indeed a warm day: a few early bees buzzed among the hyacinths which filled the large stone pots placed at intervals along the low terrace wall. Hester drew a deep breath of pure happiness and peeped at her silent companion below her lashes, overcome by a feeling of unwonted shyness. He returned her regard gravely for a long moment. All was quiet, save for the faint sound of Miss Stanhope's voice which floated back to them from the further end of the rose garden as she disappeared from view behind a hedge.

Hugo relaxed, his green eyes glinting in the sun.

"Mama was quite right as usual. You do look ravishing today, Miss Vane. Like a creature of spring in that ridiculous bonnet. Mama likes you, you know. That was why she sent me out here to talk to you. She thinks that I am not very good at communicating with females, but she has hopes that you will get under my guard and make me more human. She has already observed a marked mellowing in my demeanour since you reappeared in my life. But let us not linger here, there is much to see. I am afraid the roses are not yet in bloom, but if we follow this path to the right we shall presently come to the Gothic ruins by way of the topiary. Of course if you prefer we may follow the others through the kitchen garden and park to the ornamental lake, but I am sure they will understand your predilection for ruins."

Hester gasped at his effrontery and was about to protest when she found her elbow firmly gripped. His lordship maintained a flow of informative commentary as he steered Hester along mossy paths, between hedges carved in strange shapes of birds and beasts. She found the place oddly sinister and was not surprised when Hugo, pointing in the direction of a large dragon rampant, remarked,

"The family crest. 'Twas beneath that beast, according to legend, that the first Baron Montfort was murdered. His ghost is said to haunt the garden and the ruins on moonless nights for his death was unavenged. The family motto 'I will arise again' dates from that incident."

Hester shivered despite the warm breeze, but resoluterly shook off her unease.

"I have heard something of the tale. I imagine it could be a useful story for some folks, even in our present enlightened days," she said dryly.

Hugo nodded calmly.

"Not for nothing are you a spinner of gothic romances and intrigues, Miss Vane. I see from the gleam in your eye that you perceive possibilities hereabouts which are hidden from lesser mortals."

"I hope so," said Hester tartly. Obedient to a slight pressure on her arm she followed Hugo to the end of the walk. She scarcely noted the path for her thoughts were suddenly in chaos, the deeper preoccupations of the past few days rising to the surface, stirred by the ominous atmosphere of their surroundings. At length they emerged among the Priory ruins. Hester sighed with relief as her eyes rested on the old, weather-beaten stones, just now bathed in warm sunlight, for the new leaves on the trees offered little shade. Her foot, in its trim kid boot, caught in a rabbit hole and she fell forward with an involuntary cry. At once Hugo's arm was about her, arresting her fall. He set her gently on her two feet and put her bonnet straight. She put up her hand to tuck back a stray lock, but he seized the hand, saying huskily,

"Leave it, I like it as it is. Now, come and sit down, I have something to ask you. Let us clear the air for the time for misunderstandings in past."

Hester suffered him to lead her to a grassy knoll, topped by smooth stones. She seated herself and folded her hands docilely in her lap. Hugo smiled fleetingly as he seated himself beside her.

"Are you warm enough?" he enquired abruptly. She nodded and he continued, "Good. Now perhaps you will tell me at last, why did you flee from me without a word six years ago in London?"

Hester looked up indignantly and her expressive eyes sparkled with anger as she replied,

"I did not flee from you, my lord, I would scorn to do such a thing. You were under no obligation to me, sir, none at all. It was clear from your demeanour during that Season that you found the prospect of marriage a dead bore. Your father made it plain to mine that a virtually penniless female would be no fit bride for his son and heir and your own manner was so stiff and unapproachable that I concluded you shared your father's views. When Papa was killed in that dreadful race my mother was completely overset. Our financial and other circumstances were such that we had no alternative but to quit the metropolis as speedily as might be. Your father had made it clear that all thought of an alliance between our two families was at an end, but I did write you a note telling you of our loss and of our impending departure for the country. I received no reply, not even a note of condolence. What could I do but assume that all ties, even those of common courtesy, were to be severed henceforth?"

As he listened Lord Montfort betrayed a variety of emotions, incredulity and anger being uppermost. He waited with barely controlled impatience until Hester had finished speaking and then sprang to his feet and took a rapid turn about the grass. Finally he came to a halt a yard from where she was seated. He stood towering above her, breathing heavily and she shrank a little from his wrathful countenance, the lines about his mouth set rigidly and his eyes as cold and smouldering as a stormy sea. He observed her fear and sank to the ground at Hester's feet, his back to the rock on which she was sitting. For a space of time there was silence save for the merry twittering of the birds in the trees above their heads. Hester's courage began to revive and she placed her gloved hand lightly on Hugo's tense shoulder, saying bracingly,

"Come, my lord, all this is long past and should be forgotten."

Hugo reached up and clasped the small hand, then with a quick movement placed a kiss in the palm.

"But not forgiven," he said, very low.

Hester looked down at the bent head, with its thick dark hair and a wave of tenderness swept through her.

"And forgiven," she said firmly.

At her words, Hugo looked full into her face, the light of hope springing into his eyes. He leapt lithely to his feet and seated himself once more by her side.

"You are most generous, for my behaviour must have seemed — was — unpardonable. But I must tell you that I never received your note. My father probably intercepted it. I was out of town when your father was killed, for I was escorting my mother to Bath in an effort to improve her health. It is true that I was uncertain of my feelings at that time. My travels to Europe had given me a taste of freedom and a knowledge of the wider world. When I returned I found London stultifying, I was not ready to settle down and when I observed the cynical marriages of convenience of the majority of my acquaintance I was reluctant to enter into a similar arrangement. I felt that many people courted me for my fortune, not my person. My father, acting I am sure in what he believed were my best interests, informed me of your family difficulties. He was a stern man, but he adored my mother and wished me to find a like happiness. Forgive me, but I must tell you that he had little patience with a man like your father, whom he regarded as an idle and irresponsible gamester. To a degree I shared his views, but I was aware that our respective mamas cherished the prospects of a union between us. I was torn between duty and inclination when I met you again and this must account for my stiffness of manner. I believe you also found the situation uncomfortable for you comported yourself with the utmost formality and coolness in my company. Only occasionally did I glimpse a trace of the charming child I remembered, as in the instance of the kittens? I observed you with other friends and could see that away from me you were still your own wayward and enchanting self. What could I do but believe that my suit was unwelcome to you? I determined to remain aloof, but I was hurt by your indifference for we had once been good friends. Fool that I was, I did not realize the depths of my feelings until you disappeared, leaving, as I thought, no word of farewell. I spoke to my father when I returned from Bath and heard of the tragic accident which had befallen you. He assured me that he had spoken to your father but a few days previously and they had agreed that a marriage between us was undesirable. According to my noble parent, Sir Montagu had cut up incredibly stiff and had announced that his beloved daughter had no desire to be wed to a cold, proud young cub like myself; not for any great estate would he see his child condemned to a lifetime of unhappiness. Of course he may well have been provoked, for I now suspect that my father told Sir Montagu that a union was out of the question if your only settlement was a pile of debts. Of course he would not have done such a thing had I given him reason to suspect that my affections were seriously engaged, but he had no inkling of the situation. I realized my loss only when I thought the situation irretrievable. I had no word from you, you evidently shared your father's opinion of me. Bitterness overwhelmed me. I wrote to you several times, but tore up every message. I abandoned myself to a whirl of excesses until my father lost patience and sent me to the Americas. We parted with harsh words and I never saw him again. However, my time in America was profitably spent. I had a variety of educational experiences and learned how to make a fortune in my own right. I learned independence and self-reliance. Then my mother wrote to tell me that my father was dead. She begged me to return and take charge of my inheritance. I came back and took up my old life, but with a difference. I had acquired an interest in politics and many new insights into the conduct of war. I offered my services to the government and was accepted. There is little more to tell."

Hester shook her head and smiled at the end of this narration. Her heart was singing with joy, but she forced herself to say calmly,

"I suspect there is a great deal more, which you do not intend to tell me, my lord. Your tale is much as I might have supposed, and I apologize for misjudging you. I am so relieved that now everything is comfortable and we may be friends again."

Lord Montfort looked down at Hester, who was tranquilly surveying the ruins. His eyes twinkled, but his voice was perfectly serious as he replied,

"Quite so, ma'am. We were both very young and youth and folly go hand in hand, so they say. Let us begin again on a sounder footing."

Hester flung up her hand in protest, her lip quivering,

"By all means, but I take leave to inform you, sir, that I do not yet have one foot in the grave and folly is not solely the prerogative of youth. Your own behaviour of late might strike the saner members of our community as remarkably foolish."

"Yourself included, I collect, Miss Vane?"

"Exactly so, your lordship," she said mischievously.

"Minx!" he murmured, without rancour. Hester did not respond to this provocation, for a new thought had occurred to her. She shook her head soberly and tapped his lordshop with an admonishing finger,

"Pray be serious a moment, Hugo, we should rejoin the others for luncheon, but there is something which I must tell you first."

In her preoccupation she had used his first name, and Hugo seized upon it eagerly,

"With all my heart, my dear Hester, so long as you continue in this informal vein."

She frowned, remarking severely,

"This is no time for jesting, my lord — oh, very well, Hugo. Your strange behaviour has not passed unobserved of late and your enemies are aware of your identity, and your disguise. Stephen Garth is an implacable foe, with infinite resources."

A slight rustle made Hester start and hesitate, but she relaxed as her eye caught the tail end of a rabbit disappearing in his burrow close by. She saw that Hugo's expression had become grim and withdrawn. She rose to her feet, saying softly,

"Let us walk a little in open space. What I have to say must not be overheard by prying ears."

Lord Montfort responded to the urgency in her voice and followed obediently as Hester almost ran down the little slope. They skirted the hedge which bordered the topiary garden on the southern side. The path meandered beside a woodland stream, whose banks were bright with primroses. They walked in silence until they emerged at length at a point where the stream filtered into a large ornamental lake, covered with water lily leaves. Hester perceived a stone bridge spanning the lake. Half way across, the bridge widened to encompass a wooden summer house and here the rest of the party were gathered. They seemed to be happily occupied. Miss Stanhope was fanning herself, with Marietta and Hyde Abercromby beside her. Mortimer and Stephanie were out of sight on the far side of the bridge, but their laughing voices floated back on the still air to the silent couple, who stood hidden behind a large azalea bush, just above the small waterfall which marked the junction of stream and lake.

His lordship swore softly, but Hester wasted no time. She put her finger to her lips and scurried back noiselessly by the way they had come. When she judged that they were out of earshot, Hester halted. Facing Hugo a trifle breathlessly, she spoke urgently,

"My lord, Garth and his minions have struck terror in the neighbourhood. Their evil influence is widespread and I have reason to believe that their activities do not stop at smuggling, though that is bad enough. I know it sounds incredible, but I am certain that they plot against the safety of the realm. Garth and his intimates sell information to the French. I do not know how, but I presume they hope to profit if the threatened French invasion is successful." She hesitated, but Hugo remained silent, watching her keenly. Blushing a little, she hurried on, "You, sir, are a stumbling block to their plans. Garth will not tolerate your interference; now that he knows of your disguise he will seek to rid himself of the threat which you present, by fair means through his Runners, or by foul. I admit that I am frightened for you should know, my lord, that Stephen Garth is determined to wed me."

"What!" ejaculated Lord Montfort, an expression of outrage written in every line of his mobile countenance. He seized her elbows roughly. "And you, do you reciprocate his feelings, Miss Vane?" he demanded harshly. Hester stood still, her eyes twinkling, though she owned to herself that she felt weak at the knees. She was suddenly lightheaded with happiness, but this was not the time to seek to analyse her emotions. She said lightly,

"Let me go, my lord, you are hurting me. Of course I do not wish to marry Mr. Garth. My views on the horrors of matrimony and the blessings of the single state are well known. I am shocked that you could even suspect me of such an inclination when I have just this moment informed you that I fear Stephen, not to mention the fact that I should find it abhorrent to ally myself to a man I know to be a traitor to our country. What I dread is that he should find some unorthodox means to blackmail me and bend me to his will by force. He has few scruples, I assure you."

Hugo relaxed at the unmistakeable sincerity of her tone. He released his grip on her elbows, but continued to eye her intently. Hester rubbed her afflicted joints absentmindedly. Hugo smiled grimly.

"Having said so much, I think you had better tell me the whole. Whence had you this information?"

Hester was inclined to resent his commanding note, but she acknowledged to herself that it would be an undeniable relief to shift the burden of decision to his lordship's capable shoulders. She recounted as fully as possible all the facts in her possession, including Garth's association with Alice Potter, and Susan Garth's own tale of her brother's doings.

"You are quite sure Miss Garth is a reliable source?" queried Hugo, when at last she had finished her narration.

"Oh yes," confirmed Hester, "You saw yourself how her brother behaved in Church last Sunday. Susan receives all the affection which it is in his nature to give, but her love for Mr. Stone and her discovery of his deeds and methods, have created an unbridgeable rift between them."

"Not quite all his affection," observed Hugo coolly, "His would seem to be a passionate and jealous nature which cannot bear to be thwarted. Very well. Now tell me, is Garth aware that his sister knows of his treachery?"

"No, oh no! And we must not betray her confidence, for it would place her in great danger."

Hugo nodded decisively. He was once more calm and self-possessed, with a steely glint in his clear green eyes. He took her hand and placed it on his arm, pulling her gently along the path towards the lake.

"This has been a most interesting and instructive morning, my dear Hester. There is much in what you have said to meditate upon and I promise you action will be taken. I will take counsel with Andrew Minton and Abercromby at the earliest opportunity. But now, I fear, we have been absent from my other guests far too long. My mother will be displeased if luncheon is delayed." He consulted his fob watch with an abstracted air, "Hum not a moment to lose." Their eyes met and Hugo gave his rare charming smile. "It will not do for you to be in mama's black books. Hold on to your bonnet, my love."

Hester was given no time to protest at this unusual mode of address. They scampered across the wide lawns, not slackening their pace until they had mounted the terrace steps. They found the whole party awaiting them with some impatience. Hester was obliged to hide a smile as Hugo smoothly apologised for their long absence. He explained that Hester had been fascinated by the old ruins and they had explored the area with a fine toothcomb. Lady Elizabeth accepted Hester's stammered apology graciously, the brief moment of awkwardness passed, and everyone filed into the dining room, in perfect charity with one another. They found a tempting array waiting to coax the most jaded palate, and Hester, blandly ignoring her brother and Miss Stanhope's quizzical, amused glances, fell to with a most hearty, albeit unladylike, appetite.

The remainder of the visit passed for Hester in a happy haze. Afterwards she could never recollect exactly how they had spent the time, though she recalled an animated discussion with Lady Elizabeth on the subject of 'salons'. The Vanes took their leave in the late afternoon. Mortimer rode the mount with which Lord Montfort had provided him until he could buy one of his own in Brighton. The horse was a handsome brown beast with a white star on his forehead, named 'Duke'. Mortimer was delighted with his paces and said so at great length to his lordship, who rode with them to the gates of the park. Hugo encouraged his enthusiasm with good-humoured tolerance while Hyde Abercromby, who also rode with them, glanced at his friend curiously from time to time as if trying to gauge his mood. Mr. Abercromby had known Hugo Jermyn for many years, but never before had he seen him so gay and lighthearted. They reached the South Lodge gates and halted while the gatekeeper performed his office. The gentleman approached the carriage to make their farewells. Miss Vane let down the window and Hugo stepped out to take her hand. He kissed it murmuring,

"Believe me, Miss Vane, your servant always. I shall see you in Brighton next week. A safe and comfortable journey, ladies." He stood back and bowed, hat aflourish. Mr. Abercromby followed his example; as he straightened his eyes met those of Miss Stanhope, which were shrewd and twinkling. She nodded and they smiled at one another understandingly. Then the carriage rattled away, with Mortimer at its side. Lord Montfort stooped to retrieve a small white object, which had fallen at his feet: Miss Vane had dropped one of her new dainty handkerchiefs! He stuffed it in his pocket and glanced at Mr. Abercromby defiantly. That gentleman was wisely looking in the opposite direction, whistling slightly between his teeth. Mr. Abercromby was puzzled by his friend's behaviour no longer; evidently Cupid had fired one of his confounded arrows and the hitherto impervious Lord Montfort had fallen victim to love's darts at last.

Chapter 14
Arrival In Brighton

At dawn on that misty Thursday morning the commodious Montfort travelling carriage stood once more at the door of the Vanes' cottage. Hester and Miss Stanhope were ready and waiting, well muffled in shawls and cloaks against the chill air. They seated themselves opposite Marietta and Stephanie, who were both sleepy and disinclined for conversation. Hester was grateful that their maids had gone ahead with the baggage on the previous day, for the atmosphere soon became warm and close, the windows streamed with condensed moisture and the carriage jolted uncomfortably. Poor Marietta struggled gamely to overcome her sensation of nausea and Hester envied her brother and Hyde Abercromby on horseback in the fresh air. She wished, not for the first time, that she could afford to buy herself a good mount, but horses were expensive to maintain and in order to keep her independence, Hester had been obliged to practice the strictest economies. Little Merrylegs, the pony, was quite adequate for her occasional excursions about the countryside; also Squire Crossley had generously offered her a beast from his stable, but the Squire was not a good judge of horseflesh and had little that was suitable for a lady to ride. His own wife and daughters were not fond of riding, preferring to take their exercise more sedately in the barouche: Hester had borrowed an old grey mare once or twice for civility's sake, when the Squire pressed her, but the poor creature was so fat and lazy that she had had little pleasure from the activity. She sighed wistfully and spent some time in complicated computations; perhaps if her next book sold well she might indulge herself, but any royalty monies were still some way in the future. Her thoughts became gloomy as she reminded herself that Brighton was a frivolous and costly resort. Her aunt Annabelle was the soul of kindness, but Hester's pride would not permit her to be an unnecessary charge on Lady Marchant's generosity. "I must be quite firm and spend some time each morning copying out my manuscript fairly, so that I may place it in Mr. Murray's hands at the earliest possible moment," she vowed silently.

Presently the sun rose. Hester's spirits lightened perceptibly as the carriage emerged from the winding lanes and joined the Brighton road just south of Pendleton. The horses made excellent time on the smooth surface; it was only eight o'clock when they halted to change teams and stretch their cramped limbs at 'The Eagle', a busy posthouse where many London travellers stopped to refresh themselves, before crossing the South Downs.

Mortimer and Mr. Abercromby assisted the ladies to alight. Lord Montfort had left nothing to chance. Their arrival was expected and the landlord himself conducted them to a cheerful private parlour, where they found a welcome repast laid out for their delectation. Only Marietta declined all offers of nourishment. She seated herself wanly in a chair by the fire and closed her eyes, while the rest of the party partook lavishly of ham and eggs, rolls and coffee. Their hunger assuaged, everyone chatted in high good humour. Mr. Abercromby had a quiet word with the landlord and bespoke weak tea and toast for poor Marietta. He then seated himself beside the young lady and persuaded her to eat with a pleasant mixture of coaxing and firmness. Meanwhile Stephanie and Mortimer moved to the broad window seat, overlooking the cobbled forecourt, where they amused themselves by watching and commenting upon the lively scene below. Hester and Miss Stanhope remained at the table, sipping their coffee while they conversed quietly.

"At least our journey has been uneventful thus far," observed Miss Stanhope complacently, "In broad daylight one's fears seem foolish, but I must admit I was apprehensive until we joined the main London to Brighton road. One could see nothing in that mist and an ambush would have been the easiest thing to contrive. I wonder if anyone remarked our departure."

Hester shrugged her shoulders,

"I don't know, but I doubt that it signifies. We achieved our object, which was to quit Shawcross at an unexpected time and as discreetly as might be. You are too fanciful, Jane. Reflect a little. What would be the purpose of an ambush? We are not living in the days of Robin Hood. Stephen Garth is no ordinary highwayman or robber. Even had he known of our departure, which is unlikely, he could not well have overcome the whole party and carried us off to his lair to hold us for ransom! As you say, in these sane surroundings one's fears seem groundless and the whole notion of flight ridiculous."

Miss Stanhope was moved to protest.

"I cannot agree with you, my love. I am convinced that where you are concerned Mr. Garth would not baulk at abduction to force you to his will. Lord Montfort is not a man to make rash pronouncements, but he warned me yesterday that we should take particular care in Brighton, for in such a gay, crowded place, danger can lurk unseen." She shuddered eloquently and Hester was obliged to bite her lip to repress an unladylike giggle.

"I declare, I have no patience with such nonsense. Hush now, Jane, or Stephanie and Marietta will overhear you; I'm sure his lordship would not wish them to become alarmed by, or involved in, such plottings and mysteries. So far as I am aware, they have no inkling of anything amiss, though they must have wondered why we found it necessary to depart so early this morning."

"I doubt it," pronounced Miss Stanhope, adding with a sniff, "We must remember that they are strangers in this country. If they thought about it at all I imagine they concluded that such early, furtive departures are one of a piece with our other native eccentricities." She glanced from Marietta, now engaged in animated conversation with Mr. Abercromby, to Stephanie, who with a toss of her dark curls was roundly condemning some groom for his treatment of the horses. Both young ladies were fully occupied with their partners, so Miss Stanhope continued in an undertone, "They are prettily behaved girls and should give me no trouble. I suspect that they are not quite 'au fait' with the ways of our society, but that can soon be remedied and any slight 'faux pas' will either pass unnoticed in the relaxed seaside atmosphere, or will be pronounced charmingly foreign, don't you think?"

Hester smiled mischievously at her old mentor,

"Jane, you are a treasure, his lordship is fortunate indeed to have you to supervise his wards. I shall miss you sorely when our good doctor claims his own, but you certainly deserve to be happy at last. I collect that we can expect to hear the banns called before Christmas?"

Miss Stanhope sat up very straight, adjusted the brooch at her throat and concentrated on fastening the ribbons of her large, somewhat outmoded bonnet. Stephanie came to her rescue, by crying,

"Our conveyance is at the door, dear ma'am. Are we ready to depart? But I forget, in my eagerness to see this so beautiful seaside town, Marietta, how do you go on? But I need hardly ask, Mr. Abercromby has worked wonders and the roses bloom again in your cheeks."

This was indeed true, for Marietta, with the resilience of youth, had made a speedy recovery away from the swaying motion of the coach. She smiled at Mr. Abercromby gratefully, Miss Stanhope also bestowed an approving nod on that gentleman as she rose briskly to her feet.

"We are all delighted to see you in spirits again, my dear. Let us be off for we have still some tedious miles to cover, if we are to arrive in good time for dinner."

Soon they were on their way once more, trundling steadily along one of the best kept roads in England. They passed through neat villages, with thatched cottages and cobbled walls, surrounded by gardens small, but filled with flowers at the front and vegetables at the back. Stephanie remarked that everyone in England seemed to have a green thumb. The girls seemed enchanted with the gentle, rolling countryside, the hills dotted with sheep who followed the ancient chalky footpaths on the upper slopes. Miss Stanhope and Hester listened to their constant stream of chatter, observing with fresh eyes the peace and serenity of the deep hedgerows, little winding lanes, the play of sunlight and shadow and the incessant murmur of water which could be heard whenever the horses were obliged to slow to a walking pace on a steep slope. They halted for a light picnic luncheon at a high point on the Downs, which afforded a fine prospect in all directions. When everyone's hunger was appeased, the young stretched their legs in a short promenade on the springy turf. A faint, pleasant breeze ruffled their hair and Stephanie's keen, questing eyes were the first to see the deep blue of the sea away in the distance, through a gap in the hills. It was a clear day; Mortimer, standing at Stephanie's side, had no difficulty in finding local landmarks such as Chanctonbury Ring which appeared close at hand, with Cissbury further to the right. Miss Stanhope derived no little amusement from hearing him discoursing wisely (if inaccurately) on the Roman occupation of Sussex, but her brows lifted a little when he offered to escort Miss Stephanie on an excursion to view the old Roman road, which was still visible, in good repair and wide enough to accommodate a chariot, at various points on the Downs not far from Brighton. Stephanie showed an unfeigned enthusiasm for the project and Miss Stanhope's brows rose still higher. Marietta remarked that all this chalk reminded her of the schoolroom.

They travelled on uneventfully until a little past three in the afternoon when they halted at the sign of 'The Shepherd and Dog' to change horses for the final stage. A light drizzle had begun to fall, but the sharp tang of sea salt was in the air. The rain laid the dust, but the atmosphere inside the carriage was once again close and heavy with the windows tightly shut. Marietta began to droop and all the ladies were very weary. Outside the rain increased. Mortimer and Hyde Abercromby huddled in their greatcoats and pulled their hats low over their eyes. The road was busy; occasionally another carriage overtook them, but Sam Green was a capable coachman and made good time although he was obliged to stop several times for Marietta to get some air. Darkness came early that day; the ladies could no longer beguile the tedium of the journey by observing their surroundings. Marietta became agitated lest they should stick in the mud, but fortunately no such disaster occurred. At last the glimmer of lights signalled that they were approaching their destination and ten minutes later the carriage was rumbling through the streets of the small, fashionable town of Brighton. They drew up at the door of Lord Montfort's villa on the North Steyne. Hester peered out while the other ladies busied themselves in collecting their various belongings. In the flare of two flickering torches she perceived a low, white fence, with a short path leading to a square, modest residence. As she watched the door swung open wide to reveal a well-lit hallway. The rain was still falling heavily. The Vanes made their farewells hastily. It was agreed that they and their travelling companions would all meet on the morrow. The steps were let down and an orderly bustle ensued. A rather limp, weak-kneed Marietta, was escorted inside leaning thankfully on Mr. Abercromby's solicitous arm. Hester sighed enviously as, with a final wave, they disappeared within doors, leaving a sudden silence behind them. Hester had attempted, half-heartedly, to persuade her dripping brother to join her for the remainder of the journey, but Sir Mortimer declined, saying firmly that he was already soaked to the skin and did not wish to stain the elegant Montfort upholstery.

Hester patted her curls perfunctorily, then pulled on her gloves. She was already tolerably acquainted with the town, having visited it on several occasions, but she was aware that the increasing fashionableness of the resort had led to its speedy expansion. She rubbed impatiently at the misty panes and pressed her nose to the glass, but could see little in the darkness. She felt the carriage turn, bearing over to the left side of the Steyne as they approached the sea. The Steyne itself was a popular, grassy promenade enclosed by low fencing, where vehicles were not permitted. The carriage turned down St. James' Street, climbing quite steeply. Two more turns and they emerged on the lofty heights of the Marine Parade, where Lady Marchant had hired a house for the Season. Her ladyship was a great believer in the beneficial effects of sea air; she also enjoyed the ever-changing view of the sea and ships from her drawing room windows.

As she neared her destination Hester's eager anticipation was overlaid by a tremor of apprehension. She recalled their hurried departure; had her aunt received their message in time? However, she need not have worried, for when Pringle, Lady Marchant's London butler, opened the door, he immediately set all qualms at rest by informing Sir Mortimer and Miss Vane that her ladyship had arrived in Brighton on the previous day and would be delighted to welcome them as soon as they had rid themselves of their travel dust. Dinner had been kept back and would be served at seven. Hester and Mortimer exchanged mischievous grins on hearing this news, well knowing their aunt's hearty appetite. The two young people were conducted to spacious bedchambers on the second floor of the tall, narrow house. Hester noted with approval the tasteful simplicity of the furnishings. She was delighted to find, on entering her bedchamber, that she had been allotted a room at the front of the house, overlooking the sea. Martha awaited her, brimming with gossip. As she chattered the little maid busied herself with pulling off Hester's boots and outer garments. She enfolded her mistress in a warm red wrapper and persuaded her to sit by the fire of spluttering sea coals, while she rang for the little scullery maid to bring the hot water for Hester's bath. It was very soothing to ease her tired limbs in the waist-high tub; Hester felt quite sleepy as she emerged to be quickly swathed in warm towels. The delicious scent of strawberry lotion filled the room, as Martha rubbed her briskly. Contentedly, Hester sipped the hot wine posset of Mrs. Blossom's own brewing. She listened with half an ear to Martha's account of her journey, the kind attentions of Lord Montfort's second footman, and her impressions of the big city, which the country-bred girl was seeing for the first time. Of course she had not had much time to look around, because she had been so busy unpacking miss's things, but in the afternoon the housekeeper, a Mrs. Datchett, had asked her if she would mind fetching some witch hazel from the apothecary for her ladyship's sore eyes. The whole household was still at sixes and sevens and she had been glad of the excuse to escape for a little while. She had seen the fishing fleet, oh, a vast quantity of ships, set out on the evening tide, and she had lost herself looking for the apothecary, but a very kind gentleman had taken pity on her bewilderment and had himself given her the direction. She was sure Miss Hester would enjoy all the fine shops. Lady Marchant was very kind, and had asked her a lot of questions when the flowers came, and given her a whole shilling to spend for herself! Hester listened in sympathetic amusement, marvelling at the change wrought in her usually self-contained maid, by the new surroundings. She sat up abruptly when she heard the word 'flowers', her glass tilting precariously,

"Cease thy prattling for a moment, Martha. What flowers came?"

"Why Miss Hester, didn't I tell 'ee. The roses from his

lordship, o' course. Beautiful they be, miss, all yellow, with lavender ribbons in a wicker basket. Her ladyship has them downstairs in the drawing room. She said they complemented the wall hangings, miss, and she wanted to see your face when you read the note. I don't think she meant me to tell you that, Miss Hester, but I thought you ought to be warned," she finished loyally.

Mistress and maid smiled at one another in complete understanding.

"My thanks, Martha. How should I go on without you? Tomorrow you shall accompany me and see a little more of the town. It is indeed a pleasant place, if it stops raining. I expect it will, for the sea wind makes the weather moody and ever changing. Now, speaking of changing, I must make haste to get dressed or I shall not have time to greet my aunt before dinner. What have you laid out for me tonight? My orange sarsenet? That will do very well."

Martha brushed and dressed Hester's hair with quick, dexterous fingers, before slipping the light, soft gown over her head. The underdress was of pale orange, sprigged with rosebuds, covered by a tunic of a deeper shade. Hester seated herself while Martha laced her gold sandals, and draped a gold fringed shawl round her shoulders. She also knotted a gold ribbon in her heavy curls which were dressed in a very creditable imitation of the fashionable Grecian style. Although she did not care much for jewellery, Hester chose a thin gold chain and small earrings of the same metal, in deference to her aunt, whose gift they had been. Lemon net gloves, reticule and a dainty chicken bone fan completed her toilette.

"You look very pretty, miss," said Martha sincerely. Hester bestowed a light kiss on her cheek,

"Thanks to you, Martha. Don't wait up for me, but be sure you wake me by eight. I have much to do tomorrow."

The girl bobbed a curtsey.

"Certainly, Miss Hester. It's always a pleasure to serve you."

With a friendly smile, Hester passed through the door; Martha watched wistfully as she descended the curving stair, thinking how elegant her mistress looked in these grand surroundings. She hoped that she could justify her elevation to lady's maid, so that Miss Hester would take her with her when she married Lord Montfort as surely she must before long. They would make a handsome couple, and perhaps Martha would get an opportunity to meet that nice footman, Mr. Mark, again soon. Dreamily she closed the door and set about laying out her mistress's night apparel.

Meanwhile, Hester was hesitating on the first floor landing, having forgotten to enquire the whereabouts of Lady Marchant's drawing room. She was about to go back and ask Martha, when she saw Pringle mounting the stair, puffing heavily beneath the weight of a large tray. The butler perceived her at the same moment: he permitted his round, rather solemn face to widen into an ear-splitting smile, for he had known Hester since childhood.

"One second, Miss Vane, I will announce you to her ladyship."

Pringle set down the tray carefully on a small side table, revealing to Hester's astonished gaze an imposing array of small sandwiches and sweetmeats. Evidently her ladyship did not intend to starve while she awaited her niece and nephew's pleasure. Pringle crossed the hallway with stately, measured tread, Hester following in his ample wake.

"Hold on, Pringle old fellow, I'll join you directly," called a cheerful voice above their heads. A clatter of footsteps, muffled to a degree by the thick pile of the red stair-carpeting, heralded the approach of Sir Mortimer, resplendent in a coat of dark grey superfine, with knee breeches of a delicate fawn and a waistcoat of the same shade. Hester nodded at her brother approvingly, noting the crisp damp curls which bore mute evidence to the rigours of the journey; in every other respect his appearance was immaculate.

"Thank Heaven Cousin Tom's man was here to lend me a hand," whispered Mortimer in her ear, as Pringle opened the drawing room door, intoning loudly,

"Miss Vane and Sir Mortimer Vane, my lady."

"Come in, my dears, come in," trilled a familiar, welcoming voice. They entered a fairly large, high-ceilinged room, tastefully appointed with a carpet of grey Wilton, complemented by soft lavender furnishings. Here they found Lady Annabelle Marchant, reclining confortably on a day bed drawn close to the fire. She had been pursuing her favourite late afternoon occupations of devouring chocolates and Mrs. Radclyffe's latest novel in equal proportions. Her ladyship was far too indolent to rise, but she tossed aside her book and stretched out her plump, heavily-ringed hands to greet her sister's children. Hester found herself clasped to Lady Marchant's ample bosom when she bent to bestow an affectionate peck on her aunt's soft cheek; a strong scent of lemon verbena engulfed her. The younger lady stood up as hastily as circumstances would permit, to allow her brother to bow gallantly over the warm hand extended to him.

"Sit down, children, sit down and tell me everything," cried Lady Marchant, waving them to chairs on either side of her couch. Her large, brown eyes darted inquisitively from one to the other, taking in every detail of their appearance, as they seated themselves obediently. Hester hoped secretly that it would not be long before dinner was announced for she found the heat of the fire and the glow of the many candles almost overpowering. Pringle must have noticed her discomfort; he carefully placed a small, oval firescreen between her chair and the blaze. Hester smiled up at him gratefully, thanking him softly for the small service. Under her ladyship's fascinated eye, the portly butler beamed down at her niece.

"A pleasure, Miss."

Lady Marchant broke in impatiently,

"Well Pringle, where are the refreshments which I requested? See to them at once. Am I always to be neglected in my own house?"

The portly butler immediately assumed his accustomed impassive demeanor.

"I have them in the hall, my lady," he said expressionlessly. He withdrew at once; only his quivering calves betraying his indignation at his mistress's sharp words.

Lady Marchant rolled her eyes to the ceiling.

"Heaven preserve me, now I have hurt his feelings. He will be in the sulks for days! But it is too provoking to see him making sheep's eyes at you when he has not favoured me with even the glimmer of a smile since we left London. He abhors Brighton — some incident in his youth, I fancy," whispered her ladyship confidentially, as the elderly butler returned, a tall footman in tow. A formidable array of tidbits was set out for their delectation in silence, Pringle supervising with awesome dignity. When the doorman had been dismissed, the butler bowed primly.

"Will that be all, my lady?" he enquired stiffly.

Hester was obliged to suppress a giggle at her aunt's expression of dismay. Mortimer also restrained a chuckle; obviously the time had come to intervene.

"Dearest Aunt Annabelle, you must not blame Pringle for the tardiness of your refreshments. It was all my fault because I kept him gossiping when he brought me a splendid hot drink which has probably saved me from developing an inflammation of the lungs, for you must know that I was quite soaked when we arrived. I have not yet had an opportunity to tell you how much I appreciated his thoughtfulness."

Lady Marchant struggled with conflicting emotions, but her natural kindliness and real concern for the welfare of her dependents triumphed over baser feelings of pride. She looked up in some trepidation at the imposing personage who was gazing fixedly before him, apparently deaf to his surroundings.

"Pringle," she shrieked with a high-pitched croak. She paused and lowered her tone to its normal level, "Pringle, you heard Sir Mortimer's explanation, I trust. I am happy to know that you have attended so assiduously to the welfare of my guest. I think that we had best forget the whole incident, it has been a trying day, but you are wonderfully adept at making the household comfortable in new, perhaps rather cramped, quarters. His lordship shall learn of your good offices, Pringle."

Offended though he felt himself to be, the butler could not withstand her ladyship's clever blend of coaxing and flattery. He unbent sufficiently to say,

"So long as your ladyship understands my dilemma, I am content."

"Yes, well, that is splendid. You may go now, Pringle."

They held their breath for a long moment until the drawing room door was closed with the smallest possible click; then Mortimer and Hester could contain their pent-up mirth no longer. Her ladyship sighed plaintively as she waited for their merriment to subside.

"Have you no respect for me at all, you heartless children?" she scolded at last.

Hester dabbed her eyes.

"Of course, dear ma'am. But tell me, how did you get here so soon and does my cousin accompany you?" she asked hastily, as Mortimer threatened to go off in another paroxysm of gaiety. Her question introduced a welcome change of topic. Lady Marchant settled back comfortably among her cushions; she selected a minute sandwich, nibbling daintily, but steadily, while she talked.

"I have been feeling rather low and out of sorts recently," she commenced, "Your uncle Arthur has been much occupied with affairs in the House and London has been unusually thin of company, so many people have been sick with the influenza. In March I contracted a putrid sore throat and was confined within doors for several weeks. I had just begun to go about again when Mortimer visited us. The notion of removing to Brighton was not mine. Your uncle consulted my physician for he was concerned that I could not shake off my listlessness. He persuaded me that a change of scene would be beneficial and knowing that I cannot abide Bath, he suggested the sea. The journey is shorter and the company more lively; so we fixed upon Brighton. Thomas offered to accompany me, he has friends in the Prince's circle. Really my dears, I have been quite worried, for he and his father do not see matters in the same light politically and I was constantly obliged to intervene to prevent a foolish rift. They are so alike, stubborn beyond belief. When Thomas declared that the moment was ripe to introduce a Regency at dinner the other night — foolish beyond permission, he did not even wait until the port — I thought Arthur would have an apoplexy. You see long ago, when Arthur first came into the title he became passionately interested in two things, improvements in agriculture and the plight of the poor. His interests shifted to the diplomatic sphere with the rise of Napoleon Bonaparte, but prior to that he was almost wholly engaged with domestic affairs. As you know he was born and bred a Whig. In our poor King's better days he and 'Farmer George' passed many a happy hour discussing agricultural improvements which were designed not only to inprove techniques, but also to alleviate the miserable condition of the labourers and to save as many as possible from the fate of going to the cities to seek work in the new factories. Recently, my dear husband has recognized that the movements of the people cannot be reversed and we have become much involved in various charitable institutions in London. There is so much to be done and so much resistance to the efforts of well-meaning people that we have been obliged to restrict ourselves to the next generation. Arthur and I believe that education for the masses is the key to peaceful progress. As you may surmise this view is in advance of most people in our circle, whose apathy in the face of so much misery is equalled only by their fear of revolution if the populace is not kept firmly underheel. They have no notion that discontent breeds revolt and that it is much better to divert and occupy men's minds, to give despairing parents the hope of a brighter future for their children.

"Good Heavens, how I do run on with my favourite hobby horse. Forgive me my dears, this is not to give you a lecture, but all by way of explanation. To be brief, your uncle is a good friend of the King, but he is also a staunch supporter of Mr. Pitt and the present war is like to make Tories of both gentlemen. The present disordered state of our government dictates that rational men must at times forget their instinctive loyalties for the good of the country. When I left town it seemed virtually certain that Mr. Pitt must soon supplant Addington, but a new Pitt ministry will split the Whigs and I gather that many of Mr. Pitt's supporters in a new government will be men of Tory leanings. As you can imagine this is all very distressing to many of our acquaintance. Arthur could not leave town at this juncture, but he wished to know what is said in the Prince of Wales' circle and this is my real mission, although health is the ostensible reason for my being in Brighton. Now, I cannot get about as much as I would like, but I depend upon you both to bring me news; I charge you with this as a solemn duty which I am persuaded you will not shirk. Your Cousin Thomas has a blind devotion to the Prince of Wales. It is ever the way with young men to oppose their fathers, but unfortunately Tom does not have your uncle's political acumen and I fear his partiality to the Carlton House set may lead him into foolishness. I have tried to persuade Arthur to buy him a commission, but he is adamant that, as an only child, Thomas must remain in England and learn to care for his estates. This he has no interest in doing while his friends are all in regimentals. It is a situation which almost parallels the Prince's own, with similar consequences — both have become fashionable fribbles, idling away their time and fortune in extravagant pursuits for want of some rational and satisfying occupation. Loath though I am to admit it, my husband is also to blame for he will not delegate any of his many duties to his son. You, Mortimer, are mature beyond your years and I have noticed effect a pleasing restraint on Tom's excesses. Tom is a good boy, but misguided." Lady Marchant sighed deeply.

A short silence ensued, during which Mortimer and Hester glanced at one another uneasily. Mortimer spoke in defence of his cousin.

"Tom is a very determined fellow, ye know, Aunt Annabelle, but there's not an ounce of harm in him, and he is most sincerely attached to you and my uncle," he paused uncomfortably, for it was foreign to his character to speak easily of the deeper emotions. However, after a moment he continued gamely, "I'm very fond of you all myself; find it infinitely painful to distress you further, but ma'am, Tom's my friend and I share his enthusiasms. I couldn't possibly consent to spy on him and his acquaintance, not even for the good of the country. Why don't you let me post up to town? I'll seek my uncle and do my best to persuade him that Tom needs a spell under the colours, 'tis the only solution as far as I can see, my dear."

This earnest entreaty caused Lady Marchant to whisk out her lace handkerchief. She dabbed her eyes.

"I'm sorry, Mortimer, I see that I was wrong to try and involve you. I should have known how it would be. Heaven knows I have heard enough of men, their honour and loyalty of recent weeks. Enough to last me a lifetime. You would merely waste your time by calling on your uncle just now. We parted in some bitterness on this very subject. Our family will be split asunder by this quarrel. I declare I do not know which way to turn now that you have failed me!"

Mortimer stood up in acute embarrassment as his aunt dissolved into a prolonged fit of weeping. Hester patted her hand encouragingly until the outburst abated. Finally she said gently,

"Mortimer is right for once in his notions of honour, dear aunt. We simply cannot spy on our cousin and his friends. With regard to Tom's own future we must let matters take their course, it is not for us to interfere. Perhaps this situation is not so desperate as you believe. I have not seen Tom recently, but he was never a fool in my estimation — I should rather have said that he did not tolerate fools gladly than number him among them. I think you can trust him to make his own decisions, ma'am."

"Thank you, my fair cousin, you are quite correct in your assumption," remarked a smooth, faintly amused voice from the doorway. The three by the fireside spun round to see the Honourable Thomas Marchant, only son and heir to Lord Marchant, advancing upon them quizzing glass raised and a supercilious smile hovering about his lips.

Chapter 15
Sea Breezes

Lady Marchant was the first to recover. She raised her chin defiantly.

"Eavesdroppers never hear any good of themselves," she observed tartly. "I thought you were engaged for dinner this evening, Thomas?"

"I was, but I cried off in order to have the pleasure of greeting my cousins. I have already spoken to Pringle, so I trust there will be no difficulty at the table, mama," replied Thomas easily. He turned to Hester who was vexed to find herself blushing furiously.

"You do not stand in need of sea air to bring roses to your cheeks, cousin," he murmured wickedly as he kissed her lightly on the cheek. He and Mortimer exchanged a quick, firm handshake.

"I trust I am not *de trop*," he next enquired blandly, as he seated himself beside Hester, crossing his legs and disposing himself as comfortably as his tightly-fitting garments would allow. His roving gaze fell on the large basket of lemon rosebuds which graced the rosewood table in the centre of the room. "Whence comes the floral offering? Which of your admirers has abandoned the comforts of the Metropolis to brave the perils of this raffish resort for your sake, mama?"

Lady Marchant frowned reprovingly at her son. She wished fleetingly that he would not make constant gibes at the married state. Her own marriage had been an unusually happy one, but she feared that Thomas had no aptitude for domestic felicity. He had no patience with insipid society damsels, preferring to seek his pleasures among the expensive muslin company or with older married women. Although not precisely handsome, his tall, swarthy elegance and considerable fortune made him an eligible *parti* in the eyes of matchmaking mamas, but he went his own reckless way, scorning all attempts to ensnare him, and now, at six and twenty, found himself incredibly bored by fashionable society. The marks of dissipation, disappointment with life in general and boredom, combined with a certain hauteur of manner, gave the impression that he was much older than was in fact the case. Hester regarded her cousin with frank curiosity, for she found him much changed since their last meeting several years previously. She was surprised at the freedom which he had used in addressing her aunt, but her wandering thoughts were abruptly recalled by that lady's next words, accompanied as they were by a coy glance at Hester herself.

"You are mistaken, Thomas, in supposing that the charming roses are mine. They arrived this morning for your Cousin Hester. I believe the man said they were from Lord Montfort of Huntsgrove, but I have been sadly remiss with all my chatter, for I have quite forgot to give you the note until this moment, Hester my love. Pray excuse me." As she spoke, Lady Marchant sorted energetically through a small pile of cards and letters which lay on a silver tray at her feet. With a little crow of triumph she pounced on an imposing gilt-edged missive, bearing the crest of the sable dragon and addressed to Miss Hester Vane in a familiar black scrawl. Thomas rose to his considerable height with alacrity in order to pass the interesting communication to his cousin. She received it composedly and made to slip it in her reticule to be perused at a more convenient time; however her aunt cried that she must not stand on ceremony and bade her open it at once. Hester could not refuse to comply with such an injunction, so with a murmured word of apology she slit open the envelope.

Hugo had written:

"Please accept this small token of my regard and esteem. Have a care until we meet again, which shall be as soon as I can contrive it. Ever your devoted, Hugo Jermyn."

"Is it indeed from Montfort, Cousin? I had no notion he was a beau of yours," remarked Thomas teasingly. Hester blushed, momentarily at a loss and Lady Marchant made haste to intervene. Unlike her son, she well remembered Hester's London season and had long regretted that nothing had come of her efforts to encourage a match between her niece and Lord Montfort. In the turmoil following her brother-in-law's untimely demise, she had been unable to ascertain, amidst the general despondency, the degree of Hester's affection for her noble suitor, but she had later concluded that she must have overestimated their attachment. Her curiosity had been aroused when her niece's letter had informed her that Miss Stanhope was to reside at his lordship's house to chaperone his wards, but all else was conjecture and she was determined to tread delicately. Therefore, she observed casually,

"You should not leap to conclusions, Thomas. It is not kind to embarrass your cousin. You may recall that Shawcross is but a few miles distant from Huntsgrove and the families have long been acquainted. Hester's companion, Miss Jane Stanhope, is settled in North Steyne to chaperone the Montfort wards. It is only correct and civil that his lordship should send a small posy to thank Hester and welcome her at the end of her journey."

Thomas raised his quizzing glass to survey the large basket of flowers dubiously.

"If you say so, ma'am, though for myself I would not call that mass of blooms a small posy!" He eyed Hester speculatively, but refrained from further comment.

"Does Lord Montfort expect to join his wards in the near future, my dear?" next enquired Lady Marchant.

"Yes, no — I have no certain knowledge, aunt," exclaimed Hester struggling vainly to hide her confusion. Mortimer was puzzled by his sister's reticence until he recalled the mysterious circumstances surrounding their departure. He broke in to say cheerfully,

"Of course he will come soon. He was obliged to go to town for a few days, but he has lent me the most magnificent horse, Tom. You must see the beast. I only hope I may find one half as sweet a goer as 'Duke' when I come to purchase my own mount. I shall be glad of your advice in that matter, Tom, for I know you are an excellent judge of horseflesh."

The two gentlemen became immersed in technical discussion and Thomas mentioned a friend of his in the regiment with a horse which he was desirous of selling to pay some gambling debts. Hester was grateful to her brother for the diversion and, having recovered her composure, engaged her aunt in a comfortable gossip. Nothing loath, her ladyship cheerfully dissected the latest modes, speculated on the company that would be in Brighton for the season and made plans for their entertainment until dinner was announced. The evening passed uneventfully and they retired early to bed.

Hester entered the breakfast parlour rather later than her usual hour the next morning. She found the room empty, but an appetizing smell of coffee lingered in the air, suggesting that some members of the household were already astir. She rang the bell and ordered toast and fresh coffee.

"Has my aunt already breakfasted, Pringle?" she enquired doubtfully. Her knowledge of Lady Marchant's town habits had not led her to expect an early appearance by that lady.

"Oh no, Miss Hester," murmured Pringle, quite shocked at such a suggestion, "Her ladyship always keeps her room in the morning since her illness. Jervis, her maid, just took up her morning chocolate, and I'm commissioned to ask that you will visit milady in her dressing room when you have breakfasted, miss. 'Twas Mr. Thomas that went out, about half an hour ago."

Hester nodded her thanks and the butler withdrew. Left alone, she strolled idly over to the window; being on the ground floor her view of the sea was somewhat obstructed by solid, wrought iron railings, but she was encouraged, on looking up, to perceive that the sky was blue with scudding white clouds. The rain of yesterday had blown over and it was a fine spring day. Dreamily Hester began to weave the plot for her next novel; the new environment was stimulating, she would set it in Brighton. The hero should be a faithless soldier. Here she caught herself up short, realizing that the hero was taking on unusually positive features in her mind. She chided herself severely when this figment of her imagination was found to have eyes as green as the sea. It had always been her practice scrupulously to avoid using friends or acquaintances as characters in her novels and the mental lapse troubled her, even though Hugo no longer seemed faithless and could therefore bear little resemblance to the dashing, scarlet-coated, heartless gentleman she had visualised. Unbidden, in various guises, his lordship was intruding in her thoughts with monotonous regularity. She turned from the window and went to peer in the small looking glass, which hung above the fireplace. Her reflection gave her some satisfaction for her new lemon cambric, with its blue sash became her well. Her complexion was clear, her eyes large and luminous and her hair thick and shining.

"The sea air must agree with you, sis, you are in capital looks this morning," remarked a sleepy voice from the doorway. Hester laughed happily, meeting Mortimer's appraising glance in the mirror. She turned and seated herself at the table, her brother advancing languidly to take a chair opposite. Pringle reappeared bearing a large silver coffee pot, while a maid and footman set out a number of covered dishes on the sideboard.

"May I recommend the devilled kidneys, Sir Mortimer," said the butler in sepulchral tones. Mortimer eyed that worthy uneasily,

"Oh aye, if ye say so, Pringle. Bit blue devilled yerself? Smile man, do. The rain is over and gone, ye know."

"Yes, sir," said the man obediently, permitting his lips to turn up the merest hint at the corners. "It is indeed a fine day, but I fear I cannot appreciate it on account of milady's French chef, that Mounseer Andree 'ee calls hisself. He can't cook kippers, you understand, sir, he will poach them with a 'leetle light sauce'. Well, every self respectin' Englishman knows they should be biled and served with butter. I nigh choked myself on a bone and consequently don't feel quite the thing.

It's crooel 'ard for a man to smile when 'is throat be all lacerated with coughing and spluttering, hif you follow me, Sir Mortimer."

"Thanks for the warning, old fellow. I won't touch the kippers at any price," replied Mortimer solemnly. The butler bowed in acknowledgment and departed for the nether regions, much heartened at having had his revenge on his enemy.

"Mortimer what a terrible tease you are," exclaimed Hester, as soon as they were alone. "He looked so doleful I was quite worried." Mortimer grinned as he rose to inspect the breakfast dishes.

"Do you care for a coddled egg, Hester, or some ham and fried eggs? By Jupiter, these muffins look excellent. I think I shall essay the kidneys."

"Just a muffin for me, please, love. Shall I pour you some coffee?"

Mortimer nodded and a moment later returned to the table his plate piled high with a startling mixture of edibles.

"The sea air evidently has a beneficial effect on your appetite," observed Hester, shuddering delicately.

"You don't know what it's like dining in hall every morning. 'Tis enough to ruin one's digestion for life. Thank heaven Oxford is behind me," retorted her brother irrepressibly. Hester watched in reluctant admiration as the pile of food steadily diminished. She waited until she judged the inner man to be replete and then enquired casually,

"Did you have any plans for this morning, Tim? I thought that I might walk to call upon Stephanie and Marietta to see how they go on. Pringle informed me that Tom is already out, so I thought you might care to accompany me."

Mortimer met his sister's innocent enquiring gaze with a narrow, suspicious look. However, the possibility of again encountering the lively Stephanie was a sufficient bait. He responded cautiously,

"I've no objection, in fact I would welcome a stroll through the town, but don't be thinking I'll be forever squiring you on polite jaunts for I have other activities in mind."

"Of course, you must not imagine that I wish to be seen with only my brother for escort above three times a week at most. Good gracious, I have my own reputation to think of, to be always with you would be dull and tame beyond description and would doubtless give rise to unwelcome comment," pronounced Hester decidedly, more than a tinge of sarcasm in her tone.

Mortimer was unmoved.

"Thou art a shrew and no mistake, sister mine, but I am content if you understand that I do not intend to appear at Public Teas at the

Assembly Rooms on Sundays, nor to sully my ears by listening to screeching violins at private musical evenings — to mention only two of the traps which lay in wait for the unwary."

The vision which the mention of these two horrors conjured up was so unlikely that they both giggled.

"Never fear, I shall be sure find other companions for those occasions," gasped Hester, when her merriment subsided. "I shall go and get ready before you change your mind. I must speak with my aunt, but I shall not keep you waiting above a quarter of an hour."

With these words, she bestowed a light kiss on his brow and whisked out of the room, leaving Mortimer to enjoy his third cup of coffee in peace.

After a brief colloquy with Lady Marchant, in which it was decided that Hester should call at Thomas's Circulating Library to sign their names in the visitors' book in order to obtain invitations to the social life of the town, she ran to her room to make ready. She chose to wear her dark blue redingote with gold tabbed fastenings and a small cape with a high-standing collar. She tied the ribbons of her hat securely beneath her small, firm chin, slipped her large swansdown muff over her left arm and ran downstairs to join her brother, a glow of happy anticipation on her face.

They set out arm in arm in the direction of the Steyne. Hester exclaimed in delight at the freshness of the salty air, but informed her brother in no uncertain terms, that she had little desire to bathe on the pebbly beach in the early hours of the morning. Her remark was prompted by the sight of the bathing machines, with their bonnet-shaped modesty hoods which covered the steps to enable the hardy to descend into the sea unobserved by the other sex.

"Invigorating it may be," she declared, "But I am convinced that dipping in those chilly waves would do my health more harm than good. After all, I have the benefit of country air all the year. I see no necessity to take such extreme measures for I am not seeking to overcome the ill-effects of a dissipated town life. I must admit that I prefer a hot tub to a cold sea any day."

Mortimer could not quite agree with his sister.

"Pure rationalisation, m'dear, to justify your own inclinations. For myself I shall bathe tomorrow morning."

"Well, I would prefer that you do that rather than ogle the poor females through telescopes as many a 'gentleman' did last time I was here. One cannot appear to advantage in those hideous flannel smocks wallowing in an unfamiliar milieu. And one is supervised more severely than in the schoolroom by those dreadful women attendants."

Mortimer was compelled to acknowledge the force of these arguments. Hester had the last word as they reluctantly turned inland. The force of the wind dropped abruptly and they found that they were almost shouting at one another.

"If men and women had been meant to swim they would have been given tails," announced Hester at the top of her lungs, causing several heads to turn in their direction. She fell silent in confusion, but Mortimer only laughed. They strolled slowly across the grassy expanse of the Steyne. It was some time since they had visited the town and they noted with interest the changes and additions which had been made to the royal residence. The Pavilion was no longer a simple country house. It had become an outlandish fantasy, its facade constantly being changed and extended at the whim of its proud owner. They speculated idly on the possibility of an invitation to view the interior.

"Not sure you should accept even if you are invited, sis," observed Mortimer, as he frowned disapprovingly at yet another lapse in royal taste which had caught his eye, "Prinny has a roving eye for the ladies, though you're not quite large enough for his usual style." He surveyed her from his superior height with brotherly candour.

Hester laughed, saying teasingly,

"Tim, I had no notion you were such a prude. I vow you only need a quizzing glass like Cousin Thomas to throw me quite out of countenance. I admit I have a curiosity to see inside the Pavilion. I wonder if his lordship could procure an invitation for us. In the press of people I am sure I should go quite unremarked by his Highness, but should I go, I promise to take you for my escort and to behave with great circumspection. Does that satisfy you, sir?"

"Myself or Montfort. He would know how to ward off unwelcome advances. Good Lord, there's Mrs. Pennyfeather, friend of my aunt, met her in town, an unconscionable gossip. Knew it was a mistake to come." Mortimer tugged at his sister's arm, but before they could do more than take a few steps, Hester perceived a formidable, turbaned lady bearing down upon them like a ship in full sail, a trio of fair, pastel-garbed damsels at her heels.

"Sir Mortimer Vane, I declare," trumpeted the turbaned lady, her purple plumes nodding vigorously. Perforce the Vanes awaited their approach and Mortimer bowed over the black-mittened hand which was graciously extended to him. He begged to leave to present his sister to Mrs. Pennyfeather, the ladies curtsied politely and then the fair daughters were summoned with an imperious jerk of the head, which made Hester fear for the safety of the waving plumes.

"Miss Vane, pray allow me to introduce my daughters, Cleo, Hera and Philomene. Make your curtsies, my loves. You recall Sir Mortimer in town, of course. He is cousin to Mr. Thomas Marchant and was kind enough to stand up with you, Cleo, for the country dance at Lady Glenvale's ball."

Hester glimpsed a fleeting expression of anguish as Mortimer sought hastily to recall which of the three indistinguishable girls was Cleo. He was saved when the tallest of the three smiled coyly and fluttered her lashes at him, saying eagerly,

"Yes, of course, mama. It is nice to see you again, Sir Mortimer, do you stay long in Brighton?"

"My plans are somewhat uncertain, Miss Pennyfeather," responded that gentleman hastily, "But my sister is fixed with Lady Marchant for the season."

"In that case we shall call on her ladyship soon," announced Mrs. Pennyfeather augustly. "We must not detain you, but will hope to meet at the Castle Assembly on Monday. Good-day, Miss Vane, Sir Mortimer. Come girls, I see Count Benedict approaching with Lady Frome."

The redoubtable lady marched away, her daughters dutifully in tow. Cleo smiled over her shoulder at Mortimer in what she evidently intended to be a beguiling fashion. As soon as they were out of earshot, Mortimer emitted a long sigh of relief.

"Dreadful woman. She pursues one like nemesis with those three fates at her heels. No half-way eligible man is safe from their clutches."

"There's safety in numbers, my dear," murmured Hester soothingly, as she watched the now-distant Mrs. Pennyfeather swoop down on the hapless count.

"She's well-named. The whole family is in dun territory, not a feather to fly with and that eldest girl has already been on the market for three seasons, Tom told me."

"Thomas is not always very kind, I think, but I am surprised to hear you speak so harshly, Mortimer," frowned Hester, "No doubt the prospect of Mrs. Pennyfeather as a mama-in-law must be a considerable deterrent, but one should feel some compassion for those down-trodden girls. At least I can sit comfortably upon the shelf, with no apprehension that I shall be forced into an unwelcome marriage, but females in that situation with forceful mamas are often obliged to accept old and even repulsive suitors in order to escape from home and, if possible, to marry money. A lifetime of unhappiness is a high price to pay."

Hester spoke feelingly and Mortimer had the grace to look abashed; however he replied obstinately,

"There is much in what you say, but I assure you I ain't about to get trapped into matrimony with any designing female. Too much compassion can soon put the noose around one's neck." He ran his finger thoughtfully round the inside of his neckcloth. Hester's momentary anger gave way to amusement.

"Let us not quarrel, love. It is too fine a day. Should you object if we but glance in the shop windows? I promise you I do not intend to make any purchases today. I hope we do not meet many more of your acquaintances or we shall not have time to call at the Circulating Library and visit Jane and the girls before luncheon."

Still somewhat chastened, Mortimer made no objection. Accordingly, they promenaded at a sedate pace along the eastern side of the Steyne, surveying the bow-fronted windows of a number of small shops which offered all manner of fopperies to attract the fashionable visitors. The wares varied from china, lace, millinery, ribbons, muslins, chintz, cambricks and tea, but true to her promise Hester did not succumb to these enticements and they shortly arrived at the door of Thomas's Circulating Library. As they entered they found that even at this early hour the establishment was thronged with well-dressed people, since the library was used by persons of quality of both sexes as an informal club. Here, in addition to finding the latest books and periodicals, one could pass an idle hour exchanging gossip or writing letters. The Vanes attended to business at once and signed their names in the large visitor's book. Glancing casually at the previous page, Hester noticed a number of familiar names, including that of her cousin Thomas, who had also signed on behalf of his mother. Other visitors approached the table whereon reposed this invaluable social document and Hester moved aside to examine some sketching materials. While hesitating over her selection, she was startled to hear her name pronounced in eager tones. Half-turning she perceived two elegant ladies bending over the page of the visitors' book where she had written her name.

"Miss Hester Vane! See Alicia, oh I wonder if she is still here. I would so love to meet her. You remember last Christmas, John gave me *The Master of Crumbling Keep* and I lent it to you. It was the most diverting tale, did you not think? She must be a lady of powerful imagination and strong sensibility. If only I knew what she looks like!" The two ladies scanned the well-filled room closely. At length the lady addressed as Alicia replied, prosaically,

"Well, my dear Rebecca, since we have no notion what her appearance may be, I fear you are doomed to disappointment, at least for the present. In this crush we can hardly approach all the possible ladies. Perhaps it is as well, for pray consider, she may be some eccentric little old lady or a terrifying blue-stocking who overwhelms us with her penetrating intellect!"

Hester remained at the sketching table until the two ladies passed on, still animatedly discussing her book and possible character. She felt a shock of excitement to know that her fame had gone before her, for it was the first time she had received recognition as an authoress by persons unknown to her. After a few moments she went to join her brother, a mischievous smile transfiguring her countenance. Several gentlemen glanced with interest at the attractive lady as she slipped past the chattering groups with a murmured word of apology, but Hester remained oblivious to the attention which she provoked, her mind in a whirl and her eyes darting to and fro in quest of Mortimer. She found him in the card room, engaged in earnest conversation with a gentleman of sporting appearance, some twenty years old. On perceiving his sister at his elbow, Mortimer performed the necessary introduction with as much enthusiasm as his languid social manner would permit.

"'Low me to introduce Mr. Montagu Sprague, m'dear. Monty to his friends. We were up at Oxford together. Lady Sprague is a close friend of our aunt; families connected in some way. M' sister, Hester, writes novels, ye know, Monty," concluded Mortimer wickedly. A look of undeniable alarm overspread Mr. Sprague's round, cherubic visage as he absorbed this offhand information, but his years of training and good breeding stood him in good stead and he executed a surprisingly elegant bow before taking the hand which Hester graciously extended.

"I am happy to make your acquaintance, Mr. Sprague. Pay no heed to my tiresome brother, my scribbling is a family secret which I try never to discuss in company," said Hester kindly, correctly interpreting Mr. Sprague's expression as springing from a deep-rooted fear of clever females. A warm smile suffused the gentleman's pleasant brown eyes, it was irresistible and Hester found herself smiling back gaily.

"Can see you're a right 'un, ma'am. Tim was just trying to gammon me."

Monty Sprague rounded indignantly on his grinning friend. Mortimer stepped back throwing up a hand in mock dismay.

"No, no, old man, wouldn't dream of it. Couldn't resist letting the cat out of the bag and by Jove it was worth it just to see your face! But it ain't something to worry about. Hester don't go around prattling of it the whole time. Sensible female!"

"Mortimer, you are incorrigible," cried Hester, half-laughing, half-angry. "Let us talk of something else. Are you fixed long in town Mr. Sprague?"

It seemed that this was not altogether a welcome topic, for a cloud descended upon the youthful brow.

"As long as it takes, Miss Vane," he responded mysteriously. Hester was wondering if it would be tactful to enquire further when Mortimer intervened.

"It's his sister that's the problem, ain't it Monty? We were just talking of it before you came."

"Oh, if it is a private matter, please excuse me," said Hester quickly, preparing to depart.

"No, no, happy to tell you, if it won't bore you," protested Mr. Sprague. He peered over his shoulder to make sure they were not overheard, then lowering his voice to a confidential whisper, he continued, "M'sister, Agatha, nice girl, ye know, fond of her. Well, m'mother has a match for her, bit embarrassing, but Aggie will have none of it. Came post-haste down to Brighton in pursuit of him, m'mother that is, and Aggie begged I would come along to support her, so here I am."

Hester listened in amused puzzlement to his tale. As Mr. Sprague halted with the air of having told all, she began,

"I'm sure it is very splendid of you. Agatha is lucky indeed to have such a brother, but . . ."

"What Hester means, Monty, is give us a plain tale, without roundaboutation. Who is the proposed groom and what can you do to help?" interjected Mortimer impatiently.

Monty fiddled with his fob, adjusted his intricate cravat, surveyed his brilliantly striped waistcoat doubtfully, and finally enunciated, "Thought you knew. Your cousin Thomas, he made an offer, Aggie begged for time to consider, is in despair, says he don't love her, mama very put out, had gone to great lengths to bring the match about, down to the sea we all came, atmosphere very tense, devil of a coil, excuse me, Miss Vane, but there it is."

Hester smiled sympathetically at the agitated young man, then reached out impulsively to tap his arm,

"Your affection does you credit, Mr. Sprague. Perhaps we can help. Pray don't be uneasy, I don't wish to meddle, but tell me, does your sister love my cousin, or is there some other impediment?"

"Oh, she loves him, has done ever since she was in the schoolroom, but feels he is above her touch, discrepancy in wealth and all that. Don't want a marriage of convenience. Thomas is a very difficult man to know. Never showed her any great partiality. She believes he is merely fulfilling a family obligation."

Hester nodded, feeling that the parallel with her own youthful situation was remarkable. She suggested tentatively that perhaps Mr. Sprague would introduce her to his sister. The young man agreed eagerly and offered to bring her to call the next morning. Hester shook her head firmly,

"No, Monty, may I call you Monty?" Receiving a delighted affirmative, she went on, "Well, then, it behoves us to move cautiously, until we have ascertained the feelings of both parties, we cannot risk a chance encounter at my aunt's house. Let us meet here at noon."

It was arranged and the Vanes took their leave of Mr. Sprague at the library door. He walked off with a sprightly step, his dejected air quite vanished.

"I like Mr. Sprague very much," observed Hester as they set off briskly towards the North Steyne.

"So do I, but don't think we should get involved in this affair," replied Mortimer disapprovingly, "Thomas is quite capable of managing his own love life."

"I wonder. I do not recall any hint from Aunt Annabelle, surely she must be aware that he has made an offer to Agatha Sprague. Yet if not, it would be a hopeful sign. Perhaps his affections are engaged and he is not seeking Miss Sprague's hand to oblige his parents."

"Tom is very independent. He goes his own road for his own reasons. Aggie Sprague isn't at all in his usual style, though she's a taking little thing. Can't see him falling for her, best keep out of it, sis," counselled Mortimer, with unwonted sternness.

Hester, glancing askance at his wooden countenance, decided not to press the matter further for the moment. Instead she recounted the conversation she had overheard between the ladies in the library and they were soon laughing together as they thought of her two admirers trying to deduce her character from her novel.

It was nearly noon when they arrived at Lord Montfort's villa. They were admitted without delay and found the two young ladies but just returned with Miss Stanhope from a perambulation upon the Steyne. They all sat down, speculating as to how they could have missed one another in such a small space and professing themselves much delighted by the fresh sea air and interesting company which Brighton offered. Mr. Abercromby's absence was explained. It appeared that he had not stayed the night, but had halted merely to see the ladies safely ensconced before posting up to London on a matter of business. He had promised to return with Lord Montfort and with that they had to be content.

The girls chatted on; Stephanie was in particularly lively spirits, stimulated no doubt by Mortimer's undisguised admiration. He listened, without restlessness, to her raptures over the charming, 'chic' little shops, Marietta, in her restrained way, was also very happy to recount her morning's impressions. They had ventured into the Circulating Library where Miss Stanhope had entered their names in the book. Marietta did hope that the Master of Ceremonies would find time to call before Monday, so that they could attend the Castle Assembly ball. Stephanie announced that in spite of Miss Jane's sniffs she had purchased some raffle tickets and dear Hester's novel. With a mischievous grin at her preceptress, she ran to her chamber to fetch the volume and requested Hester to autograph it for her, for she declared she had heard several people speaking of it and she wished to boast of her friendship with a real authoress. Hester began to feel uneasy and was relieved when Miss Stanhope stated firmly that Miss Stephanie would do no such thing. Stephanie pouted, but promised to remain silent on the subject of Hester's writings unless directly questioned, when it was pointed out to her that she would otherwise cause her friend considerable pain and embarrassment.

Stephanie brightened a moment later, declaring,

"Of course, dear ma'am, it shall be as you wish, but I do not think it will be long, because once everyone knows that Hester is here, they will all be talking of her and desiring introductions. The gentleman who packaged the book for me, told me that they are ordering more copies, the demand is so great."

Hester arose in some agitation, saying that they must leave. She found that her spirits were quite disordered by Stephanie's artless chatter. She had been totally unprepared for the possibility of so much recognition outside her own circle and felt that she needed some time in private to compose herself and come to terms with her reputation. She was grateful when Miss Stanhope ordered the Montfort carriage to convey them back to Lady Marchant's house. Mortimer considerately discoursed soothingly on unimportant subjects until they reached home and Hester was able to flee to the sanctum of her chamber.

Chapter 16
The Castle Ball

Hester found much to occupy her thoughts during the next few days. Aside from her own problems of how to deal with her unexpected popularity and the anticipated arrival of Lord Montfort, there was also the enigma of her cousin Thomas. Her aunt's confidences concerning her son's behaviour and character, combined with Hester's own, admittedly limited, impressions of her cousin were not easily reconciled with the rôle of ardent suitor for the hand of Agatha Sprague. However, Hester dearly loved a mystery and could not resist an attempt to unravel the puzzle. She took the first step on Saturday morning, the day appointed for her meeting with Miss Sprague. Her brother stood firm in his resolve not to meddle in Tom's affairs, either emotional or political. Instead he rode out with his cousin soon after breakfast. The gentleman intended a gallop upon the downs, so that Mortimer could demonstrate Duke's paces, to be followed by a visit to the military camp, where Tom had a number of cronies.

Hester remained at home with her aunt and received several callers, for news of their arrival had leaked out. The ubiquitous Mrs. Pennyfeather was among the first to arrive, accompanied by her eldest daughter, Cleo. The two ladies barely concealed their chagrin, on finding that the two gentlemen of the household were not present, but were somewhat consoled when the imposing Mr. Wade, Master of Ceremonies for the '*ton*', made his appearance and issued invitations to Lady Marchant and her guests for various social functions. Having received assurances that Lady Marchant and the Vanes would certainly attend the Castle Assembly on Monday evening, Mrs. Pennyfeather and her daughter departed, leaving Lady Marchant to chat comfortably with Mr. Wade about various friends and acquaintances who were currently in Brighton, drawn hither by the presence of the Prince of Wales. Mr. Wade was an elderly man, of distinguished appearance. He had held undisputed sway as social arbiter in the fashionable town for many years and was held in considerable respect, although it was rumoured among the younger set that his influence had begun to decline. He and Lady Marchant were old friends and Hester listened with interest to their flow of reminiscence, until a glance at the gold ormolu timepiece reminded her that it wanted but a quarter of an hour to noon. She excused herself to her aunt, who dismissed her with a vague nod. Mr. Wade bowed politely and she left them immersed in a sweeping denunciation of the manners and morals of the younger generation, which they would evidently enjoy a great deal more without her inhibiting presence.

It was exactly noon when Hester, accompanied by a breathless Martha, arrived once more at Thomas's Library. Mr. Sprague and his sister were equally punctual and they met upon the steps. Hester immediately dismissed her maid, sending her on an errand to deliver a dinner invitation to Miss Stanhope and her charges. Martha trotted off happily, hoping for an opportunity to renew her acquaintance with Lord Montfort's second footman. She promised faithfully not to linger in too many shops on the way and to return within the hour. The necessary introduction having been made, Hester then accompanied her new friends through the bookshop and cardroom. Mr. Sprague found seats for the ladies on a secluded sofa near the window. After a few minutes of polite conversation, Miss Sprague adjured her brother to go and gossip with his sporting friends who were gathered in the cardroom, so that she and Miss Vane could converse in peace. Hester was a little surprised at this abrupt dismissal, though Mr. Sprague acquiesced with easy good nature, bowing and excusing himself to Miss Vane before wandering off in the direction of a noisy, cheerful group of young men whose shouts of laughter redoubled when he joined them.

Hester cast an appraising glance at her companion, noting the modish pelisse and bonnet, the tall, but slender figure and well-cut, regular features. Agatha Sprague was elegant, rather than pretty, possessing an indefinable air of maturity and poise which belied her youthful appearance. Hester guessed that she must be several years her brother's senior. Miss Sprague returned Hester's look frankly, her deep blue eyes sparkling with amusement.

"Monty is a dear, but sometimes his delicacy and excessive propriety get in the way of real conversation," she explained, "I hope you don't mind my sending him away, Miss Vane, but I do so wish that you and I may be friends. You must not think that I am always so impulsive, but I have heard a great deal about you from Monty and from your brother when we met in London. Sir Mortimer is very proud of you, though I must confess that he gave me quite a false impression when he described you as a lady novelist living in seclusion in the country. Your brother told me of it during a dance at Almacks, but Monty did not know that you were a writer until he met you yesterday; he was quite overcome, for he has a horror of what he calls 'the blue-stocking brigade'. My mother's salon was famous when we were children and we were often summoned to give an account of ourselves before earnest ladies who squinted or sallow gentlemen in dishevelled attire who spoke with foreign accents. My mother believed in mixing the sexes at her gatherings, following the fashion set by Lady Elizabeth Montfort. Monty conceived a dislike of intellectuals which he has never been able to outgrow. I might add that I did not share my brother's feelings, on the contrary, being fortunately possessed of a ready tongue, I was much petted and rather enjoyed being the centre of attention. I had an indulgent upbringing, my parents were kind and did not relegate me to the schoolroom once I was of an age to converse sensibly, so you see Miss Vane, I grew up rather fast and was quite at ease in adult society long before my come-out. That was how I came to know Thomas when I was fifteen. I believe Monty told you of my dilemma. Do forgive my burdening you with all this on our first meeting, but I have a feeling that you are a kindred spirit and I am much in need of a confidante."

Miss Sprague paused to take a deep breath, and smiled wistfully at Hester. For a moment there was silence, then Hester said, with an easy laugh,

"Dear Miss Sprague, I am honoured by your proffered friendship and delighted to be your confidante, but I should warn you I am an incorrigible matchmaker. It is one of the chief reasons why I write novels for, on paper at least, I can always be certain of achieving a happy ending. Now, tell me, in what way may I be of service to you? I understand that my cousin has made you an offer and that your parents favour the match: wherein lies the difficulty?"

Agatha Sprague's expressive dark eyes clouded and one large tear rolled down her cheek and fell unheeded to her lap. She looked suddenly much younger and very vulnerable. Hester's sympathetic heart was wrenched by the misery in her new friend's face. She waited patiently for Agatha to regain her composure. At length the younger lady managed a watery smile.

"I beg your pardon, Miss Vane, you must think me very foolish. I assure you I do not often succumb to such displays of emotion, but I have been under considerable pressure recently."

Hester nodded understandingly and moved a little on the sofa to shield her companion from the gaze of the curious.

"Do call me Hester if you will. I already exchange Christian names with your brother and it makes things so much more comfortable if one is not set at a distance by formality." Agatha nodded eagerly in agreement. Hester continued, "Let me say at once that I am somewhat at a loss to comprehend your predicament. Can you not return my cousin's regard?"

"That is not the problem," Agatha replied hesitantly. "I have loved him always. But, although I have been out for several seasons and received two quite eligible offers, I am convinced that Thomas still looks on me as a little sister. He teases me, admonishes me quite severely on my behaviour upon occasion, dances with me regularly, but in no way singles me out beyond the bounds required by civility to an old family friend. In short, my dear Hester, his manner is perfectly proper, but hardly *loverlike*!"

"I see. So you had no inkling that he would make you a declaration?"

"That is the whole point," cried poor Agatha despairingly. "He has not done so, at least not to me. Very correctly, he approached my papa and requested his permission to pay his addresses, but only the previous week I had seen him in the Park with a notorious high-flyer, the Comtesse de Chérault. Perhaps you have heard of her? She is an émigrée, supposedly of good birth, but her background is mysterious. She is received everywhere. I cannot and will not compete for his affections with such a woman." Agatha's lips were set mutinously and Hester wondered uneasily if the match were not doomed before it had well begun.

"Perhaps," she suggested tentatively, "Do you think it possible that you might have mistaken the relationship between Thomas and this shadowy lady? I have not moved in London society for some time and am not *au fait* with the latest *on dits*, but it occurs to me that many gentlemen pay court to such ladies to be in the fashion. Frequently it does not mean a thing. Tell me about the Comtesse. How long has she been in society? Is she beautiful?"

"You will soon be able to judge for yourself, for I believe she is in Brighton," muttered Agatha sullenly. Then she shook her head and to Hester's relief her mischievous smile peeped out. "Oh my friend, pray excuse me for being so disagreeable. A jealous female is quite the most spiteful of creatures. Do advise me. My parents are eager for the match and my mother almost literally dragged me to Brighton in Thomas's wake. I dread meeting him, for I cannot believe that his affections are seriously engaged. He masks his true feelings so well, his countenance is so inscrutable, that I am truly at a disadvantage."

Hester rubbed her nose pensively, her gaze resting meditatively on

Agatha's drooping form.

"This will not do, my dear, you will mope yourself into a decline. You must fight back. There is only one way to ascertain Thomas's feelings and that is to test him a little. In other words you must make him jealous. No, do not protest, if he does not rise to the bait at least you will know what answer to give. You must fend off the declaration for a while. Do not be alone with him. I may give you one small piece of encouragement. I have reason to believe that my aunt does not know of Thomas's approach to your father. To her mind he shows no indication of wishing to settle down and establish himself. Surely this must mean that he knows his own mind and is not merely fulfilling family expectations, obligations or what you will."

"It may be so," replied Agatha doubtfully, a small gleam of hope brightening her eye. She straightened her shoulders. "I do thank you. Will Thomas be at the Castle Ball on Monday?"

"Yes, I am almost certain that he intends to accompany us. Now behave to him as always, be friendly, but a little distracted. There is no need to have just one beau, several would probably be safer. Do you know of any likely candidates in Brighton, the sort who enjoy indulging in a mild flirtation? Mortimer would do very well, so long as he doesn't suspect a plot."

The prospect of action had brightened Agatha's spirits immeasurably. She looked a different girl from the forlorn creature of ten minutes ago. They saw Monty wending his way towards them through the press of people. The two ladies had been so absorbed that they had failed to notice how crowded the rooms had become.

"Leave it to me," Agatha whispered in Hester's ear. They rose as Monty reached their secluded corner. They shook hands.

"Adieu, my dear Hester, we shall meet on Monday. My thanks for a most stimulating conversation." Agatha was once more her cool, elegant self. They parted, Agatha with Monty in tow.

The remainder of the weekend afforded Hester no opportunity to divine her cousin's intentions. She was much occupied in attendance on her aunt whom she accompanied to church on Sunday morning. In the early evening Lady Marchant and her niece promenaded in the Assembly Rooms and partook sparingly of the Public Tea. Mortimer and Thomas had dutifully attended Morning Service, but declined resolutely to visit the Assembly Rooms for such a tame gathering, preferring a brisk walk by the sea, followed by a dinner party given by that rising star of the Tenth Light Dragoons, Mr. George Brummell. Hester noted Mortimer's military preoccupation with concern, but also with resignation. It was evidently something which had to be endured. She could only hope that a close exposure to life in the Brighton camp would give him a distaste for any form of military enterprise. She did not have much time to brood, for the Assembly Rooms were unexpectedly crowded. It was a dull, grey day, with a keen wind, the weather being more appropriate for March than for May, and many people seemed to have decided that fresh faces and conversation were just what they needed to raise their flagging spirits. Accordingly, Lady Marchant found herself greeted by a number of friends to whom she naturally introduced her niece. In no time word circulated that her ladyship was accompanied by the lady novelist whose latest volume was on everyone's lips and coffee tables. A new face was always welcome in the narrow, exclusive world of the *Ton* and there were few who remembered Hester's undistinguished London season, though many gallant gentlemen wracked their brains to recall a possible meeting place. Of course, hardly any of these gentlemen had read one line of Miss Vane's works, but possibly one or two had done so, and she was informed on good authority (by no less a person than the Prince of Wales's beloved Mrs. Fitzherbert) that His Royal Highness had a copy of *The Master of Crumbling Keep* beside him at this very moment and that he was enthusiastic in its praise. Hester wondered how she knew, for it was rumoured everywhere that the long-standing love affair was at an end, but she conceived an instant liking for the dumpy, yet commanding litte figure who seemed too sane and sensible to have ensnared the erratic Prince, and they passed a pleasant ten minutes in conversation, several ardent gentlemen listening respectfully to their literary discussion, before their talk was interrupted by the tinkling of the bell which summoned everyone to the tea tables. Hester found herself seated beside a very young gentleman with a high, stiff neckcloth who was obviously much in awe of her. After a few trifling attempts at polite discourse, which met with strangled, inarticulate replies (whether caused by the neckcloth or her forbidding reputation she could not decide), Hester, in common humanity, desisted from her efforts and relapsed into silence, while the young man devoted himself to an astonishing number of cucumber sandwiches, until she began to fear for his digestion. On glancing around discreetly, Hester was pleased to see an animated Agatha Sprague doing her best to converse with three eager and handsome young men at the same time. When the ritual of tea was completed at last, Hester seized the opportunity to have a quiet word with her friend as they donned their pelisses and wraps.

"I have made excellent progress, I am already engaged for the first five dances and the supper dance tomorrow night," reported Agatha in a whisper, smiling mischievously. "I only hope mama does not eat me, she has been watching my antics disapprovingly for the past hour, but fortunately she was seated too far away to overhear my conversation. I am in danger of becoming a shockingly fast female."

Before she could say more, a tall, elegant lady, well-muffled in furs, bore down upon them. Agatha's expression sobered instantly, assuming its normal mask of detached indifference. The elder lady was an exact replica of Hester's friend apart from the greying hair at the temples and the network of lines about the eyes and mouth. Hester did not require Agatha's formal introduction to realize that she was in the presence of Lady Sprague.

"My dear Miss Vane, I am delighted to make your acquaintance at last. I have heard so much of you from your charming brother and from my great friend, Annabelle Marchant. I understand that you are staying with her?" Her ladyship extended her hand graciously for a moment, before tucking it snugly back inside her enormous sable muff. The large echoing hallway was too draughty for a prolonged conversation and the ladies soon parted to seek their respective carriages. As she hesitated, wondering where her aunt might be, Hester caught Lady Sprague's clear, carrying tones remarking to her daughter,

"'Twas most odd, I could swear Lady Marchant had no notion that Thomas had offered for you. I did not like to mention it directly, although I hinted several times. And while I am on the subject, Agatha, I feel obliged to point out that your behaviour this evening was hardly in keeping with that of a young lady who is spoken for."

"But mama, I am not betrothed to Thomas yet. Pray lower your voice, everyone will hear us," cried Agatha urgently. The Spragues' carriage was announced and Hester heard no more. Lady Marchant chatted happily on the way home. She praised Agatha as a pretty, unaffected girl and hoped that her head would not be turned by too much adulation, but she gave no indication of having a personal interest in the matter. Hester was puzzled and began to view the ball on the morrow with some trepidation.

The problem preyed on her mind intermittently for the next twenty-four hours, and as she made her toilette on Monday evening she suddenly nodded resolutely at her reflection in the looking glass. By hook or by crook, she decided, she must take the bull by the horns and contrive to speak privately with Cousin Tom. The necessary seclusion was not easily achieved, for although Thomas solicited her hand early in the evening for a country dance, the intricate figures offered little opportunity for anything but the most casual conversation. Hester schooled herself to be patient and sought distraction, in the intervals afforded by the movements of the dance, by glancing about her. She marvelled at the change wrought in the Assembly Rooms' appearance. The difference in the attire of the company, the number of candles, and the activity upon which the guests were engaged made the spacious, elegant chambers appear a fairyland, compared with the rather sombre atmosphere of the Sunday Public Tea. Hester loved to dance, and she waited, her foot tapping gaily, for her turn to move down the long line of dancers, Thomas at her side. There were four main rooms at the Castle, the principal ones being the ball-room and a card-room. The ballroom was a double cube in its proportions, with a high ceiling. It was about eighty feet long, with recesses at the ends and a row of columns on one side. The walls were decorated with delicate plaster reliefs and the whole effect was exceedingly agreeable. It formed a tasteful background to enhance the rainbow colours of the ladies' silks and muslins and the darker hues of the gentlemen's formal evening wear. Hester gave a sigh of pure pleasure as Thomas returned her to her aunt's side at the conclusion of the dance. It was so long since she had been to a real ball with good musicians and she had not realized how much she had missed it.

"You look radiant tonight, cousin," said Thomas thoughtfully, his dark eyes resting on her flushed cheeks and parted lips.

"She does indeed," confirmed Lady Marchant complacently from her chair on Hester's left. "Pale green is very becoming on you, my love. I was right to have Jervis dress your hair in a high knot. The prevailing mode for tight little curls would not suit you at all. I sometimes think Jervis must be a witch, she certainly has magic in her fingertips. I wish you had consented to borrow my emeralds."

"No mama, that simple chain is perfect," interrupted Thomas authoritatively. He raised his quizzing glass, "Ah, I see Miss Stanhope and her charges approaching. Delightful young ladies! I encountered them on the Steyne this morning. But I fear they are already bespoke, Mortimer is before me. Who is the gentleman behind them? Good Lord, can it be Montfort? I understood he was in Town."

Thomas was standing, and his superior height gave him the advantage. Hester remained seated by a firm effort of will, her hands tightly clasped. Outwardly at least she was quite calm and collected, if a trifle pale, when the Montfort contingent arrived at their column. She rose and curtsied, was dimly aware of greetings being exchanged. The musicians struck up a waltz and suddenly she found Hugo bowing before her, requesting the pleasure of the dance. In a daze, she rested her hand lightly on his arm and allowed him to lead her on to the floor. She felt his arm circle her waist; for a moment the room receded and his green eyes swam before her. She stared fixedly at the top button of his white waistcoat. His gloved hand tightened on hers.

"Well, Miss Vane, have you no word for me? Thomas Marchant was regarding you with a very proprietary air. Is there, by any chance, an understanding between you?"

This was not the opening conversational gambit she had expected. Astonishment took her breath away. She realized with a shock that he was actually jealous. The knowledge steadied her. She intended to take her time about replying, but when she glanced up the anguished expression in his eyes caught her heart. Gently she wriggled her crushed fingers and his clasp immediately relaxed to become light and impersonal. She murmured playfully, in tones that she hardly recognised as her own,

"My lord, do stop making a cake of yourself, as Mortimer would say. Thomas is my cousin and I have known him since I was born. He has every right to regard me with a 'proprietary air' if he wishes, but you. sir, do not. To further disabuse you of any unjust suspicions which you may be harbouring, I will tell you in confidence that he has recently made an offer for the hand of my friend, Agatha Sprague. Now, my lord, do not mar your countenance with that fierce frown, or you will frighten all my beaux and I shall be a wall-flower for the rest of the evening. Tell me, instead, why we have not received word of your arrival. We did not expect you until the end of the week."

Hugo listened intently to this speech, his piercing eyes fixed on Hester's face. Perversely, she refused to meet his gaze. They swirled dizzily and finally came to a halt at the end of the long columns beneath a large frieze depicting 'Dawn'. Hester pretended to study the painting, her breath coming rather fast. Hugo drew her into the shadow of the fluted column and gave her shoulders a little shake.

"You can stop my-lording me, my girl, or I — I shall kiss you right here in the Castle Ballroom," Hugo declared grimly. Hester gave a small gasp compounded of dismay and amusement; her hand flew to her mouth, the delicate ivory fan swaying precariously on her wrist. Hugo seized the small hand and implanted a kiss on the palm.

"Take that to be going on with," he commanded. "Now, you look flushed, allow me to procure you a glass of orgeat. Sit here, I will return directly." The dance was not yet over, but Lord Montfort threaded his way through the swaying couples and reappeared with the necessary beverage in a miraculously short time. He swept up his coat tails and seated himself beside Hester, his habitually saturnine expression transfigured by a broad grin.

"You must be the devil himself to pass unscathed through such a press," remarked Hester lightly, as she sipped the welcome liquid. She was experiencing a heady sensation of happiness. For the moment it was enough to sit by Hugo's side and let him take charge of the situation. Even when confined by evening dress, he looked immensely capable.

"Did you receive my flowers?" he enquired abruptly.

"Yes indeed, I must thank you for them. They were quite beautiful," returned Hester warmly. They sat in companionable silence, Hester marvelling at how astonishingly at ease she felt after her earlier discomposure. It was a moment of tranquillity which was to linger long in both their memories. At length, stirred by the possibility of interruption, she felt obliged to ask,

"Was your mission in London successfully accomplished? Have you had news from Shawcross?"

Hugo's dark brows drew together and Hester felt a twinge of apprehension.

"The London end of the affair was no problem, and I have set certain influential wheels in motion," he replied softly, his lips twisted in a rueful smile. "However, I found a letter awaiting me here from Andrew Minton. The situation in the country has developed more quickly than I had foreseen. That rogue Garth is up to some trickery. Susan Garth has disappeared and Jedediah Stone is beside himself with anxiety. Minton fears he may resort to desperate measures."

"Oh, poor Susan, where can she be?" exclaimed Hester, in dismay, all her peace shattered by this revelation. She felt guilty that in the enjoyment of new impressions and surroundings she had almost forgotten the dark deeds which had been the cause of their removal from Shawcross. The gay ballroom faded and in her mind's eye Stephen Garth's menacing face appeared to threaten her with disconcerting vividness. She felt a strong premonition of danger; although not normally a timid female who jumped at shadows, she found that she was trembling uncontrollably. His lordship regarded her with deep concern, but he only said in even tones,

"I was hoping that you might advise me on Miss Garth's possible whereabouts. In fact I thought that if she had run away and not been locked up, she would have come to you immediately."

She snatched at this straw.

"Yes, I think she would come here, but she might have come by devious routes. Did Dr. Minton mention the day of her disappearance?"

Hugo frowned in an effort of memory.

"No-o, I believe not, but I gather that he wrote as soon as he heard of the occurrence. His letter was dated last Saturday."

They were recalled unwillingly to a consciousness of their surroundings by a general bustle as the waltz ended.

"I must take you back to your aunt. Let me know at once if you receive word of Miss Garth."

As they promenaded sedately down the length of the ballroom Hester confided suddenly,

"I cannot understand myself. I am not usually such a widgeon, but I must confess that the mere thought of Stephen Garth sends shivers down my spine."

Hugo glanced down at her, but could see nothing beyond the thick brown hair threaded with silver ribbon. A feeling of protectiveness almost overwhelmed him but he forced himself to respond lightly,

"Indeed, I am quite envious of Mr. Garth. It is my ambition to create a similar sensation, though perhaps for different reasons."

At once the queenly head lifted; Hester surveyed him with marked indignation.

"I did not expect you to jest upon such a subject," she declared reproachfully. Satisfied that he had achieved his object by distracting her, Hugo was about to make a teasing reply, when his eye was caught by some person across the room. His brow grew thunderous.

"What the devil is she doing here?" he demanded wrathfully. Puzzled, Hester followed the direction of his gaze. The floor was temporarily clear of dancers and she had no difficulty in discerning at once the lady to whom he referred, although she did not recognize her. She saw a woman past her first youth though still of great beauty, with pinched aristocratic features and enormous, tragic dark eyes. Her extreme pallor was accentuated by her jet black hair, and she wore a flimsy, low-cut gown of a rich gold, long black mittens and a glittering black and gold necklace. Hester could sense the magnetism of her personality even at a distance and it was obvious that many others shared her feeling. Gentlemen of all ages were vying with one another to pay court to her, as she sat regally enthroned on a small, high-backed gilt chair. The lady sat still as a statue, apparently lost in meditation. The thought flashed through Hester's mind that it was like the beginning of a play, with everyone waiting for the curtain to go up.

Even as she watched the lady moved, flirted her fan, dropped her handkerchief and bestowed a smile of peculiar charm upon the fortunate gentleman who retrieved it. The gentleman, she noted without surprise, was Cousin Thomas.

Hugo stood as if rooted to the spot.

"Who is she?" whispered Hester urgently.

"Thérèse Marvin, Comtesse de Chérault," replied Montfort grimly.

Chapter 17
La Comtesse De Chérault

At that moment, alerted perhaps by the intensity of Montfort's regard, the Comtesse looked directly into Hugo's eyes. Forgotten in the wings, Hester watched expectantly. Clearly some unspoken signal passed between them. The lady's hand faltered at her bosom for a second, then she lifted it in a gracious gesture of greeting; her eyes sparkled mischievously as she beckoned Hugo imperatively to her side, patting the seat beside her invitingly. The Comtesse was apparently impervious to the bevy of gentlemen thronging about her. His lordship inclined his head stiffly, then turned to Hester in time to catch a flash of anger in her frank grey eyes. He smiled down at her in the special way which he reserved only for her and she was obliged to suppress the temptation to pinch him or tread on his toe. Absorbed in one another, they quite failed to notice the stricken look on the Comtesse's expressive features, but others had seen and tongues were already wagging as his lordship returned Hester to her aunt's side.

"Do not bite me," he murmured as he bent over her hand. Aloud he thanked her for the dance, then departed in the direction of the card room, stopping to exchange a few words with Mortimer and Stephanie on his way. Hester would have been glad of a few moments of peace to collect her racing thoughts, but she was allowed no such luxury. Her hand was claimed for the next set by one of the gentlemen whom she had met at the Sunday Tea and she was obliged to concentrate on the demands of polite conversation. It was with relief that she stood up with Monty Sprague for the supper dance, which happened to be a waltz once again. Monty was an excellent dancer guiding her lightly, but firmly. She felt quite at ease with him. They chatted cheerfully of inconsequential subjects for several minutes and Hester was caught off her guard when Monty observed casually,

"I'm a lucky fellow to have secured your hand for this dance, Hester. Had a notion Montfort might be taking you in to supper, but I see the Comtesse waylaid him. Dangerous female that, breaks hearts as easily as our cook breaks eggs. Ruined many a good man's peace of mind, quite unscrupulous too, no thought for repercussions, so long as she can make another conquest. Ought not to be talking of it, but fear she may have your cousin in her toils. Agatha's been on tenterhooks all evening, though she's done her best to hide it, poor soul, by languishing after your brother. Only safe place for a woman like the Comtesse is a nunnery. Surprised to see she has her claws in Montfort though, thought he would have had more sense," he concluded bitterly.

With an effort, Hester managed to reply with an air of detached interest,

"At least you do not appear to have succumbed to her charms, Monty. She is a remarkably beautiful woman. Are you sure you are not being unfair? She cannot help attracting attention, but it may not be what she desires. Is there no one whom she prefers above the others? It must be very hard to be the object of so much admiration. I know nothing of her, indeed I never set eyes on her until this evening. Tell me, is she widowed? Has she been in England for long?"

Monty looked down at Hester, his kind face assuming an unwontedly stern cast.

"Shouldn't be saying these things to you, especially at a ball," he muttered uncomfortably, "But it's right you should know and be on your guard. I was desperately, foolishly in love with Thérèse myself for a while, and she used me to get an introduction into several houses where she would not normally have been received, including that of your aunt, Lady Marchant. She then threw me over in favour of your cousin Thomas. She uses everybody quite ruthlessly. Her past is shrouded in some mystery. It appears she was married at an early age to the Comte de Chérault, a man old enough to be her grandfather. Her birth is obscure, but when the Comte died, not long after they were married, she was left a woman of enormous wealth. She moved to Paris and became influential in her own right, during the late eighties. She saved herself during the Terror by becoming the mistress of several important men in turn, but with the advent of Napoleon the situation changed. She played her cards badly and her intrigues made her vulnerable. She fled to Switzerland, then Italy, but could not settle. She arrived eventually in Naples, fell deeply into debt and to escape her creditors, stowed away on one of the ships of the Mediterranean squadron. She must have been well-informed because she chose a ship which was ordered back to England with dispatches and she appeared on the London scene about a year ago, since which time she has created havoc in many a happy household. She was not well received at first, but rumours of her undeniable beauty and intelligence and her refusal to be cast down by hardship and suffering, came to the ears of the Prince of Wales, who always pities the lot of the French émigrés, and she was adopted by the Carlton House set. She seems to have money enough now, though where it comes from, I would not care to hazard a guess."

The music ended with Monty's narration. Hester had listened in fascination and the tale held her in thrall as they walked slowly through to the supper room, where light refreshments awaited them.

"You seem to know a great deal about her? Are you sure your information is accurate?" whispered Hester, as they paused to let the press of people squeeze through the narrow entrance.

"Oh yes," returned Monty, with a twisted smile, "I was so in love, I wanted to marry her. M' father was alarmed by my obsession, made it his business to discover all the relevant facts. Of course, by the time he had them in his possession, the situation had changed. Thérèse knew that I would have been cut off by my family if I had married her. Without money and influence I was of no use and she told me so, quite plainly. She said that she had had enough of starvation and poverty to last her a lifetime, and besides she could not return my affection. She wants security above all, but she is a woman of a passionate nature and her affairs are notorious. I had a narrow escape, but 'tis my belief she will wed some wealthy, older man, if she weds at all. At present she shows a strong preference for Montfort, but he is not an easy man to deceive and I fancy he sees through her. Unfortunately, I seem to have a penchant for females who are unattainable, your lovely self for example. Tell me, is Mortimer fixing his interest with the lively Miss Stephanie?"

For a moment Hester was nonplussed by the abrupt change in subject. Monty pressed her hand slightly as he seated her at a round table near the window and said in an undertone,

"Do not let me embarrass you, Hester. You should not be such a sympathetic listener. Forgive my impertinence and tell me what I can fetch to tempt your appetite. You must be famished after waiting so long to find a table."

Hester did not feel in the least hungry, but she strove to match his bantering tone, thus proving that she was not offended. Having commissioned him to procure her some cold ham and salad, she sat back to survey the scene. What she saw gave her little satisfaction. At the far end of the room Hugo was bending assiduously over the Comtesse, apparently engaged in earnest conversation. Hester wrenched her eyes away and in an effort to divert herself looked about for Mortimer. Despite her inner agitation she could not help smiling when she spied him seated side by side with Cleo Pennyfeather. Cleo was fluttering her eyelashes and waving her fan to such a degree that Hester could see Mortimer's hair lifting, even at a distance. He wore an expression of ineffable boredom, but his innate politeness obliged him to give his full attention to his partner, which was perhaps as well, for when Hester sought his lordship's wards she found Stephanie flirting outrageously with Thomas Marchant, while poor Agatha Sprague, on Thomas's other side was darting dagger glances, first at Stephanie and then at Mortimer, who had deserted her for Miss Pennyfeather, completely ignoring her own partner, a rather pallid youth with a very high cravat, who was unknown to Hester. Only Marietta gave no cause for alarm; she was sitting demurely by Miss Stanhope and Lady Marchant, a contented smile giving a glow to her usually pale features. From time to time she fingered her reticule lovingly and Hester guessed that Hugo had brought her a letter from Hyde Abercromby.

What a muddle. Nothing was working out as she had hoped and the evening which had begun so well was beginning to turn into a disaster. Unwillingly her eyes strayed toward Lord Montfort and the Comtesse. Hugo happened to glance in her direction at the same moment. Her face froze and she looked away to welcome Monty so warmly that she quite took his breath away. Mr. Sprague set down two laden plates and seated himself beside Hester with alacrity. He, too, glanced around the room, his eyes resting briefly on Montfort and his companion who were once more engrossed in conversation. He nodded comprehendingly, as if he had solved a problem to his own satisfaction, then tilted his head to look askance at Hester. She was in the act of biting a morsel of ham when she met his penetrating gaze, and immediately coughed, choked and grew red in her confusion. All concern, he patted her gently on the back and offered her some water.

When she was somewhat recovered, Monty murmured half-mockingly, as if to himself,

"I see it is as I thought — quite unattainable. I despair of inspiring any emotion deeper than friendship in one of the fair sex. My parents tell me 'tis time I looked around for a wife. I'm young, not less endowed than the next man in looks and worldly wealth, yet no woman has ever regarded me in that special way which would indicate she is mine for the asking. Lucky dog, that Montfort. Dear Hester, pray enlighten me as a mere male, what is the secret of his success with the ladies? Is it that indefinable thing called 'charm'?"

Hester blinked, hesitating whether or not to reply seriously to his teasing questions. She sipped some more water.

"If 'charm' is indefinable, I do not think I can answer you precisely," she offered cautiously.

"Come, don't prevaricate, I beg. You know my meaning well enough, I think."

"Well, sir, you are very persistent and will not be put off. But, I cannot tell you the secret of his lordship's charm for I love him, as I believe you have guessed already. Love is not something which can be subject to reason and analysis, but it has little to do with 'charm' beyond the initial attraction. Love is a meeting of minds and hearts, a shared sense of humour, a similar outlook on many subjects, a feeling of incompleteness when separated from the beloved object, a sensation of happiness and contentment when together. I am describing it very inadequately, but when you experience it you will know. But, how foolish of me, you were in love with the Comtesse, so you do not require my definition."

"According to your definition, I was never in love with Thérèse," said Monty wryly. "I see now that it was little more than an immature infatuation with her beauty and presence. I was not at ease in her company for she was always laughing at me, not with me. But perhaps my disappointment has made me bitter and impossible to please."

"Nonsense, it has just made you a little more wary. You must have confidence in yourself. Consider you have a most gentlemanly air of distinction and poise, in addition to wit, health and wealth. In sum, you are what matchmaking mamas call an 'eligible *parti*'."

They both laughed.

"Great heaven, with all these qualities and advantages how can I fail! I shall re-enter the marriage stakes with renewed enthusiasm. My thanks to you. What a bore I have been, prosing on. Have you had enough to eat, do you care for a pastry? No? Then let us return to the ballroom and see how matters have been progressing. In your wisdom can you suggest any suitable young lady? What say you to Miss Cleo Pennyfeather?"

Hester shook her head emphatically and they re-entered the ballroom arm in arm, laughing merrily. Their arrival was observed by several interested persons who had taken note of their exclusive suppertime *tête-à-tête*. Lord Montfort was standing a little to the left of the double door, the Comtesse still at his side. Hugo pounced at once, informing Hester that the Comtesse de Chérault had expressed a great wish to be made known to her. Hester acknowledged the introduction civilly, but with restraint, aware of Monty frowning at her elbow. Before the two ladies had time to do more than exchange one or two commonplace remarks, Lady Marchant swept down upon them, her normally placid brow wrinkled forbiddingly. Very much the 'grande dame', she barely noticed the rest of the company, but announced to her niece in frigid tones, that it was time they were leaving. Quite dismayed by the arctic atmosphere which her ladyship generated, Hester made her farewells. However, not one to be easily intimidated, she curtsied gracefully to the Comtesse and offered Hugo her hand, before joining her aunt, who awaited her at a little distance, her foot tapping impatiently. Monty escorted them to their carriage and Hester was glad of his supporting presence, for the small incident had attracted a good deal of attention and many eyes were upon them as they travelled the length of the ballroom. She lifted her head, keeping her eyes straight ahead, as she vainly endeavoured to forget the two high spots of angry colour on the Comtesse's cheeks and Hugo's fierce scowl.

Cousin Thomas rode home with them in the carriage, but Mortimer remained behind to squire Stephanie. The sight of Thomas, lounging at his ease on the soft maroon velvet squabs, temporarily distracted Hester. She reminded herself that she had still not fulfilled her intention of having a private word with him on behalf of Agatha Sprague. Her aunt's indignant voice interrupted her meditations.

"Whatever can have possessed Montfort to behave so improperly? He must know that that designing hussy is not fit company for you. How dare he foist her society upon us? Don't you laugh, Thomas, my son. I saw you dangling after her, like the rest of those fools."

Lady Marchant paused in her tirade to reach for her handkerchief, giving Thomas the opportunity to say, without heat,

"My dear mama, of course. Here, in this stronghold of the Prince of Wales it would be taken as the deepest insult to His Royal Highness himself if one did not lay siege to the beautiful Thérèse. Besides she was by far the most amusing woman in the room. Your pardon, cousin, present company excluded I assure you." Thomas leaned forward, seemingly untroubled by the rattling movement of the carriage. His stern tones made Hester shiver as he continued, "You have done yourself and my cousin no service by incurring the enmity of the Comtesse. She and H.R.H. are thick as thieves and she could make your stay here very uncomfortable if she chose to do so. I was glad to see that you, Hester, had more presence of mind and there is the chance that she will not include you in her displeasure. This is not London, mama. Society here is more tolerant, more lax if you will, but you will quickly find yourself shunned if you do not abide by its *mores*. Make no mistake, the Comtesse is a woman of great power and influence. For my sake, if you wish me to have any future in politics (Whig though I may be), and for my cousin's sake, I beg you to reconsider your attitude. You must invite her to tea, or better still, to dinner. Montfort too. Your slight to him was unpardonable. Do but reflect, dear ma'am, Hester's morals are not likely to be affected by a woman of doubtful virtue, but if the Prince frowns on Hester because of Thérèse, my cousin may as well return to Shawcross for all the society she will see here."

This far from tactful speech fell somewhat short of its object. By the time Thomas finished his lecture, both ladies were in a state of seething rage. The carriage arrived at their villa and no word was spoken until they were upstairs in the drawing room. As soon as the door was closed, Lady Marchant rounded on her son,

"I am deeply distressed by your attitude and by the lack of filial respect displayed by you this evening, Thomas. You have spoken plainly and I claim the same privilege. I will not receive that woman in my house. Since we are to speak in crude terms of power, I will remind you that I am an earl's daughter, your father's wife and not entirely without friends and influence at least among the older generation. Your threats and insinuations have wounded me; my feelings are unchanged. Thérèse Marvin may take tea with Hester in some other place, perhaps at Montfort's residence, if she so wishes. There is a grain of truth in what you say and I would not stand in Hester's way, though I believe you underestimate your cousin's own friends and abilities. Hester may speak for herself. I shall retire. It has been an upsetting evening. Goodnight, my dear niece; Thomas."

When the door had closed behind her ladyship Thomas smiled ruefully at his cousin.

"Oh lord, now the fat is in the fire. Mama's feathers are seldom ruffled, but when they are it takes a long time to smooth them down. Am I sunk too low in your esteem or will you accept my apologies for some thoughtless remarks, Hester? Mama is quite right, Thérèse Marvin is not really a companion for you, but if you could bring yourself to be polite to her, it would be better for everybody, including your friend Montfort. Oh dear, it is my night for making tactless remarks, I can tell by your face! Come, listen, sit down and take a glass of wine, while I explain a little — you must let me try to make amends. Mama can be intolerably high in the instep occasionally, but I hope you are more reasonable, cousin. Strange how lovely females can be so unapproachable. Do come down off your high ropes, and smile."

His pleading voice was accompanied by a winning smile of his own. Drawn by curiosity, Hester could not resist saying,

"Oh, very well, but I wish you will explain to me why you pursue the Comtesse at the price of your own happiness."

Thomas glanced at her from under his brows as he set down a glass of white wine at her elbow.

"You speak in riddles, cousin. In what way is my happiness at stake?"

"Have you not made an offer for the hand of Agatha Sprague? Why, I cannot guess. If you love her you have a strange manner of showing it. You made her very unhappy this evening, Thomas."

Hester's accusation seemed to affect the gentleman powerfully. He sank down on the chair beside her, a thunderstruck expression on his dark face.

"My dear Thomas, have a care for your coat. It will become quite crumpled if you sit on it like that!" exclaimed Hester, in tones of exaggerated concern.

"Never mind my coat. Kindly explain yourself, if you please," exploded Thomas, all his affectations forgotten. Hester was amazed at his reaction. She mentally apostrophised herself for betraying Agatha in her anger and wished uncomfortably that she had taken Mortimer's advice and refrained from meddling. However, it was too late now to draw back, so she said as calmly as she was able,

"I do not wish to interfere, Tom dear, but Agatha is my friend and I am fond of you both. You cannot expect Agatha to believe that your intentions are serious when you ignore her the whole evening and spend your time dancing attendance on the Comtesse. Such behaviour does not hold much promise of future marital bliss."

"Since you are in her confidence," pronounced Thomas bitterly, "perhaps you can tell me why she did not save me a dance, though I asked her early in the evening, and why she flirted outrageously with more gentlemen than I care to number. Finding myself unwelcome, I naturally sought consolation elsewhere."

Hester was momentarily at a loss how to reply, without betraying her friend further. She smoothed her skirts and sipped her wine, while hastily rearranging her tactics.

"I think Agatha may have been indulging in a mild form of tit for tat," ventured Hester at last, "If you truly desire to make her your wife, why have you never singled her out for special attention or told her that you love her before approaching her father? Agatha is well protected by her family. Her parents are not desperate to push her into an unhappy marriage merely for the sake of an advantageous alliance in the eyes of the world. Your reputation . . ." she paused, uncertain whether to proceed.

Hands clenched, eyes flashing dangerously, Thomas prompted between gritted teeth,

"Yes, cousin — my reputation? Why do you hesitate? You would say my libertine propensities, my political leanings, my dilettante dabblings in art and literature, and my general lack of seriousness do not inspire confidence in my probable husbandly qualities. I do not gamble and have no more than trifling debts, but these are small items in my favour compared with the weights in the scales against me. Do I have it in a nutshell, Hester?"

Her head was beginning to ache, her nerves stretched taut in reaction to the many intense emotions of the evening. Almost past caring she replied tiredly,

"Do not let us quarrel. No doubt these are considerations which have occurred to Lord Sprague and his daughter, but I understand his lordship favoured your suit. After all such a description could apply to most men of fashion, who waste their talents, finding no outlet for their abilities in their restricted social circle. I am convinced that many men who seek escape in dissipation can and do settle down to become useful members of society, married to the right woman. But the nub of the matter is that Agatha is an intelligent girl who will not marry you unless she believes that you want her for herself. At the moment she has the impression that you are fulfilling a family obligation; you need a wife and you have selected her because she is known and liked by your family, has a respectable portion, impeccable birth and all the other attributes generally desired by a gentleman contemplating matrimony. She is under great pressure from her mother to accept you and I honour her for her determination not to countenance a marriage of convenience. If you truly desire to wed her, you must work a little, court her, not take her for granted as if she still idolised you from the schoolroom. She is an attractive lady who must be won and I warn you it will not be easy to atone for past neglect and flirtations elsewhere. But if you love her, I think she will forgive you, in time. Now, cousin, I am vastly fatigued and must bid you goodnight."

She rose, but before she could take a step, she found her hands clasped and felt a firm kiss implanted upon her brow. Thomas murmured into her hair,

"Hester, you are a treasure. I must thank you for showing me that I am the biggest fool in Christendom. I have always thought of Agatha as someone quite special and unique, but I have known her so long that I do not stand on ceremony with her and I admit that I have always taken her affection for granted. I see now that I have failed to make it clear that I regarded her as more than a friend. Can't think how I can have been so blind, but I meant it as a compliment, treating her as a person, not a woman, quite forgetting what irrational creatures women are."

Relieved to hear the familiar note of mockery creeping back into his voice, Hester raised her head, absentmindedly thinking how unfair it was that a mere male should have such wonderfully long, curling lashes. They smiled ruefully at one another. She wriggled one hand free and thumped Tom commandingly on his elegant waistcoat with one small fist.

"Now do not rush things, or Agatha will be suspicious," she admonished severely.

"I'll be as cautious as a cat," he promised solemnly, as he escorted her to the door. He paused, his hand on the knob, "Tell me, is there something I can do for you in exchange? I consider myself deeply in your debt. Forgive my impertinence, but is there aught amiss between you and Montfort? No, do not answer, but remember, not everyone courts the Comtesse for the sake of her 'beaux yeux'. Intrigue, political as well as personal, is the breath of life to the divine Thérèse. So far she has led a charmed life, but she dabbles in dangerous pies. Montfort finds her a useful tool, a source of information, nothing more, I assure you. Do not let her haunt your dreams with vain imaginings, sweet coz!"

Thomas opened the door and bowed gracefully. Hester giggled, curtsied and ran lightly up the stair, her headache completely forgotten.

However, the mysterious Comtesse was not so easily dismissed. The very next day, when Hester returned from her favourite walk along the seafront, she found a message from Hugo, inviting her to take tea with himself and the Comtesse under Miss Stanhope's auspices at three that afternoon. She carried the note thoughtfully into the drawing room, stripping off her gloves as she went. Preoccupied, she failed to observe Thomas enter the room behind her and she gave a jump when he drawled,

"Shall you go, Hester?"

She rounded on him, speaking sharply in her fright,

"I suppose I have you to thank for this, cousin? You do not let the grass grow under your feet."

"You wrong me. 'Twas the merest hint, when Montfort called. Very put out to find you from home. Something required. Common civility suggested a tea party. He took me up on it at once."

"I see," said Hester acidly, "Is my aunt included in the invitation?"

"Good lord, no," Thomas feigned astonishment. "You must know she needs time to recuperate after a ball. I suggested it might lift her spirits, if Miss Stephanie and Miss Marietta were to call. Mr. Abercromby arrives this forenoon and I believe he may accompany them. A fresh face is always welcome to mama in the comfort of her own drawing room."

Presented with a *fait accompli*, Hester accepted the situation with equanimity and set out alone in the Marchant carriage a little before the appointed hour. Lady Marchant had made no objection to the arrangements. Thomas and Mortimer remained at home to help entertain their guests and she left the three of them ensconced by the fireside, Thomas chatting amusingly on trivial subjects and exerting himself to please his mama, which he quickly succeeded in doing with considerable skill. Her ladyship's ruffled feathers were quite smoothed down and Hester was free to concentrate on her own affairs.

The tea-drinking which took place in Lord Montfort's elegant yellow salon was an unqualified success. Each lady was aware that she looked her best and none felt at a disadvantage. Hugo's masculine presence injected the necessary stimulation to raise the talk above the level of feminine trivia. Initially Hester was inclined to be a little stiff, but Hugo steered the talk smoothly through the first awkward moments, ably supported by the Comtesse who expressed an eager interest in Hester's writing. Miss Stanhope interjected a few sly, provoking comments from her seat behind the tea table and Hester, unable to resist their combined onslaught, found herself gaily describing her methods of work, the problems of research and the difficulties of publishing. Hugo was delighted to find that Hester's usually sunny disposition had reasserted itself and she basked in the warmth of his smile and gentle teasing. Hester in turn was pleasantly surprised to discover that the Comtesse was an interesting and intelligent person who made no attempt to divert the conversation or to attract Hugo's attention to herself. It was left to Hester to change the subject, which she did by expressing a sincere regret that she had never travelled abroad.

"I'm afraid you must find English people very insular, Comtesse," observed Miss Stanhope, tilting her little birdlike head enquiringly.

"Perhaps a leetle," admitted the Comtesse, "But they have been so kind to me, a poor exile and then, of course, you know many gentlemen have visited my country on their Grand Tour. That was how I met his lordship, in Paris, oh, so many years ago." She sighed, but smiled immediately, dimpling mischievously at Hugo. Hester suppressed a quick pang of envy and said sympathetically,

"You must miss your own country very much, Comtesse."

"I do, of course, but in France it is not the same any more. There are so many *problèmes* and no one knows his place. It is so uncomfortable. Sometimes I long for my friends, to hear my own *belle langue*, but I find many people here will indulge me and let me speak to them in my mother tongue. It can be a great relief, a relaxation, not to guard one's words, for the nuances of language are very subtle and the humour here, it is not at all the same and *très souvent*, oh, so frequently, there are the little misunderstandings, which make me impatient with myself."

"But your English is excellent," protested Hester.

"You must meet his lordship's wards, they are from Luxembourg," remarked Miss Stanhope, "Perhaps you saw them last night?"

There was an infinitesimal pause. Everyone looked at Hugo, who said calmly, after a moment's hesitation,

"Yes, indeed. I am sure they would be most happy. There was no opportunity to introduce them last night. Your brother monopolized Stephanie very successfully, Hester. Did you know that my friend Abercromby has arrived in Brighton?"

"Why yes, Thomas informed me. How does he go on?" replied Hester, ignoring the ladies' raised eyebrows at Hugo's familiar use of her first name.

Hugo launched into a detailed account of Mr. Abercromby's journey and went on to give a brief description of the political ferment in town. He also remarked that it was rumoured in certain knowledgeable quarters that Napoleon intended to make himself Emperor of the French.

"He is a strong man, but I fear such an ambitious step is of *la folie*, how do you say? — ah yes, thank you, milord, unwise," vouchsafed the Comtesse thoughtfully. The dark lady's face assumed a brooding expression, preoccupied with her own thoughts. Hester decided it was time for her to leave. The Comtesse remained with Miss Stanhope, while Hugo accompanied Hester to her carriage.

"Thank you for coming," he said sincerely, "did you like Thérèse? I could tell that she was quite taken with you, which is not often the case with her own sex."

A slight breeze had sprung up. They were standing by the carriage steps and Hester lifted her face into the wind, sniffing happily. She felt in charity with the world.

"If you are correct, I am honoured by her approbation. It is too soon for me to pass any worthwhile opinion, but I thought her interesting, charming and elusive. I would like to know her better. Does that content you, my lord?" She grinned up at him and Hugo flicked her cheek affectionately.

"You are generous. I shall see you very soon, what say you to a drive in my curricule tomorrow morning?"

It was agreed and Hester departed in high spirits, well satisfied with her afternoon's work.

Chapter 18
The Sketching Party

The curricule drive with Hugo had to be postponed because of bad weather. For several days Lady Marchant's snug house on the Marine Parade was lashed by rain and gale force winds. Being largely confined within doors, Hester seized the opportunity to assuage her nagging conscience by devoting every morning (while her aunt lay abed) to copying her manuscript and making final changes before sending it off to the publisher. She made good progress and was pleased with her sense of accomplishment. Thomas teased her, calling her a little Puritan. She laughed, but admitted it to be true that she became bored if the round of entertainment were not leavened by some solid endeavour. However, on Friday she was by no means unhappy to discover that the gale had blown itself out during the night and that a bright sun shone on the boats of the fishing fleet bobbing (rather than tugging) at their moorings below Hester's bedchamber window.

"What a glorious day!" exclaimed Hester, turning from the window. She clasped her arms about her silk wrapper and took a twirl around the room, her thick hair swinging loosely to her waist. Martha smiled tolerantly as she poured hot water from the ewer into the flowered china basin.

"That it be, Miss. What will you be wearing this morning?"

It was still quite early and Hester was seized with a sudden longing to go for a drive out of town.

"How warm is it, Martha, do you think it would be possible to picnic outdoors?" she enquired, seating herself at her small writing table and drawing a sheet of paper towards her.

The little maid frowned doubtfully,

"I suppose so, Miss Hester, but be sure and take lots of rugs and wear something thick. Sea weather can be very contrary."

"Hum," nodded her mistress absentmindedly, as she dashed off her note. In a few moments she had finished, sanded the sheet and sealed it with a wafer. "Have this sent over to Miss Stanhope without delay, there's a dear. Tell the man to wait for a reply. Then come back and help me dress. That should be warm enough to satisfy you."

"Ne'er cast a clout till May is out," pronounced Martha solemnly, as she whisked out of the room, Left alone Hester proceeded to perform her toilette. She had barely finished when Martha returned to slip the blue gown over her head and tidy her hair. She was sipping her second cup of coffee in the breakfast room when Simmonds, the footman, returned from his errand. He presented Miss Stanhope's reply on a silver salver and retired. On reading the neat missive Hester learned to her satisfaction that the ladies would be delighted to join her in a sketching party and *al fresco* luncheon at Hove. His lordship and Mr. Abercromby proposed to escort the chaise on horseback and they would present themselves at Lady Marchant's at eleven thirty to take up Hester.

A glance at the clock revealed that the hour was already advanced towards ten. She rang for Pringle and gave orders for hampers to be prepared. It was arranged between them that, subject to her ladyship's approval, two menservants were to go on ahead to Hove and prepare for their arrival in a spot well-known to Pringle. He assured Hester that it was a popular location for picnics, owing to the fine views which it afforded and the sheltered sunny aspect. After giving detailed directions concerning the contents of the hampers, Hester sped upstairs to consult her aunt. As she had anticipated her ladyship made no difficulty, merely repeating Martha's advice, adjuring her niece to wrap up warmly and not return too late as they were engaged for the play that evening. Next Hester knocked on her brother's door and entered to find Mortimer already up and dressed for riding. It appeared that he and Thomas had laid plans the previous night to attend a pugilistic display at some village a few miles inland. At first he was reluctant to forgo the promised spectacle, demurring that sketching parties were not much in his line. However, after some hesitation, he allowed himself to be persuaded by Hester's entreaties and the prospect of spending a whole day in Stephanie's company. The party was completed when Thomas, finding that his companion for the day proposed to desert him, begged that he too might join the expedition.

Punctually at eleven thirty the Montfort chaise arrived. Hester took the vacant seat beside Miss Stanhope, her back to the horses, and the gentlemen clattered along behind. They followed the coast road, the whole party in gay spirits, exhilarated by the beautiful weather. The drive was accomplished without incident, even Marietta suffering no ill effects in the open vehicle. The ladies were obliged to open their parasols to shade their eyes from the bright sunlight. A little beyond

Hove they turned inland and followed a winding track into the foothills of the Downs, until they came to a wooded copse where they left the horses in charge of the coachman and continued on foot. Following Pringle's directions they crossed a stile, skirted a sheep-filled meadow, ignored an illegible weatherbeaten signpost and pursued a chalky uphill path for perhaps five minutes. Finally, just as Miss Stanhope was beginning to wonder volubly if they had mistaken their way, the path forked abruptly to the left. Somewhat breathlessly they emerged on a greasy plateau, sheltered by a rocky outcrop. A small waterfall splashed and gurgled merrily in the far corner; beside it Pringle's two menservants were busily engaged in laying out the picnic equipment.

"It's perfect!" exclaimed Stephanie and Hester together. Everyone laughed and agreed.

"It's strange," confided Marietta shyly to Abercromby, "The countryside in England is not wild, or grand or — or romantic, but it is so tranquil and green. I do not think I shall ever tire of it. I love to draw and to paint, but I do not see how I can capture a scene like this. It is so different from my own familiar countryside at home."

"Oh come now, Miss Marietta, you must try. The English landscape lends itself particularly to the medium of watercolours. Let us find a suitable place to settle ourselves and I will bore you with a history of English painting, while you make a preliminary sketch before luncheon."

Apparently oblivious to the kindly amusement which they had aroused, the couple made themselves comfortable a little way up the waterfall, Mr. Abercromby coping expertly with the impediments of rugs, sketching materials and parasol.

"I do like a masterful man," observed Miss Stanhope approvingly to nobody in particular.

"Then I am the man for you," declared Thomas, grasping her sharp little elbow firmly and piloting her to a rug spread out under a tree, conveniently near to the picnic hampers.

"You should have been a general, Thomas." Miss Stanhope did not stand on ceremony with a young man she had known in short coats. "I could not have chosen a more strategic site myself."

She sat very upright, taking her duties as chaperone seriously, but Thomas stretched beside her, lazily chewing a blade of grass, his customary sneering smile on his lips.

"You must relax, Miss Jane. This is a picnic, not a ballroom. One is allowed a little more licence on such occasions, surrounded by the beauties of Nature."

Miss Jane pursed her lips. "A dangerous precept. However, on this occasion, as you say . . ."

"Exactly so," confirmed Thomas, following her gaze. The party had split naturally into couples. Marietta was already busily sketching the waterfall and laughing happily at some remark of Hyde's. Stephanie and Mortimer had wandered back down the hill to look at the horses, while Hugo and Hester had scrambled to the top of the chalky outcrop to admire the view and select a suitable object to be immortalised on paper. "You cannot be everywhere at once, Miss Jane, so I suggest it is your duty to entertain my humble self, as the only unattached member of the party."

"Nonsense and ungallant in you, young man. The boot I think should be on the other foot," chided Miss Stanhope, hiding a smile by rummaging in her capacious bag for her embroidery.

"A just reproof and indeed I am well known to have a penchant for older women," said Thomas wickedly. "Do you not sketch, ma'am?"

"No, I am aware of my limitations and drawing has never been one of my talents."

They sat in comfortable silence as Miss Jane perched her spectacles on her small, tip-tilted nose and selected a crimson skein of silk carefully. When this was accomplished she threaded her needle and peered at her companion over the top of her spectacles.

"Do you number the French Comtesse among your conquests, Thomas? I noticed you dancing attendance on her at the ball. But then you flirted with Stephanie quite assiduously too. A case of the devil making work for idle hands, perhaps?" She poked viciously at her work, pricked her finger and gave vent to an exclamation of annoyance. Thomas sat up, laughing boyishly and retrieved the fallen cushion cover. Miss Stanhope was sucking her finger vigorously, but she glanced at him curiously.

"What an excellent governess you must have been! I can just see poor little Hester stabbing away at her sampler with her grubby fingers and chanting to herself, 'The devil makes work for idle hands'. No, no, don't be angry, I do not mean to provoke you. If it will give you peace of mind, let me assure you that my motives are unimpeachable. The Comtesse and I have a business relationship, nothing more. As for Stephanie, she is inexperienced, but charming. I would not take advantage of her, but it is good for her to have a little light flirtation and it will do Mortimer no harm, merely a prod in the right direction, 'tis clear they are meant for one another, don't you agree? As to myself, my heart has already been laid at another lady's feet, perhaps Hester told you?"

"Hester has told me nothing since we left Shawcross," grumbled Miss Stanhope, "She's eating her heart out for Montfort, of course, but that Comtesse bothers me. She came to tea the other day and although she is clever she could not quite conceal her feelings from me. She is jealous, she means to have Hugo by hook or by crook and I fear she will not scruple to trample over Hester to get him."

"Are you certain?," enquired Thomas thoughtfully.

"Oh yes. After Hester had gone she attacked her quite spitefully, calling her a poor country mouse. She praised her as well, so that Hugo could not take offence, but she somehow twisted everything to make it appear in the worst possible light, saying that of course Hester must be on the catch for a rich husband. She implied that the writing of novels was a most unladylike occupation and pitied Hester for having been 'on the shelf' for so long. She hinted that Hester had several strings to her bow and suggested Monty Sprague as the most likely candidate. Her insinuations were the most consummate piece of artistry and innuendo it has been my misfortune to hear in a long while."

"Did you say nothing in Hester's defense, ma'am?"

"How could I, silly boy, I was listening at the keyhole," replied Miss Jane impatiently.

"I see. What of Hugo? I cannot believe that he made no protest at these aspersions."

"Only a token one," sniffed Miss Stanhope, "He said that Miss Vane was a lady of considerable independence and spirit who liked her single state and that while she may not be wealthy he can find nothing mouselike in her demeanour. Then he changed the subject and I was obliged to move for fear one of the servants would catch me snooping."

Thomas nodded.

"You may feel that his reply was inadequate," he said understandingly, "But pray consider, the Comtesse is well known to him. He must be aware that she can be both vindictive and cruel. He would not think it wise to defend Hester too heatedly, 'tis better the Comtesse regards her as an insignificant figure and believes Hugo to be indifferent to her. Then Thérèse's enmity will not be aroused against Hester."

"True enough, but one has only to see Hugo and Hester together to realise the bond between them," objected Miss Stanhope.

"It is certainly apparent to those who know them well, but you must remember that the Comtesse does not. At least not Hester. She may suspect, but so long as she remains unsure, she will be careful. Have you mentioned the conversation you overheard to my cousin?"

"No. I was afraid to meddle."

"I will drop a hint to her, she should be on her guard, I think. But let us talk of other things, luncheon for example. Do you care for a glass of wine? I see Simmonds has chilled it in the stream. The others all seem so happily occupied it would be a pity to disturb them just yet."

Miss Stanhope acquiesced graciously and watched with amusement as Thomas supervised the opening of the bottle. Several twigs and burrs had attached themselves to the back of his grey morning coat, there were specks of mud on his shining boots and he looked out of place and yet somehow quite as ease in the rural setting. When he returned with two brimming glasses, cursing the clumsy man who had filled them so full, Miss Stanhope diverted him by enquiring about the young lady who had captured his wayward heart. With very little prompting he launched into an enthusiastic description of Miss Sprague and mentioned Hester's advice on the matter of courtship, which Miss Stanhope endorsed unreservedly. So absorbed was she, that she quite failed to keep track of her charges, which suited those young ladies very well.

From her perch on a rock at the head of the waterfall Hester noted her erstwhile governess's dereliction from duty and commented on it to her companion. He smiled, without looking up, being intent upon the neat, businesslike sketch he was making of a bee in a clump of clover. Hester nibbled the tip of her pencil irritably. Her own drawing was not shaping well and with a quick, restless motion, she crumpled the paper and arranged a fresh sheet on her board.

"You need a broader canvas and a big brush to encompass your chosen subject," remarked Hugo, finishing his own work with a few brisk, competent strokes. He leaned back against the rock with a sigh of satisfaction, pulling his hat forward to shade his eyes.

"How aggravating of you to be always in the right. I fear sketching is not my métier. I become too impatient, particularly with vague countryside scenes such as this. I need a focal point, a ruin, or a well, or some small animal."

"All good pictures need a focal point," agreed Hugo. He twisted round to face her. "I wish that I was truly gifted! It would give me great pleasure to capture you as you are now, chipstraw bonnet, chewed pencil and all. Do you remember the last time we sat side by side upon a rock?"

"In the Priory garden? Yes, of course. It was the last time we spoke together undisturbed. We talked of the Garths — which reminds me, have you any word yet of Susan's whereabouts?" Hester felt a little flustered by the ardent expression in Hugo's eyes, but her attempt to change the topic of conversation was unsuccessful. The Garths were summarily dismissed on the grounds that there was no news and Hugo adroitly steered the talk back into more personal channels.

"You are so hedged about with relatives and admirers of the lady novelist it is difficult to come upon you alone. Tell me, did I do aught to offend you at the ball? Your manner has been cool and I had the feeling you were avoiding me this week."

"Did you? Well, perhaps I was," she admitted honestly, "You see you are a very distracting person and I had to copy my manuscript and attend to my aunt, and then it has been raining. But I did come to tea and I saw you at my aunt's dinner party on Wednesday."

"You hardly spoke two words to me all evening. Come, I will not be put off, is it the Comtesse that troubles you, Hester? Has Mortimer been telling tales? He saw me with La Belle Thérèse at the theatre last night."

"Yes, he mentioned it, but not in the way you imply, he was *not* telling tales, it slipped out by accident and I'm sure he wished it unsaid, for he closed up like an oyster immediately, which was silly of him for I'm sure you may go to the theatre with whom you choose. Is it a good play? We go tonight. And indeed perhaps we should go and see about luncheon, for I promised Aunt Annabelle we would not be late back and the servants must have unpacked the hampers by now. I'm quite hungry with all this sweet, fresh air, so refreshing after the rain — and I told Pringle to be sure and include some asparagus tips just for you." Hester rattled on, hardly aware of what she was saying. Not looking at Hugo, she gathered up her sketching materials and jumped to her feet. Hugo rose too; before she had taken two steps he caught her in his arms and swung her round to face him, pushing up her chin with one firm hand. For a breathless moment they stood still, then Hugo bent and kissed her lips hard and lingeringly.

"Oh!" she said inadequately, when at last she could speak. She raised her hand to her mouth and rubbed her bruised lips gingerly. Hugo stood back, still holding her shoulders. Below, seemingly from a great distance, they heard voices calling them.

Hugo laughed shakily,

"Let there be no more misunderstandings between us, my love," he murmured. "Now listen, and believe me, Thérèse is beautiful, but she has a heart of stone. There are reasons why I must cultivate her friendship and when I have time I will explain them to you. Now, let us go and seek the promised asparagus tips." He kissed her once more, lightly on the tip of her nose, then seizing her hand in a warm clasp, he guided her carefully down the steep, uneven path.

They found the rest of the party seated on rugs in circular fashion, around a vast, snowy white damask tablecloth covered with all manner of tempting delicacies. When everyone had eaten their fill, the hampers were repacked with the remains of the feast. There was not much left, so it did not take long. Reluctantly, they made ready to return to the carriage. The *al fresco* picnic expedition was generally pronounced to have been a great success; Hugo's and Marietta's sketches were examined and admired and they all agreed that another such outing should be arranged in the near future. Hugo suggested that they should visit the Devil's Dyke on the next occasion. This idea was greeted enthusiastically, for although the dyke was a popular place for a short drive with Brighton visitors, none of the ladies had yet visited it.

"Why is it called the Devil's Dyke, *mon cousin*?", enquired Stephanie as she walked down the hillside beside Hugo.

He glanced down at his ward affectionately. It occurred to him that she was like some small, bright butterfly tripping along beside him, her red ribbons fluttering in the wind.

"I did not know you cared for history, Stephanie," he said teasingly.

She dimpled up at him, her eyes sparkling vivaciously.

"Well, I do, a little. But with such a name it must be legend not history, I think?"

"True, although at times it can be difficult to separate the one from the other. The story goes that the dyke was dug in the chalky downs by the Devil so that the sea could swamp the churches of the Weald. It is not known whether or not he achieved his object, but it is my guess he was frustrated in his design. You will understand when you visit the place, for although the ravine has steep, grass-covered sides, it is unlike other watercourses in the Downs for it is closed at both ends, giving no access to the sea. It is a haunting spot, its past shrouded in the mists of time. Even on a clear, sunny day there is something imposing in the atmosphere, people instinctively lower their voices, as if in church. On a grey, windy day it must be awesome indeed, though I have never visited it under such conditions."

"Say no more, already I am shivering in my shoes. Clearly it is an environ of the most sinister. But Hester will like it, she will find it romantic. Me, I am a practical person."

Hugo's lips twitched.

"If you say so, my dear Stephanie, though I have noticed you are susceptible to some romantic influences. How do you go on with young Vane, is he a congenial companion?"

Stephanie glanced suspiciously at his lordship's impassive countenance. Then with a toss of her dark curls, she replied dismissively,

"Oh, he is well enough. He is amusing and très épris with his so-beautiful horse. I wish that I could ride here."

It was obvious Stephanie wished to keep her own counsel, so Hugo charitably refrained from pressing her on the subject of Sir Mortimer, though it was his private conviction that that gentleman had fixed his interest to an unwonted degree on the pretty filly (to employ a stable metaphor) at his side. Hugo promised his ward that he would buy her a suitable mount when they returned to Huntsgrove Priory and they passed the remainder of the walk in discussing her precise requirements. By the time they reached the carriage Stephanie found herself more in accord with her aloof cousin than she had previously believed possible.

Hester was seated next to Stephanie on the drive home, but the two girls spoke little, each being preoccupied with their own thoughts. Hester had walked down the hillside with Thomas, who had taken the chance to set Hester on her guard against the Comtesse de Chérault by hinting that Thérèse regarded Montfort as her exclusive property, and would be unlikely to relinquish her claim without a struggle. To Thomas's chagrin, Hester appeared unmoved by his warning. With the memory of Hugo's kiss fresh in her mind, her earlier jealousy had been replaced by a feeling of compassion for the unhappy exile. She told her cousin confidently that she had enjoyed her conversation with the Comtesse and was certain they could deal comfortably together. She refused to listen to any more malicious gossip concerning the lady, saying sharply that she had often observed that men were more spiteful than women, especially if their proffered attentions were spurned. In the face of Hester's unexpected championship of Thérèse Marvin, Thomas decided not to repeat the conversation which Miss Stanhope had overheard. It was quite probable, reflected Thomas cynically, that Hester's generous friendship would spike the Comtesse's guns more effectively than open hostility. A woman with few, if any, female friends, might be drawn irresistibly by Hester's unaffected liveliness and warmth. Thomas had stifled his doubts, while Hester, ashamed of her momentary outburst, exerted herself to assure her cousin that she was still very happy in her single state and that therefore, by implication, the Comtesse had nothing to fear from her neighbourly association with Hugo. This solemn nonsense proved too much for Thomas, who had been watching closely when Hugo and Hester rejoined the picnic party. He hooted with laughter and roundly bade her not to talk such fustian to him. Hester had retorted indignantly that it was no such thing and turned the conversation by demanding the answer to a question which had been puzzling her, why had Thomas not told his mother of his intentions regarding Agatha Sprague?

As the carriage left the lane, and swung east, following the coast road once more, Hester smiled to herself, recalling Thomas's ludicrous expression as the force of her query went home. His brows had drawn comically together and he had clasped a hand to his head, leaving Hester stranded half way across the stile. She had brushed a burr off his shoulder, and at once, recalled to a sense of his social obligations he lifted her down, before owning that, dash it all, she'd given him quite a leveller, for it had never occurred to him to tell his mother until his suit had been accepted. Patiently Hester had taken his arm, and pacing slowly along she had done her best to explain that his remissness was in fact a favourable sign so far as Agatha was concerned, for until she had known that Lady Marchant was in ignorance of Thomas's marital intentions, Miss Sprague had been convinced that he was merely obeying his parents' wishes in paying her his addresses. When at length he understood, Thomas had been inclined to be angry with Agatha for thinking him such a 'spineless milksop', but Hester succeeded in convincing him that Agatha's apprehensions had been only natural in view of the long friendship between their families and his own apparent indifference.

The sun disappeared behind a cloud and the subsequent chill roused Hester from her meditations. The gulls wheeled overhead, emitting plaintive, piercing cries. As they neared Brighton the carriage traffic increased and at one point their driver was obliged to halt to allow a string of donkeys to pass, on their way home from the beach. Two ragged, sunburned boys drooped wearily on the backs of the foremost beasts, while a man walked ahead, flourishing a stick and whistling cheerfully to the tune 'Hearts of Oak'. The ladies viewed the little procession with interest.

"The donkeys look better cared for than the children," observed Marietta thoughtfully, as the chaise moved on.

"They were certainly very thin, but perhaps they are just growing fast," suggested Stephanie, "Surely there can be no shortage of food so close to the sea." She glanced meaningfully down at the row of fishing boats which they happened to be passing. The boats were drawn up above the high tide line and the fishermen, bare to the waist, suntanned and weatherbeaten, were laying out their nets to dry. One of the men looked up and seeing the carriage containing three attractive young ladies, he leered and bowed in an exaggerated manner, his white teeth flashing. There was something indefinably evil about him, and Hester was relieved when his companion kicked him, pointing to the four gentlemen riding behind. Immediately he shrugged and turned away, revealing a long, jagged scar reaching from his right ear to his shoulder blade. As the vehicle moved on, Hester found herself wondering curiously how the man could have been injured in such a position. And then it was unusual for a fisherman to have tattoos of parrots and seashells on his arms; he might have been a sailor at some time, for now that she reflected, his behaviour had been more in keeping with that of a seaman than of the fisherfolk, who were often taciturn and tended to keep themselves to themselves. Perhaps he had been an impressed man, who had deserted from the Navy. She recalled Mrs. Lightfoot, sitting in her neat kitchen at Shawcross, telling her tales of life at sea. Her husband had been a gunner on a sloop of war and there was no denying that daily life on the King's ships was incredibly hard; draconian discipline was often essential to force the crews to endure the harsh conditions and long absences from land, but there was no other way to maintain the defence of the realm and keep the trade routes open. No one could live near the sea, as Hester had done most of her life, and be unaware of the cruel methods employed by the Press Gangs to drum up vital recruits. In wartime there were never enough volunteers and the Press Gangs roved the countryside using force, persuasion and trickery to trap able-bodied men, often with little reference to their domestic circumstances. Once seized, these unfortunate men were passed from ship to ship, never allowed to set foot on land for fear they would escape. Naturally some men did try to get away, despite every precaution, often drowning in high seas when they made the attempt. Few sailors could swim.

Absorbed in her reverie, Hester was quite surprised when the carriage halted at Lady Marchant's door. The other ladies also planned to attend the play that evening, so they did not linger, but paused only long enough to allow Hester to alight. Thomas and Mortimer rode their horses round to the stables, while Hester entered alone.

She was about to run upstairs to remove her bonnet, before presenting herself to her aunt, when Pringle cleared his throat and announced portentously,

"There is a young person begging to speak with you, ma'am. She has the accents of a lady, but is very dishevelled in her attire, hif you follow me. Being uncertain what to do with her, I put her in the bookroom, she was very persistent you see, Miss Hester," he concluded apologetically.

Hester listened in astonishment and growing excitement, but she managed to reply calmly,

"Yes, of course, thank you, Pringle. I'll go to her at once. Is my aunt at home?"

"Her ladyship is in her room, dressing, miss. The young person arrived only a few minutes ago, so I have not had an opportunity to mention her presence to milady."

"Very well, pray don't disturb her ladyship. I will inform Lady Marchant myself, when I have spoken to the visitor."

Pringle seemed inclined to hover in the hall, but Hester dismissed him firmly before making her way to the small book-lined study, which stood opposite the breakfast room on the ground floor. She opened the door softly, quickly scanning the room, which was dimly lit by the light of a single candle. There was a rustle of skirts and a small body ran forward to seize her hands, near-sighted brown eyes peering eagerly at her face.

"Susan," gasped Hester, staring in dismay at her friend's dirty, crumpled gown and the tumbled ratstails which had replaced the bright, golden curls. Even in the faint light, the change in Miss Garth's appearance was remarkable, there were black streaks on her face and deep hollows under her eyes, as if she had not slept for a week. The room was chilly, for Pringle had not thought it necessary to set a match to the fire for so unprepossessing a guest.

"You poor dear! You must come upstairs and we will set you to rights and then you must tell me the whole," exclaimed Hester, recovering somewhat from her first shock, "Are you alone, Susan?"

"My maid, Nellie, is on watch outside, to make sure we were not observed. We may be followed, you understand. Oh Hester, I am so relieved to be with you!" cried Susan, giving vent to her pent-up emotions in a flood of tears.

Chapter 19

An Unexpected Revelation

It took Hester some time to soothe her overwrought friend. Once in the sanctum of her bedchamber, Hester summoned Martha to her assistance and between them they did their best to alleviate Susan's physical sufferings. They bathed and bandaged her blistered feet, brushed her tangled hair and settled her comfortably between the sheets in one of Hester's own nightgowns. She was clearly exhausted and Hester insisted firmly that her tale could wait until she was rested. Susan protested feebly, but already her eyes were closing. Gently, Hester removed the glass of warm milk which tilted precariously in Susan's slack grasp. Then she blew out the bedside candle and retreated to the fireside, beckoning Martha to sit beside her on a little footstool.

"You were splendid, Martha, thank you," whispered Hester.

The little maid glowed with the praise. She smiled at her mistress and shook her head.

"'Tweren't no trouble, Miss Hester. Poor Miss Garth. Do you think she's run away? Her brother can be turrible fierce. I know 'cos Nellie, Miss Garth's maid, used ter tell me. Everyone's afeard of him."

"Good heavens, I've just remembered, Nellie is outside waiting for her mistress!" exclaimed Hester in dismay.

"Doan't you worry, miss, I'll fetch her in. She's strong, Nellie is, a bit o' walkin' won't have harmed her. Will you still be goin' to the play tonight?"

Hester hesitated, glancing at her friend, who was now sound asleep.

"Yes, I think I will go, but I must send round a message to Lord Montfort. I'll write it while you let Nellie in. Then come straight back here. You and Nellie must sit with Miss Garth this evening and make sure that she is not disturbed. Hurry now, and send Pringle to me, there's a dear."

Hester was sealing her letter to Hugo, informing him of Susan's arrival, when Pringle tapped on the door. She stepped out into the corridor, closing the door softly behind her and handed the letter to the butler, with instructions to have it delivered into his lordship's own hands immediately. As Pringle hesitated, obviously hoping for further enlightenment, a number of doubts suddenly assailed Hester. She had been too occupied to consider the matter previously, but it now occurred to her forcibly that Susan might be in some danger. In a flash, she recalled her own hurried departure from Shawcross and shivered at the thought of Stephen's ungovernable temper. Susan was his most prized possession, he would never let her go without pursuit. What could have happened?

Pringle coughed discreetly and Hester hastily pulled her wandering wits together. It was essential to enlist Pringle's aid. She summoned a beguiling smile, which she hoped conveyed absolute trust in his strength and abilities.

"Pringle, my whole dependence is on you. The young lady who arrived earlier, Miss Susan Garth, is my very dear friend. I am not at liberty to reveal all the circumstances, but I believe she is in considerable danger and it's vital that no hint of her presence here goes beyond the household until I have consulted his lordship, Lord Montfort that is, not my uncle. If anyone comes asking for Miss Garth you are to deny all knowledge of her whereabouts. You must also beware of intruders who may seek to gain admittance, either for force or by guile, you understand me?"

Despite the seriousness of the situation, Hester could not help being amused by the varying expressions registered on the butler's normally immobile countenance. His initial disapproval changed to bewilderment and then excitement; his small, black eyes lit up at the mention of possible intruders. He threw out his tightly waistcoated chest, so that Hester feared for his buttons, and flexed a muscle.

"Your friend will be safe in this 'ouse, Miss Hester, you can rely on me. No one can cross the threshold unbeknownst to me. I shall be vigilant night and day. You may not be aware, miss, but in my misspent youth I was a champion exponent of the pugilistic art, before I took up wi' the Wesleyans and was taken on by Lord Marchant. Your uncle, he were very kind to me, miss, 'e understood 'ow 'ard it were fer me to give up the 'game' you see. But it will be a pleasure to be of service to you, if needs be, Miss Hester, quite like old times. You go and enjoy the play, I'll look arter things here an' there'll be no tattlin' below stairs, neither."

So saying, the intrepid ex-boxer executed a small bow and almost scurried away to see to his duties. His speed reminded Hester that she too had no time to lose. She heard the click of her aunt's door further down the passage and hurriedly slipped into her own chamber. In a remarkably short time, Hester re-emerged clad in a new evening gown of apple green silk, with a gauze overskirt. She had decided, while dressing, that her aunt must be taken into her confidence, but the evening afforded no opportunity of speaking privately with her ladyship. The play was an inferior comedy which held few people's attention. Lady Marchant was popular and her box offered a welcome diversion, though the visitors found Miss Vane unaccountably *distrait*.

Hester had hoped that Hugo might have received her message in time to accompany his wards to the theatre, but she found, on scanning the audience carefully during the first intermission, that none of the Montfort household was present. The play seemed interminable, but at last it was over.

Lady Marchant, despite her easy-going manner, was far from unobservant. When they arrived home she waited while her niece enquired eagerly if there were any messages. Pringle handed Hester an envelope and her ladyship's sharp eyes recognized the Montfort seal at once.

"Shall we take our nightcap together in the drawing room, my dear?", she suggested, walking purposefully in that direction.

"Yes, Aunt Annabelle, I should like it of all things. I will join you in a moment," replied Hester, lingering in the hallway. As soon as her aunt had disappeared, Hester signed to Pringle, who was waiting at a little distance. He approached and murmured in her ear that the evening had been uneventful. Miss Garth was still sleeping. Martha had caused another bed to be made up in the same room for Hester. Reassured, Hester dismissed him with a grateful smile; then, with a quick glance at the half-open drawing room door, she unsealed the note and scanned its contents with deepening dismay. It was brief and to the point,

"Forgive hurried departure. On no account leave Brighton.
You may contact me at the 'Horse and Groom'. Inform me at
once if Susan G. comes to you." Signed "Hugo."

She realized that he must have left before receiving her own letter. What was to be done? She tucked the paper away securely in her reticule and was about to go to her aunt, when she heard a thundering on the door. Her heart missed a beat, but she controlled herself with an effort and went to peep over the bannister. To her relief it was only Thomas and Mortimer, returned early from an insipid evening at cards. She noted with interest that Pringle had two sturdy footmen in attendance when he opened the door and that a serviceable-looking bludgeon reposed on the hall table. Thomas must have remarked it too, for Hester heard him question Pringle.

"Miss Hester's orders, sir," replied that worthy calmly. Hester waited to hear no more. She fled to the drawing room, pausing long enough to draw a deep breath before entering.

"Ah, there you are, my love. Come and have a comfortable coze," said her ladyship, patting the seat beside her invitingly. She waited for Hester to be seated and then remarked casually,

"By the way, it had quite slipped my mind until this moment, but I believe you have a visitor. My maid mentioned that a young lady had arrived just as I was leaving for the play. Is she staying here? Why did she not accompany us this evening, or perhaps she had another engagement?"

Hester started guiltily, uncomfortably aware that the usual social courtesies had not been observed. She hastily marshalled her thoughts, leaning forward to clasp Lady Marchant's plump hand.

"Dear Aunt Annabelle, it is a long story and rather difficult to explain. Thomas and Mortimer have just come in and I would like them to be present, with your permission," she hesitated. Lady Marchant was puzzled and intrigued, but she could not withstand the expression of entreaty in Hester's deep, grey eyes.

"By all means, if you think it necessary. You had better send Pringle to intercept them before they retire."

Hester jumped up at once, but stopped with her hand on the bell-pull, for at that moment there was the sound of voices on the stairs and a second later the door swung open to reveal the two young men.

"May we come in, mama, or do we interrupt a *tête-à-tête*?", enquired Thomas, grinning engagingly.

"Come in, Thomas and you Mortimer, we were just about to ring for you," declared her ladyship, waving her hand amiably towards two large chairs. "Your cousin has some information which she wishes to impart to me and she desired that you be present," she continued, settling herself more comfortably among the numerous tasselled cushions and nodding to her niece to signify that she might begin.

"Most of my tale is familiar to Mortimer," began Hester, glancing apologetically at her brother, who raised his brows, but made no comment. Without more ado she launched into a detailed account of the happenings in Shawcross prior to their departure. She omitted only the part that Hugo had played, in his rôle as the 'Beau Chevalier', when he had held up Mr. Abercromby's coach, for that episode still puzzled her considerably. She also forbore to mention Mortimer's meeting with Hugo at 'The Horse and Groom', but she hinted at the enmity between his lordship and Stephen Garth and concentrated on the difficulties of Susan and her fiancé, Mr. Stone. She described the way in which Garth and his followers terrorised the neighbourhood and went on to explain Garth's courtship of herself, which had necessitated her own hurried departure from Shawcross. She concluded her tale with a brief account of Susan's arrival in Brighton earlier in the day.

"So you see, my dear aunt, I felt that I must take you into our confidence, for it is possible that Mr. Garth will pursue his sister here. I do not yet know why Susan ran away, but clearly something of a serious nature must have occurred. I took the liberty of requesting Pringle to deny all knowledge of her presence until I had had time to consult with Lord Montfort, but now unfortunately I cannot do so at once, for his lordship has been obliged to leave Brighton; I received a message from him a few moments ago."

For a moment there was silence, the faces of Hester's three listeners registering a mixture of emotions. Mortimer was flushed with excitement and anger at Garth's ill-treatment of his sister. He could not imagine bringing Hester to such a pass that she would be obliged to flee from him, covering her feet with blisters and utterly destitute. It was unthinkable. Lady Marchant appeared bemused, as if she had been listening to some fairy tale that could not possibly happen in real life. Thomas's reactions were the most complicated for, unknown to the others, some aspects of Hester's story were already familiar to him. He realised that she had suppressed certain information and was curious to know why. He was also surprised for he had not suspected that his quiet country cousins would have become involved in such a tangled affair, which promised to have far-reaching repercussions.

Thomas swung his fob watch reflectively.

"One sees now why Pringle is patrolling the entrance hall armed with a bludgeon," he observed, throwing a mischievous side-glance at his parent. A look of horror replaced bewilderment as her ladyship absorbed the meaning of this laconic remark. Matters were moving too quickly for Lady Marchant's taste. Before she could speak, her son continued, "I wonder if I should remove myself. I could go and stay with the Spragues. There may be a little awkwardness, you see, for under the circumstances I feel it my duty to inform you that I am already acquainted with Stephen Garth and his sister met me once at Hatch End. It was a difficult evening and I doubt if Miss Garth would care to renew the acquaintance. She must have been desperate indeed to come to this house, but of course she may have forgotten my name or failed to realise the connection with you, mama. Garth is not a man to be trifled with," he concluded grimly.

"But Thomas, I don't understand, why did you not visit us, if you were in the vicinity?" exclaimed Hester.

"Yes, and what reason can you have had to have dealings with such an undesirable character?" broke in Lady Marchant sharply. Mortimer said nothing; he lounged back in his chair, his elbows resting on the arms and the tips of his fingers together, regarding his cousin shrewdly through narrowed lids. He was beginning to see daylight.

Thomas rose restlessly and took a turn about the room before coming to a halt beside the fireplace. He tugged uneasily at his faultlessly arranged neckcloth and was about to speak when Pringle appeared, with hot chocolate for the ladies and a decanter of canary wine for the gentlemen. When the refreshments had been served, the butler bowed himself out. Thomas waited until the sound of his footsteps had died away, then he tiptoed over to the door and threw it open. All was quiet, he closed the door again gently and returned to the group around the fire. Before anyone could venture a comment, he placed his finger to his lips and said softly, but earnestly,

"It is vital that what I am about to divulge go no further than these four walls. A great deal will depend on your discretion. Have I your assurance?" They nodded, puzzled and curious to know the reason for elaborate secrecy. With a hint of his familiar crooked smile, Thomas addressed his mother, speaking in quiet, even tones, "You must steel yourself for a shock, dearest mama. Your son, not to put too fine a point on it, has been engaged in espionage." He paused; Lady Marchant gazed at her son, sensing the tinge of bitterness and defiance underlying Thomas's simple statement. She jumped up with surprising agility and threw her arms around his neck, an unusual display of affection, for of recent years, Thomas's relations with his parents had been reserved and undemonstrative.

"My darling boy, how perfectly famous! Your father will be so proud. I always knew you were not a mere dilettante, but it distressed Arthur to see you frittering your time away with Prinny's set." Her ladyship would have run on for some time, but Thomas gently disentangled himself and stood back, retaining a loose clasp of his mother's hands.

"No, mama, it will not do. Papa's attitude towards me must remain unchanged; his hostility is essential if I am to retain the confidence of my, er — accomplices. Recollect he is an influential member of the Whig party. He must continue to regard me as an idle fribble, at least until this affair is over. Your letters may be opened, you must write as usual, deploring my behaviour and the company I keep, wishing I would settle down and marry Hester, or some other nice girl — you know the sort of thing."

Lady Marchant was dumbfounded.

"Have you been reading my private correspondence?" she demanded.

"Of course," confirmed Thomas sardonically, "But I work to serve our country, remember. Spies are sometimes required to perform most distasteful tasks in order to fulfil their mission. The work is often hazardous and that is the chief reason why I have been unwilling to contemplate matrimony, at least until such time as the present threat of invasion is averted. I have good cause to believe that this desirable object may soon be accomplished, and then I will marry Agatha Sprague, if she will have me, but just now I must have as few emotional ties as possible. However, the advent of Miss Garth is an unexpected complication. It is right that you should be on your guard, in case anything happens to me."

"But Thomas!" cried Lady Marchant and Hester together. He waved them to silence.

"No 'buts' my dears, it is futile to protest and too late to draw back, even if I wished to do so. Now listen and I will a tale unfold. What a night of revelations it is to be sure. Well, first we have it from a reliable source that Napoleon will declare himself Emperor of the French in the very near future, if he has not already done so. This will cement his authority absolutely and raise hopes in the bosoms of many émigrés in this country — vain hopes, but there are a number of misguided individuals who cherish the expectation that an Emperor will restore titles and estates lost during the reign of terror. Such people are trying to win favour by sending information, for it is well known that one of Napoleon's foremost ambitions is the subjugation of England. I have been keeping a discreet eye on several suspect French exiles, working in conjunction with senior Foreign Office officials, the Admiralty and Bow Street. We have unearthed an extremely daring conspiracy designed to facilitate an invasion of the South Coast. The enterprise is well-planned; the plotters wait only for the signal, which is to be the declaration that Napoleon has accepted the imperial title. Of course the émigrés are not strong enough to manage alone, but they are cunning. They have taken advantage of the unrest and dissatisfaction among the poor and have enlisted the support of several influential Englishmen, willing to be traitors to their country, bribed by the promise of large rewards when the new régime is successfully installed. The plot is well-conceived. The government has cried wolf so many times, that the threat of invasion is no longer taken seriously. The country has been lulled into a false sense of security, but careful preparations for a friendly reception of the invaders have been made in nests of traitors all along the South Coast. I am not concerned with them all, my task is to concentrate on Brighton and its environs, in conjunction with certain other agents, including your friends Montfort and Abercromby. It is here that the first shock of invasion is expected." Thomas paused, trying to gauge his hearers' reactions. The ladies had grown pale as the full enormity of the situation was borne in upon them. Mortimer said thoughtfully,

"I presume Garth has a finger in this pie. He has a lot of men in his pocket, men of all classes, for one reason or another."

"Men and women," nodded Thomas, smiling at his cousin. Hester glanced from one to the other, listening closely.

"The Comtesse!" she exclaimed triumphantly, "How scatter-brained I have been, but then I had no reason to suspect . . . that is why you have all been courting her so assiduously." She rounded on Thomas, shaking her small fist at him accusingly.

He raised his hand teasingly, to ward off the threatened blow.

"No need to put yourself in a pucker, Hester, sweet coz. 'Twas necessary to throw everyone off the scent. You do understand that now, do you not?" he finished earnestly.

"But what is to be done? How is this disaster to be averted?" interrupted Lady Marchant impatiently, "Arthur should be told at once. He will know what steps should be taken. This hole in the wall activity is all very well, but Napoleon may not wait for you to unmask the plotters. I must write to your father at once."

"Remember your promise, mama," said Thomas warningly. Then his stern features relaxed and he grinned, "Your faith in papa is touching, m'dear, but he is already informed. We are not quite so unprofessional as you appear to believe. However, my noble parent does not know and must not be told of my involvement. There is no need for alarm: the troops are ready, the invasion will not succeed; but my part is not yet finished. Our agents must round up the conspirators and for that we lack proof until the time is ripe. There are one or two missing links. For the present we must all go on as usual. The Comtesse must not guess that she is suspected, for in truth we are uncertain where her deepest loyalties lie. She is known to have been the mistress of Napoleon, but they apparently parted in bitterness.

"Garth is another matter. Montfort is dealing largely with him, but not in a friendly way. He has adopted a disguise to mask his activities, whereas I am accepted by Garth as a fellow conspirator. That is how I came to be at Hatch End. I was sent down to keep an eye on the Runners, summoned by Garth after the highwayman's attack on Abercromby's coach. You probably recall that incident?"

Hester and Mortimer nodded assent, avoiding one another's eyes. Thomas remarked their reticence, but forbore to press them. He continued,

"Well, as you may have discovered, Watson and Peabody are not the sharpest of individuals, but they were not above a little bribery and I gather Garth paid them handsomely for their dubious services. I had supper one evening at Hatch End. Miss Garth was present, obviously unhappy. She pleaded with her brother to leave the vicar in peace, even offered to marry some choice of Garth's if he would guarantee Stone's safety. Garth was very harsh with her, told her she would do as she was bid, and so would Stone if he knew what was good for him. He appealed to me for support, even hinted that I might be a suitable candidate for Susan's hand, once the new régime was installed. Forgive me, mama, but he's a demmed thickskinned fellow, hide like a rhinoceros. I did my best to depress his pretensions, but it was not politic to offend the man, so I fear Miss Garth formed but a poor opinion of me. It would be intolerable for her to be here under the same roof with me."

"Yes, but Thomas, she will be obliged to meet you. Brighton is but a small town," objected Lady Marchant, grappling valiantly with the complexities of the situation.

"Excuse me, Aunt Annabelle, I believe Susan must be told at least some of Tom's activities," interposed Hester, rubbing her nose meditatively, "We do not yet know why she ran away, but if she meets Tom by accident, not knowing his true position, she will flee again in all probability. However, I agree it would be wiser for Tom to remove, for if Garth or his spies hear of his and Susan's presence under the same roof, they could not fail to be suspicious and we must not jeopardise the plans at this stage. I am truly sorry to have added to your burdens, but Susan is my friend and she has nowhere else to go."

"Oh, what a tangled web we weave when first we practise to deceive!" declared her ladyship despairingly, "Miss Garth must remain, of course, but is she to go into society or become a recluse or what?"

"I think 'twill be safer if she goes into society, but with care and always in company," replied Thomas.

"Does Montfort know of your activities?" enquired Mortimer, following his own train of thought.

"Yes and no. He is aware that we are both working for the same end, but we do not collaborate closely, our rôles being rather different, as I have explained."

Mortimer listened carefully, then addressed his sister.

"Montfort should be told of Susan's arrival, and other matters. Do you know where to contact him?"

"Yes, he said that he may be contacted at 'The Horse and Groom' or through Peter Lightfoot or Ned Potter, I suppose," said Hester slowly.

"Are you wise to entrust me with such information. I might have told you a great many untruths this evening?" interjected Thomas, smiling bitterly. Hester and Lady Marchant looked indignant, but Mortimer said, a trifle roughly,

"We've known you forever, Thomas, I'd trust you with my life. Pray heaven our faith is justified. Now, I set off at dawn. Hester, you must speak with Susan and ascertain the reason for her abrupt departure, so that I may tell Montfort. Thomas, you should leave this house tonight," he finished decisively.

"As you wish," replied Thomas, bowing ironically, to hide a sudden rush of colour.

"Perhaps the army is the place for you, Mortimer," remarked Hester lightly, to ease the tension, "You issue orders to the manner born. Excuse me, dear Aunt, I will go to Susan, there is no time to be lost." She sketched a curtsey and hurried away, Thomas soon following, leaving Mortimer to restore his astonished aunt with a fortifying glass of canary.

"I presume Garth thinks you're under the same roof with me to keep a watchful eye on my movements?" said Hester softly, pausing at the head of the stair, as Thomas joined her.

"Ask no questions and you'll be told no lies," replied her cousin, smiling enigmatically. "Believe me, it's safer so."

"Provoking creature!" murmured Hester cordially, "But have a care. Hugo's sudden disappearance must mean that something is afoot. Well, I will not tease you, but let me know if there is aught I can do to help. Goodnight, dear Tom, tread gently with Agatha if you go to the Spragues."

He looked at her searchingly for a moment, then gave her a sudden hug, and turning on his heel, strode down the passage to his bedchamber. Hester opened her own door quietly. Martha was nodding by the fireside, the candle burning low in its socket. Susan stirred in her sleep and Martha woke up. On perceiving Hester she jumped to her feet, but Hester laid a finger to her lips. She allowed Martha to help her undress, then dismissed the maid and approached the bed, carrying a freshly-lit candle. The light roused the sleeping girl, she blinked and raised her arm to shield her eyes.

"Susan, wake up, I'm sorry to disturb you, but the matter is urgent," whispered Hester, shaking her friend's shoulder. Unwillingly Susan opened her eyes, then, as awareness returned, she sat up in alarm, pushing back her tumbled curls.

"What is wrong, oh Hester, is my brother come?" cried Susan, pale with fright.

"No, no, nothing of that nature, pray calm yourself," replied Hester soothingly, "It is just that my Lord Montfort has had to leave town. I wish to send him a message assuring him of your safety, a verbal message, Mortimer will take it, but I need to know why you ran away. I do not wish to pry, my dear, but larger matters may be at stake."

"Of course, I have no secrets from you," said Susan, shaking her head in an effort to clear the mists of sleep. She recounted her adventures in a low hurried voice, plucking the sheet nervously from time to time in her agitation. The tale was long, but Hester listened patiently, making no attempt to interrupt for fear of breaking the thread. It appeared that Stephen Garth, mightily incensed by Susan's betrothal, had made life intolerable for Mr. Stone and his fiancée. In order to prevent the marriage he determined to send Susan to stay with her aunt in Yorkshire; when she refused to go, he locked her in her room, under close guard. With the aid of her maid, Nellie, Susan had contrived to escape on the Saturday after Hester had left Shawcross. Nellie had drugged the guard with a sleeping potion obtained from Andrew Minton and they had slipped down the back stairs and out into the night, while Stephen was preoccupied with one of his numerous late night visitors. There had been an unusual number of comings and goings at Hatch End, while Susan was confined to her room and not the least of her troubles during her flight had been a constant fear for her beloved's safety. However, there was nothing she could do alone and she had come to Hester because she did not know where else to turn in her hour of need. Dr. Minton had been kindness itself. She had changed into one of Nellie's gowns at his house, but it was out of the question for her to remain in the neighbourhood. The doctor had promised faithfully to send word if anything happened to Mr. Stone. She and Nellie had walked to Brighton, following tracks frequented only by sheep, and sleeping in hedgerows. Susan was not accustomed to such a hard life and her sore feet had hampered their progress. Several times they had followed watercourses for miles out of their way, for fear Stephen would seek to follow them with his dogs on the scent. More than once they were hopelessly lost and the severe gales and rain had made the journey exceedingly miserable. Without Nellie, Susan would have been obliged to seek aid and shelter in a cottage, but Nellie had proved remarkably resourceful. Disguising her voice in a gipsy whine, she had begged for food, and had obtained enough to survive on, for Susan had no money and had not thought to ask Dr. Minton for a loan. Once, when Nellie entered a village, she had seen two of Garth's men going in and out of cottages, obviously conducting a search, but she had managed to retreat unseen. It had taken them almost a week to reach Brighton, concluded Susan.

"It is strange that your brother did not look for you here," observed Hester, when Susan fell silent. Susan lay back wearily among the pillows.

"Perhaps he did," she suggested, "He would not have expected me to take so long to cover such a short distance."

"No-o," replied Hester thoughtfully, "I don't think so. I expect Thomas was the reason."

"Thomas, who is Thomas?" asked Susan, puzzled.

Hester took a deep breath. She had decided to confide in her friend. Susan listened wide-eyed to Hester's summary of Thomas's activities, in so far as she knew them.

"'Tis strange," she remarked at length, "I had no notion that Mr. Marchant was your cousin, but I liked him better than my brother's other 'gentlemen' visitors. Of course, as he told you, I encountered him only once, but he seemed sensitive and sat silent when the others taunted me about Jedediah. Indeed, he intervened to protect me. He did not fit in with the usual pattern, but Stephen respects him. He stayed late discussing private affairs when the others had left. I was sent upstairs after a while, he held the door open for me and gave me a very reassuring smile. I did not see him again. Please tell him that I bear him no animosity and he must not quit his mother's roof on my account. I think he is a very brave man to mix in such company. What will happen to Stephen, Hester, will they arrest him?"

"I don't know, my dear. It is very probable. Try not to think of it till you are stronger. I will tell Thomas what you have said, but I think he will remove in case your brother becomes suspicious of his loyalties. Your advent must have complicated the situation for Tom, but he will not betray you. I have a notion 'twill not be long before the whole plot is unravelled. We must be careful, but you need not be confined to the house so long as you do not venture out unescorted. Now I must go and speak with Mortimer. Try to get some more rest. I will be back soon. Tell Martha if you require anything."

Hester spoke briefly with her brother and retired to spend a restless night, a prey to a thousand imaginative fancies. Mortimer snatched a few hours sleep, then, armed with the necessary information, he set out at dawn, two well-primed pistols in his holsters.

The ladies passed the next few days uneventfully. They diverted themselves by undertaking a round of social engagements. Thomas avoided them, but they received word of him from time to time by Monty Sprague. Monty reported that he was comfortably installed in the Sprague household and was doing his best to monopolise Agatha's time and attention. Susan and Hester strove valiantly to be patient, but they jumped every time they heard a knock upon the door. On Wednesday their peace was shattered. Mortimer returned from Shawcross and reluctantly informed the anxious women that Jedediah Stone had disappeared.

Chapter 20
The Devil's Dyke

"Oh Hester, what can we do?" cried Susan, for the thousandth time, as they sat together in the drawing room on the morning after Mortimer's return.

"Nothing," replied Hester firmly, as she busied herself tying the knots of the large parcel which contained her completed manuscript. Usually this task would have given her a thrill of satisfaction, but today she was distracted by a feeling of foreboding and she felt as if her fingers were all thumbs. The grey weather matched her spirits and she was worried about her friend, who sat listlessly by the fire, her shadowed eyes enormous in her pale face.

"Be a dear and lend a finger to help me tie these knots," she commanded briskly, "It is always better to be occupied, brooding will not solve matters and I'm sure Mr. Stone is quite safe. Mortimer left word with Peter Lightfoot and by now his lordship will have taken action. You may depend upon it he will know just what should be done."

She spoke with an assurance which she did not feel, but Susan seemed comforted. She rose and came to the table, placing her finger as Hester directed. Between them a neat parcel was soon achieved. Hester addressed the label and rang for Pringle for the dispatch of the manuscript to London. It was a relief to be rid of the burden of work which had been with her for so long, to know that any decision was now out of her hands. She took a lighthearted twirl about the room, but halted in sudden contrition as she perceived Susan's quivering shoulders. She joined her friend at the window and placed her arm around the smaller girl's waist.

"You are fortunate indeed to be so talented, so self-sufficient," sniffed Susan, dabbing her face with a minute handkerchief, "I cannot think of anything but Jedediah; I keep imagining him beaten, perhaps dying, with no one to succour him."

Her voice rose hysterically: Hester decided that stern measures were in order. Gently, she detached herself and sat down by the fire.

"By all means indulge in a fit of the vapours if you wish, but I believe Mr. Stone has a right to expect more restrained behaviour on the part of a prospective clergyman's wife," she remarked prosaically, pausing to let the full import of her observation penetrate Susan's overwrought mind. "As for your earlier comment, it is nonsense to say that anyone in our society is self-sufficient; I am extremely dependent on my family and friends for affection and rational company. My books would be poor things indeed if I lived like a hermit in seclusion, cutting myself off from all civilised pursuits and avoiding emotional entanglements. I write to please myself and to provide a little light diversion for other people; I am not greatly talented, but I am vain enough to be flattered and happy at the success of my works. I need the approval of my friends. Dear Susan, forgive my plain speaking, you are one of my dearest friends and you are undergoing a great ordeal, but for everyone's sake you must strive to overcome your emotions. I share your anxiety, perhaps more than you know, but we both have a duty to those around us to comport ourselves as usual. It is all that we can do, but we must do it to the best of our ability."

Hester did not relish her rôle as mentor, but to her surprise Susan responded to her admonitions by squaring her shoulders and achieving a watery smile. In a flurry of skirts, she flung herself at Hester's feet and clasped her hands.

"What a selfish beast I am to wallow in my own troubles. I quite forgot how acute must be your anxiety for his lordship. You still have a partiality for him, do you not?"

"I love him beyond expression," replied Hester evenly, in low tones.

For a moment they gazed at one another in silence, sharing a sympathy deeper than ever before. Then Susan leaped lightly to her feet, tugging Hester up with her.

"Let us go for a walk. We could call on Miss Stanhope and see if there is any news; surely we must hear something soon. Besides, Miss Stanhope is always a good antidote to the dismals and Marietta has promised to lend me her latest copy of *La Belle Assemblée*. I like Marietta extraordinarily well, and Stephanie too, of course, if only she would not talk so much of horses. Marietta is quieter, but very interesting. We had a long conversation after dinner the other night and she told me about Mr. Abercromby. She feels for him just as I do for Jedediah, we have a great deal in common. She knows how it feels to run away from home with hardly a stitch of clothing to one's name and — oh, so many things!"

Susan rattled on cheerfully all the while they made ready for their walk. She was a different person from the sad little waif at the breakfast table. Hester encouraged her as much as possible and they were deeply engaged in an animated discussion of how best to make over one of Hester's ball gowns for Susan's use at the next Assembly when they arrived on the Steyne. They were approached, almost immediately, by the Comtesse de Chérault, regally attired in a coat of midnight blue, trimmed with white fur, a matching bonnet set at a becoming angle on her dark curls. It occurred to Hester that the Frenchwoman's dress was more suited to a Russian winter than an English Spring, but she curtsied politely and offered some innocuous comment on the weather. Quelling a momentary feeling of unease she made Miss Garth known to the Comtesse. The two regarded one another curiously for a moment; then the older lady turned back to Hester and requested the favour of a few minutes private conversation. Susan excused herself prettily, saying that she would await Hester in the milliner's establishment nearby as she wished to purchase some trimming for her straw bonnet.

"I am fortunate to have found you so easily, mademoiselle. I 'ave a message for you from your admirer, milord Montfort," said the Comtesse in low, hurried tones as she fell into step beside Hester, "He asks me to tell you to meet him by the old hill camp above the inn at the Devil's Dyke at sunset today. You are to bring Mees Garth with you and I will accompany you in my carriage."

Hester listened to these words in growing suspicion and disquiet. Hugo had told her on no account to leave Brighton. Surely he would not choose the Comtesse as his messenger. She replied warily, raising her eyebrows sceptically,

"What proof have I that it is Hugo himself who sends this message? I understood that he was in London."

The Comtesse nodded calmly as if she had anticipated some opposition.

"My dear Mees Vane, you are a lady of great imaginative powers. I see I must tell you a leetle about myself. Forgive me if you find it tedious. You must know I fled from France some years ago, and after many vicissitudes I arrive in England. I 'ave been mos' grateful for the 'ospitality of your country, yes. When I come, I 'ad many friends, but no money. One must live," she paused, spreading her hands in an eloquent, pathetic gesture, "Well, me I do not like to take and not give something in return. I 'ave been obliged to deal a leetle with the smuggling fraternity. Also, in order to bring about the overthrow of the upstart Napoleon and to bring about the return of the true king, I 'ave 'elped your government spies insofar as it is possible for a woman with my reputation. I am a person of resource and I see and hear much. Milord Montfort has been mos' interested in my information concerning the French plans to invade England. You too have 'eard the rumours, perhaps?"

The Frenchwoman looked sharply at Hester, who had given an involuntary gasp. Hester hesitated, her mind racing, could it be possible, as the Comtesse herself had hinted, that she was a double agent, and if so, where did her true allegiance lie? It was a question of the utmost importance and the only way to find out was to accompany her on the proposed expedition to the Devil's Dyke. Should she risk it? A sudden ray of bright sunshine broke through the clouds. Hester took it for a good omen, coinciding as it did with her longing for some form of positive activity. She wondered if the Comtesse had received news that Napoleon was about to be crowned Emperor, but restrained herself from enquiring, for she feared to betray the depth of her own knowledge in that direction. Instead she observed quietly,

"You honour me with your confidence, madame. It is all most interesting, but I am at a loss to understand the purpose of the proposed meeting. What can I do and why must Miss Garth accompany me?"

The Comtesse shrugged in an expressive, yet indefinably elegant, gesture.

"That I cannot say. I am merely a channel for information." She slipped her hand inside her muff and drew forth a small packet, which she gave to Hester. "This is a token of my good faith, open it in private and destroy it at your discretion. I obtained these damaging articles, not without some difficulty, from a mutual acquaintance, Mr. Stephen Garth." She raised her voice as they approached the milliner's, having completed a circuit of the Steyne; Susan was waiting for them on the steps in conversation with Agatha and Monty Sprague. "It has been so pleasant to 'ave this opportunity to further our acquaintance, chère Miss Vane, au revoir." She stopped some ten yards from Susan and the Spragues.

"Here I take my leave. My carriage will call for you at 3.30 this afternoon. Do not fail me, much depends upon you."

The Comtesse's forceful dark eyes rested compellingly on Hester's thoughtful face for a moment. Then, with a quick nod and a graceful wave, she turned on her heels and was soon lost to view on the far side of the grassy promenade. Hester was left with a troubled sense that she had been outmanoeuvred. She must consult Susan at once; she joined her friends and learned with some dismay that Cousin Thomas had been called out of town on urgent business. She had hoped that he might advise her. The chilly wind did not encourage lingering conversation and after a few minutes the Spragues departed, while Hester and Susan proceeded to the Montfort villa where they hoped to find Miss Stanhope. In this they were disappointed. Miss Stanhope and her charges had driven out to the Camp to view a parade, accompanied by Sir Mortimer, who had appeared as the ladies were about to leave and had volunteered his escort. His lordship's butler vouchsafed this information and upon further enquiry, told the young ladies that the household had received word from his lordship in London only that morning; it was understood he would not be returning to Brighton for several days. Susan and Hester glanced at one another in perplexity. Hester had told Susan of the Comtesse's proposal on their walk to the North Steyne and it appeared that all their allies had deserted them.

"We cannot consult my aunt, for she is spending the day with Mrs. Fitzherbert. It is unfortunate above all things!" exclaimed Hester in vexation, as they hurried home.

"It's as if there is a conspiracy against us," agreed Susan, alomost running to keep pace with her friend.

"You may speak more truly than you know," replied Hester wryly, "I think you should remain in Brighton and give the alarm if I do not return by a reasonable hour. The more I reflect on the matter, the more foolhardy it appears. Do but consider, Susan, the Comtesse was so vague, she spoke of a message from Hugo, and insisted that it was a situation of the utmost seriousness, life or death even, but how can we help? And does it not occur to you that it is very odd for his lordship to send a message, a verbal message, by the Comtesse, when it was his firm injunction that we should on no account quit Brighton? I am but a pawn in the game, my dear, but you are Stephen's sister and once we leave the town we are unprotected, in countryside terrorised by your brother and his men. I cannot, in good conscience, allow you to accompany me."

Susan's exquisite little face puckered obstinately; she caught Hester's arm as they were about to mount the steps of Lady Marchant's residence. Her voice held an equal blend of determination and pleading.

"And I cannot, in good conscience, allow you to go alone. You have been so kind to me, you have given me clothes, money, shelter and listened to my nonsense. It is a debt which I can never hope to repay, but if, as you imply, there is a trap, Stephen must be involved and I can restrain him. Suppose he should force you to wed him? It is unthinkable that you should go alone. And then there is Jedediah, perhaps if I return Stephen will release him; even if I cannot marry him, he will be safe. I cannot stand idly by, my duty is plain, if you go, I go too." She lifted her chin, her appealing brown eyes meeting Hester's unwaveringly.

"But you forget, the Comtesse will be with me, I do not go unchaperoned," Hester protested, but her voice lacked conviction.

"In the event of a plot, how long will she remain?" enquired Susan scornfully.

Hester shrugged, but persisted,

"She cannot think us so naive that we will run off without leaving a message for our friends. The days of waiting have made us overwrought. There must be a simple explanation. I am persuaded that Hugo will be at the Dyke to meet me."

"He cannot be in two places at once, his butler heard from him in London only this morning, recollect."

"Oh, that may be a ruse to cover his tracks. He told me to send word to him at 'The Horse and Groom', so he must be in the country." Hester spoke with more confidence than she felt. Susan nodded calmly.

"Very well, then I shall accompany you as he requested. He did desire my presence, did he not?"

"Oh heavens, we are arguing in circles. Do as you wish. I cannot deny that it will be comforting to be together," Hester capitulated, giving her friend's hand an affectionate squeeze.

The decision having been taken, they entered the house and separated to make preparations. Alone in her chamber, Hester pulled out the small packet which the Comtesse had given her in token of good faith. Her hands trembled as she tore off the oilskin wrapper and she blinked in surprise as two items dropped lightly on to her bed; carefully she examined the objects: a man's black velvet mask and a ring, bearing a familiar heraldic device, a sable dragon rampant. Her mind flew back to the day at the Priory when she and Hugo had stood in the topiary garden surveying this same ancient beast and Hugo had told her of the untimely end of the first Baron Montfort. She shivered, but whether with some sense of fear or premonition she was unable to decide. She felt very close to Hugo and could almost feel his physical presence when she slipped the heavy ring on her finger. It was much too large for her slim fingers and she stood cradling it in her left hand, surrendering herself to a deep longing for his love and companionship. She rarely indulged herself in this way for she had been badly hurt once before and could not quite believe that a more satisfactory ending might be in view this time. Troublesome thoughts intruded. How had the Comtesse obtained Hugo's ring? Was he in danger, was it a trick or a *bona fide* token? Fears and suspicions chased away her mood of happy nostalgia. She was roused from her reverie by the hall clock chiming the hour of two. She wrapped the ring carefully in a handkerchief, ready to be tucked in the bosom of her gown when she had changed for the drive. The mask she burned, poking it carefully down among the coals until it had quite withered away; then, seating herself at her writing table, Hester wrote two notes. One she addressed to Mortimer, informing him of the Comtesse's message from Hugo and stating the destination of the afternoon drive. The other she sent to Miss Stanhope, desiring her to take no action unless she heard from Mortimer or Hugo himself, in the event that she and Susan did not return that evening. Time was passing; hurriedly, Hester selected a warm, grey carriage dress, kid half boots and gloves, and, after some hesitation, her heavy, dark travelling cloak with a fur-lined hood. It would be cool on the Downs in the late afternoon and it was as well to be prepared for eventualities. She placed the ring in position, touching it like a talisman for good luck, and checked her reticule to make sure that she had adequate funds against possible need. She combed her hair without troubling to summon Martha's aid; as a finishing touch she settled a small, neat bonnet with a yellow ostrich feather on her head, tied the ribbons beneath her chin and, taking up her notes, descended to the drawing room a few minutes before the appointed hour.

Susan, also warmly clad in shades of green and russet brown, was waiting for her. They smiled conspiratorially at one another, their eyes sparkling with mingled excitement and apprehension.

"I feel quite hollow, I couldn't eat a thing, but perhaps I should have attempted it," said Susan, clasping her hands nervously.

"How foolish, I didn't even think of it," exclaimed Hester in dismay. "Well, it is too late now. Perhaps we may obtain something at the inn on the Dyke if we arrive early. An empty stomach makes one feel so defenceless, now that you mention it."

"Not quite. I have my pistol, you see," announced Susan, drawing forth from her muff a small, serviceable-looking weapon. Hester blinked incredulously.

"Can you use it?" she asked, curiously.

"Oh yes, indeed. Stephen believed that it was essential when one considered the company we were sometimes obliged to keep," replied Susan casually.

"What a very unusual accomplishment for a parson's wife," murmured Hester teasingly, but she eyed her friend with a new respect.

"I wish I had a weapon too."

"Why don't you take this?" Susan picked up a small, jewelled paperknife from the escritoire by the window. Hester slipped the knife in her reticule. A moment later, they heard a loud knock on the door below. They waited tensely, listening to Pringle's steady footsteps approaching.

"The Comtesse de Chérault's carriage awaits you, ladies," pronounced the butler, a hint of disapproval in his stentorian tones. "Will I tell my lady you'll be in for dinner, Miss Hester?"

Hester hesitated, uncomfortably aware that Pringle was regarding their heavy cloaks with surprise.

"Yes, that is, I'm not sure. We may dine with the Comtesse. Please give this note to Sir Mortimer, and have the other sent round to Miss Stanhope as soon as possible. Thank you, Pringle. Are you ready, Susan?"

The Comtesse's tiger, a small black boy of some fourteen years, sombrely arrayed in black and silver livery, jumped down to hand the ladies into the carriage. They seated themselves with more haste than dignity as the vehicle set off almost at once, rattling down the hill towards the centre of town at a smart pace. The interior of the carriage was dark, but luxurious, being upholstered in the Comtesse's favourite black velvet, with silver tassels. When their eyes became accustomed to the gloom they realized that the carriage was empty, save for themselves. They speculated uneasily on the Comtesse's whereabouts and were greatly relieved when the vehicle swung away from the main thoroughfare to draw up before a tall porticoed house on Charles Street. Seconds later, the nearside door opened to admit the Comtesse, swathed in a voluminous black cloak. She settled herself opposite Hester and Susan with much flurry of rugs and draperies. A footman set a hot brick tenderly at her feet, the door clicked shut and they were off once more, slowly at first due to the exigencies of town traffic, but, as soon as they were clear of the main streets, the coachman sprang his horses to such a degree that the occupants of the vehicle were obliged to cling to the silver tassels to prevent themselves being thrown to the floor.

"Comtesse, why this excessive speed?" gasped Hester, when the pace slackened a trifle as they began the ascent in the foothills of the downs.

"I told you, my dear Mees Vane, it ees a matter of life and death," responded the Comtesse, her eyes glittering wickedly in the half light.

"It may well be so, and before we reach our destination," retorted Hester tartly.

"Relax my dears, my coachman, he is very experienced. Tell me, are you quite warm, would you care for a rug?"

Hester and Susan declined civilly. The Comtesse shook her head in amusement, her black lace mantilla fluttering about her pale face.

"You English ladies are so 'ardy. I come from a warmer climate. My estates were in the Rhône Valley and 'ere I am always cold. The chill breezes of La Manche, they reach through to my bones, I do not find them invigorating, not at all. It ees sometimes *très triste* always to be an exile." She sounded so wistful that Hester exerted herself to converse. Susan stared fixedly out of the window, offering no help, but Hester adroitly turned the talk to the old days in France before the Terror. The Comtesse became quite animated in describing her ancestral home. She mentioned briefly, but without apparent regret, her husband who had fallen a victim to the guillotine and concentrated in her reminiscences on the happy days of her youth. Hester listened with real interest, forgetting her uneasiness, but Susan sat quietly in her corner, making no comment.

The drive was accomplished smoothly, the Comtesse's confidence in her coachman's ability proving fully justified. Conversation languished as they made the final approach. Hester, sitting on the seaward-facing side of the carriage, was awed by the majesty of the panorama spread out before her. The well-beaten road ran along the top of the downs, the fields on Hester's left falling away in gentle undulations. By craning her neck to look back, Hester could see Brighton, small in the distance, nestled between folds in the surrounding hills, with the sea a shimmering streak on the far horizon. Closer at hand she saw sheep and ploughed fields, the landscape dotted here and there on the high ground with windswept stunted trees. Thick clumps of yellow broom were in May flower.

"That must be the Dyke. What a strange, deep gash it has gouged in the smooth slopes of the downs!" exclaimed Susan, breaking her long silence. Hester turned eagerly to peer through the opposite window, but her view was obscured by a hedge of yellow broom as the road curved around the Dyke.

"How do you call that tree, with the so delicate white blossom?" asked the Comtesse as they clattered over the chalky yard, which formed the forefront of the small inn on the Dyke.

"It is called May. One wonders how it survives in the high winds up here," replied Hester, catching her breath as the Comtesse's tiger pulled open the door; he was obliged to hang on to the handle with all his strength to prevent it swinging shut again, for the sea breeze had attained almost galeforce proportions on the high ground. The Comtesse laughed and tapped the boy lightly on the cheek as he handed her down, his back pressed firmly against the door. Hester and Susan followed quickly. The wind caught their bonnets as they moved away from the comparative shelter of the carriage.

"Run child, bespeak me a private parlour and some refreshment, make haste," ordered the Comtesse, almost shouting to make herself heard. Beckoning to her companions to follow, she tripped across the uneven ground to the left, skirted some low outbuildings, and halted on the far side of a rough construction, which might once have been a pigsty. Here they were out of the wind, the sudden stillness making their voices sound unnaturally loud.

With an airy wave of her hand the Comtesse indicated a small footpath which meandered along the side of the downs in the direction away from the Dyke, which lay on the other side of the inn. Their eyes followed the path for a distance of perhaps five hundred yards before it dipped out of sight behind a rocky outcrop.

"That is the track which you must take. It leads to the site of the ancient fort, very interesting it is, *on me dit* that it was there before Caesar crossed *La Manche*. Me, I like the present, and I 'ave no desire to see it, so I will await you here in whatever warmth and comfort this hostelry can offer."

With a regal gesture the Comtesse drew her cloak about her and sailed away, giving Hester and Susan no opportunity to protest. They looked at one another in dismay, taken aback by the sudden desertion of their chaperone. At this hour the place was very lonely and quiet; Hester felt a small wave of panic which she resolutely suppressed. She could see nothing for it but to put a good face on it; the carriage had disappeared, should they rejoin the Comtesse and beg her to accompany them? While she hesitated a man emerged from one of the outbuildings and began to scatter grain. At once he was surrounded by dozens of hungry, clucking fowls. Reassured by the normality of the scene, Hester drew a deep breath; from somewhere close at hand a cuckoo gave a plaintive cry.

"Come, Susan, we must make haste before it gets dark," she said, bunching her billowing skirts firmly in her right hand and clutching her bonnet with her left. Her reticule flapped violently against her arm and she was forced to bend her head against the wind, as she stepped forward. Susan followed her, the long grass swishing against their legs. They crossed a patch of rough ground until they reached the chalky path indicated by the Comtesse. The ascent was steep and they climbed for some minutes in silence. Half way between the inn and the rocky outcrop the two friends paused to catch their breath. Looking back, they were amazed at the beauty of the darkening valley; twinkling lights had appeared in the lower windows of the inn, emphasising the loneliness without; no other human habitation was in sight. Accustomed though they were to the solitude of the countryside, the girls were unprepared for the awesome, eerie atmosphere of the place.

"Shall we turn back?" asked Susan, shivering despite their energetic climb. Hester hesitated.

"No," she replied at last, "We have not come so far to be deterred by a few ghosts. Roman legionaries and ancient Druids cannot harm us. See, over there on that hilltop is Chanctonbury Ring. We will just go a little further, and look around the big rock. If we cannot see Hugo on the fort site, then we will return to the inn."

They hurried on, Hester a little ahead, for the path was not wide enough to accommodate them side by side. They rounded a small bend in the path and Hester stumbled. At the same moment Susan, who had been glancing over her shoulder, cried out,

"Hester, a carriage is leaving the inn courtyard, it looks like — oh heaven, it cannot be — the Comtesse is deserting us!"

Before Hester could recover her balance a musty blanket was thrown over her head; from Susan's scream, abruptly stifled, she gathered that the same misfortune had overtaken her. Hester felt herself half dragged, half carried over the uneven hillside for some distance. Very soon she ceased to struggle, being wholly preoccupied with the effort to breathe. She must have fainted, for when she became once more aware of her surroundings, she found that she had been slung over a pony's back. Cords bound her at wrist and ankle and she was blindfolded, but she was relieved to know that she was still alive and could breathe freely. At least their captors had not murdered them outright. Nevertheless the long journey was excessively uncomfortable and she felt bruised in every limb when the pony finally halted in response to a pressure on his bridle. Almost beyond thought, Hester found herself lifted in strong arms; she was carried, not ungently, for perhaps twenty yards. A door was pushed open, followed by a rush of warm, foetid air. She was deposited on a pile of sacking, still blindfolded, and for a while she was content to lie quietly, listening to the bustle around her and striving to regain her composure. At length she heard footsteps approaching, the blindfold was untied by deft, sailorly fingers and she blinked in the sudden light of two candles, one set at each end of the long, low room.

A curious calm descended on Hester as she took stock of her surroundings. A strong smell of salt and fish assailed her nostrils; she saw lobster pots, nets and seamen's boots stacked neatly in a corner. Susan was lying, apparently unconscious, on a pallet directly opposite her. The middle of the room was deeply shadowed. Cautiously, Hester turned her head; two men were sitting at a rough table near the door, which was heavily bolted. The men were engaged in a whispered conversation, their heads close together. Both wore thick seamen's jerseys, woollen tasselled hats pulled low over their eyes, and they were in their stockinged feet. One of the men stirred and Hester hastily averted her eyes. Through an uncurtained window at the other end of the room she could see that it was now quite dark; the second candle glowed on the window sill. Sitting quietly on the sacking, she became aware of an unexpected sound, a murmuring hiss, changing every now and then to a thunderous roar. Realisation came abruptly: It was the crashing of waves on a pebbly beach. The sea was very close.

Wincing with the effort, the cords cutting painfully into her flesh, Hester wriggled to an upright, sitting position, her back resting against the wall. She frowned, indignation at the highhanded audacity of their abduction temporarily overcoming her physical discomfort. After a while her anger subsided and she began to speculate on the lateness of the hour; how long would it be before Mortimer and Miss Stanhope instituted a search party? She wondered if the ponies had left any tracks and decided that it was unlikely. The ground was very dry. Her mind racing feverishly, Hester reviewed the situation. Obviously the kidnapping had been planned, the Comtesse acting as an intermediary to lure them with Hugo's false message. How could she have been so foolish as to fall into the trap? She raised her hands to feel the signet ring, pressing against her bosom. That had been the deciding factor; how had the Comtesse obtained it? Had Hugo been tricked as she had been, or was he injured, even dead? Involuntarily she gave a small gasp. The two men looked up, a chair scraped and the larger fisherman came to bend over her.

Hester overcame a strong impulse to huddle down among the sacking. Instead she sat up very straight, lifted her chin and met the man's gaze unflinchingly. The lower half of his face was masked, but to her astonishment, Hester sensed something vaguely familiar in his stance, head a little to one side. She looked hard at his dark eyes, but the light was dim and the feeling of recognition faded.

"Make yerself aisy, mistress. There's a gennelman a-comin' to see 'ee afore lang," said the man gruffly. He did not linger, but withdrew to the table, where his companion produced a pack of greasy cards and set a bottle on the floor beside them. The two men were quickly absorbed in their game, Hester watched them covertly. At first she puzzled over the identity of the larger man, but failing in this she turned her attention to the other guard, who was seated with his right profile towards her. He stretched out his arm to place a card, revealing a cluster of tattoos. She raised her eyes to the man's neck; as she half-expected a jagged scar was just visible below his ear before it disappeared beneath his jersey. There was no doubt about this man; he was the fisherman who had leered insolently at their carriage on the way home from the sketching party in Hove. Vividly, Hester recalled his mocking bow and her own irrational feeling of disquiet, even fear. How unfortunate, to say the least, to be at this man's mercy. He seemed to have a weakness for the bottle, but she was relieved to find that his larger accomplice had some control over him. At one point in the game the half empty bottle was replaced by a pitcher of water. Tattoo, as Hester mentally designated him, objected forcefully, but his companion shook his head firmly. No word was spoken, but the vociferous protests subsided immediately and the game progressed. The tension and animosity between the two men was almost tangible. It occurred to Hester that she might try to enlist the sympathy of the gruff-voiced fisherman. She had decided that she and Susan must depend upon their own wits to escape, for she could not believe that help would soon be forthcoming from any other quarter.

Hester's gaze rested meditatively on her friend, who was still lying, white and still, on the straw pallet. She hoped that Susan was not seriously injured. Fortunately, this anxiety was soon allayed. Susan opened her eyes, actually winked at Hester, then closed her eyes again and moaned feebly.

Hester took her cue.

"Can you not see that my friend is sick? Could you have the goodness to procure her a glass of water. If you will unbind my cords, I will see what I can do to restore her." Her sharp tones roused the card players.

"Cain't do that, miss. Orders is orders, ye see. But I rackon some water woan't do no harm," observed the large, gruff man, rising and taking up the pitcher. His movement was arrested by the sound of footsteps crunching over pebbles close by. The two fishermen, in unspoken accord, pulled out long, curving knives, and Gruff Voice took up a position behind the door. There came a sharp soft rapping, three beats, a pause, then two more taps. The guard relaxed and the smaller man leapt forward to remove the bolts. A moment later, he was thrust impatiently aside as a gentleman attired in riding dress, precise and neat as a pin, strode into the centre of the room. His entrance was somewhat marred by an unexpected encounter with a jagged beam. The newcomer staggered, but recovered his balance with a remarkable effort. He glanced round quickly, his eyes fell on Hester and he swept her a low bow, his long dark cloak swinging rakishly.

"I am delighted to see you again, my dear Miss Vane," said Stephen Garth.

Chapter 21
Return To Shawcross

For a moment there was a curious silence in the room. Hester was temporarily bereft of speech and it was Garth himself who made the first sound: a muttered oath as blood dripped into his eye from the nasty gash below his hairline, caused by his encounter with the beam. He fished in his pocket for a handkerchief to staunch the flow; Susan chose this moment to utter an agonised groan. Garth swung round at once and dropped to one knee beside his sister. He put his free hand to her brow, the other being still clasped firmly to his own. In other circumstances Hester would have laughed for the scene contained undoubted elements of melodrama. Garth soon removed his hand and nodded, apparently satisfied.

He said bracingly,

"Come Sukey, this will not serve. You are not feverish and this is no time for the vapours. Bestir yourself, I beg."

Susan allowed two weak tears to trickle from beneath her closed eyelids. She winced and rolled over to face the wall. Hester felt that the time had come to intervene.

She exclaimed indignantly,

"Sir, how can you be so unfeeling towards your own flesh and blood? This churlish treatment is quite outrageous. Kindly explain what you mean by it."

Buoyed up by anger, yet Hester shrank back as Garth towered menacingly above her. He realised his advantage and laughed triumphantly. He lingered, savouring his victory, Hester at his feet. His obvious delight in the situation, his mastery over two helpless women, stiffened Hester's backbone. With as much dignity as she could muster, she said quietly,

"Will you not be seated, Mr. Garth. I have sufficient aches and pains without adding a crick in my neck to the other discomforts."

He grinned down at her appreciatively, his expression transformed. Hester was reminded of earlier days when she had believed Stephen Garth to be her good friend. Involuntarily her face softened and he, perceiving this, abruptly ordered the two guards to wait outside. Obediently the fishermen pulled on their boots and clattered out. Garth waited until the door closed behind them, then squatted on the sacking beside Hester. She found his proximity disturbing, but reflected that he would hardly try to force his will on her with Susan present. He leaned back against the wall, his eyes resting meditatively on Hester's averted profile. Coolly, almost negligently, he reached and caught Hester's chin in his lean, strong fingers, forcing her to turn her head and meet his look. Irrelevantly, it occurred to Hester that she had never before realized that brown eyes could appear as steely as blue.

"That is better, m'dear. Charming though your profile is, I cannot bear to be ignored. Good! those flashing eyes suggest hatred rather than indifference. I like spirit. You look splendid, almost Junoesque, despite the straws and general dishevelment."

"You are impertinent, Mr. Garth," cried Hester hotly, jerking her chin from his grasp, "especially since 'tis you who are responsible for my disordered appearance."

He shrugged, his eyes veiled to hide a sudden gleam of desire.

He replied gently,

"What you say is very true. I regret, infinitely, the necessity for bringing you to such a ramshackle hovel, but when a lady chooses to appear unwilling, a man of decision must seize his opportunities as they arise."

With an effort Hester choked down her indignation. Realising that guile was her only weapon she allowed her head to droop wearily.

"Oh Mr. Garth, I am so tired," she sighed, "Pray come to the point, sir. What good can it avail you to abduct an unwilling female? I am convinced that a personable man like yourself can have no difficulty in making yourself agreeable to any number of attractive ladies. I have no wish to be indelicate, and dislike raising the matter, but I feel I must remind you that I rejected your suit only a short time ago and nothing has happened in the interim to change my decision."

Stephen Garth listened approvingly, a smile touching the corners of his mouth.

"So sweetly reasonable, my dear Hester. I vow I had not suspected you of such duplicity, but you cannot fool me, my girl. I know you are seething inwardly, quaking too, your quivering lip betrays you." He eyed her a moment longer, then driven by some irresistible impulse, he seized her in his arms and kissed her fiercely. Hester knew that it was useless to struggle, so she took refuge in complete passivity. Her attitude of disdainful endurance infuriated Garth. He released her by flinging her back viciously against the wall, and laughed harshly as Hester gave a cry of pain.

"Mine is a nature which thrives on overcoming obstacles," remarked Garth in casual tones. Hester said nothing. She could sense the banked-up fires of passion beneath the light words and feared to rouse him again. She wondered what Susan was thinking. Surely she could not have fallen asleep, she must be biding her time. Garth was speaking softly, his eyes flickering dangerously in the dim light.

"Cease this trifling, Hester Vane. You are mine and the sooner you become accustomed to the notion the better it will be for you. I do not intend to moulder in Sussex all my life. I am going places and you are coming with me, willing or no. Now, time presses. Listen carefully. A woman of your remarkable intelligence will have guessed that it is not solely for the pleasure of your company, great though that is, that you and my sister are here. You are to be decoys. The details need not concern you. Suffice it to say that certain important ventures of mine are being jeopardised by two interfering gentlemen of your acquaintance. The time has come to end their little game. No one will mourn the disappearance of that rash highwayman known as the 'Beau Chevalier' and as for Jedediah Stone, my sister's nonsensical infatuation must be curtailed once and for all — it will be a way of — let us say — killing two birds with one stone, as it were."

Hester felt her flesh creep at his grim tones, but managed to ask calmly,

"I see, and what is to be our fate, mine and Susan's? I presume that knowing so much, we cannot be allowed to live. Incidentally, purely as a matter of curiosity, do tell me, what is the rôle of Thérèse de Marvin in all this?"

Garth grinned, running his hand through his thick hair. After a moment's hesitation, he seized Hester's bound wrists, absentmindedly fingering the cords, while addressing her earnestly, almost pleadingly.

"Do not mistake me, ma'am. I mean you no harm. It is my intention to wed you and so give you the protection of my name. In that way I can gain an entrée into fashionable circles and also ensure your silence through your involvement with my affairs. Stone will wed us early tomorrow. I have a special licence already."

Hester's heart beat fast. She blinked in an effort to clear her thoughts, but before she could speak, Garth continued,

"As for the Comtesse, she is a lady of many parts and I have had the privilege of being of service to her on several occasions; in a nutshell she is in my debt. Not to put too fine a point upon it, she is also a rival of yours for the affections of that demmed, stiff-necked Lord M. and I'm sure you do not need me to tell you that a woman scorned can be the most dangerous of all enemies."

Hester digested this information quickly. Two salient facts had emerged: Mr. Stone was still alive, but in Garth's clutches, and the Comtesse was her implacable enemy. Evidently the Comtesse did not know that her beloved Montfort was the 'Beau Chevalier', for surely even in spite she would not hand him to his death at Garth's hands. The interesting question then occurred to Hester, did Garth know that Montfort and the mysterious highwayman were one and the same man? She suspected that he did — had he not mentioned the 'Beau Chevalier' as an 'interfering gentleman of her acquaintance'? Stephen Garth had assumed what Mortimer used to call his 'pettifogging legal expression'. Hester was possessed of the uncomfortable conviction that her erstwhile lawyer could read her thoughts with ease. In a feeble attempt to divert him, she said warily,

"How neatly you have contrived to pull your puppets' strings, Mr. Garth. And what of Susan?"

Her captor shrugged and frowned at his sister, who had remained rigid and still throughout their conversation, her back towards them.

"Sukey will do as I say," he replied tersely.

Hester raised her brows sardonically, but Garth was no longer looking at her. He had extracted a handsome gold watch from his waistcoat pocket and was regarding it thoughtfully. Hester held her breath as the seconds ticked by. After an interminable pause, Garth replaced the watch, nodded his head decisively and sprang to his feet, brushing Hester with his long cloak.

"Come ma'am, no more of this gossip. It is time for us to leave. Do you go willingly or as a sack of potatoes?"

Hester looked up at the figure towering above and replied with a hint of amusement,

"It is hardly a matter of choice, but since you phrase it so, I would prefer to be spared the sack."

"A wise decision, Miss Vane, but I am taking no chances. One moment, if you please."

He turned to take up his hat, gloves and whip from the table, then tapped imperatively on the door with the whip. The gruff fisherman reappeared and was ordered to unbind the cords which bound the ladies' feet, but to leave those on their wrists. The man knelt before Hester, removed the rope efficiently and was about to rub her ankles to restore the circulation, when he was pushed roughly aside as Garth himself bent to perform the service. The fisherman glanced resentfully at his employer, but made no comment. Hester's ankles tingled and she staggered when Garth pulled her to a standing position.

"Sit on this chair while I attend to Susan," he commanded, swinging Hester off her feet and depositing her by the table. "You had better silence her, Bates," he added over his shoulder. The man nodded, took up a scarf and gagged Hester efficiently. He then feched her cloak, which he draped gently about her shoulders. The reticule he stuffed into his own capacious pocket. 'Bates', the name was familiar. Hester recalled the faint sense of recognition which she had experienced earlier. Could this burly fisherman be young Tommy Bates who had run away from Shawcross rather that be sent to school by her father? But no, it was impossible, he had been drowned at sea. Yet reports were occasionally wrong. She searched her memory; how old had Tommy been when he ran away, twelve, thirteen? He was about three years younger than herself. His colouring had been unremarkable, brown, no, more sandy with freckles, good-natured and big for his age. It must be at least ten years since he left Shawcross; he had travelled widely, sending infrequent, misspelled letters to her father. He had said little of the hardships of sea life, but it had been clear that he suffered acutely from homesickness. The wonders of the Orient had been disparagingly compared with the delights of his native downland. After a while they had ceased to hear from him, and the news of his death came indirectly through Ned Lightfoot shortly before his own death at the Battle of the Nile. Try as she would, Hester could not recall the details, but she knew that Ned had befriended the lad and missed him sorely. She had a vague feeling that Tommy had been washed overboard in a sudden Mediterranean storm. Anyway it did not signify. She raised her eyes and surveyed the fisherman thoughtfully. He was occupied with filling a much-battered pipe, but becoming aware of her regard he met her gaze. The lower half of his face was still masked, but his eyes twinkled and after a moment he winked deliberately. She turned quickly away, astonished by her discovery, but almost sure that her instincts were correct.

A rustle in the corner created a diversion. Stephen Garth had succeeded in rousing his sister, but she refused to speak to him. Hester heard him say,

"You cannot have expected that your presence in Brighton would go unremarked. What a widgeon you are. I trust you benefitted from the change of scene. In fact it suited me very well to have you absent from Hatch End for a short period. Now, since you are so weak, I will untie your wrists, but I warn you, it will go hard with you if you try any tricks. I am your guardian, Sukey; the law will uphold my authority."

Susan compressed her lips, but made no reply. A spasm of pain crossed her face and Hester began to be seriously concerned for her friend's condition. Evidently Garth had the same doubt. He addressed Bates sharply.

"I expressly commanded you to refrain from ill-treating the ladies. Why is Miss Garth in such distress?"

Bates shrugged his shoulders and replied more gruffly than usual,

"Doan't be blamin' me, maister. 'Twere that Spanish fool, Pedro, wot 'ad her in charge. Ye didn' say which o' the leddies was to be given special treatment an' I noticed 'ee were a bit rough loike."

The accent was unmistakeably Sussex, thought Hester, listening carefully. Garth accepted the man's word without question, but a fierce scowl settled on his brow, which boded ill for the absent Pedro. Garth wrapped Susan in her cloak and carried her to the door. Bates retrieved her muff from the pallet. He weighed it thoughtfully in his hand, then passed it to Susan.

"'Tis loikely you'll be needin' this mistress, 'tis a blustering night," he observed nonchalantly. Susan received the soft fur object with a whispered word of thanks. Bates held open the door and Stephen stepped outside, his sister drooping in his arms.

Hester, watching this by-play from her seat at the table, felt absurdly comforted. No-one could have held Susan's muff, containing the small, elegant pistol, and failed to have noticed the extraordinary weight of the item. Yet Bates had given it to Susan without hesitation and had even told her that she would probably be glad of it. The scarf over Hester's mouth was infuriating as well as uncomfortable. If only she could have spoken she would have been able to verify her suspicion.

As Garth swept out into the night, Bates approached Hester.

"See if'n ye can stand now, miss," he urged, placing a firm hand under her elbow. Waveringly Hester came to her feet. "Try an' walk, do, 'twill give you strength, otherwise ye might fall out 'o yon saddle."

Hester tottered out. She waited, stamping her feet, timidly at first, but with increasing confidence until the Spanish man, called Pedro, appeared, already mounted, from behind the shack, leading two horses. Garth tossed Susan up before him and told Bates to follow with Hester. Pedro brought up the rear; he did not appear to be a very good horseman for his beast stumbled frequently and the man swore profusely in a mixture of tongues. Fortunately her own companion seemed at home in the saddle. He guided his horse firmly through the dark, windy night, encouraging the nervous animal with pats and soothing words. Lulled by the steady movement, Hester drowsed fitfully and lost all sense of time. She awoke to startled awareness, numb and chilled, to find that the little cavalcade had halted. Peering into the surrounding gloom, Hester made out a group of pack ponies, heavily laden. Several shadowy figures approached Garth's horse, one figure carrying a covered lantern. A whispered colloquy ensued, then the ponies and men disappeared into the darkness and she felt their horse move forward.

Wakeful now, Hester looked about her. A break in the scudding clouds allowed a silver streak of moonlight to illumine the surrounding countryside. She gave a gasp of recognition; they were crossing the green in her own village of Shawcross.

All was quiet as they proceeded cautiously through the churchyard and drew rein behind Vine Cottage. Hester sniffed the fragrant air. It was lilac scented, a pleasant change from the tang of salt. She felt a wave of homesickness for her own little cottage. Hugo's lean, dark face flitted before her mind's eye and she realized with breathtaking certainty that, come what might, she could never wed Stephen Garth. As one in a dream, she allowed Bates to assist her from the saddle and followed in Susan's wake through Mrs. Lightfoot's vegetable garden to the back door of Vine Cottage. Garth tapped softly on the door. Waiting in the shadows, Hester wondered briefly how it could be that Mrs. Lightfoot had become involved with Garth, but the answer to the riddle was not hard to guess; her son, Peter, was one of the smugglers. A further unwelcome thought intruded: Shawcross Church was uncomfortably close and convenient for a midnight wedding.

There was no time for further meditation. Mrs. Lightfoot's visitors heard the sound of bolts being withdrawn, then the door creaked slightly and swung open to reveal the lady herself, fully dressed in a dark, grey gown. No one spoke. Susan and Hester were pulled quickly inside and followed their hostess along a stone-flagged passageway, past the pantry and scullery, to the cheerful room at the front of the cottage where Hester and Mortimer had taken tea on their last visit. Pedro had disappeared with the horses, Bates remained on guard at the back entrance and Stephen Garth followed the ladies.

The room was softly lit by a single lantern and the newcomers hesitated while their eyes adjusted to the comparative brightness. All at once, Susan gave a low cry and ran to the corner of the room where little Sally Lightfoot was lying asleep, The child was propped up on cushions on the inglenook seat beside the dull red embers of the fire. She had one arm folded in a snowywhite sling and there was an ugly, black bruise on her cheek. Hester was unable to speak for the gag which still constrained her, but she swung indignantly on her heel to face Stephen Garth, her eyes flashing accusingly. Mrs. Lightfoot stood behind Garth, her face drawn and grey, her hands nervously clenching and unclenching. She looked years older than she had done when Hester last saw her. Hatred smouldered in her once-bright eyes and Hester saw her gaze rest thoughtfully on a long kitchen knife, which happened to be resting on the table. Garth appeared to have a sixth sense for danger, for he too turned and took in the situation in a moment. He reached out and grasped the implement, shook his head sorrowfully at Mrs. Lightfoot and advanced upon Hester, still holding the knife in his hand. She shrank back, but Garth seized her hands and with, one swift stroke, severed the bonds at her wrists. Unhurriedly he replaced the knife on the table, then returned to Hester's side and untied the scarf which sealed her lips. She choked, moistering her lips with her tongue.

"Kindly procure a glass of water for Miss Vane," he commanded, not troubling to glance in Mrs. Lightfoot's direction. She scurried out and Garth bent over Hester, "Let this be a warning to you, my dear Hester," he murmured, gesturing significantly towards Sally. Before Hester could reply, Susan sprang to her feet and rushed at her brother, pummelling him with her fists and shrieking hysterically,

"You brute. You are responsible for that poor child's sufferings. So sweet, so innocent. I hate you Stephen! From this day on I shall never call you brother or speak to you again. If I had not seen it with my own eyes I would never have believed that you could be so cruel, so heartless. And it is not only Sally that you have hurt, think of her mother, and Hester and my own dear Jedediah . . ."

She broke from him and flung herself down in a chair, burying her head in her hands in a storm of weeping. Hester moved to comfort her friend, Susan rested her head on her shoulder and remained so for some minutes. At length her sobs abated, Mrs. Lightfoot returned with the water and both Hester and Susan sipped some gratefully. Garth remained standing at a little distance, silent and inscrutable. He was roused by a low growl; Sally's faithful dog, Toby, jumped from his resting place at his mistress's feet and ran to scratch on the front door. Seconds later, the listeners heard a rhythmical tapping on the window pane.

"Restrain yon animal, lest I do him a mischief," recommended Garth imperatively. Mrs. Lightfoot scooped the little dog up in her arms as Garth opened the door and stepped out into the night. There was a slight lessening of tension in the quiet room, but before the women could speak their tormenter returned. He addressed himself to Hester.

"I must leave you for a while. You will be quite safe here and Mrs. Lightfoot will tend to your needs. Do not attempt anything foolish. I leave guards posted outside and I have influence everywhere."

He was pulling on his gloves as he spoke. He raked them with one final, comprehensive glare, then caught up his whip, saluted Hester with a flourish and disappeared once more into the darkness.

Sally stirred and whimpered in her sleep. Mrs. Lightfoot bent over her anxiously, but the little girl did not wake. She snuggled down more comfortably on her pillow and her mother transferred her ministrations to her guests. She gathered up their cloaks and shawls, clucking sympathetically meanwhile. Hester was relieved to note that she seemed much more like her useful, cheerful self.

"I'll just give the fire a poke and then I'll make some tea," announced Mrs. Lightfoot, suiting the word to the deed and bustling about to good purpose. The fire blazed up merrily and the copper kettle on the hob responded to the increased heat by boiling in record time. While the tea steeped, Mrs. Lightfoot sliced wafer-thin bread with the kitchen knife, now restored to its proper calling. She placed flowered cups and plates, fresh butter and strawberry jam on a white cloth and summoned the ladies to the table. To their surprise they found that they were very hungry. The bread, butter and jam disappeared with unladylike despatch and they settled down to a second cup of tea with sighs of contentment.

"What time can it be? I have no idea," said Susan, smothering a yawn.

"Nor I," agreed Hester, "But we have been travelling for hours. Surely it will be light soon."

Mrs. Lightfoot nodded in agreement.

"It's a shocking thing, my dears, when folk can't sleep sound in bed at night, for fear o' those murdering scoundrels. I tried to warn you, Miss Vane, the last time you was here, I truly did, but I could not do much. My Peter, 'ee's mixed up in it, though 'is 'eart bean't in it, but there be no-one hereabouts can say nay when Mr. Garth calls. 'Ee's like a devil, beggin' your pardin Miss Garth, for he's your brother when all's said. But when 'ee treats 'is own flesh 'n blood the way 'ee's treated you, and allows one of 'is men to attack my Sally, all because she was playin' in the wood behind the church and overheard them talkin' — well, it ain't Christian and that's a fact."

The good soul paused to wipe a tear from her eye. Susan interposed sharply,

"Did Sally tell you what the men were talking of, Mrs. Lightfoot? Did they mention my — er, Mr. Stone, by any chance?"

Mrs. Lightfoot's voice dropped to a confidential whisper. She leaned close across the table and replied,

"Why yes, Miss Garth. Oh, the poor gennelman. It seems they've been tryin' to make him do their bidding loike an' one o' the rascals said, "Tonight is 'is last chance." That were yesterday, leddies, about noon time, 'cos I were out weedin' me vegetables an' I heard Sally give a scream and then, all in a flash, a big man in a stocking mask appeared, with my Sally in 'is arms. 'ee saw me and dropped 'er by the lavender bed an' run off mighty quick, but o' course, I were so busy with her and Toby barking something frantic, so I didn't see no more and that's all Sally said she heard."

Hester and Susan glanced at one another. Hester spoke softly, but decisively.

"We cannot just sit here, without making a push to save ourselves and those others whom we love. I have a plan. I left a note at home and by now my aunt and my brother will be seeking us. I told Mortimer to ride first to the 'Horse and Groom' to contact a friend of ours there. Tell me, Mrs. Lightfoot, do you think Peter will be at the inn tonight?"

"I doubt it, Miss Hester. 'ee generally has charge of the pack ponies on nights like this."

"I see," said Hester thoughtfully, "Then I must contrive without his aid. I have no wish to be wed to your brother tonight, dear Sue, but perhaps a wedding is not altogether averse to your taste, my friend. So you, Susan, will remain here and meet Mr. Stone when he arrives, as I feel sure he will. Mrs. Lightfoot, I do not wish to jeopardise your family further on our behalf. Did you know 'twas Tommy Bates on guard outside?"

Mrs. Lightfoot nodded and smiled, almost mischievously.

"Aye, the lad spoke whiles I was fetchin' the water. Quite shook me, I can tell you, but I doan't know how far we can trust 'im, nowadays."

"Best not," confirmed Hester. She rose and set a chair in the middle of the room. "I think we should bind you to this chair, dear Mrs. Lightfoot. Susan can stand guard over you with your redoubtable kitchen knife. I will take your pistol, Susan, and seek help at the Priory. Bates still has my reticule stuffed in his pocket, so I cannot take my paper knife. Now let us make haste, or it will be too late."

"Of course you must take the pistol, Hester, but for goodness sake be careful. Can you handle it?"

Hester nodded more confidently than she felt.

"Theoretically. Mortimer, you know, will not let me touch his, but he did once explain the manoeuvre to me."

"But how will you go? Do you know that guard, Bates, did you call him?", asked Susan, puzzled.

Mrs. Lightfoot and Hester exchanged mysterious smiles.

"Why yes, I know Bates, but that is another story. It was very foolish of your brother to leave me on my home ground," responded Hester lightly, as she caught up her cloak and gloves. Susan found the pistol in her muff and Hester slipped it into her cloak pocket.

"I must go. Wish me good fortune. Make haste and tie Mrs. Lightfoot in the chair. My love to Sally when she wakes."

While they were speaking, Mrs. Lightfoot had been busy in the far corner of the room. Quietly Hester and Susan joined her. The older lady was on her knees, having pushed aside a rocking chair and rag, hooked rug. Mrs. Lightfoot's nimble fingers ran along a small crack between two flagstones. Soundlessly the right-hand stone slid aside on well-oiled wheels, revealing a dark hole and a rough rope ladder.

"Have a care, Miss Hester, that you do not twist your ankle. Remember, there is a little drop at the bottom. There are candles and a tinder box in the niche to your left as you face the ladder."

Hester kissed the two anxious women quickly.

"Have no fear, I'll be as speedy as may be," whispered Hester. She swung herself down cautiously. It was very dark, but she found the tinder box after a moment and groped for the candles. Susan and Mrs. Lightfoot peered down into the hole.

"I'm quite safe. Replace the flagstone quickly. Farewell," called Hester softly, her voice echoing hollowly in the emptiness. She waited for no more, but turned and hurried along a damp, earth-walled tunnel. She was obliged to stoop low to avoid the wooden posts which shored up the roof. She followed the twists and turns of the secret passage, reflecting that she had grown considerably since her last visit. The distance seemed interminable. Once she heard footsteps overhead and halted in terrified suspense until they passed on. She trod in a puddle, and was grateful for the protection of her half boots. After perhaps ten minutes the passage swerved abruptly to the left and rose sharply. Her candle guttered and went out in a slight draught. For a moment Hester succumbed to a feeling of sheer panic. She hugged her cloak close about her as she felt the wall of darkness pressing in upon her. She took a few hesitating steps and bumped her head hard on a large metal object.

"Heaven be praised," she sighed in relief. She searched feverishly for the metal lever, found it and heaved with all her strength. It moved easily, a door opened and Hester fell out on her knees in the damp dewy grass. She took several deep breaths of cool, fresh air, gasped, gulped and glanced about her. She was seated among the gnarled tree roots in the copse behind her own cottage. She longed to take a peep at her home, but dawn was at hand and she dared not linger. She pressed the familiar spring knob in the little grassy mound among the roots and waited as the trap door closed slowly. Quickly, she tossed an armful of last year's leaves over the entrance to the hidden passageway. Having removed all traces of her presence so that even a keen countryman's eye would remark nothing unusual in the copse, Hester removed her boots and stockings, skipped lightly over a tangled web of roots and jumped down into a small, fast-moving stream. The water was cold and the pebbles hard, but she moved with the ease of long familiarity, and soon reached the farther bank. She stumbled, but caught herself in time. It would never do to get her pistol wet. Her knowledge of firearms was extremely hazy, but she recalled Oliver Cromwell's famous maxim about keeping one's powder dry. Or was it the Duke of Marlborough? She needed Miss Stanhope to set her right. Dear Jane, how worried she would be. The thought spurred her as she made haste to rub her feet dry on her cloak. Pulling on her boots once more, she remarked resentfully the red weals which the ropes had made in her tender skin. That men could be so heartless! It was wonderful to be free and alive on such a morning. The first rays of sunlight were glinting through the trees. She wondered what Tommy Bates would do when he discovered her escape. How soon would he raise the alarm? She decided not to follow the familiar mossy path through the woods, but slipped along taking a parallel course darting from tree to tree. The early morning mist was rising quickly and Hester shivered with cold and fear. She felt as if she were dreaming. Surely she would wake in her own comfortable bed and laugh at her wild imaginings. The distance to the Priory on foot was only too real. She was wasting valuable time; oh — if only she could borrow a horse.

As if in answer to her unspoken prayer, Hester heard the muffled thunder of hooves approaching uncomfortably fast. Without hesitation she ran for cover. She reached a gorse thicket and crouched down behind it with not a second to spare. Peeping cautiously from her hiding place, she watched as the rider, heavily booted and spurred, reined in just below her, his horse stamping and snorting at the sudden halt. So preoccupied was she, that she quite failed to notice the snap of a twig behind her. A hand clasped her around the waist and the other covered her mouth. 'My freedom was shortlived indeed', thought Hester despairingly, as she struggled in vain to escape. The iron grip relaxed a trifle and a well-known voice muttered in her ear,

"Peace my darling, for your life, make no sound."

Chapter 22

What Befell At "The Horse and Groom"

Fortunately, astonishment rendered Hester speechless. She felt quite weak from the cumulative shocks which she had sustained during the past twenty-four hours and it required a considerable effort for her to reach up and tug gently at the strings of her captor's mask. The world receded as a wave of tenderness and delight swept through her; still holding the mask, Hester rubbed the back of her hand along his lordship's stubbly cheek.

"You!" she whispered, wonderingly, "Oh Hugo, is it really you?"

For answer he bent his head and kissed her hard, but briefly. The next moment he pulled her close within the shelter of his arm and drew his cloak about her. Hester heard stealthy sounds nearby; she felt Hugo grow tense and rigid, he fumbled with his free hand for his pistol. Scarce breathing, they remained motionless, listening to the muffled sounds of feet and hooves passing by not ten feet from their hiding place. At length, after a seemingly interminable period, all was quiet once more. Hester stirred, but Hugo shook his head warningly. She snuggled closer; minutes passed, the birds began to sing again and Hugo leaned forward, pushed the leaves aside and peered warily about.

Apparently he was satisfied for he sat back, flexing his cramped limbs. His brow was furrowed in thought. Hester remained silent, content to wait upon events now that the immediate danger had passed. She gave vent to a sudden yawn and realized that she was fatigued to the point of exhaustion. Her mind wandered back to the old days at Shawcross Manor, before her parents died, when she and Mortimer had risen to go fishing. She had never been a good early riser and often succumbed to yawns of monumental proportions when she had accompanied Mortimer on his early-morning forays. Hester was abruptly recalled to the present by her companion giving her a fierce shake.

"This will not do, you looked fagged to death. Whatever are you doing here? I've been beside myself with anxiety ever since I met Mortimer on his way to the 'Horse and Groom' last night, bringing word of your disappearance and little else." Hugo growled in her ear. Giving Hester no time to reply he continued in the same gruff tone, "But we can talk of that anon. You must return to your cottage and bar the doors until I have run Garth to earth and dealt with him as the fellow deserves. Why the devil did you not remain in Brighton as you were bid? Your're a confounded nuisance and that's the truth."

Hester's hackles rose at once in response to this unloverlike speech. Firmly suppressing some inner qualms as to the justice of his lordship's observations, she drew herself up with as much dignity as she could muster, met the glinting green eyes unwaveringly and retorted with spirit,

"I quitted Brighton at your behest, my lord, or so I believed. My aunt and my brother were from home when I received your urgent message relayed by the Comtesse and there seemed no choice but to come myself. You cannot reproach me more than I do myself for meddling in your dubious affairs. Unfortunately I cannot return to Shawcross, for it is crawling with Garth's men and I desire to wed Garth even less than I desire to marry your so noble self. Therefore, if you will excuse me, I shall trouble you no further."

Hester made as if to rise, but Hugo caught her firmly around the waist and held her pinioned at his side.

"Ouch, you're hurting me. I bruise very easily. Release me at once, my lord," protested Hester, wincing. Hugo shifted his grip, but retained a firm clasp. He remarked through gritted teeth,

"Now, my fair termagant, perhaps you will explain to me where you intend to go and how you came to be such a sapskull as to believe I would send you a message by that she-devil, Thérèse?"

Suddenly the humour of the situation struck Hester forcibly and she giggled a trifle hysterically as she perceived his lordship's outraged countenance. She groped for the handkerchief containing his signet ring, untied the knot and flourished the token of good faith under Hugo's haughty, aristocratic nose. He stared at it in surprise for a long moment.

"Proof positive, you see," said Hester triumphantly, tilting her head sideways to regard Hugo mischievously.

"No, minx," he replied decisively, "but a deuced clever ruse. 'Tis a perfect copy of my own, which is in its usual place, you see." He held out his left hand and Hester blushed as she recalled the loving care which she had lavished on the false ring, believing it to be Hugo's own.

All such pettiness was swept aside the next moment, for his lordship was addressing her gently, an unaccustomed note of pleading in his deep voice.

"Come, Hester, let us cry a truce. I appreciate that you acted with my best interests at heart and I thank you. We must linger here no longer. Since you cannot return home and it is manifestly unsafe for you to wander about the countryside unaccompanied, I suggest that we take our chance together, but before we leave you must promise to obey me implicitly, otherwise I shall — er — knock you over the head and leave you beneath the leaves until all danger is past. Do you agree?"

Hester hesitated,

"I will obey your instructions so long as you are free and able to defend me," she replied firmly. Hugo was not quite satisfied, but observing the mutinous set of Miss Vane's pretty mouth he gave in with a good grace.

"Very well, so be it. Come now and tread as quietly as you can. My horse is nearby."

Hand in hand they followed an overgrown track through the woods, bending low to avoid overhanging branches. They had been following a course directly opposite to the one taken by the smugglers for perhaps five minutes, when they reached a sharp fork. Here Hugo plunged unhesitatingly into the deep underbrush. Hester followed blindly, amazed to own herself completely lost, for hitherto she had prided herself on her knowledge of the woods and fields around Shawcross. She commented on this when Hugo paused to let her catch her breath. He grinned wryly down at her,

"A highwayman must needs be acquainted with his locality in ways not required of the ladies of Shawcross Manor. I fear your taste for low company may lead you into some strange places, my dear."

She looked up sharply at the ironic, bitter note in his voice, but Hugo waited for no reply. He strode ahead and Hester had to run to keep up with him, the brambles catching at her cloak and hair with uncomfortable persistence. Breathless and dishevelled, she stumbled against Hugo, who had halted suddenly by a large oak tree. They listened alertly; peering round his lordship's large form, Hester was entranced to see a small clearing with a pebbly stream running through it. She sniffed the wild woodland fragrance of moss and violets. A great black horse, ready saddled, stood patiently, tethered to a tree near the stream.

"Cassy, old girl," murmured his lordship softly. As he approached the mare whinnied with pleasure. He patted her lovingly and produced a sugar lump from his pocket, then turned to look for Hester. The rays of the rising sun picked out her bedraggled appearance, but Hugo noted that her head was held high and her eyes sparkled. Impulsively he held out his hand saying,

"Foolish Miss Vane, why can you not leave such adventures to your heroines?"

Relieved to find that his dark mood had disappeared, Hester responded gaily,

"There is no substitute for experience, my Lord Montfort."

"Come then, trust me a little longer and we will see if we can achieve a happy ending for you, my lady," replied Hugo teasingly, his hand still outstretched. Hester placed her hand in his and allowed him to lead her to the waiting mare. Hugo kissed her hand before releasing it and tossing her up on Cassy. He waited a moment for her to settle herself, then swung up behind and urged the mare forward at walking pace.

"Put your hood up and keep your head low until we clear the woods," he commanded briskly. This was good advice as Hester soon found, for the overhanging branches were more troublesome on horseback and once Hester was nearly unseated, but Hugo quickly encircled her waist with his left arm and the danger was averted. They rode on steadily and soon cleared the woods, Hugo kept in the shelter of the deep hedgerows as they skirted fields and farms. The early morning sun grew stronger.

"Great Heaven, it is good to be alive on such a morning," remarked his lordship, breaking a long silence.

"Everything is fresh and bright except my humble self," sniffed Hester, tartly, for she was overwhelmed by weariness and did not share his lordship's enthusiasm. Hugo glanced down at the small, pale face bobbing against his shoulder. He cursed himself for having landed them both in this mess, but betrayed none of his inner anxiety to his companion. Instead, he said encouragingly,

"Take heart, my brave girl. We shall be at the 'Horse and Groom' within the hour. You will feel more the thing with some hot coffee inside you. Hold tightly to the pommel, for I fear we must make haste to find Abercromby and Mortimer, or this night's labours shall be in vain."

Hester was puzzled and intrigued by these words, but she had no energy to spare for thought. Thoroughly awake now, she was obliged to cling to the saddle as Hugo swung the mare on to a broader track over the downs and gave Cassy her head. Hester gasped and heard Hugo laugh exultantly as the pace increased to breakneck speed. The term 'breakneck' assumed a very real significance as Hester hung on for dear life. She was about to declare her inability to 'hold on' one moment longer, when Cassy's rider miraculously slowed the mare to a walk. Hugo slipped to the ground and led the way cautiously, supporting Hester with his left arm, for which she was grateful. She felt so weak that she was assailed with a sudden doubt concerning her ability to stand on her own two feet. They were following a grassy footpath behind some cottages. Hugo glanced up, laying his finger to his lips. Hester nodded understandingly, for she recognized the location. It was Pen Village and yonder, round the next bend, lay the 'Horse and Groom'.

They emerged from the footpath on the main London road directly opposite the inn. Smoke coiled lazily from the twisted chimneys and wreathed in the still morning air.

"Good, Ned's astir," muttered Hugo, urging Cassy forward.

Dazzled by the bright sunshine, they crossed the road to enter the cobbled forecourt. Cassy insisted on drinking thirstily from the water trough. Hugo let her have her way; holding the leading rein loosely over his arm, he turned his back to the inn and reached up to help Hester dismount. Then everything happened at once: footsteps clattered hurriedly from the side of the inn and Peter Lightfoot appeared, calling desperately,

"Have a care, my lord, Mr. Garth is here before you!"

The words of warning had no sooner left Peter's lips than a shutter swung wide; the three stood frozen in dismay as Stephen Garth leaned from the casement, gripping a pistol in his right hand. In cold, menacing tones he commanded,

"Come in, Miss Vane and join your brother. You too, Montfort, or should I say 'Monsieur le Beau Chevalier'. Do not attempt anything foolish. I have you covered and two officers of the law await within to do their duty."

Hugo was the first to recover. His hands still circled Hester's waist. With a shrug and a smile, his eyes met her fearful ones. Ignoring the onlookers, he spoke to Hester as if they were alone.

"Pluck up, dear heart, all will be well," he promised softly. His words, coupled with Garth's impatient "Make haste there," stiffened Hester's backbone. Her chin well up, she placed her hands unhurriedly on Hugo's shoulders and slipped lightly from the saddle.

"Give Cassy a good rub down, Lightfoot," commanded Hugo. He gave the mare a final, loving pat before surrendering the reins to Peter, then turning to Hester he took her hand with a reassuring squeeze and led her across the cobbles to the inn.

They found the entrance somewhat obstucted: the two Runners, Peabody and Watson flourished blunderbusses. Ned Potter and the maid Bessie lurked close behind. Of Alice Potter, the landlord's shrewish daughter, there was no sign, but the group in the doorway heard Garth call, "Await me there, I'll join you presently," over his shoulder as he pounded down the stairs. He paused on the bottom step, his brown eyes glinting with suppressed triumph as he surveyed the upturned faces. In a moment of curious stillness, they heard the unmistakable sound of the door slamming and of a key grating in a lock above stairs. Lord Montfort's icy voice, enquiring irritably of Potter if it were his custom to keep his patrons dangling on the doorstep all day, broke the spell cast by Garth's sudden advent. The Runners fell back overawed by his lordship's aristocratic demeanour; Bessie bobbed a curtsey and ran forward to assist Hester with her cloak, while Ned Potter hurried ahead to usher the party into his cozy inner room. To be totally ignored was the last thing Stephen Garth had anticipated. He glared after the retreating backs of his captives; with an effort he calmed himself, allowing his features to adopt a bland noncommittal expression which he had found useful in trying circumstances in the course of his pursuit of the legal profession. Thus composed, he strove to regain mastery of the situation before it slipped through his fingers. With firm, deliberate tread, he strode through the public taproom to the little private parlour beyond, the same snug room where Sir Mortimer Vane had first made the acquaintance of the 'Beau Chevalier'.

The scene that met Mr. Garth's eyes gave him some satisfaction; but this was quickly dispelled when his forehead met the low lintel with a sharp crack. No-one paid any attention to his angry cry of pain, followed by a string of oaths. His lordship had cast aside his cloak and stood revealed in all the splendour of full evening dress; the Runners, stationed strategically one on either side of the door, were watching the noble lord's darkening brow with expressions of mingled apprehension and wariness, but his lordship gave them no heed. His concentration was centred on the Vanes, brother and sister. Mortimer was seated at the dining table, his hands tied behind his back with stout ropes; Hester was kneeling at his feet beseeching him to tell her if he was in any way hurt.

"Not a whit, m'dear," Mortimer was saying, soothingly, with a rueful smile, "Though I confess my pride is somewhat bruised. Here came I, seeking you, after I received your note, and walked straight into the arms of yon ruffianly fellows." He nodded in the direction of the two stalwarts by the door, who cast down their eyes sheepishly.

Heartened by their evident discomfort, Mortimer addressed himself to Hugo. "Mighty glad to see you and Hester safe, old fellow. Can't think what the countryside is coming to. Be so good as to have these Robin Redbreasts release me. I'm dev'lish sharp set, I can tell you, and my arms all pins and needles. Ned, bustle about and dish up some breakfast, daresay I'm not the only one who is hungry. Must fortify the inner man, ye know."

The landlord had been watching the proceedings with an ill-concealed grin on his cherubic countenance. He now winked slyly at Sir Mortimer and looked to his lordship for guidance.

"By all means, Potter, do as Sir Mortimer suggests. And bring us a pot of coffee at once, strong and sweet if you please, Miss Vane must be nigh dead of fatigue and worry." Hugo's concerned expression hardened to one of steely disdain as he surveyed the Runners through his quizzing glass in leisurely fashion. Watson, the older man, squirmed and shuffled uncomfortably beneath the disconcerting gaze, but Peabody puckered up like a game cock and glanced at the silent Garth for an encouraging signal. Before the lawyer could respond, his lordship took the offensive. Drawing himself up haughtily, Hugo enquired sternly,

"Well, gentlemen of Bow Street, if such indeed you be, kindly explain yourselves. For what reason did you permit this fellow, Garth, to menace Miss Vane and myself with a pistol, and why is this lady's brother so rudely treated? Name his offence, sirs, and it had best be as you say, or I shall see to it that you rue the day you were born. I am well acquainted with the Chief Magistrate of Bow Street and I do not suffer fools gladly. Miss Vane has suffered enough tonight at the hands of this villain," his eyes flickered towards Garth, who was angrily grinding his teeth; unmoved, Hugo continued, "And I would not have her further distressed. Pray make haste and untie Sir Mortimer's bonds, unless, of course, you can *prove* that he is indeed the rogue you obviously mistook him for."

The Runners, feeling the ground shift beneath their feet, glanced at one another uncertainly. They drew sighs of relief when Stephen Garth stepped forward to the centre of the room. He was about to speak when Ned Potter clattered in and began pouring coffee. The landlord completely ignored the tense atmosphere, but commented cheerfully on the brightness of the morning, and the prospects for the crops, while Bessie set down a plate piled high with buttered muffins and passed the cups around.

Impatiently, Garth raised his fists, but meeting the landlord's bright unwinking eye, and noting the pugilistic set of his jaw, he lowered his arm. After a momentary hesitation, Garth advanced to within two feet of Hugo and spoke in cold, firm accents.

"I denounce you, Hugo Jermyn, Lord Montfort, as traitor to the realm and plotter with the French for the invasion of these shores. I further declare that you, in the guise of the 'Beau Chevalier', notorious highwayman, did attack the coach of one Mr. Hyde Abercromby, at Staleybridge in this county and did take information from him plus certain valuables, which you then sent on to a French agent through a certain lady, known as the Comtesse de Chérault. For these, and diverse other deeds, listed here," he waved a long sheet of parchment, "I, in my legal capacity, do authorise, nay command, you gentlemen of Bow Street, to arrest Lord Montfort and hold him at the King's pleasure."

Hugo smiled grimly.

"Well, Mr. Garth, that is the most consummate farrago of truth and lies I have heard in a long time and I have heard a good many. As a lawyer I feel sure you must be aware that the courts will require more tangible evidence of my guilt than you have so far produced. And furthermore we await some explanation of Sir Mortimer's uncomfortable situation. Is he too under arrest and if so, on what charge? I believe he was put under restraint yesterday evening and am at a loss to understand why, that being so, he is still held in a common inn. In such cases, it is customary to proceed to the nearest jail, which would be in Pendleton. Such laxness should be reported to your superiors."

He nodded affably in the direction of the two Runners, who shifted their feet uncomfortably, but made no other move.

"Yes, by heaven, not only laxness, but inefficiency," declared Mortimer, scowling ferociously, "It's unpardonable. Not a word of explanation has been vouchsafed so far. These scoundrels seized me and have kept me trussed up like a chicken all night. Not one wink of sleep have I had. If you want my opinion, Hugo, these fellers must be dicked in the nob."

Mortimer subsided, shaking his head sagely. Impelled by the injustice of the accusation, the Runner, Watson, spoke up ponderously.

"That's as mebbe, Sir Mortimer, but in matters o' deep-dyed treachery and wickedness we 'ave to use the tools at our disposal, in a word, you sir, you was the sprat to ketch the mackerel, 'is lordship bein' our chief hobject." Watson paused for effect, eyeing Lord Montfort keenly. Forgotten in her corner seat on the floor beside

Mortimer, Hester sipped her coffee, feeling the warmth flow through her. Mentally alert she followed the discussion closely and was mildly amused to note a distinct resemblance between Watson and her aunt's butler, Pringle, both in voice and manner. What a splendid butler Watson would make! She watched him purse his lips and puff out his chest, preparatory to launching on a further speech. His next words dispelled her amusement.

"My lord, Mr. Garth has given us written ewidence that you and the notorious 'ighwayman known as the 'Bew Cheevaleer' are one and the same. 'Twas he, sir, that told us you would be at Staleybridge on the night in question and he that winged you. 'Tis likewise known as how Miss Hester Wane did aid an' shelter you on aforesaid night last April. There be witnesses to the fac' that Mr. Garth has undertaken to produce, includin' Peabody and myself, who was present at the scene. Peabody followed you, my lord, right to Miss Wane's werry door, an' wiv his own eyes saw her remove your mask before callin' for help. 'Tis further suspected that Miss Wane and her brother be your accomplices in treason, for Miss Wane has been much in your company since the ewent, and if you remember Sir Mortimer, you was here at this werry inn on the Friday night a-followin' the accident at Staleybridge, and you and Potter diddled us finely and kept his lordship 'id, but we found the mare, the black mare in your house in Shawcross, the same one 'is lordship rode at Staleybridge. 'Twere Mr. Garth that drew our attention to these facts and he has been most assidiwus, you might say, in aidin' our inwestigations. He even went so far as to court Miss Wane and discovered your mask in her bedchamber secreted in the pocket of the gown she wore when you arrived wounded at her gate. The country is indebted to Mr. Garth for his work in uncoverin' your plottings. Last night, he told us that we would find Sir Mortimer Wane 'ere in the final fling of your desperate endeavour to bring about a French inwasion and so feather your own nests. All this bein' known, 'twill be better fer you gennelmen if you give yourselves up easy like an' come quietly to Pendleton to await trial. Miss Wane too, o' course." Watson finished his speech triumphantly and flourished his truncheon surmounted by a little crown to enforce his authority.

The response to these accusations was not quite the one which the Runners expected. Instead of hanging their heads in guilty shame, the Vanes appeared first thunderstruck, then furiously indignant. Hester jumped impetuously to her feet and ran to Hugo's side, exclaiming,

"Hugo, we must put a stop to this nonsense at once. I never heard such a series of sly misinterpretations in my life!"

His lordship smiled down at her flushed, angry face and gently pushed aside a lock of hair. Behind them Ned Potter poked the fire vigorously, while the Runners and Stephen Garth waited tensely for Hugo to speak. Hugo flicked an infinitesimal speck of dust from his sleeve, raised a sardonic eyebrow at Garth and drawled softly,

"Mr. Garth has been busy it seems. May I see the written evidence and also the warrant for search which Mr.Garth used to enter Miss Vane's abode. I like everything to be legal and above board. I'm sure you agree, er — Watson, is it not? In exchange perhaps you would care to peruse these documents of mine; this one, signed as you will see by Mr. William Pitt, gives me the authority to ferret out a nest of traitors, led by the chief smuggler, who has terrorised the downland area for some time, one Stephen Garth. No, don't interrupt me, Mr. Garth, I am almost done. You may have wondered, gentlemen of the law, why no action has been taken to arrest me before this, on the strength of Mr. Garth's evidence. No doubt he told you all must wait until the plotters were so deeply embroiled that the net could close and trap them all."

"But, the 'Bew Chevaleer', the Frenchie 'ighwayman, is leader of the smugglers, and speaks French like a native, as you do, my lord, 'acos of your mother, Lady Elizabeth bein' French," spluttered Watson, shaken, but hanging on gamely.

"Read the papers, man," commanded Hugo impatiently, his eyes never leaving Garth's face, "In particular the one with the red seal, from the Chief Magistrate of Bow Street, no less. I take it you are acquainted with his signature. Good."

A tense silence ensued. Watson shuffled the papers, scanning them slowly, the fire crackled, but neither Garth nor Hugo moved a muscle. Peabody stood guard in the doorway, his bulk filling the frame, his right hand gripping his truncheon in readiness for action as soon as he knew in which direction his duty lay. Hester, shivered uncontrollably and sank down on the fireside settle. She leaned back against her cloak, which Bessie had carelessly draped over the arm. Something hard thumped against her elbow. With a small thrill of excitement, Hester recalled Susan's pistol tucked in the side pocket. Could she reach it without being noticed? Her heart thumping, she slipped the cloak about her shoulders quietly and casually. No-one paid any attention. Watson dropped a paper and stooped to retrieve it. The momentary diversion afforded Hester the opportunity to wrap the cloak closely around her, the voluminous folds covered the pocket and she slipped the weapon into her right hand, still hidden, as Watson straightened. The Runner looked worried and undecided; Hester felt a twinge of pity for the unfortunate man, trying to unravel such a tangled coil beneath the merciless gaze of two such adversaries as Garth and Montfort. Miserably torn, Watson decided he must get support from 'higher up'. Relieved to have found a solution to his difficulties by shifting the responsibility, he announced almost cheerfully,

"Such weighty matters cannot be settled in a public inn. I must hask you all to accompany me to Pendleton, where fuller enquiry can be made in the presence of reliable witnesses."

Watson's small, bright black eyes beamed jovially at the assembled company. Undeceived, Hugo eyed him sharply, but could make nothing of his bland expression until the Runner deliberately winked at him with his left eye. Less perceptive, Mortimer protested irascibly,

"Dem it, man, are we all your captives, or none of us? If no-one else is to be bound, perhaps you'd be a good fellow and untie these bonds. They're ruining my wrist bands. And what about breakfast before we go. We'll all feel better on full stomachs."

Hester giggled, but Garth, stung to fury by the delay, turned wrathfully on Watson, who stood his ground calmly. His features distorted with anger, Garth shouted bitterly,

"I see what it is, Watson, you're a two-faced scoundrel in the pay of this noble lord. But I will see justice done, a few forged documents do not convince me. While we dither here a French invasion may be taking place. I'm off to put a stop to it, single-handed if necessary." He made for the doorway, still blocked by Peabody. Garth reached to push the Runner roughly aside, but at that moment a gentle click in the panelling behind Hester halted Garth in his tracks. The panel swung open slowly to reveal Hyde Abercromby's head, with Tom Marchant peering over his shoulder.

"We have heard all that has gone forward," remarked Mr. Abercromby, slightly smiling at the astonished faces before him. He gestured to Watson, "Runner, do your duty, I assure you we now have enough witnesses of his perfidy to hang Stephen Garth ten times over. Marchant . . .," Mr. Abercromby glanced over his shoulder at his companion and in that second Garth leapt at Hester, brandishing his pistol wildly. Dragging Hester after him, his left arm about her waist he backed towards the window, which stood ajar. None of the other occupants of the room dared move as Garth jumped up on the window seat. He shouted loudly,

"Alice, my horse."

His eyes blazed as he surveyed the room. Dangerous, cornered at last, yet every inch a leader of men, Garth held his enemies spellbound.

His forceful personality exuded power and defiance, as he proclaimed in ringing tones,

"Well, noble lord and commoners, I pity you, for you are men without vision, no revolutionary fervour will ever stir your feeble spirits, you'll die content in the stations to which ye were born, the rich man in his castle, the poor man at his gate, too stuck in your mud of privilege and prejudice ever to sail with the mighty winds of the age. Mine was the greater impulse! — a fair share of earth's bounty for all — a vision that brooks no petty constraint, no by-your-leave! Enough, it is better to have tried and failed than never to have tried at all. I will hie me to a land where persons of energy and enterprise are encouraged and appreciated at their true worth. No, not to France, where the steeds of Revolution have been harnessed to a Dictatorship. If the French had come here — oh, what a chance England has missed — properly guided this island could have combined the best of both nations, our industry newly fired by their enthusiasm. We could have learnt from their mistakes! We could have made this land one of comfort and plenty for all, overthrowing the wealthy parasites, giving government to the professional classes — those most fitted for it! No, I see it is not to be, England's hour has not yet come. I forsake this hidebound island and will seek my fortune in the Americas." He paused as a clatter of hooves sounded below the casement. In a different tone he continued hurriedly, "Hester, my dear, what a helpmeet you would have made; intolerable to relinquish you to the arms of that devil Montfort. Such a calamity must be averted at all costs. Forgive me, my dear, 'tis for your own salvation." A fanatic gleam in his eye, he pointed his pistol at Hugo's chest. Sensing his intention Hester jerked her arm and fired. Her bullet hit a beam with a resounding thud. In his surprise, Garth slackened his grip and Hester stumbled forward and fell against Hugo just as Garth released the trigger. A searing pain ran down her right arm; dimly she was aware of an outburst of shouts, pandemonium reigned and in the midst of the confusion a third shot rang out, and Hester heard, rather than saw, Stephen Garth give a choking cry as he sank to his knees, toppled over and lay still. A cat howled indignantly, footsteps approached and Hester swooned away with a blurred vision of Hugo's anguished face above her.

Chapter 23
A Tangled Tale

"Dead! Bullet through the heart," pronounced Watson solemnly, after a cursory examination of Garth's recumbent form. Peabody peered bemusedly over his colleague's shoulder and nodded in confirmation.

Hyde Abercromby took charge of the situation, rubbing his hands briskly.

"Pity, fellow would have made a great general, leader o' men, ye know, but a twisted heart." He placed his still-smoking weapon carefully on the table and smiled ruefully at the two Runners. "Sorry, my dear fellows, no choice, had to save the lady. Come, let us tidy up this mess," indicating Garth with an airy wave of the hand, "and make Miss Vane comfortable. Explanations afterwards."

Mr. Abercromby's military bearing, the hint of steel in his good-humoured, even tones, quickly produced the desired impression. Hugo, cradling the still-unconscious Hester in his arms, was roused from his abstraction by his friend, who gripped his shoulder and murmured encouragingly in his ear, "Buck up man, she'll be fine, but her wound needs tending. Take her upstairs and have a maid settle her. Assure you, she'll soon feel more the thing. Potter can send one of his lads for the doctor, eh, Ned?" Mr. Abercromby glanced enquiringly at the landlord, who nodded eagerly and bustled out, calling in stentorian tones for Peter Lightfoot and Bessie, and brusquely ordering his weeping wife to see about breakfast for everyone. "But what about my poor Alice?" protested his lady, still sniffiing. In a harsh, unaccustomed voice, Ned Potter replied,

"Let her cool her heels awhile. Yon foolish girl has made her bed and now she must lie in it, in Pendleton jail belike."

Poor Mrs. Potter fell to weeping copiously once more, but she went obediently to the kitchen and her receding sobs ceased abruptly as a door slammed in the distance.

Meanwhile Mr. Abercromby released Mortimer, and left that young man flexing his muscles to restore the circulation while he supervised the Runners' removal of Garth's body to a less public spot. He chose an old, derelict carriage at the back of the stables for this purpose and, having seen all arranged to his satisfaction, he returned to the Snug in search of sustenance, accompanied by Watson and Peabody, who were mutually agreed that it would serve no useful purpose to stand guard over a dead body, and that a pint of Potter's home brewed ale was just what they needed to clear their addled heads, which were spinning with the various revelations of the morning.

Ned Potter took pity on the Runners and saw to it that they were settled comfortably in the outer taproom; he tactfully left the door to the Snug ajar so that they could keep Sir Mortimer and Mr. Abercromby under their eye, reflecting that no useful purpose could now be served by alienating the Redbreasts and something might be gained by propitiating them: he was worried about his daughter's fate, uncertain of the exact degree of her involvement with Garth. While the Runners had been outside with Garth's body, he had seized the opportunity to slip up and have a quiet word with Alice. She had remained in her room throughout the stirring events downstairs, making no attempt to bring the horse round when Garth called urgently for her aid, although her door was locked only on the inside. So he surmised that it had been young Lightfoot in the yard, directing a traveller, when the sound of hooves had been heard by Garth as he attempted to escape. Potter was concerned at his daughter's reception of the news of her lover's sudden demise; she had listened to his brief account impatiently, and her reaction had been anger at Garth's incompetence and jealous spite towards Miss Vane, but no vestige of grief had crossed her sharp little face and no tear had dimmed her fine, dark eyes. As he busied himself with familiar breakfast tasks, Potter brooded on the unkind chance which had saddled him with nought but a pretty shrew for a daughter. However, the good landlord was not much given to introspection and he managed to rid himself of futile speculations by concentrating exclusively on the care and comfort of his guests. And it is true there was much to be done; Miss Vane gave little trouble, for she remained in a deep sleep, but Lord Montfort enquired for the doctor every five minutes, and the other gentlemen were almost equally solicitous for her welfare once their hunger had been assuaged.

Potter reassured them as best he could, although he privately considered that it was nigh on impossible for Dr. Minton to return with Lightfoot before noon.

Little conversation of any importance took place among the four gentlemen in the snug parlour. They discussed the situation in a desultory way and satisfied one another's curiosity on minor points of detail, but at Abercromby's insistence they deferred any serious decisions or action until the arrival of two necessary witnesses, namely Mr. Jedediah Stone and Miss Garth, whom Abercromby had arranged to meet at the inn at ten o'clock.

They were just broaching their third pot of coffee and beginning to think of something stronger when a clatter of hooves on the cobbles brought Hugo restlessly to his feet.

"Stone and Miss Garth, at last," reported Hugo over his shoulder as he peered through the narrow casement. He watched a moment longer, then exclaimed in surprise, "Devil take it, they have young Bates with them. Stone and Miss Garth look very cheerful. This is an awkward coil, Hyde, who will break the news to her, you or I?"

"Leave it to me," advised Mr. Abercromby in an undertone, as Potter ushered Susan and her companions into the room, followed by Watson and Peabody, now refreshed and ready for duty.

In the centre of the room Susan hesitated, glancing from one solemn face to another. Her radiant smile faded and she looked to Mr. Stone for support.

"Perhaps you would like to be seated, my dear," he suggested gently, placing a chair for her and stationing himself behind it. Tom Marchant and Mortimer made their bows and murmured conventional greetings, but Hugo remained standing, his broad shoulders resting against the wall and his hair almost brushing the low ceiling. Hyde Abercromby occupied the hearthrug, feet well apart and one hand behind his back. With a gesture he took charge of the proceedings and made the Runners known to the new arrivals. These civilities being over, Mr. Abercromby addressed himself to Susan, saying simply,

"I fear I am the bearer of sad news, Miss Garth. I am sorry to have to tell you that your brother is dead."

Susan turned a little pale, but replied steadily enough,

"I see. I half-expected it, I suppose. It is a shock, but not a blow, Mr. Abercromby. Stephen and I were estranged by his cruel opposition to my dear Jedediah and my brother's recent behaviour has destroyed all my former regard and respect for him." She sighed sadly.

There was a short silence, none of the gentlemen being quite sure of the appropriate reaction to these artless disclosures. Mr. Stone was the first to recover; he offered a short prayer for the dead man's soul, then enquired curiously,

"But what has happened here? We came as you requested, Mr. Abercromby. In what way may we be of service to you?"

"And where is Hester?" added Susan, who had just remarked her friend's absence.

"Unfortunately, Miss Vane met with a slight accident. She is upstairs resting," answered Mr. Abercromby calmly. Susan cried out in dismay at these words, but upon being assured that Hester's hurt was not serious and that she was indeed sleeping peacefully, she consented to remain awhile and hear Mr. Abercromby's tale, instead of going at once to her friend's bedside. Hugo threw her a look of deep gratitude for her concern and Susan smiled back a little uncertainly. Mr. Abercromby now asserted himself and in a few terse sentences put the newcomers in possession of the salient facts surrounding Stephen Garth's last activities and death. His recital ended as Dr. Minton arrived upon the scene. Susan rose immediately, saying that she must offer the doctor her assistance. She thanked Mr. Abercromby with quiet dignity for sparing her feelings as much as possible and added, with a hint of a shy smile in Hugo's direction that she would bring word of Miss Vane's condition at the earliest opportunity.

There was a little bustle in the Snug following Susan's departure. When everyone was settled, Watson addressed Mr. Abercromby.

"I hassume that the Reverend gennelman an' his lady are the witnesses we 'ave been waitin' for, sir?" On being assured that this was so, Watson drew himself up, thrust his thumbs into his buttonholes, and allowed his shrewd little eyes to roam over the company. Satisfied that he had their full attention, he proceeded,

"Now, Mr. Stone, sir, perhaps you can oblige us wiv a plain tale concarnin' your whereabouts of late an' your inwolvement wiv the smugglin' fraternity in this wicinity. My inwestigations after your disappearance and the fac' that you are a gennelman of the cloth, do hincline me to think that you are an honest man, but I must warn you that it will not do to circumwent ewidence, nor to suppress facts, Mr. Stone."

Mortimer suppressed a grin at the little man's pomposity, while Hugo chafed impatiently in his corner, but Jedediah Stone nodded calmly,

"Of course. I'll be as brief as possible. I was seized by Garth's ruffians more than a se'nnight since, as I crossed the churchyard on my way home from Evensong. I was taken to a fisherman's hut somewhere along the coast and kept in uncomfortable captivity until last night. I saw Garth himself but once. He told me that I was a fool, but a meddlesome one; he tried both threats and cajolery, but when he found I was adamant both in my desire to marry his sister and in my refusal to co-operate by hiding kegs in the churchyard and staying within doors on certain nights, he revealed himself as my implacable enemy. I told him that it was absolutely contrary to my precepts to skulk at home when needed by one of my flock, no matter what the hour of day or night. I also said that my love for Susan was deep and long-standing and that although Garth might be his sister's guardian until she was twenty-five and not twenty-one, as she and I both believed until the banns were called, I was yet ready to wait for Susan to gain her freedom.

When Garth realized that I was firm in my determination, he sneered, 'All very fine and loverlike, but I have other plans for you, as you shall learn anon'. I didn't see Garth again until last night. In the meanwhile I was transferred from the fishing hut, to make way for Susan and Miss Vane, as I later discovered. I was brought back to my own house in Shawcross under cover of darkness and kept closely confined in my bedchamber for two days and nights. Garth needed a clergyman close at hand to conduct the marriage by special licence, which he planned to unite him with Miss Vane. When all was in readiness, he came to me with the news that Miss Vane and Miss Garth were lodged with my house-keeper, Mrs Lightfoot. He was in a strange mood, but good humour predominated and he set himself to charm me and so bend me to his will. He began by assuring me that he was prepared to overlook my previous recalcitrance; he promised that I should have tangible evidence of his gratitude if I would but oblige him in one or two trifling matters. He attempted to flatter me, remarking that he had always respected my principles; he also said that it grieved him deeply to see his beloved sister so unhappy and that, on reflection, he had decided to withdraw his opposition to our marriage.

At this point in our conversation, I enquired sceptically as to terms. Incredibly, Garth seemed genuinely hurt by my bluntness; he protested that for his sister's sake he desired to foster good brotherly relations by furthering my career, even unto a bishopric, which eminence would be well within his power to grant when all his plans came to fruition. He painted a glowing picture of our mutual rise to power and influence in the land; he was captivated by his vision and as I listened I grew cold with fear, for he was clearly dangerously unbalanced. He talked wildly of the glories of the French Revolution which were about to be transported to English soil, until I felt constrained to remind him of the unhappy fate of the Church in that country. He brushed my objections aside, saying that of course there would be local modifications in keeping with national traditions. Abruptly his rhetoric ceased and he came down to plain demands; in essence my rôle would be one of intermediary between him and various French agents since my reputation was above reproach and my former attitudes would keep me beyond suspicion until our new French masters were securely established. But first I must wed him to Hester Vane forthwith. He became increasingly confidential as he warmed to his theme, revealing that the Vane fortune was intact, but under his control, though Sir Mortimer had set various lawyer fellows in Brighton on the track. He insisted that if Miss Vane were his wife, her fortune would be legally under his direction and Sir Mortimer would hardly wish to create a family scandal by challenging his influential brother-in-law's financial dealings. In any event he could easily be bought off with a commission in the new revolutionary army. The money was Hester's, willed to her by her maternal grandmother and hence not entailed on the family estate to pay her father's debts."

At this point in the recital Mortimer emitted a sound midway between a cry of outrage and a yelp of excitement. Tom Marchant patted him sympathetically on the back while Watson interposed smoothly,

"Such facts can be easily werified, Sir Mortimer. Proceed, Mr. Stone, hif you please, sir."

Jedediah Stone went on with his tale in quiet, even tones.

"The rest is soon told, gentlemen. I informed Garth without roundaboutation that bribery as a form of coercion did not appeal to me; I refused absolutely to take any action to aid or further his illegal and treasonable plans though my life and happiness depended upon it. He realised at once that I was adamant in my decision. At first I thought he would strike me, so great was his fury, but he curbed himself and said that he would give me ten minutes to reflect on my hasty words: the choice before me was simple — co-operation or death. Five minutes passed in gloomy contemplation, knowing that Garth had made no idle threat. In my parish work I have seen many sad examples of punishment meted out by Garth's henchmen and my own knowledge of Garth's plans was now so great that I could not hope for any mercy. I was attempting to dismiss all worldly thoughts from my mind and to prepare myself to meet my Maker when I heard a loud knocking below. Then ensued a nerve-wracking silence, I rose from my knees and waited tensely. Imagine my utter astonishment and relief when I heard voices calling my name. I hammered on the door, within seconds I was freed by Bates here, with Mr. Abercromby and Mr. Marchant at his heels. We wasted little time in explanations. Mr. Abercromby I knew slightly as a close friend of Lord Montfort and I readily followed his suggestion that I should concern myself with Susan's safety and, with

Bates' aid, keep my parishioners within doors, while the hunt for Garth and his inner circle of strong-arm men took place. I agreed to bring Susan to this inn at ten o'clock this morning and that is really the end of my tale, gentlemen."

Everyone relaxed at the conclusion of Mr. Stone's narrative. Hyde Abercromby helped himself to more ale and sipped meditatively before nodding in the direction of the Runners.

"I trust you are now convinced that Stephen Garth was a plotter against the safety of the realm, Watson. Are there any further points which you would care to have clarified?" he enquired affably.

"One or two, sir," replied Watson firmly. "I haccept without reservation that Stephen Garth was engaged in treasonable activities. In fac' I'd already done so earlier this mornin'. But jes' for the record, Mr. Abercromby, who is this man, Bates, an' what were you an' Mr. Marchant 'ere doin' last night?"

"Perfectly reasonable questions, Watson and I shall endeavour to satisfy your very natural curiosity. Bear with me, certain information which I am about to disclose is highly confidential and must go no further than this room. As you know, Lord Montfort, Mr. Thomas Marchant and I are all government servants and we have been engaged in unravelling a potentially dangerous conspiracy. To this end his lordship assumed the guise of the highwayman known as the 'Beau Chevalier', Mr. Marchant courted the French agents and through them gained entrée to Garth's inner band of plotters, while I remained my respectable self but kept my ear close to the ground. Bates was born in Shawcross, served in His Majesty's navy, fell overboard in a fog, lost his ship and returned through war-torn Europe to his native land, assisted on the last stages of his journey by members of the smuggling fraternity known to him as a lad. Being a bright adventurous fellow he kept his eyes open and his mouth shut while he felt his way. He had changed considerably in his long years at sea and his old friends did not recognise him. He kept them in ignorance being uncertain whether the Navy Officers would catch up with him and charge him with desertion from the service, for his story, though true, was hard to prove. By the by, Bates, I can set your mind at rest on that score. Mrs. Lightfoot has a letter written by her husband which totally absolves you from any accusations of desertion. Your courage on the occasion in question, when you tried to save a drowning friend, was reported and you are more like to get a medal than a hangman's noose."

Tommy Bates flushed to the roots of his sandy hair at this unexpected encomium, but Abercromby pressed on eager to be done with the tedious business of exposition.

"Well now, let us pull all these threads together without more ado. Bates has been crucial to the success of our mission, for 'twas he who first became aware of the range and scope of Garth's ambitions. Through his childhood friend, Peter Lightfoot, he contacted Lord Montfort and so the network of counter espionage spread to Tom Marchant and myself. We have watched and waited since early spring, both in London and along the coast; we had time to spare for we knew that the French hoped to organize their invasion to coincide with the crowning of Napoleon as Emperor in May. Of course Garth's circle was not the only one preparing a welcome reception for the invaders, but his band was important owing to its location, for it was expected that the main French army would land in Sussex. The weather and French logistical problems delayed matters, Napoleon's coronation came and went unheralded by the conquest of England, but it remains a cherished ambition. The new Emperor has been urging his military people to make the attempt and this week the conditions of tide and moon have been propitious. Garth received instructions from the Comtesse de Chérault to have all in readiness and a diversion was created by the abduction of Miss Vane and Miss Garth. This suited Garth very well, for his private plans were also maturing and he hoped to tidy everything up neatly in one blow, by wedding Miss Vane so gaining her fortune, by bending Mr. Stone to his will in such a way that he would assure his silence and yet rekindle his sister's affection towards himself and by destroying his chief rival and political enemy, Lord Montfort. His self-confidence was boundless, but he overestimated his ability to manipulate his victims for he failed to realise that a rule by fear is not the best way to inspire loyalty in one's followers. Hence, when the crisis came last night, he found that he could not be everywhere at once, he was distracted by personal concerns, and without his guidance his men crumbled in the face of the Excisemen brought by Marchant and myself, the signals were not given and the puzzled French fleet retired to mid-Channel. We all owe a great debt to Miss Vane. She showed remarkable courage and initiative in escaping from under her captor's nose. Marchant and I were able to use this information, brought to us by Bates, to lure Garth away from Mr. Stone's house. You must remember that Garth trusted Marchant and Bates implicitly; I kept out of sight while Bates reported Miss Vane's escape. I must say Garth showed considerable qualities of leadership in this crisis. He sent his bully boys off under Marchant to give the expected signal to the French fleet and Marchant led them neatly into the Excisemen's ambush. Bates was left to guard Mr. Stone and to ensure that the villagers did not meddle, while Garth himself set off in pursuit of Miss Vane, cursing himself for having been foolish enough to give her too much dangerous information. He correctly anticipated that she would attempt to contact her friends at the 'Horse and Groom'. Before he left for the inn, Garth told Marchant that he would collect the two Runners from their lodging in Pendleton in order to cover his tracks. He hoped to retrieve the situation by adding the weight of Bow Street to his own authority. At first his ruse appeared to succeed. You, Watson and Peabody, accompanied Garth, Sir Mortimer walked straight into your trap and you waited for Miss Vane. Garth met a snag, for Alice Potter, his mistress and accomplice, refused to co-operate. She had heard from Peter Lightfoot, the ostler, that Garth planned to marry Hester Vane and she was consumed by jealousy. Time passed, Garth chafed at the inactivity, but Alice, who was known to his men and had been his frequent messenger, would not leave the inn. In his anger he struck her, but before he could take further action, Lord Montfort and Miss Vane arrived.

"Meanwhile, Marchant and I had arranged to meet Mr. Stone, Miss Garth and Bates here at the inn this morning. Then Marchant rounded up the bully boys of Hatch End from their billet in the stables and led them forth at a good pace to meet their fate at the hands of the Excisemen. I followed at a prudent distance, when Garth had disappeared in the opposite direction. It was a demmed dark night and I had much ado keeping my saddle, for the men eschewed the open downlands and kept to ancient wooded tracks. The destination was that notorious hut by the sea, which had been used as a place of captivity for Mr. Stone and the ladies. Bates had told us of it and the Excisemen were in a position when we arrived, having already overpowered a sizeable contingent of the local smuggling 'gentry'. Garth's ruffians fought well, but they were taken by surprise. Three men were killed and several others wounded; we completed their capitulation by telling them that their leader was already a prisioner. The little Spaniard Pedro sued for mercy, offering to turn King's Evidence; before we could prevent it he received a fatal thrust from a long knife, the others submitted in sullen silence. At this juncture welcome reinforcements arrived in the form of a troop from the Tenth Hussars led by a friend of Marchant's, Andy Fanshawe. Marchant had sent them a message before leaving Brighton, but they had lost their way and were on the point of returning to town when they heard the sounds of firing. It was a useful object lesson to them on the virtues of mastering local terrain;

perhaps in the future they will spend less time on the parade ground and more on manoeuvres rooted in real conditions."

Tom Marchant snorted irrepressibly,

"Not while our noble Prince is in command."

Mortimer sighed ruefully,

"If only I could have been with Fanshawe instead of cutting a rather inglorious figure here. How did it end, Hyde?"

Mr. Abercromby flashed him a wicked grin,

"I'm afraid His Highness's pretty uniforms became sadly mired. The troops were sent through some muddy woodland country to destroy the illegal pitch and furze beacons set close together out of sight of any habitation. When all was under control, Marchant and I left Fanshawe in charge and rode back here as fast as possible. Lightfoot intercepted us in the land behind the stables with the news of Garth's arrival and we hid in the panel a few moments before Lord Montfort and Miss Vane appeared. By the by Hugo, it was fortunate that you found your lady in all the confusion last night."

"Perhaps. I could wish she had remained in safety at Shawcross. Minton has been with her an unconscionable time."

"Never fret, Hugo," said Tom encouragingly, "My cousin's spirited actions served her country well. You would not have her otherwise and she's stronger that she looks, she'll recover, see if she don't. And thinking of the ladies reminds me, someone should make haste to Brighton to reassure poor Miss Stanhope and my own Agatha, not forgetting dear Mama. What's to be done about the Comtesse, shouldn't we make haste to get her under lock and key?"

"I believe you'll find that elusive lady has already left on her travels, but make the attempt by all means, Tom. Take Mortimer with you. Abercromby and I will tidy up the loose ends here. Pray tell Miss Stanhope that I shall have Hester transported to the Priory the minute Minton pronounces her fit enough to travel."

Mortimer jumped to his feet eagerly,

"Action at last. Come, Tom, bustle about man. We can't let the Comtesse disappear. She's a foreign agent, a menace to society! I know I'm leaving Hester in good hands, Hugo; and she would never forgive me if I did not try to stop the Comtesse — why, the witch betrayed you to Garth and all but made an end of you, and what Hester would have done then I cannot imagine."

For the first time that morning Hugo laughed heartily and clapped a hand on Mortimer's shoulder.

"God speed in your witch-hunt, Mortimer, but do not allow yourself to be caught in her toils if you come up with her, for I believe you may soon have that commission you crave."

The two Runners had been listening open-mouthed to the rapid sequence of events. Watson now gave way to a series of wheezing chuckles which shook his entire frame.

"Finely diddled we've bin, sirs, an' a merry dance you've bin leadin' us, but I ken see 'twas all for the good of the country that the rogue Garth should have us in his pocket, as 'twere, an' I'm not one to bear a grudge, all bein' well, that's well ended, eh, sirs?"

"Very decent of you to take that attitude, Watson. I suggest you and Peabody prepare to accompany me to Pendleton to make your report. You have conducted an arduous mission in a most commendable way. I assure you that your superiors shall hear of it." Hyde Abercromby nodded graciously as the two men bobbed themselves backwards from the Snug. The five gentlemen looked at one another and spluttered with suppressed mirth, but Mortimer soon recovered his composure.

"I think I'll just run up and see how m'sister does. Then we can be off, Tom."

He hurried through the outer taproom, but returned almost at once accompanied by Susan and Dr. Minton.

Hugo strode across the low room to make them welcome.

"How fares you patient, sir?" he enquired anxiously.

Dr. Minton eyed him sternly beneath his bushy eyebrows. Then he relaxed, smiling cheerfully at the company.

"She'll do, your lordship. Aye, she'll do now. A brave lass, for 'tis sure a painful thing to have a bullet extracted. I've given her a sleeping draught, Miss Garth has consented to remain with her and will administer various medicaments which I have prescribed. I will return tomorrow morning." Dr. Minton delivered himself of this speech standing in the doorway. Over Hugo's shoulder he espied Mr. Stone.

"It's good to see you safe and sound, my dear sir. We've all been mightily perturbed about you. But I gather from Miss Garth that there have been stirring deeds going forward under my very nose?" The doctor glanced round enquiringly.

"All in good time, sir. You'll stay for a glass of wine with us?" Hugo asked politely, his innate good manners coming to his rescue. Inwardly he felt that he would explode if he were obliged to listen to any further account of Stephen Garth's misdemeanours. The doctor eyed him keenly for a moment.

"You look as if a glass of wine would not come amiss yourself, my boy. You're worn to the bone. Get between the sheets, that's my advice."

Hugo smiled wryly. "Very good advice I'm sure, sir. But first tell me, can Hester be moved to the Priory, with the greatest of care, of course?"

"Don't see why not, but I should leave it till tomorrow. Wounds like this take time to heal, as you know, my lord," replied the doctor, with a twinkle. His bright eyes wandered to the other side of the room where Susan was sitting side by side with Jedediah Stone. "So great a happiness is good to see and richly deserved."

Hugo nodded, but before he could reply, Mortimer erupted at his elbow.

"Tom and I are leaving, Hugo. We'll keep you posted. Good-day to you, Dr. Minton."

"Not so fast, young sir. When you see Jane Stanhope, er — remember me to her, if you please."

"I'll do better than that, sir, I'll bring her to you, as soon as my mission is accomplished," grinned Mortimer.

"Good lad," beamed Andrew Minton. Hugo detained Mortimer a moment longer.

"Kindly tell your aunt that Miss Vane will be cared for by my mother at the Priory until she is well enough to return to Brighton. I will have messages conveyed to report her progress. Incidentally there is no need for my wards to return to the country until the end of the season. They would be very much in the way."

Mortimer executed an impudent bow,

"Your words are my command, my lord. I'll to horse," he cried, suiting the deed to the word.

Mortimer's departure gave the signal for the company to disperse. Dr. Minton stomped off to the stables, having secured a promise from Hugo that he would satisfy his curiosity on the morrow. Hyde Abercromby set out for Pendleton with the Runners and Garth's body, taking Alice Potter in tow guarded by Peter Lightfoot. Mr. Stone and Susan looked up from their whispered conversation and were surprised to find the room empty, save for his lordship who was finishing up the final dregs in his glass while a bedchamber was being made ready for its distinguished guest. Hugo felt unutterably weary, but he smiled sleepily at the two lovers on the window seat.

"The 'Beau Chevalier' will disappear?" Susan asked softly, as she approached and laid a gentle hand on Hugo's arm. He placed his warm hand over hers, his green eyes glinting down at her.

"Indeed, ma'am, I fear he must. His work here is accomplished."

"You will miss him?" Susan persisted.

"Why no, Miss Garth, I have er — other things to occupy my mind at present."

Mr. Stone interposed, coming to stand on Susan's other side,

"I think we can perhaps guess. Susan and I would like to wish your lordship a happiness as great as our own."

Susan and Hugo both laughed merrily.

"My lordship thanks you for your kind wishes. I trust they may shortly be fulfilled. I hope that you will call to see our patient and Miss Garth at the Priory whenever you can, Mr. Stone."

"Thank you, my lord. You may rely upon me to avail myself of every opportunity."

The happy couple withdrew, leaving Hugo to find a surcease of care in deep, refreshing slumber.

Chapter 24
Happy Ever After!

It was mid-morning, some three weeks after Hester's arrival at Huntsgrove Priory. Despite the advanced hour, she still lay abed, propped up among her pillows in the pleasant, sunny chamber assigned to her by her hostess, Lady Elizabeth. Her thoughts far away, Hester absentmindedly took a sip from the cup of morning chocolate which Martha had placed on her nightstand a while since. She grimaced. Faugh, how horrid, the milk was stone cold and tasted almost as vile as one of Dr. Minton's potions — almost, but not quite! Hester reflected that she had had more than her fair share of potions, possets and cordials since her injury, but at least it was good to have dear Martha to fuss over her once more, for the little maid had packed and quitted Brighton in a welter of bundles and boxes the moment word of Hester's mishap reached Lady Marchant's household. Her eye rested on a gaudy, moon-faced, china cat, occupying the place of honour on the mantleshelf, its expression of disdainful composure unruffled by the dainty Dresden shepherds and shepherdesses which flanked 'Moonface' on either side. Martha had insisted that the cat would cheer Hester during her convalescence and indeed he had done so, for she had always admired the complacency and self-sufficiency of cats. He was Martha's most treasured possession, being a fairing gift presented to the maid by her gentleman follower, Lord Montfort's second footman. No poor words of Martha's were equal to a description of her sweetheart's prowess on the fairground stalls, for besides the cat he had won a quantity of coconuts, some ribbons, a peacock brooch and a gingerbread heart with a little glass set in it, all of which tokens he had duly offered to Martha.

It was Martha's cherished hope that her mistress and his lordship would make a match of it, thus bringing the maid and her lover under one roof, where she could keep her eye on him and ensure that matters developed as she intended. Martha's sojourn in Brighton had been an enriching experience for the country girl; in the common way with devoted servants, she had been quick to guess Hester's secret and had watched the progress of the affair with deep interest, accurately gauging its ups and downs by her mistress's moods and demeanour.

Sunk in comfortable lethargy, Hester smiled wryly as she recalled the many hints which Martha had let fall of late. She stifled a sigh; it was strangely depressing to witness the happiness of those around her, especially Martha and Susan (for Susan was to be wed at Christmas, after waiting a decent interval for the talk to subside); tears trickled down Hester's thin cheeks, tasting salty on her tongue. She seized the hand looking-glass from the bedtable and regarded herself critically. Mentally she apostrophised the pale, thin face, with enormous grey eyes, which returned her regard solemnly. "This will not do, Hester Vane, you're hagged as a witch; silly as any schoolgirl in the throes of calf love. At your age you should know better than to over-refine on a gentleman's apparent sentiments in moments of crisis or distress. You must learn to forget (as he no doubt has done, no word in three weeks, merely hot-house posies with no note attached, polite but nothing more!), resume your normal life, go home to your cottage, take up your pen and use your newfound wealth to make your brother happy by sending him off to buy a commission." At this juncture in her homily, the tears began to flow thick and fast. Aghast at her weakness, deserted by her sense of humour, Hester threw aside the revealing glass and buried her throbbing head among the pillows.

In this sorry state she was shortly discovered by Susan, who entered softly lest her friend should still be sleeping. Encompassing the situation at a glance, Susan ran across the wide floor, jumped up on the counterpane and grasped Hester's heaving shoulders in comforting arms.

"Don't cry, love 'tis bad for you," she whispered, "You're thin as a rail. Oh! I feel so guilty when I consider 'twas all my own brother's doing! Come, let us think of more cheerful things, see I bring you a letter."

Hester stiffened; in a voice muffled by the coverlet, she enquired thickly, "A letter, from whom, not . . .?"

"From Mortimer," replied Susan firmly, repressing a bright smile, which Hester, lost in her own sad thoughts, failed to observe. Understanding full well the source of Miss Vane's low spirits Susan continued cheerfully, "Here, let me plump up your pillows so — and now you can read it. Oh, I long to hear all his news, does he write from London or Brighton?"

Listlessly Hester suffered Susan's ministrations; she wished devoutly that her friend would cease her prattle and leave her alone with her misery, but Susan seemed determined to stay. Resignedly she unfolded the crackling sheets and peered at the closely-written scrawl.

"I cannot make it out very well. He writes from London, I think," Hester complained fretfully. However, as she read on her frown disappeared and she chuckled several times. At length she looked up, her eyes sparkling through her tears. She patted Susan's hand remorsefully, "Forgive me, my dear, I am a shrew. Listen to this, he writes first to reassure us that the Comtesse Thérèse is safely under lock and key, chiefly by his own contriving. Where is it? Oh yes, "Tom and I went first to the Comtesse's lodgings on Charles Street, as was to be expected the bird had flown. Tom was eager to call on Miss Sprague, who by the by is a very jolly girl and should suit our cousin well — as I was saying we went from Charles Street to the Sprague's house, where we also found Miss Stephanie enjoying a *tête-à-tête* with Monty, which confirmed me in my fears that she (Miss S.) is a lost cause so far as I am concerned. Agatha and Tom enjoyed a rapturous reunion and I, feeling very much *de trop* with all these lovers, took myself off to visit Andy Fanshawe and the Regiment — Miss Susan will have told you by now of his part in capturing Garth's rogues. I had a notion that Andy might prove helpful in my quest for the Comtesse — correctly as you will hear. I felt convinced that she would have delayed her departure until news of Garth's success or failure reached her. The French are always prudent, so I guessed that the Comtesse would have her plans well laid; she was acquainted with many officers of the Regiment and would have had no difficulty in discovering information about the abortive French invasion when the troops returned to town; I surmised that she would have left town early the next morning, but where would she have gone? Andy told me that one of his brother officers, a dark-avised fellow, disliked for his superior overbearing ways, had disappeared that same morning and had later been found with a knife in his back some miles to the East on Pevensey Beach. It was little enough to go on, but following my hunch I quitted Brighton almost at once, leaving Tom to explain matters to my aunt and Jane Stanhope! Poor fellow, my conscience still plagues me on that score, but I am sure he acquitted himself well. Do not scold me, dear sister, to say truth, I craved a little excitement after my long confinement. My eagerness was almost my undoing. I refused Andy's offer to accompany me, but accepted the loan of a mount, as Hugo's 'Duke' was nigh floundered by the long rides to and from 'The Horse and Groom', for we returned to Brighton at a very fair pace, I assure you. I lay overnight in Newhaven and arrived in Pevensey about 11.00 the next day. I went first to the old village, huddled in the shadow of a great ruined castle — you should visit it, Hester, for I thought it a likely setting for one of your books — for my part, I drew blank, no-one had seen any strangers in the vicinity resembling the Comtesse. The local priest suggested I should make enquiries among the fisherfolk in the hamlet near the sea, about a mile from the castle. Thither went I, across a flat, marshy plain. On arrival I found the coast to be well-defended by newly-constructed Martello Towers; the people were close-lipped as oysters, smuggling folk without a doubt and hostile to outsiders. I tried approaching the watchers in the Pevensey Tower, which is an interesting round, flat, bomb-proofed, building intended to hamper the disembarkation of supplies and artillery in the event of an invasion. I doubt its utility in an emergency . . . but I digress, the Martello men proved co-operative — they had seen the officer's arrival, accompanied by a heavily-veiled lady and two servants, all on horseback. I cursed myself for not accepting Andy's offer of help, somehow I had expected the Comtesse to be alone, save perhaps for her maid. I learned that the unknown officer had tried desperately to find passage on a fishing vessel, leaving the lady to shelter at the Tower for she was very weary. The hospitable fellows welcomed the diversion and sympathised with the couple, whom they guessed to be eloping. The officer did not return. At the lady's urgent request, the men instigated a search and found his body on the beach. It is thought he was slain by fishermen when he attempted to commandeer their boat by force, or guile. On hearing this news the lady surprised them by throwing a tantrum. In her fury she slipped on her long train and fell headlong, crashing her head on the stone floor. Immediately her two servants, round-faced, tough, little men with the look of pugilists about them, seized the lady and carried her off into the night, offering no word of explanation. I pressed my informant for a description of the lady and soon felt sure that it was indeed the Comtesse, though the man had believed her to be Spanish, largely because she wore a high, black mantilla. Somewhat sheepishly he admitted that he had made no attempt at pursuit, feeling that it was none of his affair and his first duty was to keep watch in his tower. He had sent a message to the officer's regiment, for he recognized his uniform. I cogitated awhile, not my favourite occupation as you well know — I was puzzled that news of the officer's death had reached Fanshawe yesterday — the man must have died the night before, and I had been out in my calculations by a day, for obviously the Comtesse had quitted Brighton when the troops rode out to meet Tom and Abercromby, not, as I had previously supposed, when they returned. Her panic had given her a day's grace as far as pursuit was concerned. No wonder she was angry at her companion's death, for the Martello men would be bound to report the incident and her own whereabouts could be traced. But where was she now? She had disappeared in the darkness while I lay in Newhaven, twelve hours or more ago. At this juncture I had a stroke of undeserved good fortune. I decided not to bungle alone any more, but to seek help in the next town, Bexhill. Accordingly I set off, following the coast road. Just beyond the hamlet of Norman's Bay I came upon a gipsy encampment by the side of the road. The way was dusty and I stopped to ask for a drink of water. This was brought to me very civilly by a little maid and as I sipped I looked about me curiously. Imagine my delight when I spied two round-faced, sturdy fellows sitting on the steps of one of the gaily painted caravans; they wore bright gipsy garments, which seemed strangely at variance with their fair, ruddy complexions. Their caravan stood a little removed from the rest and I observed that they were given a wide berth by the other vagrant folk. I looked hastily away for the two men were watching me keenly. When I returned the dipper I asked the little maid if they would soon be moving on. She told me that they intended to rest a day or two before heading for Rye Fair. Nonchalantly I thanked her and rode on at full speed to Bexhill, where, after some coaxing I succeeded in obtaining help from the Excisemen, who, if truth be told, were not reluctant to have an excuse to examine the gipsy camp for possible contraband. We returned under cover of darkness and easily overpowered the menfolk while they slept. The Comtesse's two bodyservants fought valiantly; after some hard knocks they were taken. The Comtesse was still in a weak state after her fall and could offer little resistance; she tried to shoot herself, but was prevented. My hand grows cramped from so much unaccustomed exercise, so I will tell you briefly, m'dear, that I escorted the lady to Town, manfully resisting her wiles and blandishments on the way — for I admit it pains me to think of that wild bird in captivity. Arrived in the Metropolis, Bow Street relieved me of my charge."

Hester shook her head over the last paragraph. Susan giggled, exclaiming gleefully,

"What weak creatures men are. A good riddance, I say."

"And I also, though she possessed a strange charm, I felt it myself," agreed Hester, more soberly.

"But Sir Mortimer acquitted himself well, do you not think? He is clearly in transports to have seen some action at last — almost single-handed too. I vow 'twas bravely done."

"It has but given him a taste for it, I fear. The rest of the page is tantalising in the extreme. He wishes me a speedy recovery, congratulates me on my inheritance and hopes that the bearer of this letter will give me reassuring tidings concerning his own present whereabouts and future plans. He ends by wishing me every happiness and promises to visit me when his arrangements are completed. He remains my own loving brother, Tim. Sue, what does he mean? Who is his messenger?"

"Oh, he came with Dr. Minton. They are gossiping together in the library. You had not forgotten that the doctor promised to call this morning? He said that he would wait until you had read Mortimer's letter, for he was sure that would be a tonic in itself."

"Susan Garth, tell me at once, you wretch. Who came with Dr. Minton?"

"Who but his lordship, of course, you silly goose," replied Susan, laughing.

"Hugo, here? Oh, but I cannot see him, I look frightful!" gasped Hester agitatedly pinching her cheeks and blowing her nose vigorously.

"You cannot be so cruel as to disappoint him, when he has come expressly to see you. Why I daresay Dr. Minton is trembling for Lord Montfort's sanity at this very moment. His lordship was pacing the floor and answering quite at random when I left them together. He is anxious to tell you of Mortimer's doings, no doubt."

"Ye-es, he is most likely in haste to return to Town," sniffed Hester dolefully.

"For a sensible female you talk a great deal of nonsense. The sight of my dear Jedediah overcame all my bumps and bruises in a trice. I am persuaded Lord Montfort can perform a similar miracle for you, if you will but give him the opportunity. I give you fair warning I have promised his lordship that he will not have to wait above an hour. Do you propose to receive the gentleman in your nightgown?"

"Yes, no — I don't know! I must have time to compose myself. Is it warm outside? Then pray inform his lordship that I will join him in the Rose Garden in half an hour. Please ring for Martha, dear Sue. Oh, I vow I never suspected you of such bullying, overbearing ways," cried Hester, preparing to jump out of bed.

"I have only your interests at heart, my dear," retorted Susan; she gave the tasselled bellrope a sharp tug. "I will leave you now. Stop rubbing your eyes and be sure to wear something soft and becoming. Your rose silk, I think, definitely not white, too wraithlike in your present enfeebled condition."

So saying, Susan whisked from the room, leaving Hester to make a careful, though swift, toilette, deftly aided by a beaming Martha. All traces of woe were removed by the skilful application of an infusion of rose water followed by a light dusting of powder and her rumbled hair was brushed until it shone. Standing obediently still before the glass while Martha solicitously wrapped a light fawn shawl about her shoulders, Hester felt her spirits rise to match the change in her appearance. Her cheeks glowed delicately pink, seeming to reflect the warm rose colour of her gown.

"I will come down the back stairs with you and slip out by the garden door, Martha," said Hester, smiling mischievously at her maid's shocked countenance.

"Oh miss, it's not fitting. Whatever would Mr. Simpkins say?"

"He'll probably be in his room polishing the silver at this hour. In any event he cannot eat us. Lead on, there's a good girl."

Trembling inwardly, Martha did as she was bid. By good fortune she managed to effect her mistress's exit from the house without any dire encounters with the august personage who held undisputed sway below stairs. Thankfully, Martha closed the garden door and hurried back to tidy Hester's chamber, leaving Miss Vane to wend her way slowly through the herb and vegetable gardens. Now that the long-awaited moment was at hand, Hester found herself unaccountably reluctant to meet his lordship. Susan had told her all the details she had missed hearing in her unconscious state and she knew that his lordship had been much concerned for her well-being. She was also aware that he had been obliged to go to London to tidy matters and confer with inner members of the Cabinet. Hester found herself regretting the demise of the 'Beau Chevalier'; she wondered if Hugo would seek an outlet for his energies by going on his travels again, or, Heaven forbid, accept some diplomatic position abroad. She lingered so long staring hard at a large cabbage that the Head Gardener approached to see if she had detected signs of maggots attacking his prize produce. Hastily disclaiming any such notion, Hester praised the vegetable extravagantly and was much confused when the good man insisted on cutting the cabbage for her dinner. In reality she loathed cabbage, but she thanked him prettily and was about to hurry away when a well-known voice said teasingly,

"Jem Dutton! Have you no romance in your soul offering cabbages to a lady? Now roses I can understand . . . but cabbages! What will you do for the harvest festival, I thought this was to be your *pièce de resistance*?"

At these words Hester felt ready to sink into the ground, but Jem Dutton appeared no whit disturbed. A slow grin overspread his somewhat taciturn features as he remarked reprovingly,

"Mr. Hugo, 'tis a real pleasure to know my cabbage will come to such a good end, for there's nought like greens for someone wot's bin peaky. When Miss Vane is bloomin' in health again, then's the toime ter give her roses, an' I still have me marrer for the festival."

"Your philosophical sentiments put me to shame, Jem, but you see, to me Miss Vane looks so much better than when I last saw her, that I feel she deserves a rose as well. Be a good fellow and lend me your pruning knife before you convey that superb specimen to the kitchen."

Jem Dutton winced when he heard his lordship's designs on his cherished blooms, but nobly forbore to comment, being a shrewd man. Instead he handed over his knife, executed a neat bow and departed with dignified mien in the direction of the kitchen, the large cabbage tucked securely under his arm.

The little interlude had given Hester time to recover her composure, which was perhaps his lordship's intention. He chuckled at Jem's departing back, flourished his knife with a practiced skill and then seized Hester's hand in his own warm clasp, saying,

"Come my lady, let us seek the seclusion of the rose garden, where will I pluck for you one of the fairest roses in all England, yet not more beautiful than thine own sweet self."

Hester flung up her hand in laughing protest, replying with mock severity,

"My lord, I must insist that you desist forthwith for to laugh so gives me a pain in my shoulder. To cut that cabbage nearly broke poor Dutton's heart, I refuse to allow you to cut a single rose."

They had reached a wooden bench in a shady corner of the rose garden and here Hugo waited until she was seated, then dropped on one knee before her and gazed long and earnestly into her face. She returned his regard steadily, a small pulse beating rapidly in her throat. He was silent so long that Hester began to fear that he was about to impart bad news. Rallying, she exclaimed,

"Do sit down, my lord. You will ruin those exquisite inexpressibles and very likely get the cramp as well if you remain in that exceedingly uncomfortable position any longer. That's better. It was very good of you to spare the time to bring me Mortimer's letter. We have been starved of news and dying of curiosity these three weeks," she concluded reproachfully.

Hugo replied formally, "I beg your pardon, ma'am. I wished to give you time to recover before burdening you further. I have been much occupied, but I am happy to be able to tell you that Abercromby, Marchant and I have completed our mission satisfactorily. The threat of an invasion has been averted, at least for a time, though I suspect we must now look to our laurels at sea. Incidentally I have purchased a yacht and put Tommy Bates in charge of her. I hope you enjoy sailing, I was thinking that a short cruise might be just the thing to complete your cure."

Hester blinked in surprise.

"You are very kind, but I assure you I am quite well again. I was saying to Susan only this morning that I have trespassed long enough on your good nature and hospitality. It is high time that I returned home . . ." She faltered to a stop, glancing at Hugo under her lashes. He appeared to be in the grip of a strong emotion; he rose to his feet and towered above her, blocking the sunlight. In hurt, angry tones, he commanded,

"Look at me, Hester. Never talk such fustian to me again. I love you more than I can express, but it appears my feelings are not reciprocated or you would not speak of leaving the moment I return home. On a more practical plane I owe you my life twice over, first on the night when you found me on your doorstep and again when you sustained your injury for my sake. I had hoped that you were motivated by feelings similar to mine, but in any event I insist that you let me repay a little of my great debt. If my presence offends you, take Miss Garth or Miss Stanhope with you on the cruise. I fear I cannot suggest Mortimer as he will be otherwise occupied. I don't know how to break this gently and I expect you will be angered, but I have helped your brother to obtain a commission with Sir John Moore's Light Brigade at Shorncliffe. He is there now, but asked me to assure you that he will visit you once his training is completed." Hester found herself quite unable to reply to this speech and Hugo continued rapidly, almost pleadingly, "I am truly sorry to have distressed you so. Pray believe me when I say that I had only Mortimer's best interests at heart. I think you know he loves my ward, Stephanie, but she is not ready to settle down. A period of absence will be beneficial for them both."

Mid-way between a sob and a laugh, Hester jumped to her feet. Reaching up, she put her hands on Hugo's shoulders and gave him a small, fierce shake.

"You dear, silly, *idiotish* man, of course I love you! I have loved you for years and Mortimer is fortunate indeed to have you to stand his friend." At this point Hester gave vent to a convulsive sneeze, tears of happiness trembling on her lashes. Brushing the tears away with a watery smile, she murmured, "Oh, Hugo, this is ridiculous. I am not usually such a milk-and-water miss."

His eyes alight, Hugo raised a sardonic eyebrow, before folding her in a close embrace. Hester responded rapturously and for a long moment they stood locked together, wordlessly, joyously happy. When at length Hugo released her, Hester sank down on the bench, breathless and shaken, but tingling with delight from her head to her heels. With admirable aplomb, his lordship seated himself beside her, remarking lightly,

"Well, my lady novelist, I had almost forgot to tell you my other piece of news, your new volume will be on everyone's lips by Christmastide, or so Mr. Murray informs me. I left his letter back at the house. When I called at his office last week he asked me if you had begun work on another tale and I told him that I believed you had recently accumulated a wealth of material for your next venture. There is no substitute for firsthand experience, I suspect."

Her demure tones belied by her twinkling eyes, Hester replied slyly, "As you say, my lord, and you may rest assured that (contrary to my usual precepts) your noble self will figure prominently in one guise or another."

Hugo clasped his brow in mock horror,

"Heaven preserve me from literary females. To have my character torn to shreds for the benefit of simpering schoolroom chits and dissatisfied dowagers!" With an extravagant gesture, he seized the pruning knife and sliced off a beautiful red rosebud. This he proffered to his beloved, once more falling before her on one knee to exclaim, "How may I avert this catastrophe? I need a quiet life to restore my customary equanimity. My lady of letters, will you not have pity on a simple country gentleman and confine your quill to those dashing figments of your imagination who have proved so popular hitherto?"

Biting her quivering lip, Hester answered him,

"Arise, my lord. Plead not, my mind is made up."

Unmoving, Hugo replied, "And so is mine. Since there's no help for it, I feel we must oblige your readers with a happy ending. Hester my darling, will you marry me?"

Thoughtfully, Miss Vane twirled her rosebud between her fingers. Lord Montfort surveyed her bent head wistfully, a little anxiously. When she judged she had teased him long enough, Hester favoured his lordship with a radiant smile and murmured, wickedly submissive,

"But of course I am honoured to accept your proposal, dear Hugo, though as your obedient wife I fear my gentle readers are doomed to disappointment, for this is a tale shall never be told by me."

With a derisive hoot of laughter, Hugo once more clasped Hester in his arms, muttering fiercely into her hair,

"So be it. Let us make haste and be wed then, my love, before you change your mind!!"